THE LAST TIME I SAW RICHARD

A NOVEL BY

CRAIG FREEDMAN

WESTRY BOOKS

North Carolina ∽ Washington

WESTRY BOOKS
an imprint of Westry Wingate Group
www.wwgpress.com

Front cover image: Francisco de Goya, *Señora Sabasa Garcia* (c. 1806/1811), Andrew W. Mellon Collection. Image courtesy of the Board of Trustees, National Gallery of Art, Washington, D.C.

ISBN 978–1–935323–03–7

For Donna who made this book necessary; and for Brooke who made it possible.

... and he told me all romantics meet the same fate someday
cynical and drunk and boring someone in some dark cafe.
— Joni Mitchell

CONTENTS

1

LETTERS

"Indifferent! Oh no – I never conceived you could become indifferent. Letters
are no matters of indifference; they are generally a very positive curse."
"You are speaking of letters of business; mine are letters of friendship."
"I have often thought them the worst of the two," replied he, coolly.
"Business you know, may bring money, but friendship hardly ever does."
–Jane Austen, *Emma*

October 24

Dear Lisa,

This I hope will be a milder letter than you are accustomed to
receive from me. My feelings remain the same but I can now accept
a situation that was difficult a few months ago. I still think of you.
That cannot be helped and it is not wrong to remember. Mistakes
are made and paid for but there can be no regrets. And there is no
way I can ever regret having known you, touching you, feeling your
softness.

There is not too much I can say about my own actions. I flew over
to London with a friend. We've been here two weeks. I've applied
for a job in Nigeria … sort of like joining the foreign legion, huh?
Hard to say when I'll leave, the embassy doesn't really seem to be
sure when my interview will happen. But none of this is of any great
import to either me or you.

Lisa, I do not know how successful I have ever been in
communicating with you. I believe it's generally been a failure.
Writing is a way of marking time and that is probably all this
letter amounts to. But writing to you does serve a purpose, if only
therapeutic. It's something I need to do.

1

I hope you are settled now and that your various hassles are lessening once more. I am sorry if at times I may have caused you any unhappiness, I was not always able to act as I wished.

Softness enfolds the world about you
Walking by you, all harshness is washed away
And life awakens to the love which flows from your eyes

The touch of your hand sends planets whirling through space,
Causes gold standards to tarnish
And stops the tears of children with scraped knees.

Too kind to be harsh, but by that kindness harsh,
Are you afraid that by hurting,
You yourself will be hurt;
And that the unfolding of your love will be cut off,
Your arms unable to embrace?

Richard

November 1

Dear Richard,

What does it feel like to be in London! Certainly it wouldn't be anything like Wilmington. Write if you can of what you see; the forms and shapes, the colors, and the people. I wish you could draw it for me!

I can't tell you how much I've seen in the past 3 months. I feel re–born into such a fantastic world. A world full of things to see – and to find!

Nigeria is out of my imagination – would you be on the Gulf of Guinea? Or central?

Please write and tell me all of what you're doing? And learning too!

I've been so involved with my art. It gives me much beauty and understanding of life. I'm very much in love! I want to give you happiness! Let's see you smile and be relaxed because you know someone really cares for you.

Love,
Lisa

November 18

My Dear Friend Richard,

I haven't heard from you since my last letter, hopefully you will get both, this and the earlier one. Often my thoughts turn to you – wondering about your safety and your happiness. I wish there was some way to more positively communicate.

It's been cold and work is unending – yet there is progress that can be seen in my drawings etc. But it does go so slowly.

Thanksgiving is almost here. It seems as if this will be the first one where I will be truly thankful for everything I have and share with others – I hope to share with you Richard, my love and concern. This world is so full of beautiful beings like you – yet your soul, your life is so special to me.

As I remember you – your eyes, the sadness they hold within —

Be happy now.

Written with love,
Lisa

November 28

   My Dearest Girl,

   I am so sorry not to have written before. To be honest, I was shocked to hear from you at all. I thought you wanted nothing more to do with me. When I first got here, I couldn't seem to shake my heavy feeling of sadness. I took a bus up to Hampstead Heath to visit the Keats Museum. It's in a small house, the one he lived in before he died. I was trying to look for a trace of a Swedish girl I knew here three years ago. I think she fancied herself to be another Fanny Kemble. But of course she was gone. I told myself that it was no good trying to recapture past memories or lost loves. You can't relive what's no longer there. I was trying to let go of your image too. It all seemed so hopeless.

   Then I got your wonderful letter in the mail. If only you could be here to see the love shining in my eyes. I think I've been afraid to write to you. I can't seem to convey what I feel in words. They're so flat and lifeless. I want to make them stand up and dance for you, to sing out all my love for you. I will try, only if you promise to be forbearing. I'll describe my life here, but remember, I'm not an artist like you.

   I'm staying with a cousin of this guy I came over with. She has a flat (apartment) in central London not far from the British Museum. They call the area Bloomsbury. I think Virginia Woolf lived somewhere around here. You remember, she's the one who wrote that book we read together last spring. Anyway it's really convenient. Everything you need is on this one block; a chemist (drugstore), greengrocer, butcher, pub on either end, a florist and even an undertaker. The flat is above a bakery so the heat from the ovens keeps us warm, no central heating of course. It's sort of cramped with all three of us cooped up here but so far the cousin (Linda) hasn't complained. We certainly don't dare as she is letting us stay for free. Besides, we're seldom together. I spend most of my time walking all over London. I'm starting to know the city really well. The other day a couple of tourists asked me for directions and I was able to give them without blinking an eye. I tend to fake an accent when talking to Americans. I couldn't pull it off with the locals but it usually goes over with everyone else.

The only problem I've had is with drugs. I don't mean with the cops or anything. It's just that I am constantly badgered by people trying to sell me dope. Maybe it's the way I'm dressed. I'm still wearing that floppy tennis hat and those blue aviator sun glasses; oh yeah, and your brother's clapped out corduroy jacket. I guess I must look to be a real likely target.

The big news is my latest scheme to make money. I mentioned it in that letter I wrote you. I've been trying to get a job teaching. First I tried some private American schools in London, but they all wanted experienced people. One was willing to give me a few substitute stints, so that might still come through okay. But I figured out a new angle. I'm going to teach in Africa. Or at least I'm hoping to do so. That's what I meant by applying for a job in Nigeria. If I'm accepted the government there will pay for my airfare over and next thing you know I'll be teaching math to a lot of shining black faces. It wasn't all that hard. I just walked into the Nigerian High Commission (embassy) and after being shuffled from one bureaucrat to the next I finally found the right person. Pretty bizarre huh? It should be interesting and I don't think there will be any great risk. I'll go wherever they send me, but they speak English over there, and now that the Biafra thing is over with, the government seems pretty stable. I know I should feel bad about it being a military dictatorship but I don't want to be a lone white face during some popular uprising. I can just see myself surrounded by thousands of blacks when someone screams, "Get Whitey!" Besides, teaching math to school children isn't the same as actively supporting a repressive regime. God, my father will just shit his pants when he hears. You know how he feels about blacks. That's one advantage. I won't have my parents dropping in for a surprise visit. Being in Nigeria would totally freak them out.

I probably won't hear about this job for a few months. They've got to process the application through Lagos (capital of Nigeria), Washington, and God knows where else. So we might hop over to Paris for a few weeks to see the sights and give Linda a break from our company. At the very least it will keep Sam out of the pubs over here. All that Guinness stout is bound to blow one of his kidneys before long.

Please write as soon as you can. The thought of getting a letter from you keeps my spirits up.

All my love,
Richard

December 2

Dear Lisa,

You'll never guess what happened. We finally decided to leave for Paris and booked student fares via bus and hovercraft. Hovercrafts float above the water on a cushion of air. They take no time at all to cross the Channel. I've been on one before. You know, when I was over here with my sister doing the great shopping tour of Europe. But this time the Channel turned violent and we were pitching up and down like we were on some sort of berserk roller coaster ride. I just turned completely green. I've never been seasick before. I think most of it came from being so totally enclosed. Anyway, what I seriously wanted to do was to die. And wouldn't you know it there was some little brat watching my agony, but I refused to give him any satisfaction. He was just waiting for me to upchuck but I managed to hold it in. Still, I wasn't feeling any too gorgeous.

We checked in at this really funky, little right bank hotel, "The Hotel Metropole." I would've sent you a postcard but they didn't stock postcards; no towels or soap either. The beds were classic film noir; central valleys with a dark stain down the middle of each sheet. The window opened, with difficulty, on some godforsaken alley. The guy in the next room had a bad case of asthma, or else someone was attempting to strangle him half the night. Overall it was a tad depressing. Sam couldn't get over the toilet paper (papier du toilette). It's like wax paper, you know, the kind our mothers used to wrap sandwiches in when we were kids. Hard to get the knack of using it first off. It tends to slip a lot more than you'd want it to.

The next morning we headed for the Louvre, the Macy's bargain basement of museums. Sam wanted to stop first at the American Express office. He was expecting a letter from his girlfriend. So of course since I was there already I decided to check my mail. The clerk handed me a telegram forwarded from London, from the Nigerian High Commission. It notified me of a job interview, and get this, the interview was to begin in five minutes. Naturally this posed a bit of a problem. The numbskulls at that embassy assured me that I had at least a couple of months before it could be arranged. I didn't know what to do. I had this panicky feeling that it was absolutely necessary to get back to England but quick.

Sam calmed me down a bit and we arranged for the trip back. You would not believe British Customs. Everybody under thirty with long hair is an instant target. You practically have to get down on your knees and plead with them to let you into their tight–assed little country. Now I know how all those Mexicans feel.

So we're back here staying with Linda. She's been just terrific. What she did was to show up for my interview, you know to explain things. A secretary called out my name and inside the conference room was the biggest and blackest man she had ever seen. His skin was so dark it had this almost purplish tinge to it. He asked where I was but Linda could barely open her mouth. Every racial fear she had grown up with in Kentucky immediately leapt into her mind. She ended up speaking in a squeaky, little girl's voice.

The guy turned out to be the minister of education or some such thing. He told her that he was interested in talking to me (good sign) and would I please get in touch with the embassy staff when I returned.

So that's exactly what I did do but let me tell you I was pretty pissed about the whole deal. I couldn't make a fuss about it though because there was no sense in antagonizing their people here. But the next interview can't be arranged for at least another month. I will have to try to figure out something to do until then. I might decide to sponge off this guy I know in Spain. At least it should be sunnier there and that might cheer me up.

Please write when you can. I want to know what you are doing and feeling.

With loving thoughts,
Richard

December 10

Dear Richard,

Received your letters – did you get mine? Perhaps they are trailing after you and will catch up with you in Spain. I find that your words are not flat, but shapely in my mind of your travels and distances. And of you. This last month, dear Richard, I have had such pain grip my soul. Questions and meanings haunt me. I often speak of understanding, knowing, and seeking all, but when I truly see this world, I fright and cover my eyes and then I feel the tears of my being. Why is there no one to comfort the souls that bear the pain of others? Please, remember my eyes! Can't you see all of me within them? And yet, each soul is so totally alone on its journey – but don't you see, that I need one true soul to awaken the love I have to give. That is the cause of such intense pain.

But my sweet Richard – let me not worry you. I believe that heading to Nigeria will be right for you. Please – search hard for answers! Seek whatever there you may find true.

With great love,

Lisa

December 16

   My Own Dear Love,

   Say the word and I will kiss away all your sweet tears. Nigeria or any other place in the world means nothing beside you. If only I thought you wanted me, I would fly to you tomorrow. Is that what you want? I'm not sure if it's what you're saying. You know I've never been very good at reading your feelings. I don't want to bungle things again. Right now my soul is filled with longing for you. When I am with you no one and nothing else seems to exist. You know that I love you. But I must know if you want that love in all its fullness and physical being. Or, are you just romancing again? Don't set this up without thinking. You're not the only one with commitments. With me, though, you come first.

   I'll be leaving for Spain tomorrow. Write to me c/o American Express – Madrid, Spain. Lisa, please try to make up your mind. You don't know what this does to me.

All my deepest love,

Richard

December 23

To my sweet Richard,

Your letter spoke with such truth and even though it is difficult to accept at the present, I admire your candor and respect your most precious feelings. I know nothing of what the future holds for us. Whatever, let it hold love.

Often I try and visualize your entire face, unhappily I remember you only in parts! (eyes, mouth, etc.) but I hold clearly the feelings of the few times we were together unhassled. If it is possible to send an image (i.e. photograph) please do.

End of the semester has past – maintained a B+ average. Wow – how can a grade be put on painting! My teachers found grading me most difficult! Great! Let this be a big Christmas hug and kiss! I've spent most of this week making presents and baking. I wish for you much happiness and lots of smiles. I'll think of you especially after this Christmas time. Please write soon.

With much concern — And love for you,

Me

January 14

Dearest Lisa,

Madrid is strangely disappointing. I don't know what I expected. But after the long train ride across the English Channel and through France at night, I guess I wanted something special to happen when we reached the border early in the morning. I was squeezed in with five drunken Spaniards in my compartment. No way to stretch out. I sat with my cheek against the window listening to them talk excitedly about going home, and especially the women they had there. My high school Spanish teacher, Mrs. Pincus, would have been proud of me. Though mostly, I found their conversation rather boring.

I suppose they were nice enough. They shared their wine which helped me to pass out for a few hours. You'd be surprised how good I've been so far. Hardly ever have a drink at all. It's easier now that I'm travelling alone, now that Sam's gone back to the States. You never did say who told you that I was the second biggest drunk on campus.

Did you know you had to change trains at the Spanish border? Something to do with the track gauge. They're different from anywhere else in Europe. Unfortunately that difference proved to be significant. I should have taken it for a warning. The train crawled for hours at a walking speed. But Northern Spain is truly impressive. Beautiful is too ordinary a word to use. I don't know how to describe it. You're the one with those painter's eyes of yours.

I'm feeling that Madrid is a definite mistake. I should try to be more adventuresome and bum around the countryside. I guess the truth is that I'm scared. For one thing I don't trust my high school Spanish. It's actually gotten worse since I've been here. I've stopped paying attention to what people are saying. They can get pretty impatient when you keep forcing them to repeat themselves. The real problem is that I don't think I like Spaniards. Maybe it's just their Latin temperament. I remember what you've told me about being categorical but it's really hard to resist. I'm not sure why I feel this antipathy but there's no sense in denying it.

What I know you wouldn't like are all the soldiers guarding a seemingly unlimited quantity of nouveau fascist architecture. But you would be completely wowed by the Prado. I've never been to a more fascinating museum or a stranger one. It's in an old palace like the Louvre. But the Louvre shows no discrimination in its collection. The walls there are cluttered with too many nymphs done by a handful of boring eighteenth century Frenchmen. Maybe if I stay here a bit longer I won't be such an illiterate about painting.

Life did improve somewhat when I managed to move out of the pensione where I was staying. My bed was so totally sway backed that I spent most of the morning bent over like some cripple. I was sharing the room with these two German students. One night they got roaring drunk and were up till dawn puking into the bidet. I just packed up and left. It was so totally gross. Anyway, I finally managed to hook up with one of my ex–professors at St. Michaels. He'd been away in Barcelona. So I am currently freeloading off him and his wife. It's always dangerous to give me a casual invitation. I'm all too likely to show up.

I haven't said much about how I've been missing you but it should be obvious by now. It's just no good being apart. I find myself talking to you in the Prado or pointing things out to you as I walk in the park. Everything is colder without you. It's been so many months I can no longer be sure whether your eyes are brown or not. In any case, I long to kiss them.

So Lisa, I've got an offer for you. My sister's wedding is in three months, April 14. I've promised to fly in for it. By then I hope to know for sure about the job in Nigeria or another possibility, teaching at the London Community School — Why don't you come up for the wedding? I'll arrange it with my folks. All I ask for is a chance to talk to you. That isn't so much. If nothing else I'll get to see your beautiful face once more.

Much love,
Richard

p.s. I don't have a picture to send you. I try to avoid them. I always end up looking like such a complete goof.

January 22

Sweet Richard,

Received your letter yesterday. Please explain about the teaching position — When would it begin? Sept?

Oh, yes – fear not, my eyes are true brown! Went to the eye doctor yesterday — I had doubts about my vision, but all those visions are only in my head, not in my sight, for that sight is perfect. Your sister's wedding? Well — if you truly wish for me to go, I shall. Happily — for unions are great things!

You do understand about my living situation? — That I am living with a fantastic guy — Did you know this? Yet, I am still open to love – for love has no dimensions, no boundaries. Let your love be like the dawn with the coming of the light whose colors shine into every dark hidden corner.

My love shines for you,
Lisa

January 31

   Dearest Lisa,

   This isn't right. You shouldn't be playing games with me. Of course I know who you're living with. I'm not stupid. But neither am I a fantasy, at least not to me. You can't always have it both ways Lisa. It's easy enough when I'm thousands of miles away to pretend you love me. You can sit by the fire after dinner and let yourself feel all warm and tingly thinking about me. These last six months I haven't been there cluttering your life or trying to catch your attention, though God knows I saw you rarely enough even back then. That's not what I want. A letter once a week just isn't good enough. You were star shine and light as long as you thought I'd be safely tucked away in Nigeria for a few years. Now that I'm flying back for my sister's wedding I can hear you edging away.

   Don't do it Lisa without giving me a chance. Try to be fair to me. All I want is to be able to see you. At least to see if we can work things out.

   London is so dreary now. The sky is an angry gray and the wind continually whips across the dirty squares. I take long walks, exploring every part of the city. I sometimes think I've grown to know this place better than the locals. I find myself constantly giving directions to the theaters and museums. But mostly I keep going back to the Tate. That's where they store their modern art, though not all of it is what you'd really want to call modern. I've discovered a new painter. He's an Italian or Swiss named Giacometti. The people in his portraits seem wrapped with surgical tape like so many mummies, trapped, unable to reveal their inner mysteries. Oh, and there are these incredible seascapes by Turner, all ablaze with light. I know you'd love them. I'll try to remember to send you a postcard, but it won't be the same as seeing it for yourself. I wish so much that I could have you here with me.

   Write and let me know how you feel about us. I think of you all the time —

My life, my love,
Richard

February 7

Dearest Richard,

Your last letter spoke with such honesty of the situation. Fantasy only breeds hostility towards conflicting truths.

I still question in my mind how and why your love for me began. Our first few meetings many years back sent my heart winging. Then I had doubts that you even noticed, I was so young and backwards. When your feelings for me started to show, beautifully — they came without warning or foundation. Strangely I feel the passion of your love without knowing you as a friend. This worries me Richard. It is this caring and understanding which is still missing from our relationship. We still don't really know each other. So anyway, I'm planning on spending some time with you the weekend of your sister's wedding –o.k.? Hopefully, all is well in your life.

With smiles and kisses,
Lisa

February 15

Dear Lisa,

Oh my sweet, sweet girl. I don't know how I will manage to wait until April. I've written to my parents and they will be sending you an invitation with all the necessary information. Just think, in a little more than a month we will be seeing each other for the first time since last June. It seems so long ago. At night now I can almost smell your soft brown hair. You've made me so happy and I want to promise you that you won't regret it.

I've never loved anyone quite like you before. I think you have the knack of bringing out the very best in me. Other people say I am cynical and hard, but you know the softness that lies waiting only for the right touch. I know it's foolish, but I have visions of us walking together in flower covered fields making garlands for each other to wear. Oh I feel like such a child when I think of you. You do remember our time together. There were never any problems. You'll see at the wedding what I mean. Till then—

Think of me often,

Richard

April 2

Lisa,

I understand why you haven't written to me. There's nothing more I can tell you. I would still like you to come to the wedding. My parents are expecting you. All you have to do is give them a call when you get in. I'll be flying home on the thirteenth.

Try not to be such a coward for once in your life. At least have the courtesy of letting me know what you are thinking.

Richard.

April 16

Dear Richard,

Are you too impossibly angry with me? I just couldn't go to your sister's wedding. I kept thinking about it till the absolute last moment — even had a friend willing to drive me up. But it just wouldn't have been right. The guy I'm living with is a truly wonderful person. You'd like him Richard, really you would. We've had maybe a few rough times together, but he's been truly good to me. So I can't risk hurting him now—you can see that, can't you Richard?

I know I should have called before. I tried, really I did. But I was so upset and crying so much that I just couldn't do it. Don't think too badly of me. I truly do love you. One day I'm sure we will be together. It just can't be now. I know you'll understand Richard, you always do. So please, try to find someone else to love. There's too much beauty inside you to keep it bottled up. I'd tell you this over the phone, but you're right, I am a big coward.

You are very, very precious to me.

Love,

Lisa

April 20

NO – GOOD – LISA

Richard

2

PARADIGMS

For wee must Consider that wee shall be as a Citty upon a hill. The eies of all
people are uppon us.
–John Winthrop

On a day like today, turning off the Cross Bronx Expressway at
the Webster Avenue exit, barely noticing the high–rise slums, the
dirt and decay, I think, this city is crud and so is my life. And that,
my friend, is one helluva way to start your day.

I have one of the company cabs. Usually I do this trip by subway
and bus; hot unbreathable air, trains that stop mysteriously between
stations, crazies marching through the aisles shouting unintelligibly
to wooden faced commuters. These daily occurrences are not
symbolic: people with withered arms appearing every day as though
extras in a demented drama, point to no greater meaning. This is not
art but simply life.

More and more often I avoid these horrors by making my way into
the heart of the Bronx along its major highway. It's getting harder
and harder to find decent drivers. You have to work too damn hard
to make renting one of these shitboxes pay off. Who wants to work
hard? Sixty people answer an ad, maybe five derelicts show up for
an interview. It'd be quicker to smash the windshields myself than
to employ one of those treacherous losers.

The Third Avenue El stopped running up here a few years ago.
There it is looming ahead of me now as I make a right off of 170th;
that green meaningless structure, a form stripped of any possible
function. Somebody told me that the city plans to tear it down soon.
Sure they'll tear it down. Probably about the same time that Bruce
Adams becomes the gypsy cab king of New York.

Why do I bother? I spent four years in college discussing truth and justice to end up at a gas station in the South Bronx; smashed cabs in the back, smashed humanity out front. Everyday, jive ass blacks try to screw me out of a few bucks. Creditors pursue me like drunken sailors after a young whore. I've endured curses, threats and endless degradation—and for what? For the greater glory of my ole buddy Bruce.

Oh goody, he's here. Yep, that's his white pimpmobile parked right out in front of the trailer. Must need to skim off some more money. I should just turn around and go home. That's what I should do. The very sight of him makes me physically ill. I can picture him now, sitting inside, all freshly bathed and cologned, foot up on the desk and impatient. A new girlfriend means flowers, restaurant meals, and bars. Too bad he can't open accounts up everywhere. That way he'd never have to pay.

Well little Brucie's in for one big surprise. He's not getting a goddam cent. I haven't paid myself for two weeks. We need the little cash we have to buy a distributor, otherwise there'll be another nonworking addition parked across the street. Nothing's been coming in, maybe thirty, forty bucks a day. If it wasn't for that one loony kid who rents cabs at premium prices we'd be finished. So, the only one who skims any money out of this operation is going to be me. It's not my fault he keeps fucking up all his big time drug deals. Goddam fool thinks he's some sort of bleached out Superfly. If he wants to make money he should learn to keep his nose shut. Okay, so maybe if I don't flap my jaw he'll take the hint and go.

"Hey suds, a Cordy McNeil called while you were gone."

"No shit, Cordelia's finally in New York. I can't believe it. Did you take a message?"

"Say Richard, wasn't she one of those 'anyone for tennis' types at school?"

"Yeah, that's her."

"Which one was she, the tall one with dark hair or that dumpy kid?"

"She isn't dumpy."

"No offense old buddy."

"So, what did she have to say?"

"I think you must be holding back on your old pal ... aren't you sweetheart? When did you ever get around to poking old what's her face?"

"None of your damn business."

"Now there's no need to go and get all touchy. So your girlfriend's dumpy. Maybe she's lost some weight since then."

"Look Bruce, I'll make this simple for you, so simple even you can understand—she is not dumpy and she is not my girlfriend. Now just knock it off, okay? Well, are you going to tell me about her phone call?"

"I'll tell you what sport. You can just kneel down and suck my big fat dick ... What's the matter with you honeychil'? You afraid big bad Bruce is thinking of spoiling your fun with that fat cunt? Not to worry Richard old buddy, I wouldn't do that to an old pal like you."

"Thanks a lot ace, I couldn't stand the competition."

"You bet you couldn't Clarence, you wouldn't stand a chance."

"So what about the message?"

"Sure thing Richard but howzabout telling me something first?"

"What?"

"How does it feel when you stick your tongue into something like that? Must be pretty damn spongy, wouldn't you say so sport?"

"Listen ace, I don't really care how long you think your prick is. Just get this through your greasy little head. She is not my girlfriend and this is none of your goddam business. Now I want to know what you told her and I want to know it right now."

"Get outa my face junior."

"Bruce, I promise you one thing. I'll tear your top lip off if you don't stop fucking around. You've been pushing your luck far too long with me."

"Listen shithead, you just shut your rotten mouth. You can't talk to me like that."

"It's real easy killer ... Now why don't you just run along and kiss your grandmother's ass. Maybe she'll take you seriously, or at least give you some dough and shut you up."

"You better start apologizing now you prickhead. No one,

especially a little weaselly punk like you, gets away with crap like that."

"Well I guess that sets me straight, doesn't it Cousin Brucie?"

"I said, 'apologize,'... goddamit, I'm not going to wait much longer, Richard."

"Seems to me it's about time you did some waiting."

"Listen wise–ass, you've seen what happens when I lose control."

"Yeah, you wet your pants."

"All right you douche bag, that's it …"

"Okay Bruce, that's enough. I got no time to play. I'm sorry about your grandmother. Now let's drop it. I've got to get hold of a distributor over on Jerome Avenue before noon … Look, are you gonna talk to Dixon about the coke or not? He's fucking us over."

"I said I'd take care of it."

"You're not going to fix anything if you stick all the profits up your nose."

"It's my money isn't it?"

"Fine, do whatever you want. I've gotta run."

"Dixon took the message. It's over by the transmitter."

"Thanks, catch you later."

That was damn close. I'm not going to last this way much longer … Good thing he forgot to ask for any money. That would've completely torn it. Well, I better even up my funds and start laying plans for the future. First move is to get out of this urinal of a city.

Hah, typical Cordelia message, "Staying at the Plaza. Cordy." She expects me to remember that bozo's last name. I know he'd never let her register under her own. Lloyd, it's Lloyd something. Jensen, that's it—Lloyd Jensen … No, that can't be right, maybe it's Johnson. Okay, I know it begins with a J. Won't do any good trying to force it. I'll just concentrate on finding a phone booth first. That should be hard enough. Finding a phone booth that works in the South Bronx is becoming as unlikely as a "Mission Impossible" episode. Good, there's a phone booth with a parking spot nearby. Last time I left a cab out of eyesight it had one less tire when I got back. Jevons! Son of a bitch, it's Lloyd Jevons … Now why would anyone want to set fire to a phone book?

"Central Park Plaza. May I help you?"

"Sure, I'm looking for a Mr. Lloyd Jevons. I think he's registered there."

"One moment please, I'll check that for you."

Maybe old Lloyd won't be in. Or maybe he's sacked out with his dentures in a glass. I'm not really up for making our first meeting a phone conversation.

"Mr. and Mrs. Lloyd Jevons. Do you wish me to connect you with their room?"

"Yes, please."

Christ, someone's pounced right on that old receiver midway through the first ring.

"Hullo."

"Hey Cordy, it's Richard."

"Richard! You got my message."

"Yeah, my old pal Bruce gave it to me."

"I called you at work but some gorilla answered and said you were out."

"Low voice?"

"Like he just climbed down from a tree?"

"Dixon, one of our partners."

"But he sounded like a hood."

"Yeah, he is."

"You don't mean that, do you Richard?"

"Yeah I do, he did five years for manslaughter."

"Richard, what have you been doing?"

"Forget it Cordy, I was only crapping around."

"Are you sure?"

"Sure I'm sure. You should know me better than that."

"I don't like the sound of this Richard."

"Look, just forget it. I'm okay, really. I'm not in any danger."

"What kind of danger?"

"That's just it. There is no danger. Nothing's wrong. I couldn't be better Cordy. I'm telling you, everything's going my way." Sure it is. Next thing you know I'll be breaking into a chorus of "Zippadee do dah."

"Well, it's really good talking with you again Richard."

"A–hah."

"So, whatever happened with you and that mysterious young lady from Chesapeake Beach?

"Mmph."

"What do you mean, "Mmph"? What's wrong Richard?"

"Nothing. She just decided to stick with that guy, the one she's living with. Haven't heard a word from her since I moved here. If she's interested, it's up to her to get in touch."

"I'm so sorry, Richard. I really don't know what to say."

"Nothing to say. It'll all be okay. I'm pretty damn tough."

"I don't believe that."

"Well I am. I won't spend my life crawling after Lisa. It would just keep dragging on like it always has. What good would that do?"

"I thought she was very nice."

"I know she's very nice. Why'd you think I wasted so much time on her? Doesn't matter though, I'm giving all that up."

"What are you talking about? You're what, twenty–two, twenty–three?"

"Twenty–two I think, wait a minute, what year is this?"

"Seventy–three."

"Are you sure?"

"Hold on, I'll check. Lloyd left his watch on the table … seventy–three, it's nineteen seventy–three."

"Damn, I'm twenty–two. No wonder I've been feeling so creaky and worn out."

"Come off it Richard, you can't turn celibate at twenty–two."

"Who's gonna stop me? Besides, I only make a botch of all those things."

"You mean …"

"Not that way, Cordy. The old flipper still works. That's not the problem. I mean my relationships have all been either boring or absurd. I'm tired of that whole routine. I don't want to be second lead in some badly constructed farce any longer. So from now on, there's gonna be no more romanticism, no more hearts and flowers for this kid. I don't need it and I can damn well do without it. You're the first to know Cordy. I'm officially retired. I'm putting it on ice."

"That's nonsense Richard. You're only twenty–two."

"I know how old I am. We've just been through that. As far as I know, there's no minimum retirement age. Besides, all my best years have to be behind me. It's not going to get any better Cordy, maybe more sordid, but certainly not better. And I am past it. I can't keep up with those sixteen year old honeys any longer. After that, women just start to sag."

"Thanks a lot."

"Exceptions noted."

"Richard, I still wish I could hear that you were doing well. I'd like you to be happy."

"Christ Cordy, don't start with that happiness song and dance again. It's a total crock. Try listening to me for once. Happiness is only ..."

"Yes I know—an overrated commodity."

"Huh, I must've told you that one before."

"Richard, you're not fooling me. I know you. I know how miserable you feel."

"Cordy, now just come off it, my life has all the poignancy of a telephone directory."

"It won't work."

"Look, I'm not torn up. Actually, I should be grateful that Lisa dumped me. The only thing I know that's worse than unrequited love is requited love."

"Will you stop it Richard."

"Am I getting carried away again?"

"Yes."

"It's still true."

"Richard, you're hopeless."

"But not entirely without a certain degree of cheap charm."

"Well anyway, I want to see you tonight with or without your 'famous cheap charm.' And I do want you to remember to be nice to Lloyd."

"Why'd you register as Mr. and Mrs. Jevons? You said you'd invite me to the wedding."

"It's not till spring; but that reminds me, you'd never believe how far the Plaza has gone down the tubes. They actually had the audacity to give us this incredibly dreary little room. It's so small that even the cockroaches are hunchbacked. And I do mean cockroaches."

"Yeah Cordy, but ..."

"No Richard, I'm trying to tell you, it is not to be believed. The place has positively slalomed downhill. And don't you try to tell me anything different. We made the mistake of ordering up some club sandwiches from room service. When they finally arrived, and I tell you we had practically forgotten all about them, well I just won't bother describing what was on that tray. And then the people in the lobby Richard, I tell you I don't know where they can possibly come from. I mean I can't begin to imagine who does their tailoring."

"Maybe they don't have tailors Cordy."

"Well maybe you're right. Lloyd was incredibly lucky to find the one he did, this perfect little elf of a man named Jules over in Georgetown. When you come for a visit I'll give you his number. He's really quite marvelous. He used to do all the Kennedys' work."

"Yeah, what happened?"

"Oh you know perfectly well. There were all those messy assassinations and Rose always used a little old lady outside of Waltham ..."

"What about Teddy?"

"What about him indeed. Who'd want to dress a fat slob like that? But you almost made me forget ... Thanks for the money Richard. You always come through."

"Everything come off okay?"

"Sure, you know it's not back alley stuff in D.C. anymore."

"Well I wasn't exactly picturing you in a fifth floor walk–up using a coat–hanger."

"But now be honest Richard. Tell me how you really are. I can't help but worry about you."

Yeah, sure she worries, her and about half a dozen others I could mention. I'm not impressed. None of them loses any sleep over me. Cordy certainly doesn't. Besides, I don't think I'm exactly keen on being an object of concern, puts me somehow on the same level as that wayward brother of the Bronte sisters. Yeah, I can just see old Cordelia sacrificing her life for me. That's a real laugh.

"I told you sweetheart, everything in my life is just fine."

"No really Richard, what are you doing in New York?"

"I don't want to talk about it Cordy. It's grungy and for the most part just downright boring."

"Didn't I tell you not to get involved with Bruce? But you should've known that anyway."

"I did know it. I certainly know better than you how he operates. I knew he'd take advantage of me. And, I wasn't disappointed ... Well actually, I think I underestimated the dear boy."

"So why don't you quit?"

"It's complicated."

"Come on Richard, you must know ..."

"Of course I know. Look, I've committed myself to this garbage till October. I gave my word and I'm gonna go through with it. What else do I have left? I don't really believe in much. If I stop caring about the way I lead my life and how I do things I might as well just give up."

"But why New York? You hate New York. And anyway, who do you think you are, some sort of existential John Wayne? You know what an asshole Bruce is, tell him to stuff it and then take a walk."

"Cordy, what else do I have to do?"

"Stop it Richard. Stop reducing life to some second–rate Beckett play."

"You mean it isn't?"

"No, it isn't."

"Then it must be first rate. Is that what you mean?"

"You know darn well what I mean."

"Cordy, I'm being totally serious. If I didn't force myself to do something I'd run the risk of becoming a total lump. I'm not quite ready to succumb to the allures of lumpiness."

"Okay, but why this? There are better things you could be doing."

"I suffer from a serious lack of imagination."

"Especially getting tied up with an egotistical asshole like that Bruce. Did I tell you that the second day I was at school he came knocking at my door expecting to screw either me or my roommate? Both of us would have been even more to his liking."

"You're right Cordy, that school was unbelievable. Now who was that other jerk? Yeah, it was Stanhope Bishop the Third, that brainless English twit. I could never understand how he got all those women to sleep with him. But damn if he didn't … He must've worked his way through both women's dorms before the first semester was over. How all those women could be such total boobs … uh oh, he got you too, huh Cordy?"

"Oh stop it, Richard. It was just that he was sort of sweet, you know, in his little puppy dog way. He would look at me with those sad brown eyes and he seemed to need it so much."

"Must've been working his way through the local sheep population before the year was up."

"Don't be gross."

"Yeah … but is that true about Lloyd? Does he really have false teeth?"

"I knew I shouldn't have told you about that."

"But I mean isn't it …"

"You get use to it."

"But does he really take them off before …"

"I said, you get use to it."

"Phew!"

"Now listen Richard, I want you to be nice to Lloyd. If you give it a chance you'll like him. We're going to be married Richard. I want you two to be friends. It's important to me."

"Okay."

"So you know that Lloyd's the chief lobbyist for the Dairy Association. I don't want you to say anything about that."

"But Cordy, I mean …"

"I know what you mean and I don't want to hear anything about it. Lloyd's a wonderful man. I wouldn't be marrying him if he wasn't. He's a whole lot older than either one of us and he knows a lot more than we do."

"About cows?"

"I don't want you being nasty. He's seen more than we have. He just knows more about life."

"Sure."

"Well he does. But that's not really the point. I want you to promise me you'll watch yourself."

"I'll try."

"No Richard, that's not good enough."

"Okay, I won't ask him how much a congressman from Iowa costs."

"Be serious."

"Look, I said I'll try. You know how I get sometimes after I've had a few drinks."

"That's what I mean."

"Well kick me or something if I start acting up."

"Still not good enough."

"What else can I do? Should I order a cream drink? Do I dare to eat a peach? What if I say something nice about Nixon?"

"He doesn't like Nixon."

"You mean Lloyd was one of those …"

"Yes, but don't you dare mention it."

"But he really wasn't connected with …"

"Enough Richard, just promise me."

"How about if I goose him when he's not looking?"

"You're being impossible."

"Don't worry, when have I ever let you down?"

"Well …"

"Okay, but it won't happen this time. I promise I won't embarrass you."

"You're wonderful Richard."

"Nah, but thanks anyway."

"So listen, I have to meet Lloyd for lunch, but can you meet us for drinks later on at the bar? I know you two guys are going to like each other. You've really got a lot in common."

"What time?"

"Six okay?"

"Sure, see you at six."

"Richard, this time I'm really happy."

"Okay, you can tell me all about it at six."

"Wow, I just can't wait to see you again."

"Bye–bye sweetie."

I wonder how old Lloyd feels about being dragged up to New York for inspection. Huh, big Washington wheeler dealer needing an okay from a twenty–two year old punk kid. Maybe I should ask him the going price for a congressman. I know I promised, but fuck, why does he have to be a lobbyist? Sure it could've been worse. He could be oiling around the Capitol for those gun nuts or those goddam doctors. I'll try not to blow it, but Cordy must know she's asking for trouble. I mean we were both dodging gas canisters down in D.C. a few years back. Now she wants to marry one of those pimps.

I don't think Lloyd's going to like any of this. I wonder if he suspects something about the two of us. He's forty–two. He must suspect the worst, but this time there's nothing to worry about at all. I mean we really have only been friends. Neither of us wanted anything else. At least I didn't. I'm not so sure about Cordelia. My talent for picking up subtle emotional undercurrents has always been negligible. Anyway, nothing ever did happen. Well okay, there was that one weird time, but that couldn't possibly count. Sure it might be hard to explain, but really, it only looked that way. Besides, I passed out before anything interesting could happen. So, we'll just all have to see exactly how mature Lloyd can be about this whole thing.

Poor old Cordy, I should try to do my best for her. I still remember senior year when I was all crazy about Lisa. I would just barge into her apartment and use her phone. She would sit there while I had one in an endless series of weepy long distance conversations.

'Hey Cordy, how ya doin, mind if I telephone?' Very ego building I'm sure. Makes you feel useful, like a pair of warm socks or something. I should've forgotten about Lisa and done a number with Cordy. At least I understand her. … Maybe she was interested in me after all.

Anyway, that girl can certainly talk. My right ear is still throbbing. Think I'll go home early and take a nap. Need all the strength I can get at my age. Wonder if that sport jacket still fits?

**

What a cheap bastard I'm getting to be, walking twenty blocks to the Plaza. Okay, straighten out my tie before I stroll in. I wonder if I'll end up competing with Lloyd tonight. I'd better not. Wouldn't do Cordy any good. Christ, get two males together with one female and they start showing off. Maybe if I don't, Lloyd'll have enough sense to leave it hanging in his pants.

Well shit, the Plaza. Not my usual choice in joints. Can't remember being here for at least two years. Not since that time I stopped off with Shelly to have a drink. She was trying to land a waitress job. Rumplemyer's down the street must've been the eighth place to turn her down. So we stopped here and I tried to cheer her up. Wonder if she's okay. I'll have to get in touch with her some time soon. I'm really worried. She told me what was going on between Becky and her. Nothing I could do to help …

"Richard, over here."

Jesus, what has Cordy done to herself? All that paint and lacquer, like a badly exposed Vogue photograph. I hope she doesn't try to be brittle and sophisticated. That always leaves me feeling like a Noel Coward understudy.

"Nice to see you sweetheart."

I give Cordy a hug and a squeeze. A chair shifts, scratching the floor. Uh oh, the groom to be checking on the pressure. I release my hold and give her a modest peck on the cheek.

"Richard, this is Lloyd. Isn't he just wonderful? I've been telling him all about you and he absolutely insisted that we get together."

Old Lloyd looks about as glad to see me as Claudius was to see Hamlet. We both do our Commander Boop imitation; first a stiff handshake, then a curt nod of the head. It's just like when I was a high school fencer, 'Take your positions please, gentlemen.'

"So Cordelia tells me you drive a cab."

The boy's real quick; first sentence, first put down. "No, I usually don't drive them. I manage a cab company in the South Bronx."

"How very interesting."

"It has its points."

"I drove a cab nights in Washington when I was getting a Masters at Georgetown."

"What in?"

"I beg your pardon."

"The Masters degree, what was it in?"

"Management."

"Are you going to school here, Richard?"

"I've graduated from school. Besides, I don't have time to go to school. I'm managing a 'gypsy cab company'. I don't drive the cabs Mr. Jevons, I run the company."

"Gypsy cab company? Lloyd and I don't know what that means, do we Lloyd?"

"No dear, but I'm sure your friend Richard would be willing to oblige."

"They're not strictly legit Cordy, but they provide a service. The regular cabbies, they won't go into the South Bronx or Harlem. So there's this tacit agreement. As long as the gypsies don't try entering Manhattan everything else is cool."

"Well it sounds dangerous to me."

"Not really, Cordy. I mean the drivers get held–up occasionally, and the South Bronx isn't exactly Westchester County, but there's no use worrying about it."

Richard Davis, the cool sophisticated, existential hero of our time. Old Lloyd's trying not to roll his eyes.

"Well you should take better care of yourself Richard. I'm always telling you that. Lloyd dear, tell Richard he's being foolish."

"He's probably old enough to make his own decisions, dear."

"I don't know. I suppose you're right but …"

"Of course I am dear. Now tell me Richard, have you ever seen little Cordelia looking so fine? I do believe Cordy must just about sparkle these days."

"You're absolutely right, Lloyd. I've never seen Cordelia look quite this way before."

"Why you boys are going to make me blush. Excuse me."

Cordy gets up in search of a bathroom. Both of us rise. The son of a bitch thinks he can out manner me. He doesn't know I've read the complete works of Jane Austen twice.

"So what do you think about the wedding?"

I stare at him. "Excuse me?"

"What's your opinion of the two of us getting married?"

I thought Lloyd was supposed to be a smooth political operator. He's being about as subtle as a toilet seat. Maybe he thinks he doesn't have to bother because I'm only a kid. Well fuck that.

"I haven't given it any thought. But if it makes Cordy happy ..." I shrug my shoulders. Lloyd doesn't like that. He puts his finger between his Windsor knot and his Adam's apple.

"Okay Davis, we don't have to play any games here. I know all about Cordy and you, so let's just cut the crap."

Christ, what's Cordelia been telling him? I'm too young to be going senile. I mean, I'd remember if I'd ever screwed her. I know she didn't say anything about that one time. Technically nothing did happen. The old fart's just jealous. After all, I don't leave my teeth in a glass when I go to bed.

"It doesn't happen to be any of your goddam business, but just to set the record straight, we were never lovers."

Lloyd looks at me with disgust. That 'we were never lovers' line didn't come off at all. Too stilted, like something out of "The Guiding Light." I'm going to have to hire a dialogue coach pretty soon.

"Okay by me Lloyd, believe whatever you want."

Cordelia bounces back and we both get a chance to stand up again.

"Lloyd, didn't I tell you that you'd love Richard? Isn't he simply wonderful? He just had to be my closest friend at school. The poor guy single–handedly pulled me through chemistry, didn't you Richard? I was such a total dumdum."

How the hell did Cordy ever end up at a place like St. Michael's? You'd think she would've gone straight from that joint in Connecticut to someplace like Smith. Maybe she couldn't learn to speak with her jaw clenched.

"So how are my boys getting on together? You two haven't been talking about me, have you?"

We both smile politely.

"We've been having a most interesting conversation. Haven't we Richard?"

Lloyd reaches over and gives her arm a squeeze. Wants to make sure I know who owns who. What a sack of shit. This guy is strictly a dork … but he is buying the drinks. A waiter breezes by. I flag him down.

"Excuse me, could we have another round here?"

If I have to listen to this crap I might as well get drunk on Lloyd's expense account. Poor Cordelia.

"Did Richard tell you he's been living in London?"

"How very nice for him."

"Tell us about it Richard."

"Nothing much to tell Cordy, I was waiting for a teaching job."

"In London?"

"No, Nigeria. I was going to teach in Nigeria."

"You mean for the Peace Corps?"

"No, nothing like that Cordy. Not volunteer. I was going to work for the Nigerian government."

"So they wouldn't give you the job, is that it?" Lloyd asked.

"I wasn't turned down Lloyd. Interviews just kept getting balled up. It went on like that for more than half a year. Finally I decided to forget the whole thing and fly back for my sister's wedding. You can't imagine what dealing with the Nigerian embassy is like."

"Sure, all those dressed up coons trying to act like a government."

Wonderful. Lloyd here is one prime example of a real Virginia gentleman. This guy just doesn't miss a single bet. Poor Cordelia.

"I've always wanted to visit London. Lloyd and I were planning on going but then he had to testify before that Senate Committee."

"Now don't you go worrying your poor sweet head about that. I'm gonna take my pretty li'l button all over the world. Lloyd's gonna take good care of his precious baby girl."

Pretty li'l button?

"Excuse me." It's more than I can take. Besides, my poor bladder needs a break.

"Wait up a minute, Richard."

What's Lloyd up to? Maybe he wants to take a peek at my equipment. Well you can hardly refuse to piss with someone, can you? So here we are walking shoulder to shoulder through an over–

decorated lobby. Sort of a parody of two women going to powder their noses so they can talk over the guys.

"You don't care much for me do you?"

"I hardly think that matters Lloyd."

"It matters to Cordy."

"She'll get over it."

"Well I'm the one who's marrying her, not you."

"So I hear."

"Do you have any reason to doubt it young man?"

"Should I?" Charming conversation, I wonder if it will get much worse.

"You had your chance."

"Did I?"

"I've told you to cut the crap, Davis. You couldn't give Cordelia what she needed."

"And you can?"

"That's right sonny, I can. I understand how to treat a woman, how to give her what she needs. And what I don't need is for some punk kid to come butting his nose into my affairs."

"Don't be absurd."

"You understand me?"

"All too well Lloyd, baby."

If he keeps this up, I'm accidentally going to piss on his flannels. Uh oh, here comes the Plaza version of a pay toilet, the lurking washroom attendant. But give Lloyd credit, he is quick with the old wallet.

"Thank you, this is for you. That should take care of me and my young friend here."

Young friend, my ass. Well fuck it, if he wants to pay my way let him.

***

"I ordered another round while you two were gone."

I slip Cordelia a wink. Hard to tell if she's catching the drift. Being in love warps your perceptions something fierce.

"So Cordy, still working down at the E.P.A.?"

"Until the spring. Lloyd thinks I should give up the job. I mean he's right. I won't have the time for it. Lloyd needs a lot of support in his work."

"Now you know little girl, I don't want anything for you that you don't want for yourself."

I want to barf, that's what I want for myself. I swallow hard and face Lloyd.

"Cordelia tells me you do some lobbying …" A sharp kick brings me up short.

"Lloyd, I want to take Richard up and show him our room. Is that okay? We won't be long."

And you can examine our underwear afterward, Lloyd sweetie.

"Well I don't know honey …"

"Richard and I want to do some gossiping about old friends. It would just be a bore for you. Listen, why don't we meet in the Palm Room in fifteen minutes for a light dinner? It's okay, isn't it Lloyd?"

"Why, anything you want, sugar. I can't ever find the mind to say no to you."

Good, old honeysuckle's stuck with the check. Should be a tidy little sum by now. I wish Cordelia wouldn't tug on my arm so.

"Where the hell did you ever unearth him, Cordy?"

"Stop that. You almost ran off at the mouth just now. I really wanted you to be friends. Instead, the two of you have been snarling over me like a couple of dogs over a bone. I don't like it. My therapist says meeting Lloyd has been very good for me. It's made me face life instead of bouncing around like an irresponsible child."

"You should never have gone into therapy."

"Dr. Zalkind's done wonders for me. He's an excellent analyst."

"Wasn't he Melissa's shrink?"

"That wasn't his fault. If she had listened to him that never would have happened."

"The guy has an absolute talent for knocking out someone's props without giving them anything else to hang on to."

"Richard, psychoanalysis is important. It does people a whole lot of good."

"Sure it's important. It helps you to stop repeating your old mistakes and go on to bigger and better ones."

"Enough Richard. Do you understand what I'm saying? I've had enough."

"Okay, I want to know what you see in Lloyd. He doesn't even have his own teeth."

"He's been very kind and understanding. He can give me what I need."

"Are you sure, Cordelia?"

"I know I've said that before, but this time I really believe it. This time I've found a man who knows his way in the world, not some young frightened kid. He'll teach me how to deal with that world."

"I'm sorry sweetie, I'm not trying to be rude. Maybe it's the drinks."

"Are you getting sloshed?"

"Hell no, you call this drunk? Did I ever tell you about my twenty–first birthday?"

"Wasn't that when you were down in Clearwater?"

"That's right, being exploited by good old Brucie. Hauled produce for fifty dollars a week plus breakfast. Big improvement huh, now I get one twenty–five and no breakfast."

"I still think you're crazy doing this."

"Cordy, I want to tell you about this birthday. We can discuss the expropriation of my surplus labour some other time."

"I'm not trying to ..."

"So anyway, here's the story. The two of us drank about four bottles of champagne, Veuve Cliquot. Bruce doesn't muck around with domestic. I think his girlfriend might have had a few glasses but mostly it was just the two of us."

"You're forgetting the dope."

"Sure, it was my birthday, wasn't it? But that's not the point. I got so ripped on champagne that I could barely crawl upstairs. I passed out face forward on the bed; couldn't manage to get undressed, drink a glass of water, nothing. Next morning I work up and ..."

"There was an enormous pool of vomit next to your bed."

"No Cordy, that was our junior year in college. This time I woke up to find I'd pissed in my jeans. Not only were they soaked, but so was my wallet. I spent the morning trying to dry out dollar bills, my driver's license, you know, all the rubbish you carry around in a wallet."

"Did you throw it away?"

"Why would I throw away a perfectly good wallet? I still have it. Here, if you breathe hard enough you can catch a faint whiff."

"Don't be so gross."

"Okay, don't smell it."

"Richard, try to be serious, just for a moment. I'm really worried about you. This isn't the right life for you. How much longer do you honestly think you can keep this up?"

"Sweetheart, it's not that I don't appreciate your concern. And you're right, I am falling apart. I can't seem to read anymore. All I ever think about is getting some uninterrupted sleep. I certainly can't think coherently. And listen to me talk. I'm starting to say things like, 'I'm doing good,' and I use the word 'hopefully' all the time."

"Jesus."

"It's my environment. I spend twelve hours a day in the South Bronx. What can you expect? Well, look at you. You used to be some sort of low phosphate liberal and now you're marrying the milk lobby."

"You're not going to leave go of that, are you Richard?"

"I'm trying."

"Not very hard."

"Okay, all I wanted to say is that you can only give it your best shot. I know everyone has this belief, you know, that buried beneath a very ordinary, gauche exterior, there's some perfectly elegant, Fitzgerald type hero dying to emerge. But it just can't always be like that, can it? We're probably no better than we seem. The thing to do is to learn to accept it. Reality Cordy, is hardly ever what you'd order up from room service, but there it is. Doesn't do a damn bit of good to go around bitching about it."

"But you don't have to be so darn passive. You just can't expect some woman to come up to you and ask you to fall in love with her."

"I'm not looking to be a request line. I'm just telling you Cordelia, relationships depress me. They never change. There's always one person who's in love and some other who agrees to be loved. Sure that sounds like a trivial analysis, but life's like that. It doesn't mean shit."

"Richard, I'm not in the mood for your cynicism."

"Every time I start an affair Cordy, from the very beginning, I can taste the decay. I know that people won't let things be. They have to keep picking, like a kid picking at an ugly scab. Sooner or later it's gonna fester. People aren't really satisfied until they make themselves completely miserable."

"I really don't need to hear this, Richard."

"Sorry, I suppose we'd better get back before Lloyd has a fit."

"What are we going to tell him?"

"About what?"

"In case he asks, who are we going to say we were talking about?"

"We don't have to answer to him."

"Richard, why must you be so difficult?"

"Okay, how about Shelly? She's recuperating down near San Jose."

"God, I'm really glad to hear that. You know Richard I've tried to get in touch with her, but it's been impossible. When we were both living in New York I got to feel very close to her. Then she just sort of vanished."

"Remind me, I'll give you her number."

***

Lloyd is absolutely fuming. What the hell does he think we've been doing? Maybe I should let him sniff my crotch.

"Cordy, I was getting worried. You've been gone almost a half hour."

"Twenty minutes."

"Thank you Richard, I stand corrected. And for your information, the bar bill was one hundred and twenty dollars."

"Well, that's very generous of you Lloyd. I certainly appreciate your hospitality. ... Are these the menus?"

Driving cabs in the South Bronx by day, listening to cocktail music in the Palm Room at night. What a little jet setter I'm becoming.

And it's all paid for, thanks to a very sizeable contribution from Lloyd Jevons, Washington toady.

"How does this sound, Lloyd dear? We can all have turkey sandwiches and brandy alexanders."

"Of course Cordy, anything you want."

"Okay with you, Richard?"

"Sure, I'm game."

Lloyd still has a nasty expression on his face. He knows he's going to be stuck with another bill. Damn, it's not like it's his money. It's a goddam expense account. Does he really think I can afford the Plaza? Wonder what he's getting up for? Seems to be heading toward that woman doing the hokey piano playing.

"Thank you, my dear. We've so much enjoyed your playing. Perhaps you'd be so kind as to play "Mood Indigo" for me."

Lloyd bends over and kisses her hand. She looks mostly bored. He looks mostly down her cleavage. I guess being slobbered over by a middle aged creep with loose dentures is all part of the job description.

Cordy leans over and whispers, "Don't you think he's just wonderful, Richard?"

I give her a blank stare. Lloyd should find himself a new writer. His lines creak. I wish Cordy would stop deferring to him. I know she thinks she's in love but shit, Cordy's a bright girl, a lot brighter than that slimy old Lloyd. What does she think she is, a case study out of Dr. Freud's notebook? And Lloyd, I bet he just loves that subservient, lovely young thing routine. Probably makes him think he's grown a pair of balls. Cordy's done everything but flutter her damn eyelids. Well, maybe if I can get a little bit drunker, none of this will seem to matter.

That was quite the success. I can barely see straight. Wonder what nonsense I've been talking? Looks like it went over well. Lloyd's finally loosened up. Cordy's smiling. Get me drunk enough and I start liking everyone, even Lloyd. Alcohol seems to dissolve my better judgment.

"Richard, it's been a pleasure getting to know you."

"I'm glad we've had this chance, Lloyd. Cordelia's happiness means a whole lot to me."

"I appreciate that, Richard. I'm looking forward to seeing you real soon."

"There, didn't I tell you Lloyd, I knew you'd like him."

"We'll just see about getting your boy into a taxi now. I'm sure he has a full day in front of him."

"Thanks Lloyd, no need; I'll take care of it myself."

A cab my ass. People in my income bracket walk. I'd hate to break that news to Lloyd. But Cordy? What the hell should I do about poor, old Cordy? She wants something so badly from life and she's always been afraid of not getting it. Sometimes I think she's so scared she'll be found wanting that she ducks the whole issue at the last moment. Well, whatever it is she wants, she's not going to find it with old slimeball Lloyd. He packs all the comfort of an outdoor commode in Fairbanks. I've really got to say something, do something to put an end to this farce. And what would that get me? People have to be allowed to fall flat on their faces. You can't prop them up. Advice isn't only cheap—it's totally unwanted. Christ, you have to be so damn careful when you help people out. If you don't have just the right touch, they'll never be able to forgive you. Well, I'll try to help whenever I can. She runs into trouble, she asks for some comfort, I'll see what I can do. And she's bound to run into trouble with a douche bag like Lloyd. But, as Sigmund Freud once said to Karl Jung, "Life's a bitch."

"Thanks for everything, Richard. I knew I could depend on you."

"Sweetie, you take care of yourself. I'll be in touch."

I put my arm around Lloyd and walk with him to the door. Just as I'm about to leave I lean over until I'm nearly an inch from his right ear.

"Listen carefully, Lloyd. I'll only say this once. If you don't take good care of that little lady ... I'll have some of my boys break both your arms."

I walk out the door without looking back. New York waits for me, dark and treacherous as ever. Damn, I've gone and done it again. I completely blew that scene. When the hell am I going to find a better scriptwriter? Where the hell am I going to find a better life?

3

SOLUTIONS

Therefore mankind always sets itself only such tasks as it can solve
– Karl Marx

"Are you sure you can make that long drive by yourself?"

"Don't worry, Mom. I'll stop off at some friends in Boston."

"Do I know them?"

"No Mom, they're no one you'd know."

"Were they at that school with you?"

"Yes Mom, they went to St. Michaels but they're still my friends."

"I never did want you to go there."

"I know, but it's too late for that."

"If you'd stayed at home Richard, I wouldn't be so worried now."

"We've been through all this before."

"I told your father not to lend you that money. What was wrong with the schools around here?"

"I paid the money back, Mom."

"That's not the point. I've never begrudged you the money. That college gave you the wrong ideas."

"I have to get going, Mom. They're expecting me for dinner."

"Are you sure I didn't meet them at graduation?"

"I don't think so."

"Well, why didn't you introduce me?"

"I couldn't introduce you to everyone."

"But I like meeting your friends."

"Maybe some other time."

"Are those people married?"

"Not the last time I checked."

"They're just living together?"

"Ah, you've picked up a new expression."

"I can't accept that, Richard."

"I'll tell them that when I get there."

"Now don't get smart with your mother."

"Sorry, Mom."

"You wouldn't do that would you, baby?"

"What's that?"

"Live together without being married first."

"Sure."

"Oh Richard, how could you do that to me?"

"Mom, it's no big deal. Sex isn't all that serious."

"It is to me."

"Then I guess I'm probably not as good at it as Dad is."

"I don't like that kind of talk from you, Richard."

"This is ridiculous. I'm living alone in rural Maine. I don't have any opportunities to go astray."

"I wish you wouldn't live alone like that. It's not normal."

"I thought you didn't want me living with someone?"

"You could meet a nice girl right here and settle down."

"I probably could."

"Then you'll do it?"

"No Mom, I'm not going to do that?"

"But you just said you would."

"I said I 'could.' Now honest, I do have to get going. It's a long drive to Boston."

"Don't forget to lock your doors."

"Yes Mom, I won't let anyone jump in my car when I'm whizzing down the interstate."

"And don't pick up any hitch–hikers. It's not safe."

"I know, you sent me those articles."

"Do you need any money?"

"I'm fine, Mom."

"Are you sure I don't know your friends?"

"I'm sure, Mom."

"Well what are their names?"

"Scott and Melissa."

"I don't think I know them, Richard."

"That's okay Mom, I'll introduce you sometime."

"Call as soon as you get back to Maine."

"I don't have a phone."

"Are you sure you won't let me pay for one? It would make me feel better."

"No Mom, when I want a phone, I'll pay for a phone."

"I still don't see why you insist on living up there."

"Maybe I'm just dumb enough to like it. Look Mom, I've got to go. Say good–bye to Dorrie for me."

***

I've been on every bit of I–95 but this stretch through Connecticut has to be among the worse. Connecticut, the Nutmeg State, what the hell is that supposed to mean? Why choose something like nutmeg? Why not cinnamon or even coriander? What's so special about nutmeg? … Yeah, I can still remember old Sandy trying to get high one afternoon by snorting that stuff. She was laughing so hard that it got all over my room instead. Wonder what she's doing these days. Maybe Melissa would know. They used to be all buddy buddy. Uh uh, I don't think I should mention Sandy's name. Melissa's probably still sore about what happened, touchy woman that Melissa.

Christ, I hope Scott and Melissa are on speaking terms. If they're going through one of their bad periods I'll just pack up and leave. I don't care how late it is or how tired I feel. I won't put up with any more of their squabbling. When they're on the outs I can't handle the tension those two generate.

Who knows why people like Scott and Melissa stay together. It was mostly her idea to begin with. Scott would just as soon be off somewhere by himself painting. And Melissa is certainly a little hard to take sometimes. Should be there in another half hour. Hope they've got enough room for me. I don't really mind sleeping on their floor, but all those roaches rappelling off my stomach always keeps me awake. Don't imagine the place is any cleaner than last time. At least I don't have to worry about whether to screw around with

Melissa. Even if Scott wasn't a consideration, I can't see becoming too excited about a woman who goes to bed in a pair of Dr. Denton's.

Should I try to find some gas? Nah, the damn lines are too long. Son of a bitch oil companies finally have an excuse to stick it to us. Wonder how they manage to keep a straight face when they publicly tsk, tsk, about the Arabs. One day everyone will realize that there was no shortage, but who's going to care, or remember? People in this country just line up to be butt–fucked every day.

There's my exit anyway. I'll wait until I get to Scott and Melissa's. They ought to have the latest scoop on all the local gas stations. Well, I'm almost there anyway.

"Any trouble finding the place, Richard?"

"Nothing to it, Scott. My usual number of wrong turns."

"You missed the turn at Symphony Hall."

"Yeah, that and the one onto Heath."

"I thought you warned him about that, Melissa?"

"She did, I'm just hopeless with directions."

"You're looking good, Richard."

"And so are you, Melissa. Still driving that cab around?"

"Nope, I quit the night I got held up."

"Didn't you have one of those plexi–glass shields?"

"Sure I had a shield. What was I supposed to do if it didn't work, sue the manufacturer?"

"Why'd you do it anyway, Melissa? Driving cabs is the pits."

"It was a step up from teaching English in Roxbury; more money plus a whole lot safer."

"At least you weren't held up in school."

"It was only a matter of time before that happened."

"So what are you doing now?"

"Selling auto parts at a foreign import store."

"And you like doing that?"

"It's not something you like, Richard, but it's not all that bad. And, I'm starting to learn a little something about cars."

"Like what?"

"Changing the oil, tuning the engine; at least I won't be totally dependent on some jerk of a gas station mechanic."

"What about the newspaper, Scott, still doing layouts for it?"

"No, it folded last month. But I might end up working in a political campaign. See there's this guy, and he's just a few years older than we are, some sort of decorated Vietnam vet. He thinks he has a chance to break into Congress."

"The guy's a total loser. I keep telling you that, Scott."

"Melissa's kind of down on the idea, aren't you, Melissa?'

"Since when did you ever listen to a thing I said? But what about you Richard, you're not really serious about going back up to Maine?"

"Yeah I am, Melissa."

"I can't believe it."

"Yes you can, Melissa."

"What the hell can you do up there in February?"

"Try to stay warm."

"Scott, he's your friend, you try to explain it to him."

"Melissa, will you lay off of Richard. That's how he is. He likes being bored."

"Well how does he expect to survive up there? Just who the hell does he think he is, Nanook of the North?"

"You could just go ahead and ask him yourself. I mean, he's sitting there right next to you."

"Look Melissa, I understand that you think I'm wasting my time up there, but it's exactly what I want to be doing. For one thing it's quiet. There's no one around to pester me. I can go snowshoeing for hours without hearing a sound, just the wind moving through the trees. And the last few months, I've been getting up in time to see the sun rise. Can you imagine me wanting to do something like that? Damn Melissa, it's so goddam clean up there. And no one's looking to hurt you or keep you from walking the streets at night, or even …"

"That's because there are no streets and no one to stand on them if there were."

"Okay Melissa, I'm not gonna try to convince you. It just happens to be where I want to live."

"For how long?"

"Until I get tired of it."

"And where's all the dough gonna come from?"

"I've got a plan, Melissa."

"The only plan you ever had was to marry some rich woman."

"That's the plan. I'm getting myself a wife."

"Hey congratulations, Richard, when's the wedding? Melissa and I can be your best man."

"Well, it's still a little early for that, Scott. I have to let her know first."

"Someone you met up there?"

"Nope, youngest woman I've run into up there was fifty, and she was already married."

"Then who's the lucky lady?"

"A woman by the name of Kim Stanton."

Scott gives me a hard stare. He turns and goes into the next room. We both hear him rummaging around,

"What's he doing, Melissa?"

"How should I know? I have my own problems to deal with."

He comes back with a thin book and tosses it on the kitchen table. I glance at the title, *Thinking Backwards*. Scott nudges it toward me.

"She wrote that book when she was sixteen, Richard, her autobiography."

"At sixteen?"

"Yeah, well it's not any too good but maybe the topic wasn't all that promising."

I look at her picture on the dust jacket. A little too poignant, and scrawny, she certainly is scrawny. Well maybe she's filled out a bit since.

"She writes for the *Globe* sometimes. I didn't know about the book, Scott. Actually, I've never read any of her newspaper columns either. It's only the "Viewpoint" program I know about."

"Viewpoint?"

"Radio editorials, Scott. There's not much else to do up in Maine."

"There, he admits it himself, Scott. Only an idiot would live in that godforsaken state."

"Hush up, Melissa, no use going through all that again. Okay

Richard, so you've heard these radio solos. How does she sound?"

"Pretty much like a sap. But, it's nothing I can't handle."

"One thing I don't understand. Where did you ever run into her?"

"Well, I guess that's the real problem, Scott. I haven't."

"What! You're marrying someone you don't even know? Even Scott wouldn't try to pull a dumb move like that."

"Oh, shut up Melissa, give Richard a chance to explain."

"Thanks buddy. You see, it all happened when I was back home to see my parents. I ran across this magazine article in the *Ladies' Home Journal*. Yeah, not all that much to do down there either. I mean unless you're entertained by listening to my parents squabble. But, you know how that is, Scott."

"What are your folks doing these days? They still planning on moving down to Florida?"

"They've been about to do that for five years now. I can't make any sense of their goings on. I've given up trying."

"Stop distracting him, Scott, I want to hear about that article."

"Like I was saying, Melissa, there was this article about her. She lives up in New Hampshire by herself and she's very lonely."

"So?"

"So it's pretty simple, Melissa. I write her a letter and ask her to marry me."

"And that's all it'll take, is that right, Richard?"

"No, Melissa, of course that's not all it'll take. I'm not completely naïve. She might want to meet me first. I mean she might not want to get married till after she's seen me."

"He's being overly considerate, don't you think so, Scott?"

"That's right, Melissa. There's no need to be so modest, Richard. She's probably willing to marry you sight unseen."

"Are you saying I'm not attractive enough, Scott?"

"Look Richard, I'm not knocking your charm, but you can't just write to some woman saying, 'Hey toots, how about you and me getting married?' She's going to think you're some kind of bozo."

"Not if I do it right."

"Listen to what Scott's telling you, Richard. What sort of woman is going to accept a lunatic proposal like that?"

"It's not crazy, Melissa. I've thought it out and it's not impossible."

"Sure, and I might be cast opposite Robert Redford in his next picture."

"I kinda doubt that, Melissa."

"Well, I'm not about to start saving up for your wedding gift."

"Look, I told you, Melissa. I don't expect her to go for it right off. She's perfectly welcome to come for a visit first."

"That's very generous of you, Richard, but why in God's name should she even think of responding?"

"The letter, Melissa, wait until she reads the letter."

"No way it's gonna work, Richard."

"Scott, tell Melissa how much a stamp costs?"

"Ten cents."

"I'm willing to risk the investment. Just think of it. There she is, all alone in her little house in New Hampshire, when suddenly I enter her life. Besides, I figure she must be doing okay between the newspaper stuff and her radio spots. It's not like I'm gonna demand all that much from her. I've got modest tastes. You know that, Scott."

"Sure I know that, but what about Salinger?"

"Who?"

"You know who he is, Richard; Catcher in the Rye, Franny and Zooey?"

"So what about him, Scott?"

"The two of them, they're supposed to be having some sort of affair."

"Listen, Salinger's an old man. Why would she want to screw around with him?"

"Maybe he's that type of author. You know, like when you finish reading his work, you feel like knocking on his door and asking him to fuck."

"No problem."

"You mean no problem for your plan or are you talking about fucking Salinger?"

"Forget about Salinger. I tell you it's simple, Scott. She's making enough money for the two of us. I figure, I'll write her this sincere letter and that will be that."

"What good will that do, Richard?"

"It's going to convince her to marry me. That's my plan. I'm going to propose to her by mail. Look Scott, you didn't read the article. I tell you she's desperate, sitting there all by herself, hoping that someone will give her a ring. When my letter comes, she'll be totally swept off her feet. Then, there's only the 'happily ever after' part to take care of."

"Melissa's right, you've gone completely bonkers. You can't be serious about this."

"Not about sweeping her off her feet. But I think the whole thing is worth a try. There's not much I'm putting on the line here."

Scott looks at the picture on the dust jacket and shrugs.

"Not too promising is she?"

"Could be a bad picture. She looked better in the magazine article."

"Well she was only sixteen here."

"Be fair, Scott. Besides being a little scrawny, she's not all that bad."

"But Richard, you're not planning on asking her out to a movie. Marriage is this long term thing … well, some marriages are."

"I'm not married yet, Scott. Give me a few months, I'll end up getting attached to her. People start looking better to me once I get used to them."

"Okay, it's your life guy. Have fun with it. Now how about picking up some pizzas and beer for dinner?"

"Sure, if that's okay with you and Melissa."

"It's what we usually do, anyway. Melissa can call ahead and it should be ready by the time we finish buying the beer and driving over."

"Scott, make sure they don't put anchovies on it."

"I guess I'll see you when we get back, Melissa."

We head down the stairs, mice scampering for safety on the landing below.

"I thought Melissa liked anchovies."

"It's the cats, Richard. They start dancing on the table if you bring in anchovies."

"Put them outside."

"They just find their way right back in. They must have a key to the place."

"How do they feel about mushrooms?"

"They're lukewarm about mushrooms."

"Okay, a large pizza, lotsa cheese, lotsa mushrooms."

"Yeah, that's what Melissa's gonna order."

"Whose car are we taking?"

"Don't matter to me, Richard."

"Well if your car's still running, let's go in that. Mine's too jammed up with stuff inside."

"That's right, you'd better move it off the street if you want to see it in the morning."

"That bad?"

"People around here figure, if it's on the street, it's up for grabs. Hank's car was stripped bare overnight."

"What's that clown doing these days?"

"Harvard Business School."

"That figures."

"Well, we all can't marry wealthy women, Richard."

"No, I guess not."

***

Good thing we got plenty of napkins. Melissa couldn't find a clean plate. I suppose she didn't feel like washing a few in the bathtub. Their landlord won't fix the sink. Well, what can you expect for seventy bucks a month?

"Did you hear what Scott said, Richard?"

"What's that?"

"He said, they'll never get rid of that creep, Nixon. I say, if Agnew could be forced out ..."

"Yeah, but it took them long enough to give that doofus the boot. Scott's right, Melissa, Nixon's there for good."

"They'll get him, Richard, just like they finally got Agnew. That reminds me, did Leslie ever tell you that story about old Spiro?"

"Doesn't matter, I never believe a word she says."

"No, I think this time it's true, even if it does come from Leslie."

"Let me guess … the two of them used to meet at the Maryland Inn when he was governor."

"Be serious, Richard, even Leslie has some standards."

"Sure she does, Melissa. But, as long as Agnew was able to get an erection, he met them."

"Richard's got you there, Melissa. Remember that time by the river with those Middies from the Academy? As I recall, Leslie was being extremely selective. She wouldn't start on a new one until she had wiped her mouth clean first."

"Scott, that's disgusting."

"Sure Melissa, but try telling that to Leslie."

"You know what I mean. It's the two of you who are being disgusting. So what's it going to be? Are you finished badmouthing Leslie, or would you just rather skip the whole thing."

"Don't get so upset. Just go on with your story. Scott and I will shut up."

"Well, her uncle …"

"She doesn't have an uncle. Scott, did you ever hear anything about an uncle?"

"Okay Richard, forget it."

"No, I'm really sorry about that Melissa. I won't say another word."

"Her uncle is a contractor down in Maryland and he told her all those payoff reports were absolutely true."

"How would he know?"

"Couldn't help but knowing, Richard. He was one of the guys lined up outside Agnew's door."

"That doesn't surprise me."

"What gets me is what a sanctimonious prig he is; standing at that podium in front of nationwide TV, denying any wrongdoing."

"Did you expect him to confess, Melissa?"

"I'm not naïve, Richard. Of course he was going to lie. I just get fed up with all these self–righteous assholes having their hands stuck deep into the jam pot. Explain it to him, Scott."

"Richard, m'boy, morality is the last refuge of a douche bag."

"Is that updated Samuel Johnson, Scott?"

"No Richard, it's my exit line. I'll see you in the morning."

"Where you going Scott?"

"To bed."

"Don't you sleep here?"

"Sometimes, but I've got this apartment down the street."

"Since when?"

"Oh, about a month ago."

"Well you're coming by before I leave, right?"

"Sure Richard, I said I'd see you in the morning. Night, Melissa."

We listen to Scott picking his way carefully down the wooden stairs.

"Damn, I forgot to give him that piece of lead pipe. You can't walk around here like you were in the middle of an Iowa cornfield."

"What's going on, Melissa?"

"You know the neighborhood, Richard. It's not safe."

"I mean, what's with Scott going off like that?"

"He doesn't much care for staying up late."

"Aren't you and Scott getting it on anymore?"

"We thought it might be better to give each other a little more space."

"By living a block apart?"

"It's the intention that's important."

"So what's the intention?"

"I told you, we were getting edgy cooped up in this apartment."

"Whose idea was it?"

"That doesn't matter."

"You mean Scott was afraid he might have to make a commitment."

"Richard, you're hardly in a position to judge."

"I'm not attacking him, Melissa."

"It drives me absolutely crazy. All you guys are exactly the same. None of you ever want to open up. It's that goddam St. Michaels. That school ruins everyone who goes there."

"You know that's not true."

"Do I? What was your record there, Richard?"

"Me? What did I ever do?"

"Rachel."

"Those things just happen, Melissa."

"Sandy."

"She kissed like a guppy."

"So that's supposed to make what you did okay?"

"That's enough, Melissa."

"She thought it was."

"What do you want me to say? Okay, I was a total shit. Does that make you happy? I was a young kid and I screwed things up. I didn't know any better."

"Don't start going dramatic on me, Richard. You were never a shit, but don't try to pretend it all happened in some dim past. It was only two years ago. But I'm talking about something else, about being able to love somebody. None of you guys can do it. I've been struggling with Scott for five years now. Every time I think I'm about to bring him around, he spooks like a bird dog out on his first shoot."

"What?"

"Nothing, that's just an old Alabama expression."

"Maybe it's only all these animals you have stashed away that makes him a bit nervous. You have to admit it's a mite cramped around here."

"C'mon Richard, he's afraid, just like you are."

"What am I supposed to be scared of?"

"Of yourself. What else could it be?"

"Melissa, don't be so sure you've got me typed, or Scott either for that matter."

"I understand more than you think. What would you do if I took off my clothes?"

"Right now?"

"Sure, like this."

"Uh, could you hold on to that shirt for a minute, Melissa."

"Why, what's the problem?"

"You're making me extremely nervous."

"Don't try to tell me you're not dying to sink your teeth into my wet muff … That's the way you guys talk, isn't it?"

"I kinda doubt it, Melissa. Look, what are you trying to prove? You know Scott's a real close friend."

"He'd never have to know."

"You're missing the point. I can't operate like that."

"What's the matter, Richard? Aren't I attractive enough for you?"

"Cut it out, Melissa. You're not going to box me in like that. Okay, you go ahead, you'll only end up feeling foolish."

"Sure, Richard. But what about that bulge below your belt?"

"McChesney down there doesn't share my moral inhibitions."

"So what do you think, not all that bad for an old woman of twenty–six."

"I'm going to bed."

"You don't have to leave the room to do that."

"Damn it, Melissa, don't hit on me because you're pissed off at Scott! Yes, I would like to fuck you. Now put something on before you pick up any more of that gooseflesh."

"I didn't know that, Richard."

"You shouldn't believe everything you hear."

"How long?'

"What's that, Melissa?"

"I want to know how long you've wanted to screw me."

"Oh for God's sake, it doesn't do any good to sit here and talk about these things. Why don't you try climbing into your Doctor Denton's and then maybe we can watch an old movie together."

"Are you sure?"

"No, I'm not, Melissa, so try to help me instead."

"I think I always liked you, Richard. Maybe that's why I can't stop myself from being so hard on you."

"I know that, Melissa, but listen, you're talking to an almost married man."

"Cut it out. You're not really serious about that."

"Maybe not, but I'm still gonna give it a shot."

"I don't understand you, Richard."

"It's not as bad as it sounds. I know I've been joking around, but I think it might actually work. I was dead serious before. I do get used to people. After a while they stop looking so bad. I don't know.

I have a feeling that this Kim Stanton person might turn out to be okay. I can't tell you why, it's certainly nothing I got from reading that silly article."

"You're trying to live a fairy tale, do you realize that?'

"Well, what if I am? Look, why don't you toss me over that TV Guide and I'll see what's on. ... Hey, I don't believe it! Wait till I tell you what's on at eleven."

"Which one of your favorite junk movies are they running tonight?"

"I deeply resent that, Melissa. We're not going to watch some nasty gladiator flick. I'm talking about tuning on Zulu in just about ten minutes."

"What?"

"Trust me. It's a great movie. This is the one where hordes of African natives swarm over a British outpost."

"Must we?"

"Don't be so damn negative. I guarantee you'll love it. Besides, you don't have to work tomorrow."

"Well, are you sure ..."

"Let's stick with the TV, Melissa."

"You're a real good friend, Richard."

"I'm trying to be."

Once more the kid slips through without any major damage. Actually, Melissa looked better than I expected. But life isn't only a matter of dipping your wick ... well okay, maybe that's as good of an organizing principle as any other. The problem would be having to face Scott the next day. I would feel like a shit. Or even worse, I might not feel anything. There are still some types of truth I'd rather not have to face.

It's really not hard guessing one reason why Scott moved out. Melissa's sure no prize as a housekeeper. She's already transformed one room into an indoor potting shed. In another year or two she'll have to move out completely, along with her two dogs, three cats, and troupe of performing cockroaches.

"What was that, Melissa?"

"What was what?"

"There, crawling over Michael Caine's stiff upper lip."

"A cockroach."

"On the inside of the TV screen?"

"Yeah, they love it in there. It's a goddam cockroach paradise. About a month ago the set stopped working. Turned out one of those little buggers had shorted out a circuit. Fried it all to hell."

"Speaking about roach heaven ..."

"Damn, must've been a couple hundred back there. Totally freaked out the repairman."

"He probably wasn't too keen on having them scampering around his shop."

"Hush, Richard, I want to see what Stanley Baker is up to."

"I knew you'd love this movie."

"Where did they ever find all those Zulus?"

"The South Bronx."

"That isn't funny, Richard."

"Then stop laughing and watch the film."

***

Good, I knew three hours of the British Empire would blunt Melissa's sexual yearnings. Now maybe I can catch some sleep.

"You need any help making up the couch?"

"No thanks. My parents sent me to camp when I was eight."

"Don't mind the cats. Sometimes they get a little restless at night."

"No problem, I can sleep through anything. See you in the morning."

"Be careful, Richard. You may end up getting what you want."

"Don't be so damn cryptic Melissa, it doesn't suit you."

"You know what I mean."

"Okay, what if I do. That doesn't mean I've got to give up trying. I'm not dead yet."

"I'm not telling you what to do. But I know how you operate. You just plunge straight ahead without giving a single thought to any of the consequences. Pretty soon you find yourself wallowing in some god–awful mess."

"I can take care of myself, Melissa."

"Well, try a little harder, Richard, for me."

"Sure sweetie, now go and get some rest. I'll see you and Scott in the morning."

"The coffee's in the fridge if you get up early."

"Goodnight, Melissa."

***

Why am I up? It's gotta be too early. Bladder seems okay. That's it, that strange sound. Can't tell where it's coming from. Better get up and investigate. Hell! I certainly banged the crap out of my knee. Can't seem to focus my eyes yet. There's all that crud sticking my lids together. Sounds like it's coming from outside this door.

Turning the handle I find one of Melissa's cats sitting on the landing, pompously awaiting my congratulations. Directly at my feet are two small and very bloody creatures wriggling on the filthy floor. They're making regular, plaintive squeals, a madman's idea of a windup toy. I close my eyes. I don't want to have to see this. Another three feet away are two perfectly tailored mouse suits, lying as if their owners had just that moment slipped them off without bothering to hang them up.

"Get outta here you sunavabitch cat!"

The cat stalks off, her dignity seriously offended by my tantrum. I take one more look at the skinned mice and slam the door shut. I feel like vomiting. The right thing to do would be to finish them off but I can't. All I want to do is to lie down and pretend it never happened. The hell with it. I'm getting out of here. I'll leave Scott and Melissa a note. That way I won't have to deal with Melissa if she's in one of her moods. Scott will probably think the worst. Well, I'm not gonna sit here listening to those mice squeak their lives away. I can make it back to the farm in about five hours. If I take a nap I can finish that letter tonight.

Back on I–95 again. I'm starting to realize how much I hate driving. Maybe I liked it when I was a kid, but not after spending part of a winter in Maine. Whatever seeds of reluctance were slowly sprouting before have now become nurtured to a state of outright abhorrence by the roads and the weather up here. Forget what the state troopers try to tell you, it's snow and automobiles that don't mix. As long as you're ignorant of the danger, there's no problem. You can go rocketing along, nerves as steady as if you were sitting out on the front porch digesting your lunch. But once those nerves snap, there's no getting them back; Lucky Pierre one moment, alias Tommy the Turtle the next. These days a flurry is enough to make my palms start to sweat, even something like this piddly snow shower that's just beginning to fall …

***

Eight goddam hours of trying to keep my car on the road before I made it back home. I can still feel the adrenalin pumping. Those last fifty miles were the pits. Good thing I managed to snuggle up to that snow plow or I'd still be spinning my wheels in some ditch outside of Yarmouth. Okay, a couple shots of scotch; time to provide for my future.

How should I address her? It's important to have the right touch from the very first word. I need proper respect but nothing too formal. I don't want sloppy familiarity or sheepdog friendliness, but I can't give her the impression that I have a poker stuck up my ass. What I need is sincerity. This letter has to reek with sincerity from start to finish. I've got it, how about, "To whom it may concern"? C'mon, get serious. This isn't supposed to be an intentional goof. After all, it might work. She sounds like someone who'd go for it if she was approached in the right way. Don't forget buddy, you're writing to your future meal ticket.

I think I'll try early nineteenth century. That should catch her eye. "My Dear Ms. Stanton." Good, I like that. The "Ms." is a smart touch, adds just the right dusting of modernity. Okay, now for the rest:

I have a rather bizarre proposal to make to you. One which I hope you will find neither crass nor offensive. It will be easy enough to dismiss my letter. I realize the absurdity of it. The difficulty is in composing a letter which will convince you that I am not a crank. I do not know how to go about doing so.

That sounds about right. Put forth her own objections before she has the chance to make them herself. Better cross out "bizarre," don't want her to think I'm about to haul out the leather jumpsuits. "Unusual" should do just as well. It's one of those nice indeterminate adjectives. Now for the second paragraph:

Common sense will tell you to disregard this letter as being somewhat adolescent at best. I cannot and will not attempt to argue against such a view. I can only ask you to take a rather long chance and believe in someone. It seems that one must sometimes act according to how one thinks the world should be rather than how it may appear to be.

Okay, I've convinced her of my basic nobility. It smells honest. If she isn't convinced that I'm not a rural rapist by now, I've lost my case. Better push on with equal parts flattery and pseudo Pascal:

If my perception of you is correct, you will take such a chance. If I am wrong I lose but ten cents worth of postage.

Implying that I am risking a trifle, but have the world to gain. Should I spring the trap now? No, too early. I need to make one more stab at convincing her that I have no ulterior motives:

I have thought and considered the course of action I plan to take. I try not to undercut what I promise through easy self–indulgence. I attempt to stand by my commitments whatever the consequences.

Now ever so gently close in on my purpose. Don't want to scare her off:

Until two weeks ago I had no such thought of marriage, for it is marriage that I mean to propose. I have been renting an old farmhouse in the Maine woods since last October. Previously I had drifted, never finding a place where I felt settled. But now in my twenty–third year by moving to Maine I've discovered a place which I feel deeply about, which I do not want to leave. I will be able to manage alone, perhaps by combining teaching with some farming. Since my needs are few, this should not prove to be very difficult. When by chance I happened to pick up and read a magazine article about you, it seemed that we might do better together, that we might share our lives.

I wonder if that sounds too much like a corporate merger proposition. It's pretty modest and low key. I could say that I was instantly struck by her innate beauty and grace. No way that would ever fly. The article made her sound like a complete gawk. Should I mention which magazine I'm talking about? No, I'm sure she's vain enough to know which one. It's not likely there were any others. The question is whether I'm reading her right. Well, if this doesn't work, I don't know what will. Now I'll strike a slightly, 'gosh shucks', bashful note while daring her to take the chance:

I would like you to visit me Ms. Stanton. We might discover whether my proposal is at all possible. There is no way that I can convince you that I do not write out of desperation or boredom. You must be willing to place at least a minimum of trust in me. I can only ask you to consider my proposal seriously. It is not made lightly. This is something I have never done before, nor am likely to do again.

Either the hook is in by now or I've lost the battle. Might as well wrap it up. That Ms. Stanton bit though, that was another nice touch. Little details like that can push in the right direction:

If you are interested and would like to, you can call (207) 647–0922. I do not have a phone, but the Abbotts will relay any message. You can come by plane or bus into Lewiston. Or you can drive or hitch up Route 202, turning off on Maine State 106. My house is about ten miles south of Lawrence, a mile north of an old mill by a pond. Just look for a farmhouse and barn on a rise, right hand side of the road, mailbox says Abbott.

Please excuse the rather serious tone of this letter.

Sincerely,

Richard Davis

***

Look at it out there. Wet snow, the wind whipping round the hill; there must be bogs of semi–melted ice and snow down there big enough to swallow a horse. Damn, there goes the mailman in his yellow four wheel drive. Wonder if I should bother. Probably nothing there for me. Better to have a cup of warm milk and go back to sleep. Well, he did stop.

"You never know, this may be the day I hear from Howard Hughes." Great, now I'm starting to talk out loud to myself.

A definite mistake, my boots are full of water, I'm plastered with mud, and my moustache is clogged with frozen water and snot. Okay, what's the prize? One lousy letter, wonder where it's from? Hm, I don't know anyone in New Hampshire, Ben moved out of Durham last fall. Jesus H. Christ, it's from her. It worked! Goddam, I can't friggin believe it! I'm gonna piss in my pants, I'm so damn excited. Better not open it here, bad karma not to mention bad weather. The key is to pretend I don't really care, otherwise it won't turn out the way I want it to. I've got to try to trick fate, make an end run while it's not looking. I'll just stick it in this here pocket of mine and wait till I'm inside with my cup of hot milk and honey.

There, now let's see what Kimmie baby has to say for herself. Uh oh, I should've known not to put that hitch–hiking line in, made the whole thing sound like a put on. Hm … hm, starting to look better. Damn, I knew she'd make that merger remark. Hm … hm, what's this? Sorry she isn't adventurous enough to at least call up. Not as sorry as I am toots, though I'm probably better on paper than I am over the phone. Hah, my very sweet offer … close, I came real close. I know she almost decided to take that chance. And that would've been it. She'd never have left Maine unattached …

"Richard m'boy, you are becoming one very vain, insufferable shithead. You don't deserve to have any luck."

So another long shot doesn't pan out. Well, I'm probably gonna continue wanting to eat. I'd better start looking for something that actually pays good money. And where exactly do I expect to find a job like that up in this wasteland? Well, no matter, it's all the same really. It's just one more giant step on the treadmill to oblivion.

4

YOU CAN'T STEP IN THE SAME RIVER TWICE –
AN ELEGY

Everything flows. –Heraclitus

There are years in my life whose memories draw me back unbidden. An elicit, furtive morbidity surrounds such thoughts. I return again and again to examine each word, each feeling of those now dead conversations. I mine the slightest detail for meaning like some Talmudic scholar bent over his crumbling texts. And still, not an inch closer do I come toward understanding.

"Richard, pick up on five–one."

"Evening folks. Welcome to the Brass Rail. Relax for a few minutes, look over the menu and I'll be back to take your order. My name's Richard. Call out if you run into any difficulties ... All set now? Let me know if there's anything else you need ... Julie, scotch and soda, bourbon rocks and buy that woman a drink on my tab ... Yes, we're open till ten. Yes, that's right, two more hours ... Through with that sir? ... And how would you like that steak? Sour cream and butter on your baked potato? A side order of mushrooms, onions and peppers?"

"Richard, could you water table three–two for me? My halibut is drying out."

"Yes ma'am, lobsters are tricky little buggers to eat. No, just twist off the tail. That's right. Now poke the meat through ..."

"Hey Richard, catch a load of the knockers at five–three."

"No ice–cream, but we do have cheesecake. Yes, with strawberries, it comes with strawberries on top ... Excuse me ma'am, more coffee? ... No, don't butterfly that filet, the turkey wants it well done. Yeah, he knows how long it takes …"

"Richard, who's the yo–yo drinking scotch and ginger?"

"This is Maine, Julie. They drink Jack Daniels and Moxie up here …"

"You've got another deuce over in the corner, Richard."

"Thanks Nikkie, do you have the change from six–one?"

"Brought it back five minutes ago."

"You're a real sweetheart, Nikkie."

"Rich, some bird's been waiting at the bar for at least an hour now just to sit in your section."

"Yeah, do you know who she is?"

"Well how the hell should I know? But she seems to know her way around with you. 'Oh Miss, I would like a single in Mr. Davis' section. I'm willing to wait.' And all very la di da, if you know what I mean."

"Put her at five–one and do me a favor Nikkie, water her? Thanks sweetie."

"Don't try to sweetheart me, buster. Next time Mr.Davis, you can just take care of your female friends on your own time."

"What've I done now?"

"Nothing."

"Don't be like that, Nikkie. I want to know what the problem is … C'mon, you can tell me."

"Problem? No problem at all. Good old Nikkie couldn't possibly have a problem, now could she, Mr. Davis?"

"Give it a rest, will you … Listen to me, we can talk about this after work. I'll buy you a drink."

"And that's supposed to make everything else all right? … Well okay, but don't start taking me for granted or I'll be gone before you know it buddy."

"So how's everything going tonight young lady, first time here?"

"I want to thank you for the drink, kind sir."

"Sure, anytime. But how did you know it was from me?"

"I asked the woman tending bar."

"Well, can I buy you another one of those?"

"Maybe just a glass of white wine this time."

"What've you been drinking?"

"Bourbon old fashions."

"Hey Julie, a glass of white wine and what's the story on that woman?"

"She asked me who the drink was from and I said, "Mr. Davis." So she says, 'Who's that?' Right about then you poked your head through the window, so I gave a point. I'd say she must be pretty taken by you. I've been watching her sitting here half listening to Ebert tell his trout stories, letting him spring for the drinks, just so she could sit at one of your tables."

"You know who she is?"

"Seen her here before. Looks like a school teacher or something. Carded her the first time, turned out to be twenty–seven."

"Christ, she looks about nineteen tops."

"She's small."

"Yeah, guess that's it. Well thanks Julie, you're a sweetheart."

"Watch yourself, Richard. Don't jump in too soon."

"So what's your name young lady?"

"Katherine Hamilton."

"Okay Kathy, what would you like to eat?"

"Katherine."

"Yeah, what can I do for you?"

"You mean about dinner?"

"Yeah, that'll have to do for the moment."

"Well, you see Mr. Davis ..."

"Richard."

"I'm out celebrating tonight."

"Good for you. What's the big occasion?"

"Liberation. I paid off my Mastercharge today, so I told myself, 'Katherine, you just go right out there and treat yourself to a lobster.' But don't bother bringing the potato Mr. Davis, I'm still on a diet."

"Okay young lady, I'll see that you get everything you need tonight. Just trust me. So help yourself to a salad and I'll be right back ... What's the problem now Nikkie?"

"Boss wants to see you, Richard."

"What's up?"

"No idea. Why don't you go and ask him yourself?"

"Nikkie says you wanted to see me."

"Pretty hot little woman you've managed to snag for yourself."

"Uh huh."

"Tried to pick her up myself at Jakes last week."

"Yeah?"

"Thinking of doing a little thumping with her later on?"

"What happened at Jakes?"

"Shot me right down. But don't go telling Judy anything like that."

"No, Judy won't have to hear it from me. Don't you worry about that."

"Well, try not to wear yourself out sport. I need you working here this weekend."

***

"Here's your lobster Kathy."

"Katherine."

"Got a thing about that, don't you?"

"Kathy's a little girl's name. It's all cutsie–poo. Well I'm not a little girl anymore."

"Yeah, I've noticed."

"Thank you, kind sir."

"I'll be off in half an hour if you want to wait."

"Where?"

"Well, you can wait in the back room when we close and I'll join you there for a drink … Thank you sir. Please come again … No problem ma'am, I'll be glad to separate that bill for you … Yes, we do close shortly, now can I get you anything else, coffee, an after dinner drink? … C'mon Billy, time to go. Let's get this hole cleaned out. Let's show a little hustle."

"What's up Richard? What's the rush?"

"Got someone waiting on me. Listen, Billy boy, I've got a great deal for you. I'll clean the salad bar if you take care of the chairs and tables … Don't bother giving me those looks, just get moving."

"Yassah, whatever you say Massa Richard."

"Here's your Galliano, Katherine. Sorry it took so long."

"You got my name right."

"Yeah, I'm highly trainable."

"Do you like Galliano?"

"Not really, maybe the first sip, but not so much afterwards … You know Katherine, I don't usually bother to pick up girls."

"Nuh uh. It's me who's picking you up."

"Listen Katherine, I uh …"

"Yes?"

"Would you mind if I kissed you?"

"No …"

"I live about twenty miles north. You'll like it. The floors're too hard here."

"Okay."

"Need a ride?"

"No, I'll follow you."

***

"Christ Sally, I can't believe this last letter from Katherine."

"I don't get it, Richard. Why is she being such a bitch?"

"It's partly my fault. If it hadn't been for that accident we'd have split after two months. But there she was in the hospital all banged up and I told her not to worry, that I'd always be there, that I'd take care of her."

"That was clever."

"Well I meant it at the time, Sally. It's not like I was saying anything I didn't really feel."

"Like those last few months when you were living with her, but fucking me on the side?"

"I know I'm a shit. I've got no excuses. But it isn't like she was the long suffering little woman. Hell, I did take care of her. I nursed her, I supported her, I even changed the bandage on her scabby old ass every night."

"Bravo, Richard."

"Yeah, yeah. Look, I'm not trying to get you to believe I've got some sort of noble heart. You know better … Hey, I almost forgot, can I get you anything?"

"No I'm fine, but I still don't see why you put up with it. The two times I talked to her she was such a snotty little bitch, going on and on about all her upcoming projects and trying to lecture me on vegetarianism."

"She can't help it. She's so desperate to have a friend that she ends up driving them away by being totally compulsive and obsessive."

"Like a Catch–22."

"Yeah, she's pretty much forgotten how to deal with people. Then again, she was never too good at any of that personal relations jazz. She always pressed to hard. Even when she was being generous she still made you feel like you were being bought off. But you know, our first month together was really perfect. Though to be honest, it doesn't take all that much to make me happy."

"Thanks a lot, Richard."

"Hey Sally, give me a break. I don't have to keep shoveling compliments on top of you."

"One or two wouldn't be too many."

"Sweetheart, it's not the same. I feel I can tell you anything. I understand you. Our world together makes sense. With Katherine, I was always on edge wondering when one of my stray remarks would come hurtling back at me. It was like walking through a mine field without a map. Whatever I did, however I responded, was wrong. It was a classic no–win situation."

"Yeah, so you were explaining ..."

"At first when she was recuperating I just kept telling myself, 'She'll get better and everything will be like it was before the accident.' When she refused to let me touch her, I said, 'No problem Katherine, whatever you want.' The one time I did bring it up, she damn near drove her car into a tree.

"You know she forced me to move out of that house in Lawrence. Nearly came to blows with my old college buddy over that. Christ, I loved that place. For what it's worth, I was really happy there."

"So why'd you leave?"

"The two of them despised each other. It was becoming unbearable. Not that it was all her fault. I don't know what Sam's story was, maybe some sort of territorial imperative. But what could I do? I've always hated conflict and suddenly I had nonstop confrontation."

"Did you love her?"

"I'm not even sure about that. I know at a certain point I was sure I didn't. I felt the power shift between us. From that moment on I knew I would leave. I just didn't know when."

"What happened?"

"Well we had just rented that place on the coast with George."

"I remember."

"George and I would take off for work and leave her to fend for herself. It was freezing down there; a great place in the summer, but the absolute pits in the spring. I mean no insulation, no heat. She knew no one there, not one stinking person. Anyway, comes the big showdown. Katherine meets me after work and asks me to have a drink with her. So we go to Jakes, order drinks and she puts a quarter in the jukebox. While Rod Stewart is rasping on about his need to have a reason to believe, she tells me we're through."

"You're kidding."

"Pretty hokey, huh. It's those late night M.G.M. movies. They've ruined our entire generation. Anyway, I start begging her to change her mind, to give me another chance … sounds like we both watched the same old movie. Well, I manage to convince her to spend the night at the Motel 6 so we can talk it over. God knows what I thought would happen. There was nothing left to say.

"So she follows me to the motel office. I turn to ask her some dumb question and I see her car gunning down Eastern Ave. 'Fuck,' I said, 'this time I'm not going to run all over town looking for her'."

"You mean it happened before?"

"One night down on the coast. She was nagging me to take her out for dinner. I was working all those shifts at the restaurant and commuting eighty miles a day. I needed to relax. But of course, I gave in. So I say, 'Where do you want to go? 'She says, 'How about Novato's for pizza?' I say, 'How about taking it out?' No, she wants to eat it there. 'Fine,' I say being extremely reasonable. Come to think of it, my reasonableness probably drove her wild. The only time she was ever really satisfied was the one time I started beating her up."

"You pig!"

"Listen, when we first met she told me about her divorce."

"She was married before?"

"Huh, you ought to go see *Scenes From A Marriage* with her. I swear she relived her entire marriage and divorce in the seat next to mine – sort of embarrassing actually. Anyway, she told me that her husband had socked her, chipped her front tooth with his wedding ring ... Did you ever notice how full of cheap metaphors life is? ... So naturally at the time I was all sympathetic. The guy sounded like a total bastard, but before that year was over I was totally sympathizing with that ex of hers. I swear to God she could drive you nuts, just kept at you until your one overwhelming desire was to shut her up, to stop her infernal yapping."

"So what happened?"

"Well there was a major scene brewing all day. When I got ready to go to work, she had a tantrum. Told me I was more concerned with my work than with her, that all I cared for was my stupid job. Actually, working was the only bit of peace I ever got."

"You call waiting on tables restful?"

"Compared to my home life, it was Nirvana. But anyway, she kept up her yammering until I had to agree to take her with me just to keep from being too late. I zoom up to work. While I'm running around being polite and smiling at people, Katherine's busy making herself a pain in the ass to everyone who works there."

"I know."

"I felt bad. I mean I really felt terrible. I knew everyone was only putting up with her for my sake. It embarrassed me. ... Anyway she got so bad that I had to punch out early. So now, I'm close to the boiling point. As if she sensed it, she steps up her bitching and complaining. There we are driving back to the coast and I just start screaming at her to shut the fuck up. Of course the louder I scream, the more she lays it on and finally I start socking her."

"While you were driving?"

"She's small. Besides, it was as if that's what she was waiting for all along. She didn't even resist. I caught myself real quick but we both knew she had me by the balls. She says, 'Stop the car.' I stop the car and she gets out, crosses the highway and refuses to get back in the car. A half an hour, it took thirty minutes of me pleading and abasing myself before she coldly plopped herself back on that seat. Naturally you can guess what happened next."

"What?"

"Ran out of gas. The little shit probably felt vindicated. But what was the point of telling you that?"

"The pizza."

"Oh yeah, we get to Novato's. It's empty and it's also pretty chintzy looking. Suddenly she's not too crazy about eating there. 'Whatever you want,' I say. She goes dashing out of there like she's just been goosed by King Kong. I chase after her but she's disappeared."

"C'mon."

"I swear to God. I'm running around the parking lot of this shopping center looking for her. I even ask at the Holiday Inn across the street. Nothing. Five hours later I hear her screaming my name on a neighbor's front lawn. She's lying there drunk, she's pissed her pants and I have to carry her in, undress her, clean her up, and comfort her."

"And so?"

"And so when she ran out on me at that Motel 6, I'm depressed but I knew I couldn't do anything. I thought, 'Okay, it's finally over, I'm hurt but I'll survive.' I drive home and go to bed to sleep it off. Sunovabitch if five hours later I don't wake up to find her by my bed swearing her undying love. At that moment I knew that when the time came I would leave."

"How?"

"How would I leave?"

"No, how did you know?"

"I didn't feel anything. I heard what she was saying but I didn't feel a thing. I said all the right words but they were only words."

"So you're through with her now?"

"I've told you that, Sally."

"How can you be so sure?"

"Look, did you ever see that Truffaut film, *Jules and Jim*?"

"Sure."

"Well you know at the end after Jeanne Moreau has been driving those two guys batty for the whole film with her willfulness? You know how Oskar Werner looked when he sees her car go off the bridge?"

"Relieved?"

"Relieved. All I could think was, 'Thank God it's over. Now I can have a little peace.'"

"And you don't feel anything for her?"

"I don't feel a thing. I mean I've tried to help her. Christ knows she has no one else to turn to. But nothing she can do can make me change my mind. Not lines like, 'Excuse the tear stains on this letter, I can't help crying when I think of what I've ruined.' Not even having her begging me on her knees."

"Richard, she didn't."

"You think it made me feel good? You think I liked it? You think it made me feel like a big man? It's a matter of survival. I may feel like an old man, Sally, but I'm not suicidal."

"Forget about it, Richard, okay?"

"Okay Sally."

"C'mon, let's go to bed."

"In a minute, I'll be there in a minute ..."

5

THE ROAD TO SERFDOM

Freedom can, however, be also abstract freedom without necessity, which false freedom is self–will and for that reason it is self–opposed, unconsciously limited, an imaginary freedom which is free in form alone. – G.W.F. Hegel

"And you won't forget to feed the cat?"

"Uh, uh."

"Now don't let her out of the house. I don't want her screwing that raggedy–old Tom that's been hanging around."

"Yes dear."

"Richard, can't you even pretend to be nice? You won't be seeing me for two weeks, at least try not to spoil our last morning together."

"No dear."

My car doesn't sound right. Not exactly missing but not what I'd call running smooth; more like an M.S. victim trying to do a 'cha–cha'. Yeah, I know, I'm getting too damn paranoid, but, I'd be just shit out of luck without it. Can't expect to thumb forty miles to work on a daily basis, and Katherine's blue bomb is out of the question. I can't drive it. I'd burn out the clutch. Way things are going, I miss a few days of work and I'm permanently in the hole. Besides, it's the only escape I get from Katherine.

"… and Doctor Seaver says I may have a pinched nerve. Did you hear me Richard?"

"Hold on a minute Katherine. I'm listening to the engine."

"Do you mean to stand there and tell me that I'm not even as important as your fucking car? Are you saying that you're more concerned with how your goddamned car is running than how I feel?"

"Sh, I think the engine is missing after all."

"I said Richard, who's more important, me or your car?"

"I heard you the first time. Listen, how many cars do I own? One, right? If it doesn't run I don't get to work, right? And, if I can't get to work there'll be no more money for you to spend chatting with your doctor friends. What I'm trying to say Katherine, just as clearly as I possibly know how, is that it's goddam important that this car keeps on running. I put in a whole lot of hours every day listening to you yammering away. I think ten minutes devoted to listening to this car is not such an outrageous demand on your time. So what about it Katherine, am I asking too much? And while you're thinking about that one, I wonder where you think the seven hundred pazoolies for your lawyer is coming from? Do you think he's gonna wiggle his ass until he sees some money up front?"

"That's not my fault."

"Well it sure wasn't my grubby little hands clutching those magazines."

"I've told you Richard, it was a mistake."

"Sweetheart, nobody cares if it was a mistake or not."

"But it's not right. I didn't do anything wrong. They had no business arresting me."

"And who do you think gives a damn about that? It just doesn't matter. Listen toots, all I'm trying to do is to get you off the hook. What's wrong with you Katherine? Don't you understand, those slimeballs down at that drugstore are after your blood. Stupid goddam fucks, they're willing to lose a couple hundred bucks worth of business over a couple of magazines."

"Not fair! It's just not fair!"

"Don't be stupid, why should it be fair?"

"Screw that, Richard! You're always being so goddamn reasonable."

"Katherine, I'm doing my best to get you off. What more do you want from me?"

"I want you to believe me."

"And what choice do I really have?"

"What do you mean, what choice?"

"It's all part of the same package. If I start doubting you, if I ever feel I can't trust you, then it's over, you know like washed up, finished, done with."

"Don't you threaten me, Richard."

"And don't you tell me, sweetheart, that I'm using threats. Look, you're my girlfriend. I'm willing to take your word over some pharmacy jerk. Just don't force me to do otherwise."

"Quit grinning into that side view mirror. You could at least look at me when you're threatening to leave."

Damn, nothing worse than having my own vanity pointed out. I'm just too self conscious about how I look. If I could only stop trying to tug my hair back into place. Six years of cutting it and I still don't know what I'm doing.

"You're not supposed to notice that. You wouldn't mention it if you had any manners."

"Just because I didn't go to a ..."

"Give it a rest Katherine. You weren't some sort of disadvantaged child. It's a matter of tact. You aren't taught that, you learn it."

"Snob. Stupid, boring, insufferable snob."

"All right dear, now that we've held our usual morning conversation, is there anything else before you go?"

One more big, fat, demerit for old sonny boy. And it won't stop there. Katherine never forgets a thing. Well, who the hell does? People store up all the little slights you inflict on them. They never go away. The damn things just linger on, distorting a relationship like mindless phantoms wandering aimlessly through the deserted rooms of your life.

"You're just not interested in me, Richard. You don't care what I do, what I think. You don't even bother to pretend anymore."

"Everyone can't be totally fascinated by photography. I tried. It bored me."

"You can't wriggle out of this that easily. It's not just photography and you know it. What about my journal?"

"What about it?"

"You're one of the very few people I let read it. It's my life, Richard. Can't you understand that? It's about me, about my divorce. I turned myself inside–out to write that."

"I know you did."

"So?"

"Yes, okay, it was a very brave and honest thing to do—writing all that down. You know, you really have some clear insights into personal relationships in that journal. I was impressed. And, uh, I appreciate all the trust you showed in me. It's really something the way you were willing to let me read it and, …"

"Oh shut up, Richard. Just shut your stinking mouth."

"Now, what's the problem?"

"You shithead, you didn't even read it."

"That's not true. I'm working on it. I've still got some more to go but …"

"How much?"

"Well, a little bit more than half … Okay, I'm only a quarter way through. But it's eight hundred pages. Give me a break for God's sake."

"It's boring, isn't it Richard? Why don't you just come out and say it? You don't have the guts, do you? But that's what you think. You think my life is boring."

"Let's drop it, Katherine."

"No, I will not drop it."

"I do my best. I've been trying for over a year now. I'm beat. You've got to ease up. I won't be able to take it much longer."

"What are you saying Richard?"

"I'm trying to tell you that something has got to change or there's really no point in going on."

"What!"

"It only makes sense. What good does it do …"

Katherine goes screaming off into the back yard. At least there won't be another benefit performance for the neighbors. I'd better just sit out on the porch until she's through with her fit. I don't know what else to do. I've run out of answers. But I know this can't be how other people live. And I'm not talking about some M.G.M. version of marital bliss. I'm not looking for a June Allyson clone. All I want is some peace and quiet. Fuck the happiness routine. I'd settle right now for a little less self–laceration. Maybe I could pretend to turn catatonic. Nah, wouldn't make much difference to her. She can't hear anyone but herself anyhow.

I can feel it. It's all starting to slip away. Katherine screams at me and I try to deal with her but all the time there's this other part of me that's just watching all of this, holding back and looking at it like it was some kind of crazy newsreel. The role's so established that I don't have to put any effort into it; just a tape that loops over and over in an endlessly boring pattern. So when will it be, a month maybe two? The question is whether I split up before or after we move. It's a problem of convenience. Maybe that's what happens to love. Eventually it all muddles into finding a path of least resistance.

And here comes act two. She really looks like shit after one of her tantrums; face all rubbery, snot dripping off her nose. I'm just not attracted to the pathetic.

"Hold me, Richard. I'm afraid of losing you."

No need to be afraid. I'm already a lost cause. But, I put my arms around her. I pat her back carelessly like she was a sack of potatoes or a bag of dog food.

"I just want to make you happy. That's all I've ever wanted. But you don't care, do you Richard? You just don't care."

"I care."

"Yeah, but about what?"

"You know what."

"No, I don't know. I want you to explain."

"I care about doing things the right way."

"And you consider that to be some sort of meaningful statement?"

"It means that the actions you do are meaningless but the way you perform them counts."

"That's garbage."

"Okay, it's garbage. You asked me what I care about. That's it, that's what I care about."

"And where do I fit in?"

"You're included."

"What as, one of your goddamned performances? Is that what I mean to you?"

"I'm not getting drawn into this again. I've told you how I feel.

I'm tired of being put through a series of pop quizzes."

"You're avoiding me, Richard. All you do is avoid me. You're so goddamn closed in. When are you ever going to open up?"

"I am open. I'm totally and completely an open book. I hide nothing from you, Katherine. I'm the original Invisible Man. I'm as easy to see through as that dress you're wearing."

"And what do you see there?"

"Oh, a couple of items of interest."

"You think that all our problems are gonna vanish just by you rubbing my clitoris, don't you? ... Well, don't you?"

"No, not all."

"What then?"

"Oh, maybe the problem of you having your clitoris rubbed and me having one to rub."

"You're crude, Richard."

"But likable."

There's really nothing else we can do well together any more. It's my fault, I guess. There was that damn accident. I convinced her that this would be some sort of deep meaningful relationship. It isn't. I don't really know how to have a deep meaningful relationship. It's all those goddam films. Movie romances, wistful sighs, pressure of the hand; I made a mistake. I thought it was the right thing to do, that we were special. But we're not and neither is our commonplace little affair. It's just like thousands of other relationships, well, maybe a little worse. Katherine should either learn to enjoy what there is to it or pull out. But she can't. Sex isn't sex for her. It's a means to an end. She can't enjoy herself unless there's some payoff down the road. Her mother did one helluva job on her. I could say that it was all her problem, but it's obviously mine too ... at least for the moment.

"Richard, why don't you talk to me while we're making love?"

"I'm usually too busy."

"I don't know what you want. Why don't you tell me what you want when we're in bed?"

"What magazine did you get that crap from; *Psychology Today*, *Ms.* ...?"

"I'm serious, Richard. Would you like me to fondle your balls more?"

"Look Katherine, feel free to do whatever comes to mind, surprise me."

"You don't have to feel embarrassed, Richard. The idea is to communicate your feelings. How can I know what you're feeling if all you ever do is grunt?"

"There's nothing wrong with grunting."

"Don't get so defensive, Richard. Wouldn't you like to know where I'd enjoy being touched?"

"Not really."

"You know Richard, you have to be one of the most egotistical bastards I've ever had the misfortune of knowing."

"Listen Katherine, I'll say this to you slowly, just on the off chance that it might penetrate ... I–do–care–about–your–feelings–and–what–you–want. You can't deny that I at least try to respond to you. It's not like I'm bragging or claiming to be Maine's most fantastic fuck. I sure don't just shove you onto the goddam bed and start pumping away. So maybe I'm peculiar, but I do like a little touch of spontaneity. I don't want the whole thing blocked out beforehand. The point is to communicate with our bodies, not to try to duplicate some 'Six Steps to Sexual Bliss' handbook. Think about it. Would I really increase your ecstasy by quoting Keats while you're climaxing? Besides, my mouth is usually full."

"That's not funny, Richard. Why do you always do this to me? Whenever I try to have a serious conversation, all you know how to do is to make some crummy joke."

"What do you want me to do, Katherine?"

"Stop acting so goddamn superior. I want to be taken seriously."

"I do."

"You treat me like a stupid little girl ... comeback here Richard. I'm not through yet."

"You're forgetting something, sweetheart."

"What?"

"The workshop. It's a two hour drive up there. You're the one who's been making such a big deal about being on time."

"Okay, but we're gonna talk some more about this when I come back."

"I know. I'm not trying to avoid the subject." I pull on a shirt. "That what you taking up?"

"Uh huh."

"Let me give you a hand with that."

"Thanks ... I guess I'm ready to go."

"So, have a good time."

"I'll call you Wednesday."

"Okay, when?"

"I can't tell. Besides, why should you care? You planning on going out that night?"

"Nope, doesn't matter a bit. I'm not going anywhere."

"I'll let you know if I need my prescriptions refilled."

"Uh huh."

"Maybe I can sell some pictures up there."

"Sure."

"Don't you believe me?"

"Katherine, there's going to be umpteen other photographers all trying to hustle their goods around that place."

"Richard, my photography's never gonna come together if I act cynical and pessimistic like you. I've got to believe in what I'm doing. I've got talent, you know, I can make it."

"Why don't you just give it a rest Katherine? You can't even take a snapshot without pretending you're some sort of professional. Look, I don't mind spending the money if it keeps you occupied and away from smoking dope or gulping down valium. But it's not your damn vocation. No one's paying you to do it. No one may ever pay you a cent for one of your shots. It's bad enough turning my bathroom into a darkroom, and spending half our time together yammering away about f–stops; I don't give a fuck about f–stops! But you're making yourself look ridiculous, walking around with cameras slung over your shoulders like some *Newsweek* stringer back from the siege of Saigon. Godammit, I'm embarrassed for you, Katherine. I see how people look at you. You think I like it? I mean who in their right mind spends a Fourth of July party photographing it? People get nervous when you do that, Katherine. It makes me nervous. I'm beginning to feel like you're seeing me through a telephoto lens. I don't like it. It's a wonder you don't take the damn thing to bed with us. You could shoot us humping through a wide angle lens. That's if we ever bothered to do that sort of thing ... goddam rare enough event these days."

"Are you finished?"

"I think so."

"Now, you listen to me, Mr. Richard Everett Davis. You look at me ... I said, 'Look at me.' I'm going to make you eat every last one of those words. I know what you've done for me. You don't have to keep reminding me that I'm spending your money ..."

"I never said a word about ..."

"Shut up. For once you're going to shut up and listen. I'm not through yet; and you're not going to sneak away till I am. I know what you're thinking. It's not that I don't appreciate what you've given me. But photography costs a bunch of money, and it takes time to become good. But if you'll give me some more time I'll get there. And you're wrong. Some day I'll make it as a photographer and I'll pay back every single penny. I'm sorry I can't seem to do anything but talk about my work. But it is my work. It's not some silly hobby. It's what I want to do with my life.

"Okay, I know it's all my fault. All my life it's always been all my own damn fault. I never can get anything right. But I only wanted you to show some interest, to let me know that I'm important to you. But you just don't care and the more you don't care the harder I have to try to make it work for us. I don't like leeching off of you. I tell myself stories to make it sound all right, but I know it isn't. I don't want to depend on you, all I want is a job; a job and to have you there with me, to have you there to share our lives together.

"Say something Richard. You're supposed to be so good with words. You're the one who went to that fancy school."

I hold her and damn if I'm not as near to tears as she is. And the worst thing about it is that I mean it. My heart is going out to her. Emotions are the total pits. No use ever trying to depend on feelings. Who knows where or why they come. Maybe I'm just feeling sorry for myself. Sentimentality, it screws everything up. But at this moment I really do love Katherine. It feels good holding on to her raggedy old ass. Uh oh, there it goes. I start feeling sorry for some woman and the next thing you know I want to start screwing around.

"You slimy pig."

"Lay off, Katherine."

"No, I will not you creep. I open my heart to you, but all you want to do is to ram me up the ass."

"I can't help it."

"Well, it's disgusting. You just don't care, do you, Richard?"

"Okay honey, scream all you want, but one day sweetie nothing will happen, absolute zero. How you gonna feel about it then, toots? Oh c'mon Katherine, don't shriek. I apologize, please just don't …"

She's off again serenading those raspberry bushes round back. Lovely, light–handed touch I have. Why can't I just learn to shut up? But she keeps at me and damn, I finally let loose. That woman sure has my number. I'm just no match for her, I admit it. I can't stand up to an emotional onslaught. Best thing for me to do is to wait it out till she calms down. I've tried going after her. Only makes her more furious. Of course she's also furious if I don't go after her. Maybe I should scoot out right now. Nothing I can do when she gets in this state. Still pretty early though, maybe I'll just hide out for a while upstairs.

Sounds like her car, either that or a cheap lawnmower. She must be doing the scooting instead. I look out the bedroom window. Katherine's little blue Saab is puttering down the dirt road, kicking up dust as it disappears around the bend. I stay there after she's gone, my eyes staring unfocused out that window. It really is beautiful. When we moved here, everything was going to get better. Everything was going to be just like it was that first month we were together. What a damn fool I was to think I could recapture the past. I should leave that sort of thing to Proust and his crumbly French pastries.

If she thinks I feel guilty about parting like this, she's dead wrong and an even bigger fool than I am. All I feel is relief. I can turn over in bed tomorrow, instead of listening to her nammering away at me.

I might even enjoy living down here. I'm shelling out four bills a month for this. If I have to be miserable, I could do it for a third of that price in Augusta. I don't need the Maine coast as a backdrop. This is supposed to be my life, not an update on the *Sorrows of Young Werther*.

So first thing I do, I take me a shower then clean the place up—Katherine is an absolute slut of a housekeeper. By that time I should be ready to take off for Falmouth; play a little softball, shoot a few beers, maybe suck on some of that demon dope. See if the old boy can still party with the rest of the kids.

***

"Sum gud to see yuh Juday."

"Tuk yuh tahme getten haire Richahd. And yuh bein just down the rohd a'piece. Well gud to seeyuh anyhow. Tain't seen yuh inna munt'a Sundaes."

"Bin way tah long gurl. Whah, a week witahcha is lahk a week witout clean undawhare."

"Yuh gettin prettay gud wittat tha Maine tahk, well for a flatlanda that is."

"A–yuh."

"No, now yuh tahkin lahk sum guldang rockead from Nahampshah. It's a–ah. Long a, equal stress on each paht, but breathe in on the last."

"A–ah. I still don't see how you can talk that way. It hurts the back of my throat. No wonder people don't say much around here."

"It's all them cold wintahs we have round these pahts. Freezes up the ol' mouth organ. Trouble is, yah way tuh skinny tuh be a real Mainiac. Yessah, yuh shuld fill up on sum of them gud Maine badadoes."

"What?"

"Po–ta–toes Richard, you serve enough of them."

"Where's Doug?"

"Over there swinging three bats."

"He never gives it a rest does he?"

"That's my little Dougie."

"How's the morning sickness going?"

"Bout usual. You want me to save you some? Extra protein for that bread of yours."

"Only if I can give you those loaves."

"Look Richard, I know we haven't said anything, but Doug and I sure do appreciate what you've done for the restaurant."

"No problem."

"And where's that little Kathy of yours today?"

"Taking some photography course up to Rockport."

"Well ain't she the little dynamo. Once I married Doug, I couldn't get out of nursing fast enough … Why doncha go on over and say hello to him."

"I'll catch him later. I gotta check out the beer situation first."

I stroll over toward the batting cage. Looks like most of the restaurant's shown up.

"Richard, you scroungy low–life, have a beer."

"Thanks George, you nearly took my damn head off with that can … My favorite, warm Narragansett."

"Put back a few and it won't make a difference."

"How're things going in Augusta?"

"Nothing to complain about. We're living out by the lake in Peggy's shack. Look, how much did I end up owing?"

"There's still a hundred for the last month's rent and forty–three for the phone bill."

"Forty–three?"

"No one told you to make all those long distance calls to Connecticut."

"Yeah, I forgot. Well that's over with now. I'll pay you as soon as my insurance company settles."

"How's the leg?"

"Good, should be able to dance at my wedding."

"You know, you missed a sweet thing down there in Connecticut."

"Maybe, but I've made my decision. No sense feeling sorry for myself. What's that gonna get me?"

"So how are you and Peggy doing these days?"

"Not bad considering. The baby'll be along in seven months."

"Still no reason to marry her. She'll never forgive you."

"Could be, but we've been through this before, Richard. No way you're going to make me change my mind."

"Didn't Peggy come down with you?"

"Nah, she's with her old lady. They get pregnant and suddenly they need their mothers. Must be the first time for Peggy in two years."

"So a day off, huh, George?"

"Sure, a day off. You get that even if you do work in a restaurant … And where's your own little love bun? How'd you ever manage to loosen her grip?"

"She's honing her photographic talents in Rockport."

"Well I'm sum impressed. You know, you're a good man, Richard."

"I don't want your sympathy George."

"Don't forget buddy, I was down there for two months. I saw Kathy in action."

"It's not your problem George. I can work it out. So you really feel that strongly about Peggy. Sure, she's pretty but …"

"I come home from work Richard and you know how it feels after you've done a shift. Well Peggy hugs me and then maybe we start screwing around a little. Pretty soon I'm on top of her just plunging away and she starts moaning and making me feel special, like I'm some sort of superman. You know what I'm talking about?"

"Sure, Katherine makes me feel like a Corvair being driven by Ralph Nader."

"Richard, you are one dumb–fuck. Do you know that?"

"Yeah, I probably am."

"Well, don't worry about it slugger. Look, you feel like playing some softball? We can start you at third."

"Maybe later. I've got a few more beers to run down first. I'll see what I can …"

"Richard! Come over here and sit next to me."

"Uh oh, looks like Dina's eyeing the menu. Listen killer, you do some careful stepping around that young lady or you'll end up as the main course."

"Not to worry George, you're talking to a man with the moral fiber of a flatworm. Catch ya later."

Now ain't this a pleasant way to spend an afternoon. Almost like being a real person. I can sit next to Dina, drink a few beers, maybe even flirt a little bit. It's worth whatever it costs me to pack Katherine away for a few weeks ... Now I see why my parents were always so anxious to shuffle me off to summer camp.

"Want a beer Dina?"

"No, I've got one. C'mon Richard, pull up a patch of dirt and set yourself down." "How come you're not out there winning one for Dougie and his Brass Rail?"

"The way I hear it, it's more his brass balls than his rail that's the problem. But I'll be honest Richard, I never could stand softball ... So what's your excuse? I would've thought you were the local all–star around here."

"Nah, I'd rather just hang out and get blitzed. Doug can keep my share of the glory. Besides, the way things have been the last few months, I'm just not in shape for that kind of maneuver. I might hurt myself out there."

"You look in good enough shape to me ... But, where's that little girlfriend of yours? I expected to see Kitty hanging onto you."

"Katherine. She's off exploring her potential as a photographer."

"How nice for her."

"Yeah ... Dina?"

"Uh huh."

"You wouldn't happen to have a stick of that controlled substance. You know, 'to smoke, perchance to dream'."

Dina reaches into her halter top and pulls out a u–shaped joint. Wonder how she can manage to roll them in that shape? Oh yeah, it's those big boobs of hers. What a top heavy little number she is. Break your goddam jaw trying to mouth one of those babies.

"Pulling it out of the old storage locker, huh Dina?"

"Whah? ... Here, give it a try, it's pretty good shit."

Damn, why can't I learn to smoke a joint without slobbering all over it? Dina must just love sharing her dope with a congenital drooler. She's right though, it is pretty tasty stuff. Not all that potent but ...

That was a surprise attack! Let me see if I can re–establish some contact. Hm, colors, sounds … nice, but I need something a little more concrete. Next step, your basic associations: Okay, the sun feels warm. The beer in my left hand is also warm and tastes like the wrong end of a drainpipe. So far, so good, but now maybe a little more focus. Seems like my right hand is busy doing some missionary work on Dina's upper thigh. Hm, she's not really that bad looking. Never gave her much thought before. Well, maybe she is a bit dumpy, but not enough to make a real difference. Damn, I get some dope inside me, and my glands start singing the Hallelujah Chorus. I can't remember talking with her before. I don't think, "Dina, scotch and water to six–three," qualifies as conversation. Maybe I should give it a try, see what she has to say for herself. Besides, I like the way she's starting to rub up against my leg.

"So … Dina … where you from anyway?"

"Rhode Island. But I went to school in Maine … well at least I put in about two years over at Nasson."

"You can't be from Rhode Island."

"A hah. Outside of Providence."

"Rhode Island's too small for anyone to live there."

"You are zonked, aren't you Richard?"

"So what were you studying?"

"I was a language major, at least until my money ran out."

"Parents couldn't help out anymore?"

"No, never was my parents. It was a loan and I worked summers but things kind of fell apart after my second year. No, my parents had nothing to do with it. Mother's dead. My older sister raised the family."

"And your father?"

"My father's an alcoholic. Has been for as long as I can remember. We were dragged around from one apartment to the next. He never could hold on to a job. Sometimes when he went on a serious binge a relative would take us in for a while. I still hate that man."

This isn't quite the conversation I was planning on. I wish women wouldn't do this to me. It makes me feel like a father confessor, and I'm definitely not cut out to administer absolution.

"Do you ever see him?"

"Richard, you don't really want to listen to this. I'm depressing you, I can tell. Here, let me get you another beer."

"No really Dina, I'd like to know more about you."

"That's sweet, Richard, but I'd rather just drop it. I love my sisters. We're still really close. I can't imagine ever being separated from them. Rhode Island isn't exactly just down the road, but it's not all that far."

"How often do you make it back down?"

"About once a month and then there's the phone calls."

"You're living out in Cooper's Mills, right?"

"With Ben and Jana. You remember, they were at that party last month at Willi's. All of us met back in college. They've got this place out there now. Ben's sorta fixing it up. He's been trying to make it as a carpenter. And Jana, well she still gets some money from her folks. You know, the same old story that everyone tells around here."

"Yeah, so how come I never get a chance to talk to you? Have you been avoiding me?"

"Well you've got someone, you know, that Katherine person. Julie told me about the two of you and about the accident."

"Why would she bother telling you that?"

"Well, I guess I must have asked about you."

"How come?"

"I noticed you. Remember sticking your head in the service window and saying hello my first day at work? Everyone tells me you're a really nice guy and I thought …"

"Hey Richard, yo you there!"

"What's up Willi?"

"We're taking off. Dougie can defend the honor of the Brass Rail without us. Thought we might stop and have a few cocktails on the way back. Haul your ass into gear and let's go. Bring Dina along if that'll make you happy. And don't you worry your pretty little head Richie, Kathy ain't gonna hear a whisper from us."

"You've got a terrific sense of humor Willi. Did I ever tell you how much I admire it?"

"Where is that little Kathy anyway? You finally do away with her? Did ya knock her on the head and toss her into the bay? You'll never get away with it chump. You've got motive written all over your face. Maybe you could plead self–defense instead. Tell the judge she was about to nag you to death."

"Layoff Willi. She's in Rockport taking a photography course."

"Figures."

"Look, why don't we head to my place instead. I've got some cold Elephant beer. We can watch the sunset."

"Sure babycakes, anything you say."

"Okay, what if you meet me there in an hour ... Dina, wanna come along?"

"I'm not sure ..."

"Look, Steve and Willi will be there too ... It'd mean a lot to me if you came. ... And there's absolutely nothing to worry about. You can trust me."

"It's not that, it's ... oh hell. Sure Richard, why not? I'd love to come."

"Terrific, we'll go in my car."

***

The discovery of the wheel, Newtonian mechanics, James Clerk Maxwell, and Detroit's engineers perfecting the automatic transmission, all so I can poke along Route One with my right hand creeping up Dina's thigh. There's providence for you. Seems like a lot of effort just to let me scratch a lazy itch, but I'm not complaining, not me, I know when to feel grateful.

"It's beautiful out here, Richard."

"Yeah, George heard about it from one of his buddies. Most of the other gophers around here rent by the week."

"Have you been swimming?"

"Too cold, my skin's super sensitive."

I've been gliding around Dina so much that either my hand is getting sweaty or the young lady's turning damp. There's luck for you. First day out and I'm hot.

I turn down Heath, my car kicking up red dust on the dirt road.

Always easy to tell when someone's coming. We're talking now in low lazy tones. Fifth cottage down, screened–in porch, green with white trim ... and Katherine on her back furiously peddling her legs in the air like an upturned egg beater. She breaks off and comes running as my car slows to a stop.

Cursed, I should've known better, I'm just cursed from the start. Why can't I get away with these things like everyone else? Here I am, touched by the wrath of God, without even the meager consolation of first wallowing in one or two vile, evil fleshpots. Symbolism, my life seems cluttered with obvious if not downright tedious metaphors. Given my luck, I'd have been better off staying home and rereading I Corinthians.

I close my eyes. I still can't believe this is happening. I open my eyes. Katherine has caught sight of Dina and is swooping down on us like a banshee. She looks ready to bite my neck right off.

What should I do besides shutting off the engine? I'll lie of course. It's what everyone's expecting. The least I can do is to give my audience what they want.

"Who's that?"

"Katherine, what happened? I saw you take off six hours ago. Are you okay? ... Oh, you remember Dina, don't you?"

"No, I do not remember Donna. So why don't you just go ahead and explain to me exactly who this woman is ... and why she's sitting next to you with a very damp crotch?"

Dina looks slightly stunned, like she should be wearing a sign reading 'Innocent Bystander'. All she was planning on was a little dope induced romance. Instead she walks into an out–take from *Days of Our Lives*.

"You must remember. You met her at the restaurant. She's one of the cocktail waitresses at the Brass Rail. Remember, she came when Pammy left to train horses down in Florida. She was at the game along with everyone else. Steve and Willi are right behind us. I invited everyone over for a drink. You know how you're always after me to invite my friends over? Well we were just going to relax, maybe have a little swim later on ... But what are you still doing here? Something go wrong? What's the matter?"

Despicable, a truly slimy, unconvincing performance. I did everything short of whimpering. I've probably managed to piss off Dina as well. Maybe they'll both slap my face simultaneously. I hold my breath and watch Katherine's mind working. She's positive I'm lying. She knows me too well to doubt it. But the question is whether it's worth a full blown scene right now. The click is almost audible as she applies the brakes on her rage. Dina is staring straight ahead, glassy eyed. So that's that. We're all going to pretend we're civilized adults. Anthony Trollope, chapter thirty–two, Katherine enters the drawing room and says,

"My car broke down before I could even get out of town. I didn't know what to do. Everything's closed on Sunday. I called here but nobody was home. I kept ringing and ringing but you still weren't here. Finally Jeremy down at the Capstan gave me a ride home, but I had to wait two hours before he was through with his shift. So you're going to have to give me a ride up to Rockport. My equipment's locked in my car down at the Municipal parking lot. We can stop off on our way there. Monday, you'll have to get the car to that Saab dealer out on Cook's Corner. It's the clutch again. You can't get it out of first. Maybe one of your little friends will help you out.

"I've been waiting and waiting for you. I didn't know where you'd got to. I called the restaurant and Eric told me everyone was down at the game. You didn't say anything about a game. I had to wait here, alone, while you were there enjoying yourself. How was I supposed to reach you down in Falmouth?"

Unbelievable. Katherine is still foolish enough to try to leverage me with a ton of guilt. If she thinks she's going to make me feel the least bit guilty about having a good time, or even about Dina, she's got the wrong boy. I get little enough relaxation these days.

"As soon as Steve and Willi get here we can take off."

"I'm late Richard. Can't you at least pretend to pay attention? I was supposed to be at the workshop by two. I've been waiting here all afternoon. I waited and waited but you never came back. I didn't even know if you were coming back. It's five–thirty now. You've played your softball, you've had your fun with all your little buddies, now I've got to go."

"Katherine, there was no way in hell that I could know your car would break down ... I would rather not just leave Dina alone here by herself."

"Why? You said Willi and Steve are coming. They'll take care of her. Besides, she looks like a woman who knows how to get what she wants."

"Katherine!"

"No, it's okay Richard. Don't worry about me. Steve and Willi'll give me a ride back. I'll just sit out on the porch and watch the ocean.

"Are you sure?"

"I'll be perfectly all right."

"There's beer in the fridge. Just take anything you want. I'm uh, really sorry about all this."

Katherine is still intent on snubbing Dina. Considering the alternatives, it's all for the best ... Well so much for my little romantic flings. Somehow, in the space of a mere hour, all my wild afternoon oats have turned into this evening's cold bowl of mush.

"Okay Katherine, let's go."

Katherine picks up her camera case, gets in, and slams the door.

"Look Dina ..."

"Don't bother, Richard."

"I know but ..."

"Don't say it. Let's just not talk about it."

"Well, maybe you could wait."

"I don't think so."

"I'll see you at work then."

"Yeah Richard, that's where you'll see me."

***

Through Wiscasset, around Damriscotta and Nobleboro, Katherine has not said a word for two hours. All I've heard is the easy listening sounds of Mt. Washington. I've really got to get this radio fixed. Now she gives me a few terse directions and we're in Rockport, in front of the workshop building. I pull up and help her unload, again in silence. We carry her gear inside without speaking. It's time for me to go. We walk to the car. It's getting darker and shadows are shifting rapidly over the small harbor. I look down at her.

"So take care and study hard. I'll see you in two weeks."

She stands there silently, eyes cast to the ground. The cool of a late Maine summer is creeping up on us. I wonder if Dina will wait. No, I've blown it all around. Nothing much left for me to do but to go home and get some sleep. Katherine suddenly shifts her eyes and glares at me steadily, till I finally look away.

"I thought Richard, you had better taste than that."

Her small figure disappears into the shadows. I get in my car and reverse onto the highway. It's going to be a long drive home.

6

THE CONTRACT CURVE – A QUANDARY IN THREESPACE

Thus the utility of the contract represented by 00P0 is for Friday zero, or rather, the same as if there was no contract, at that point he would as soon be off with the bargain. – F.Y. Edgeworth

"You sure it's no problem, Richard?"

"Problem, what problem? I have to go through Hallowell anyway."

"But can you drive?"

"What kind of dumb question is that? Sure I can drive. Just look at all the licenses I have. See, I've got one from Maine, one from Maryland, one from Pennsylvania …"

"You're still fucked up from all those drinks."

"It's okay, Sally. I've been drinking coffee for the last hour, and then we stopped for those two clamburgers at Hojos … No doubt about it, I'm ready to roll."

"How can you eat that filth?"

"Upset stomach, best thing in the world to keep you awake; just cruise along listening to it rumbling, getting high off the farts, turning up the radio, rubbing your …"

"Richard, let me do the driving."

I shrug my shoulders. No need to prove my masculinity. Besides, I hate to drive even when I'm sober. So here I am leaning back in the passenger seat, waiting for Sally to zoom off. Instead she shifts and reverses directly into a utility pole. I look at her with all the drunken disdain I can muster.

"I can do that as well as you can. C'mon shove over, I'll show you

95

how to drive ..."

"Richard, wake up."

"Huh?"

"Richard, I said turn the engine off, we're here."

"Wha?"

"My place, you better come on up and try drinking some more coffee."

"How'd we get here?"

"Well you sorta worked the pedals and I tried to steer. I mean you kinda had one hand on the wheel, but it was mostly me doing the driving."

"Hey, good work there sweetie."

"Yeah, we make a great team. Now I mean it. You're not driving anywhere until you sober up."

***

Sure, now I remember ... Sally, I've been out having some drinks with little Sally ... Uh oh, you better be careful here boy, you just better be extra careful from now on. Pay some mind to those warning lights skittering across your brain.

Anyway, you should still be able to remember the way the story's gone so far. Sally stopped by the restaurant particularly to see you. She sure ain't gonna travel two hundred miles north just for her health. Remember what her friend Dana said. Sally was off somewhere and Dana comes over, points her finger at you and says, 'Richard, Sally's travelled all the way from Boston to see you. So you're gonna be a nice guy and keep her company instead of going off somewhere with someone else. Don't louse this one up. I'm keeping my eye on you.'

Well, I'd have to be pretty damn thick not to realize that Sally's interested, but Dana didn't really need to push. I've always been kinda attracted to her. I mean I like the way she looks. And I like being with her. She makes me want to laugh. I used to crack up watching her walk around the restaurant like some sort of princess forced to mingle with the hoi polloi. She's just a funny little twerp.

So what the hell, why not go ahead and do it? It's plain to see that I want to. I mean what's the difference? Don't you have to grab for everything you can get? You know, like life's short, and all the rest of that crap … Yeah, that's exactly it, that's the whole goddam problem. That stuff is just a bunch of crap. If something like this doesn't matter, if it all comes down to the same old thing, then what in the hell does count?

I'll tell you one thing. I start believing that sorta garbage and it's just down the flaming pisshole for me. There'll be no hope left. I'll be a complete and total bankrupt … Okay, okay, stop agonizing. I just won't worry about it yet. Coffee now, decisions later.

"So I was working at Friendly's and going to school at U.M.A."

"What were you studying there Sally?"

"Graphics and photography. I want to move down to Boston and learn some more. Nothing's happening around here."

"Found a place yet?"

"Only a possibility so far."

"Where abouts?"

"Do you know Boston?"

"Only vaguely."

"It's out on Huntington Ave."

"Nice place?"

"A real dump."

"You mean it has roaches?"

"Roaches are the least of the problems there."

"Sounds terrific, but listen, you never did tell me how you ended up at the restaurant."

"Well, I was fired at Friendly's …"

"You're kidding. No one gets fired at Friendly's."

"Well, I don't really think it was my fault. They had this manager see and he was always giving me a hard time, saying that I was rude to the stupid customers and then …"

"Were you?"

"Richard, that's completely beside the point. Anyway, it was only those cranky old biddies that really got me upset. 'Oh young lady, this spoon's dirty. Miss, this coffee is ice cold.' Day–in and day–out, like being pecked to death by a flock of venomous old hens.

"Well one day after work, this old fart of a manager told me that if he heard one more complaint about me he'd can my ass but quick. Said there were plenty of other nineteen year olds around to take the job. He didn't have to put up with any more of my insolence. Imagine, someone like him knowing a word like insolence."

"So ...?"

"So I climbed up on a stool and poured chocolate sauce all over his fat, greasy head. Made him look like a turnip a la mode."

"C'mon."

"Yeah, you should've seen it Richard. He went totally berserk. He turned so livid that I thought he was going to have a stroke or something. Then he started waving his arms around, threatening to call the police and have me arrested. Can you believe that? What a goddam turd ... nothing but a big fat turd."

"And then you got the job working at the restaurant."

"No, it was Dana who applied. We were living together on State Street, in this tacky little apartment—totally broke. So finally Dana walked down to the Brass Rail and talked to George."

"Yeah, I remember George being hot about some woman he'd just interviewed. Wanted to hire her right off."

"Dana thought he was a complete sleaze. She pretended not to be home when he came by."

"Hey, George is one of my buddies. He's a nice guy!"

"C'mon Richard, your buddy is a total sleaze."

"Yeah well, what does that have to do with anything? Besides, you know he's gonna marry Peggy next month."

"So what? Then he'll just be a married sleaze."

"Well look, I guess I really should be going."

"Okay."

So we stand there listening to the minutes tick by. I look down at her, down deep into her eyes. I can leave right now. I can go home to Katherine with a nice clean conscience. All I really have to do is to thank Sally for the coffee and go through that door. That's all there is to it. And if I don't, if I don't walk out in another sixty seconds, well I guess I can pretty much forget about remaining virtuous.

"Sally?"

"Mm?"

"Yeah ..."

I pull her towards me and kiss her gently. Then we kiss again and again. God do we ever kiss. We kiss as if we were going to devour each other bit by bit. Teeth, lips, cheeks working; tongues clasping in a tug of war. I pick her up and walk to the bedroom, Sally muttering directions in my ear. The room is icy, almost deadly cold. A large down comforter lies on top of a carved oak bed.

"Richard?"

"Mm?"

Sally climbs down out of my arms.

"What about Katherine?"

"I don't like an audience when I'm in bed."

"C'mon, I mean what are you going to tell her?"

"About what?"

"About this, about us! Don't play the buffoon with me Richard. It won't work."

"Okay, we can invite her to double date with us next week."

"I told you Richard ..."

"Use your head, Sally. I'm not going to tell her a goddam thing. What good would it do?

"Well ..."

"Listen, do you think anyone's going to feel better if I bring her into this? Will you?"

"I guess maybe you're right."

"I know I am."

"But Richard ..."

"Hush baby, that's enough."

So here we are having this big emotional scene and I can't even get her out of her clothes. She has on some sort of body stocking. I give it a tug, nothing. Jesus, why do women always wear things like this? This kind of stuff never happens in the movies. But what other woman besides Marjorie Main decks herself out in long johns? Can you imagine Charles Boyer stopping to look for a zipper or fumbling with a snap?

So where the fuck is the snap to this outfit? If I don't find it soon

I'm gonna start ripping my way through the fabric. Meanwhile, Sally is waiting quietly, eyes closed, head tilted back, relaxed in my arms. What the hell's wrong with her? Does she think this is all part of a long slow buildup to sex? I assure you sweetcakes, foreplay doesn't begin like this.

"Ah sweetheart?"

"Mm."

"Sally."

"Huh?"

"Where's the escape hatch on this outfit?"

"The what?"

"Look, will you kindly pull yourself out of this rig or would you rather stand there swaying passionately all night?"

She sticks out her tongue then peels off the body stocking.

"Ooh, poor wittle Dickie. Isum big bad man getting all hard and worried. Don't cry wittle boy. Auntie Sally will make everything all right. Here, show me where it hurts and your auntie will kiss it and make it all better."

I don't care if she's laughing. I'm too busy staring. God how I love women's bodies, the way they curve, all those swirling lines. And Sally's in particular, so small and compact. She definitely has a world class ass. Okay wait ... I know she's a person; I know she's not an object. I'm not just some kind of extension cord looking to plug into a spare socket. Fuck, I know all that. You think I'd be standing here creaming all over an inflatable doll? But she happens to be a person with a great ass. If I were her, I'd spend half my time in front of a mirror just looking.

Well, that wouldn't be much of a change for me. I already waste at least that much time in front of the goodam things. Mirrors, I don't know why I even bother looking. I'm never satisfied by what I see staring back. Hair is always sticking out in the weirdest way, teeth never quite clean. But I'll be damned if I don't keep right on looking; mirrors, store windows, windshields, anything that's handy. Sure I pretend I'm not. I'm always nonchalant as all hell. It wouldn't do to get caught in the act like some fixated idiot. But that doesn't stop me from looking. It's as though I really believe that if I only keep looking, if I'm persistent enough, that one special day will come when I'll see a reflection there that will make me smile.

"If you're finished polishing up my ass maybe we can get into bed."

"You look great Sally. I really mean it."

"Thanks Richard, but it's freezing. C'mon, don't you want to play with me?"

Sometimes I think I like the warm–ups even more than the main event. All that slow building, rubbing bodies back and forth till the friction makes you want to scream. And oral sex …

Rhoda and oral sex. My first real girlfriend in high school. One lucky Sunday the rest of the family was down at the Jersey shore, and Rhoda and I were sitting on the couch kissing. She was a great kisser. I mean that girl could syncopate your heart. And there was this thing she could do with her tongue and your ear that should have been proscribed by the Catholic Church. Anyway, the next thing I knew she was moaning "don't", but her panties were flying off into the potted plant. For a moment we just stopped and stared. Both of us were equally surprised to find Rhoda sitting there on her sofa completely naked. I didn't know what to do. I mean, I knew, but I never really expected to be doing it. Well, I carried her up to her bed while she protested that she'd never let any boy do such a thing to her before. I wasn't listening. I had other things on my mind. But it was so unexpected, that we just weren't prepared. I mean we hadn't really planned for this, so we could only have oral sex, you know, if we were going to play it safe. Christ, I did everything else I could think of to Rhoda except bounce her off the ceiling. My hormones were going berserk. Funny, we never did get around to actually screwing, not then, not once in those two years. I did, however, develop a very flexible tongue.

God, this is amazing. Sally has an incredibly foul tasting cunt. I mean I expect some funkiness but not the Newark Sewer System. I wonder what causes it. Not worth thinking about. Nothing I can really do. I can just picture myself saying, 'Excuse me Sally, but did anyone ever tell you that your cunt tastes like raw sewerage?' She'd try to drive my balls up through my throat and out again. Okay, just try not to spit up. There, it's all right now. My oral chemistry must be adjusting. Still not good, but no danger of gagging. Well that figures. Something always goes wrong.

I'm balanced on top of her now, arms and legs suspended in air. I think the back of my head may be coming off. Yes … there's still something to be said for orgasms … Collapsed now, soaking wet, covering Sally's body like a carelessly discarded drop cloth; maybe I should ask her to run away with me to Boise, Idaho.

"More Richard, Sally wants more. C'mon killer, let's see you do it all over again."

"It's not as easy as it looks pal."

I lean over and hug her. Amazing how relaxed you feel after a really good fuck, I mean when you've gone past the standard push and squirt routine. God, it's like being purged of all evil. We lay side by side, perfectly quiet, drifting on a large yielding cloud, removed from the world, from anyone else; just the two of us, content for the moment …

"Richard?"

"Mm?"

"I want to tell you about my mother."

"Sure."

"Did you know my mother was a dancer?"

"What was she doing stuck up there in North Berwick, Maine?"

"Her sentiments exactly. Beautiful, a very beautiful woman, about my size but the type men go crazy over."

"Don't fish for compliments, Sally. I like how you look."

"Rubbing my ass won't change the facts. See, I remember going with this guy Otto when I was in high school. Well, an aunt took me aside one day and asked me if anything was going to come of it. So I told her that I thought the guy was pretty ordinary. I really couldn't see myself getting too excited about him. So this aunt, she just looks me straight in the eye and says, 'Otto's about as good as you can expect.'"

"Poor baby."

"No Richard, I want to talk. I want to tell you about my mother."

"Sure."

"She ran away, she just up and left my dad and her five kids."

"Five?"

"Yeah, two older brothers and two younger sisters. My parents were very methodical when it came to reproducing."

"So she ran away."

"Didn't hear a word from her for two years. Though it turns out she tried to call Dad, but Jenny the operator recognized her voice and wouldn't let Mom through."

"What?"

"See, we had an operator in North Berwick. I mean the switching system wasn't automatic or anything so you had to go through Jenny. She worked the local switchboard. She knew everything that was going on because of course she always listened in. Everyone knew it, but for most people it wasn't worth making a fuss. I mean it was sort of like having an answering service. If you weren't home or something Jenny would know where you were, when you were expected back, and how to reach you. But when my mom tried to call my dad, Jenny just told her that she wasn't going to let my mom plague that good man anymore."

"But that's incredible Sally."

"You think so? You're just a big city boy. You don't understand how things work up here."

"Uh huh. So what happened to your mom?"

"When I was fourteen she was in a car accident. Went through the windshield. Decapitated."

"Poor baby."

"Listen Richard, it has nothing to do with my ass. Are you going to let me talk or what?"

"Sure."

"Anyway, there was a funeral and it was bizarre. You see, all my family and relations were there. The close relatives are mostly okay but when you get down to the third cousins, well, there's been a lot of in–breeding up around Sydney."

"What do you mean?"

"Well, they look sorta funny. They're really not all that bright and you know, they tend to drool a little too much."

"Yuck."

"Well, that's life in Maine, sweetheart. But you see Richard, ever since my mom took off I've had to be responsible for raising the family, you know cooking, cleaning. My aunts did what they could, but mostly it was my responsibility."

"What about the rest?"

"Well, the girls were too young and my brothers were worthless. They wouldn't ever listen to me. Spent most of their time working on cars. There were usually about half a dozen wrecks strewn around the yard. If I tried to tell them anything, they'd dangle me upside down over our well. ... Maybe now you understand why I've got to get away from that sort of life. I've gotta move down to Boston."

"So when are you going?"

"Next week."

"You'll let me have your address?"

"Do you really want it?"

"Of course I want it. I think you're terrific."

"Look Richard, what good is this going to do?"

"Well, I'm quitting the restaurant next month."

"How come?"

"Too long a commute from the coast. Besides, it's time. I've been around there way too long. Christ, I'm not even conscious when I work a lunch. So anyhow, I'm going to take some time off, visit friends, maybe swing down and see my family. No reason why I couldn't stop off in Boston and visit."

"But what about Katherine?"

"Look, will you stop Katherining me. If you don't want to see me, all you have to do is say so."

"Okay Richard, you know I want to see you. I want to see you again and again. I like you. I like you a lot. I think you're a really nice guy; but I mean, you are living with this other woman."

"I'm well aware of who I'm living with. It's not your problem."

"Well, I just don't know."

"I do know. Send me that address and we'll see what happens, okay? I'm not going to just let you slip away."

"If that's how you feel Richard, why don't you move down to

Boston with me?" "I'm tired of living in big cities."

"Well, you can't expect me to stay up here. Besides, what would I tell my father?"

"That you were living with me."

"I couldn't do that."

"Well, I can't move to Boston."

"Why not?"

"New York City. Did you know I lived there for six months before I moved to Maine?"

"Not good, huh?"

"The pits. The only advantage was scraping bottom at such an early age. Life can't ever be as bad as that again."

"But why not Boston?"

"The thing is, moving up to Maine saved my life. I was suicidal in the city. Didn't care what I did to myself or to anyone else. In the country everything changed for me. The life I lived down there was disgusting. I love Maine, Sally. I just love living in the country without the crowded streets and the dirt and all that tension. Christ, the tension was so thick you could hardly walk through it."

"And what do you think will happen to me if I stick around in Maine with you, maybe waitress in some other dive of a restaurant? What do you expect me to do, tell you that I adore you and want to have your child?"

"Flattering, but not entirely necessary."

"Cram it buster."

"Well you're finally grabbing onta what counts sweetheart."

"Fuck you. ... I'm being serious Richard ... You better stop that laughing. I mean it. Stop doing that ... Richard ... Screw you buddy."

"Okay, but this time you've gotta promise not to moan so much. It's distracting."

"Wait a minute, are you trying to tell me that I moan?"

"Well, what else do you call all those oohing noises you were making?"

"I do not moan."

"Hey, what do you think you're doing with that pillow? Stop bouncing it off my head."

"I do not moan!"

"That really hurts, Sally. Look, are you trying to remove my nose or something?"

"What makes you think I would moan over you?"

"Well, you're certainly worth moaning over. I mean I just grunted, but I would've moaned if Ida thought of it."

"Get off."

"Am I hurting you?"

"No, I just don't want you on me. Hey, what do you think you're doing?"

"Moaning ..."

We're quiet again. I think I was more surprised than Sally. Usually I poop out after the first shot. Christ, it's wonderful lying next to her. I wish this would never have to end. I really wish I didn't have to go. I don't want to ever have to leave, to leave Sally ...

"Fuck, it's five A.M. I gotta go."

"You sure you're okay, Richard?"

"I'm fine."

I throw on my clothes.

"Thanks for the coffee, Sally."

"Anytime, it was a genuine pleasure."

I pick my glasses off the side table by the door. Christ these glasses are filthy. They look like a troop of army ants have been holding field maneuvers on them. So typical. I'm always forgetting to attend to these small personal details; zipping my pants, cutting my toenails, wiping my ass properly. Still, no sense in cleaning them now. Can't see at night anyway.

I'm dead. Haven't reached Cooper's Mills and I'm already nodding off. 'C'mon buddy boy, keep those eyeballs open.' That's it, open the windows; more cold air, right, now the radio, louder, 'sing goddamit, open your mouth.' ... This isn't working. Okay don't panic. Try biting the inside of your cheeks. 'C'mon baby, bite harder. Bite you sunovabitch! Bite until you can taste blood ...'

Hm, now what did Sally say about me? Yeah, she thought I was such a nice guy. Great, that's all I need to hear. 'I think you're a really nice guy.' What am I doing, trying out for the Biff Loman

Chair of Congeniality? I can just hear those people round my grave saying, 'Gee, too bad, he was such a nice guy.' It makes me feel like I'm being dismissed, like I'm a total lightweight. ...But Katherine, what am I going to tell ...?

Terrific. I missed ditching the car by a split second. Lucky I woke up in time to turn the wheel and brake. Just caught a bit of the right fender. Okay, stop shaking, you're going to get through this. You're getting back in that car and then driving those twenty odd miles right into the waiting arms of your ever–loving girlfriend.

Now, get in the car ... Start the car ... Good ... You can do it sweetheart, really you can. All you have to do is concentrate. 'Goddamit, stay awake!' Please sweet Jesus, I have to stay awake ...

Fuck, how the hell did I miss that turn off? Sonuvabitch, I'm gonna have to go all the way through Rockland now ...

"Richard, Richard is that you?"

"Katherine, I didn't think I'd make it. Look at my hands."

"Richard, what's the matter? I've been so worried. I didn't know where you were."

"I was drinking after work. Okay, I know I shouldn't, but I had breakfast so I thought I was all right. I really did. Then I fell asleep near Cooper's Mills. Barely woke up in time to keep from running off the road into that ravine ... Katherine, I was so goddam scared."

I pull Katherine's small body toward me, holding on, squeezing her to reaffirm my own life. I've never wanted or needed her so badly. I shove her down on our mattress and start pumping away like a piston in a cylinder. The need to penetrate deeper and deeper is overwhelming. Only vaguely am I aware of Katherine, her body responding beneath me, her soft moaning ...

"Richard?"

"Mm."

"Are you awake?"

"Huh?"

"You fuckhead, you raped me you son of a bitch."

"What?"

"I said you raped me you god–damned egotistical bastard."

"Are you losing it, Katherine? What the hell do you think you're talking about?"

"You come storming into the house, pull me down and push your fucking dick into me while I'm still dry. You raped me, Richard. How could you do something like that?"

"Look sweetheart, I don't have to listen to this. I barely make it back home and I'm just glad to be alive. Of course I wanted to make love to you. But now you're trying to tell me that I did something wrong … And by the way honey, you responded. You were squirming and moaning like a five dollar whore. You didn't say a word about it. If that's rape, then you're the world's most obliging victim."

"It's rape you shithead! You forced me."

"Listen to me, Katherine, I've had a very hard night. I'm not about to put up with anymore of this crap. Just go to sleep and shut your fucking mouth. Ya think you can get your goddam head around that? …"

Now this, is the absolute pits. I come home from humping one woman—Christ, I was still all sticky from Sally. I come home and immediately start ramming it into another. And do I feel bad about this? Not a chance. I want what I can get. And I want it when I need it, but especially without any complaints from some little bint like Katherine.

I turn over, my back rigidly set against her, not wanting to deal with Katherine, not knowing how to approach her love, her craziness. I'm becoming an oyster safe within its shell, forming layer upon layer of protection, cutting off any remaining ties to her. And all the while I act so damn adult and so damn rational. There is no way Katherine will ever crack my facade of understanding, of cool compassion. I think that she must be suffocating under the strain of it. But I think that I may no longer even care.

I know I've become a disgusting human being. Well, I've never tried to justify myself before. I mean how can you justify your existence? That's just a bunch of crap. But this is out and out despicable, despicable because I just don't care. Christ, I should feel something. You don't go around using people like so many disposable diapers. I'm empty. I'm devoid of love or the least trace of humanity. It's just total free–fall buddy and there's no bottom left at all.

7

ONE AFTERNOON IN A SMALL TOWN IN MAINE – A ROMANTIC INTERLUDE

Nymph in thy orisons be all my sins remembered –Shakespeare

Richard often wonders if he likes the town or not. In the summer the streets are full of tourists and Route One is so blocked with traffic that he leaves his car parked for weeks on end. Winter is quieter, only the locals remain; buildings blanketed with snow, a cold wet wind whipping off the harbor. But the time of year seldom seems to matter. Whatever the month, he works a minimum of fifty to sixty hours a week. Wages may be low in coastal Maine but the cost of living comes high.

It's a rut. Richard sees that as clearly as he sees the tracks his car makes every year in the loose spring mud. Maine is a wonderful dead end. He will be spending the rest of his life like this or very close to it. There is really nowhere to go. This sense of stagnation sometimes worries him. Is it true his mind is slowly slipping, dulling as the years creep by, unused, uncared for? When he was twelve, Richard would get down on his knees and pray to God to keep him from becoming stupid. But now he is almost like the younger sister in that Chekhov play, the one who could no longer remember the Italian for window. Can he still solve differential equations or deal with Greek irregular verbs? He no longer bothers to ask.

One day a week free, and that one day comes on Monday. What can he possibly do on a Monday? Everyone else is just starting off their work week. Night watchmen and bartenders, their schedules never mesh with the rest of the world. Richard spends his late afternoons and nights watching other people relax, watching them enjoy themselves. The only people he really seems to know are other restaurant employees. It's a curious type of inbreeding, but who else works the hours he does?

Yet on a day like today, Richard can almost feel satisfied. Early autumn is the only time there doesn't seem to be some serious drawback to living in Maine; summer, heat and tourists; winter, snow and cold; spring, mud and black flies. But today he can sit quietly on a bench by the harbor undisturbed by outlandish tourists and warmed by the early autumn sun. Only the slightest hint of chill in the air reminds him of how brief this time of the year is. It will be over in a week, perhaps two. When they visited, his sister and brother–in–law could never understand everyone's preoccupation with the weather. They're city folk. Weather for them is only a minor inconvenience, not a way of life. Still, if it was always like this, then maybe, just maybe it might be okay.

***

Though he enjoys the quiet, that sense of being alone, of not being trapped in a noisy bar inhaling cigarette smoke, he knows that days like this were meant to be shared. Megan, the lovely, desirable, but never to be attained Megan, might still be at home. He doesn't think she works today, at least not till afternoon. Unless she has a morning class she might just be moping around waiting for Richard to call. He has no intention of disappointing her.

Pulling out his wallet he rifles through bits of paper with names and addresses scrawled over them. He remembers Megan giving him her latest temporary number last week. Ever since she broke up with Matt, Megan has been house–sitting for a variety of wealthy summer people; sometimes for a few weeks, sometimes for months. How does she do it? Richard pays nearly half his salary for a two room apartment in a barrack like building. At night he can hear the guy in the neighboring unit humping his girlfriend. The place is depressing and Richard has never bothered to decorate it. Nothing but white walls and a mattress greets him when he returns home from work. It's the best he can afford. There are no rich people asking him for favors. Of course, he does not look like Megan.

Richard is fascinated by her. Sometimes when talking to Megan he forgets to listen. He is too intent on watching her, becoming mesmerized by the play of her features. Yet there is something about her face which is definitely not pretty; attractive, verging on the beautiful, but in no way run–of—the–mill, yearbook type pretty. It's the fragile balance there that's exciting; as if an architect risked failure to reach for a striking effect. Her face verges on being outright ugly, of being totally wrong. Richard can never look at it without apprehension, afraid that this delicate balance, held together only by the force of her will as if by a spell, might shatter. Richard's ancestors would have burned Megan for the witch that she is.

When he was a child, Richard was given a marble the color of her eyes, a strange iridescent blue–gray. Every time he looks into those eyes he thinks of that marble. He can't remember ever playing with it, only looking and wondering.

The nearest phone booth is a few blocks away. He could take a shortcut through the Rusty Keel. He works there. No one would mind. Except, he might get trapped, end up bartending, waiting on tables, or even dishwashing. That place is an ongoing crisis, and his one day off is too precious to carelessly toss away.

The air is unusually still as he walks away from the dock up the slight incline toward Main Street. Passing the Hobbit Hutch he waves at Jill and Sam. He never could get through that book, all those dwarfs and elves with funny names. Everyone else his age has. It's probably a character defect on his part, being born with a deficient sense of the fantastic.

But a head shop in Maine, what's the sense in that? It can't be making money. Why would tourists possibly want to buy that crap up here? They can always buy it for less at home. As for the locals, Richard can just imagine some lobsterman, smelling like an old bait bag, dropping in for some jasmine incense or a water bong. If those bozos even thought about smoking dope, they would probably just shove it up their noses and light it.

***

He's heard they've been having problems. Jill's seeing some

other guy. She looks so innocent though, pure hippie naïve. Who can tell? It might be true, but he really doesn't know either one of them too well. He just serves them drinks. ... Never trust a woman who orders coffee brandy sombreros.

Richard wonders why all telephone booths smell the same way, like someone had once taken a leak inside. A whiff of stale urine always pervades that small enclosed space. Perhaps they come that way from the factory. It might even be a blue collar job at the phone company. Richard imagines workers in hob nail boots and hard hats drinking beer, then whizzing into the booths before they're shipped out and installed.

He peers at the receiver. Telephones are used by so many people. Is it safe to handle them? Perhaps a strange, highly contagious disease lurks ready to ensnare a careless caller. Does A.T.&T. worry about crazy things like this? In the distance a gull arcs, catches the morning light on its wing, circles once, twice, then heads down Union Street toward the dump.

The dime is buried deep in his jeans. Pulling it out leaves a mildly satisfying sensation. Richard listens to her phone ring as he reads the suggestions scratched on the inside of the booth.

"Richard? Oh good, I'm glad you called."

"I thought you might like to come into town. You know, we could hang out for a few hours, talk. I could show you my tattoos."

"You don't have any tattoos."

"We could find out for sure."

"I know, let's go for a swim."

"Way too cold."

"No it isn't. The ocean's the warmest it's ever going to be right now."

"Yeah, it must be at least forty–five."

"It's not that cold."

"Oh yes it is. The ocean's always freezing in Maine. Remember when it was one hundred degrees last summer?"

"Sure."

"Well I went swimming and nearly broke my bazooka right off."

"I was in yesterday. It's not that bad."

"Anyway, I don't have trunks."

"You won't need them."

"Why's that?"

"You know Gary Philmont?"

"A hah."

"Well he has this place that's right on the point. I discovered it accidental like. See, I was down there yesterday swimming around in the cove. I didn't have the slightest idea of who owned the place, but it wasn't like I was going to try to find out. I mean, why should I care?

"So there I was, stretched out in the sun, drying myself off, when I heard this noise, you know, twigs snapping. Well, about a minute later, Gary comes bouncing into the clearing wearing only that sappy grin of his, but acting like he was all cool and casual."

"Tell me, are his balls as insincere as the rest of him?"

"Sweetheart, I didn't bother to check them out for you. Most of the action was just him leering at me. I was naked too. But I am not going to play modest for someone like that."

"He's a goddam asshole."

"Focus Richard, this is the important part. He said that I was free to use his beach any time I felt like coming. Isn't that great? Let him have his peepshow. It doesn't mean a damn thing to me."

"I'm not going."

"Oh Richard, it's beautiful. We could have a really good time there."

"Sure, just you, me, and old 'good to seeya' Gary Philmont. If he came over and gave me one of his sincere squeezes on the shoulder I'd piss right on his goddam foot. You think I'm going to spend a few hours listening to his mealy mouthed garbage and watching him leer at you?"

"Calm down sweetie. You're right. Gary is a total, fucked up trip; but he has this really great place on the point."

"Megan, I don't care what he owns, he's still …"

"Richard, you're not letting me finish. I know how you feel about him. But see, the reason it'll be so great is that there's no way Gary'll be around today. He's over to Searsmont trying to swing one of his sleazo real estate deals."

"How do you know that?"

"He was trying to impress me, filling me in on all the important things he has going. The guy's a one hundred percent bogus case, Mr. Big Businessman in the flesh. I had to keep myself from laughing."

"So it'll be just the two of us, is that right?"

"You couldn't be more right."

"Just me and beautiful little you?"

"At my most dazzling."

"And we'll be alone?"

"You've finally caught on lover. It'll just be you, me, and the sea gulls."

"When do we leave?"

"It'll take me about half an hour to get ready."

"I'll wait."

"Where will you be?"

"Over by the boat repair sheds on the other side of the harbor."

***

Richard shades his eyes against the sun and watches Megan walk toward him. He remembers the first time he saw her. He was looking for a cocktail waitress. He spends every week looking for a cocktail waitress. Hardly anyone lasts. Between the fucked up lobstermen and the bullshit owner, few can take it for long. The owner prowls the bar each night looking for stray women and harassing the help. The lobstermen start by grunting obscenities, finish by becoming violent.

Megan was waiting there for him at five on a Tuesday. All the likely applicants, those who aren't lame or blind, work a shift on a trial basis. The best of the lot get the job. Sometimes he can almost sympathize with the owner. They really are pathetic.

When Richard walked in that night, Johnny said there was someone waiting in the kitchen for him. Then he winked. Her back was pressed against the serving counter. Richard mangled her name and she turned to correct him. He would always be able to remember that first smile. It was impossible to forget, impossible not to grin foolishly back. He stopped and stared, drawn in by her eyes which seemed lit by a strange light when she smiled. His heart seemed to beat irregularly and he had the feeling of drowning, of surrendering to some overpowering force.

She was dressed mostly in black; short corduroy skirt, high leather boots. If Richard could have mail ordered a woman from L.L. Bean, Megan is what he would have hoped to receive. He half expected to find a tag around her neck saying "damp iron only". Perhaps, he thought, he should offer to elope with her to Aruba.

But then he remembered his role. Taking down a soiled menu, Richard went over the routine of the restaurant. The more he chatted with her, the more he liked her. Was there some discreet way to ask her if she was living with someone? Richard babbled on, sometimes making a mild joke, often laughing with her. This middle management role would be difficult to maintain. If she turned out to be a terrible waitress would he hire her anyway? Working around her would always be a mixed game of pleasure and frustration. He wanted to find out what his chances were, but he felt obligated to be business–like and professional.

***

"You're looking good Richard, got some sun I see."

"And you're merely devastatingly beautiful today, Megan."

"That's what I like about you Richard, you're never afraid to be critical."

"Yep that's me, ruthlessly brutal to the core."

"Okay my rotten little core, I've got my car double–parked. Let's get."

Richard likes how she walks, holding her body like a precious possession, springing off her right foot, exuding a strong sensual vitality like some sleek, glossy animal. Maybe it's her diet.

"Did you hear from Harvard?"

"No go."

"Well that's completely fucked."

"Yeah, I thought so."

"Why weren't you accepted?"

"Didn't say. Just sent me a standard rejection letter."

"Yeah, but what did it say?"

"Oh you know, the usual crap. 'Thank you very much for your application to the Harvard Business School ... We're very sorry we can't accept you, bar bar bar, no reflection on your own qualifications, blub blub blub, far too many applications every year, blop blop blop, best of luck in all your future endeavors. Sincerely, Stickney Codpiece III, Director of Admissions, Associate Dork, Harvard Business School.'"

"That was it, huh?"

"Approximately."

"And you let it go at that?"

"Of course not. I'm willing to bet my scores are just as good as the bozos they let in. So, I was totally pissed. I sent a letter back demanding to know why. I mean I shelled out fifty bucks, spent all that time filling out their tight–assed application, and annoyed people for recommendations. I wanted something more than a standardized piece of fluff."

"What happened?"

"I got a personal letter from old Stickney. It read like a form letter, smelled like a form letter, and had the same thoughtful content of a form letter. So I fired off a telegram. It briefly described this guy's sexual proclivities and preferred positions."

"That tore it."

"By that time there was nothing left to tear. I'd just as soon leave them all to get butt fucked in peace."

"Don't let yourself get down about it. Harvard's as bogus as they come. It's got nothing going for it but its phony reputation. Matt went there, for all the good it ever did him. His old man was an alumnus with lotsa bucks, so he got in. Doesn't prove a damn thing."

"I'm not crushed by it, Megan. But it doesn't feel terrific to have someone tell you to get lost. Even if it's by a bunch of ass suckers like the Harvard Business School, a rejection isn't ever going to leave you feeling all too gorgeous."

"So it's California?"

"Yeah, I figure sometime near the beginning of October."

"You sure about this?"

"Of course not, Megan. It probably won't change a damn thing. But what else can I do? At the very least, it's an honest shot. I can tell myself that I haven't given up, that I'm still trying. If I stay here I'll only settle down more firmly into my rut."

"Is that so bad?"

"I don't know. Well, I suppose not. But I just wanna make the attempt, you know, like pretend that I'm still alive."

"Okay, let's park here and we can walk down."

***

Megan is wearing shorts and a scarf knotted behind her back. She slips them off. A pair of mauve bikini underpants the size of a man's handkerchief remains, a strange vestigial sign of modesty. She has small pointed breasts and a sleek slim body like an otter. Richard thinks of Circe and the spells she wove to befuddle men.

Megan has stopped shaving her legs. Richard wishes she hadn't. He feels tempted to mention the hair on her legs. Not to inform her of its existence, obviously she knows her legs are hairy. He wants to plead with her instead to get rid of the stuff. In the winter they're covered by jeans or black tights, but now she lets the dark hairs bleach in the early autumn sun. All that black hair camouflaging her legs, hair darker than his own. It just isn't right. It makes him physically ill. Logically it shouldn't. He looks down at his own hairy legs. Nothing upsetting there. But it isn't merely a matter of getting used to something he doesn't expect to see. Armpits for instance are a completely different matter. He doesn't give a damn about armpits or what goes on there. The hair could be braided. Birds could be building nests. But leg hair … no way he will ever adjust to it.

Not very progressive, but Richard doesn't give a damn about being progressive. All that right thinking business is nothing but meaningless style, like wearing the latest designer clothes. He likes to look at women's legs and he doesn't like to have that view obstructed. It's strange, it's not like he gets excited by women who primp themselves, who use make up and nail polish. He cannot imagine going out with a woman who painted her toenails. That would be too bizarre; plump little white feet in satin mules with each tootsie a Technicolor Red. It's not manufactured glamour that attracts him. Megan hasn't quite shaken free of her adolescent complexion. Richard finds those blotches charming. So, a few strands of leg hair shouldn't matter in a woman as beautiful as Megan. But it does. Aesthetics may be relative, but that knowledge doesn't stop him from feeling queasy about unshaven legs.

"Did you bring towels Megan?"

"Of course sweetie, they're there on that rock. Bring them over and we can dry each other off."

A lobster boat swings in and slowly carves an arc in the water. Richard wonders if they've come in for a closer look. If they have, what can he do? If they want to come ashore and drag Megan off in a bait bag he knows he would be absolutely helpless. Fortunately, the water's too shallow. Besides, why shouldn't they gawk at her? She doesn't mind. And what is he doing right now? Dripping salt water, gleaming in the sun, Megan more and more resembles some wild aquatic creature.

"So when I was living with Matt I started feeling like I wasn't worth being loved. He just never expressed anything. Funny, when I first started living with him, I liked that. No heavy scenes, he never came down on me at all. But then I started feeling like it must be me; he just must not care about me. It wasn't good feeling like that. So when I walked into work and there was your beautiful plant waiting for me, I started to cry and I just couldn't stop. It felt good and I felt so foolishly happy."

"Megan you deserve it. Don't you know that by now? I could never, never do enough for you, no matter how hard I tried. Don't you realize what a very special and beautiful person you are?"

"Thank you, Richard. I just don't ..."

She leans her head against his shoulder, eyes moist, swimming with tears. Richard takes her hand and carefully kisses each finger. He wants so much to take each small breast in his mouth and suck on it softly. He wants to ram his head between her legs and never pull out. He wants to make love to her right then and there until they collapse together in one sun baked, gooey mess.

But Richard doesn't understand what she wants. When they kiss, they kiss with closed mouths. And if she really doesn't want him, he'd feel loathsome trying to touch her. Silence persistently keeps them apart.

She's told him so much about her life and her feelings that he thinks he understands her. But at times like these he realizes that he knows nothing. Her feelings toward him are unspoken, unfathomable.

"Better get going."

"You can just drop me off in town, Megan, I can walk from there."

"Don't be silly."

Richard does like being driven around by a beautiful woman, or for that matter, being seen with one. It's just vanity. He knows it, but that doesn't make it any less enjoyable. It gives him a feeling of luxury. And besides, Megan is a much better driver than he'll ever be.

They pull over by the small town common and Megan hits her horn. Blond, curly headed Susannah turns, then blinks rabbit eyed and smiles in recognition. The two women met when they both were working at the Rusty Keel. Richard can never quite figure out what they could have in common. Susannah is just a kid. At least that's what he thinks. It's hard for him to tell. She's such a space cadet, and so goofy, that Richard just assumes she's very young.

"Hey Susannah."

"What you two been up to? You look sorta damp."

"Swimming."

"Isn't it too cold for that Megan?"

"That's what I said."

"Hush Richard. When are you opening Susannah?"

"I still can't get a license. You know I was going to set up in back of the Gallery, near the docks? So I went and talked to the guy, and he said it was okay with him, but then he goes and changes his mind. Wouldn't tell me why. Maybe some of the other restaurants put some pressure on him."

"I can tell you exactly who did that."

"You mean that German pig, don't you Megan? He might do something like that just to spite me. It's not like I'd really hurt his precious business by selling a few lousy falafels. What do you think Richard?"

"I think he's capable of anything. You didn't exactly leave the bar on friendly terms. Maybe you could smile at him or something."

"I wouldn't bother crossing the street to spit on him. Tell me again Richard. Just tell me exactly what he said about me."

"He wanted me to force you to wash your hair. He thought it looked dirty ... Oh yeah, he also said that your hair was too curly."

"Smell it. Go ahead, tell me if it smells dirty."

"C'mon Susannah, you don't have to convince me."

"You remember Megan telling him that she wouldn't be treated like a peon?"

"Yeah, he backed right down, no guts at all. Can't blame him though. Old Megan here is one pretty tough lady to tangle with."

"You know it, sweetie."

"God, I heard that he got mad because Megan wouldn't shave her legs. Is that true Richard?"

"I wouldn't know a thing about that."

"I thought I heard that from somebody. Guess it doesn't matter ... Hey look, why don't you two come up to my place? We can hang out for a while."

Susannah rents a small apartment on Church Street. It's the top of a garage behind a three story white clapboard house. To get to it you have to skirt a large Buick station wagon and then climb a ladder up into the loft. It's basically one medium sized room with a jury rigged kitchen and no bathroom. There's supposed to be an ocean view. Well, maybe if you could hang far enough out the window with someone holding tightly onto your feet you might catch a glimpse. And it doesn't even have the virtue of being cheap. But then nothing is cheap around there. People who work in resorts are doomed to a modern day version of servants' quarters.

Richard is behind Susannah as they climb. He looks up her skirt as they move rung by rung. At least she shaves her legs. And, even better, she also doesn't seem to be spending money on underwear. Richard has never really given Susannah much thought. Certainly screwing around with her has never entered his mind. Pretty enough, but for some indefinable reason he's always considered her somewhat asexual. Now as he carefully looks between her legs, he realizes that he might want to reconsider that opinion. Susannah turns around. "See anything up there you like or were you just browsing?"

"Well now that you ask, I wouldn't mind having one of those hairs as a souvenir."

She stares at him wide eyed. At times she can make her eyes look like blue china saucers devouring her face. Without glancing away Susannah reaches beneath her skirt, grits her teeth, and comes up with a pale curly hair. She ceremoniously hands it over to Richard.

He is slightly stunned, maybe even somewhat impressed. Smiling he mouths the words, "Thank you".

Meanwhile Megan is roaming in front of the bureau mirror upstairs. She unties the knot behind her back. With her scarf held in front she tries to rearrange her small breasts in a more seductive manner. Now that they've made their appearance for the day she no longer cares if Richard sees them or not. It's supposed to make no difference. Go try telling that to old Joe Palooka straining down there against his boxer shorts. If this keeps up much longer he might just suddenly pounce on her. The last sound she would hear is him loudly crunching on her bones. Megan probably trusts him not to stray from his prescribed role. He's supposed to be sophisticated about such things. He's expected not act like some sex–crazed adolescent. Or perhaps she just feels safe with Susannah there to act as witness. But Megan must realize that she's driving him absolutely crazy. He wonders if it's deliberate. Is she toying with him or sending out some positive signal? Richard doesn't even know if he's permitted to ask questions. It seems like he's never been told the rules to these games people expect him to play. All this shadow acting is only confusing.

"Richard, I said, 'when do you think you'll be leaving for California?'"

"Sorry Susannah, I must have been thinking about something else."

"I bet."

Richard sees Megan smile into the mirror. Did she stick her tongue out or did he only imagine it? He's certain that this is all a tease, but perhaps not. He can't be sure about anything except for his overwhelming sexual desire.

"October, I want to get over the Rockies before the winter snows hit."

"That early?"

"Well I've heard they can have bad weather before November. It's so goddam high. Why, were you thinking about coming along?"

Richard wonders where that came from. Maybe he's only trying to get back at Megan. No discernible reaction, but her eyes did seem to darken like a storm cloud covering the western sky. She certainly is listening.

It's Megan that Richard really wants to take with him to California, or anywhere else for that matter. He wishes that she would come with him but he's too afraid to ask. He wants it to happen as if by unconscious design. After all these years he is still searching for some ideal cinematic romance.

And Susannah is definitely spacey. Is he really serious about being cooped up with her for at least a week, more if he stops off to see Cordy and the infamous Lloyd in St. Paul? But it might not be too bad. She's certainly not short on looks.

"Do you really mean that Richard?"

"Sure, think about it and let me know."

He darts a look over toward the mirror and mumbles, "Try cramming that one up your wazoo, Megan dear."

Susannah for some reason seems excited about this turn of events. Richard's surprised. He never realized that she might have any interest in him. It's not as if she lacks offers from other men.

"Why don't you stop by tonight and we can talk about it. I'll spot you a drink."

Richard has just tossed himself onto the open market, and is waiting for the bidding to begin. Well, he thinks, isn't it competition that made America great? Doesn't everyone profit from it? But this still comes as an unexpected maneuver to all three players. Susannah and he would certainly make the town's most unlikely couple.

Megan, finally roused, packs away her boobs. She strolls over to the bed and manages to wedge herself in between Richard and

Susannah. Her tongue moves slowly over her upper lip, mouth opening into a hungry smile. Richard knows he will do whatever she wants.

"So sweetie, can you get tomorrow off?"

"Maybe, why?"

"Oh, I was thinking …"

"You were?"

"Yeah. I was just thinking that maybe we could go out to dinner, you know, the two of us alone."

"That'd be nice."

Megan is successfully cutting–out her best friend. She doesn't even know if she wants Richard, but for the moment, she's scared to lose his endless admiration. Her last relationship didn't work out. Too many of them haven't. She's begun to feel defective. Perhaps she worries that she's inherited some of her father's faults. And Richard is so dependable. At least he can always make her smile.

On the corner of her bed, Susannah sits watching Megan's performance, eyes wide, turning an angry red. In spite of what some people think, she is in no way dumb. She doesn't like what's going on. But at least now she understands how the game is being played. She's bought her scorecard, read the ground rules, and will wait for her chance. Megan is too sure of herself, too careless of Richard's feelings.

"Got to go ladies. Time to get ready for tonight's performance."

"I thought this was your day off, Richard?"

"Yeah, I thought so too Megan, but I promised Johnny I'd bartend for him."

"What's the scoop?"

"Nothing, he just wants some time off to be with Jeannie."

"I still can't believe those two got married."

"Why not? Two weeks, two years, knowing each other doesn't stop a relationship from falling apart."

"I just don't see the point. I like Johnny, but I don't trust her one bit."

"Jeannie? Nothing wrong with Jeannie."

"You're a guy, so you fall for her routine. But she's the type who'd fake an orgasm. And I swear she used to swipe my tips when we worked together."

"I can't believe that. What about you, Susannah?"

"Mm?"

"Is that true about Jeannie? You worked with her."

Susannah stares at Megan. "I've got nothing against Jeannie. She seems able to keep Johnny happy. That's more than some women can do."

"Yeah, well anyway, I've got to buzz."

"Hold on, I'll give you a lift home."

Richard gets up. Megan follows close by, brushing her body against his, causing his stomach to knot. This time she's not letting go.

"I'll see you tonight, Richard."

"Did you say something Susannah?"

"Well I thought we sorta had a date."

"Sure, Susannah, and I'll have that drink all ready for you. A toasted almond, right?"

"That's right."

"Never forget a drink or a pretty face."

Megan hooks her arm around his and Richard finds himself outside amidst blue skies and the faint smell of the bay. A shame to have to leave and go to work now … Richard is back home, standing with her in front of his apartment building. He works sixty hours a week to pay the rent. It's falling apart and he hates it.

Megan's eyes have taken on that strange blue–gray color that fascinates Richard. Every time he looks into them he thinks of that marble he had as a child. He could never bring himself to touch it. He only looked and wondered.

Richard wants to tell Megan of his great need for her, how he would willingly sacrifice himself to show that love. There must be some secret language which would let him communicate his burden. He doesn't think he could ever just flatly state it. That would bring everything to a point of decision. And he wants all his desires to be fulfilled without ever having to act for himself, as if life could proceed in one mystical romantic flow. What if she were to say no?

What if he was to ask and she were to say no? Megan might not be interested. How is it possible to tell, to know such things with any degree of certainty? Once voiced, it would always lay between them. Events would become determinate, moving in some definite direction, perhaps a direction he might not like and could not control. She would drift totally out of his reach. He hates not knowing but he's more afraid to find out. At such moments Richard feels trapped inside some poorly constructed Edith Wharton novel.

"I'll give you a call Richard."

"I'd like that Megan."

"Hey, wait a minute, you don't have a phone."

"Yeah, I forgot for the moment."

"Well, I'll stop by your place tomorrow. I'll pick you up for dinner."

"Where would you like to go?"

"I'll think about it and tell you tomorrow. Maybe we could go to Monhegan sometime next week. The ferry service is still open. We could picnic and spend the day out there."

"Okay, we can talk about it at dinner."

Richard will never tell Megan how he feels; too much diffidence, too much fear. There will always be some excuse; hairy legs, the wrong mood, a bad moment. … On cold winter nights he will sleep. In his dreams Richard will bend his head slowly over her pale slender body, tasting Megan's sweetness while snow drifts gently down outside his window.

8

ON WINGS OF LOVE – CALIFORNIA DRIFTING

Somehow Toto, I think we're no longer in Kansas
– Dorothy, from *The Wizard of Oz*

"So what do you do with yourself, I mean when you're not stuck in this dark old cave?"

I continue to stare for a moment, hand still wiping the counter with a grungy bar rag. Here since eleven, I've been prepping the bar, trying to scrape off some of the scum left over from last night's fiasco. Every afternoon Susan Ann Madison practices her dancing. Two nights a week she works here, a waitress hustling drinks for tips. Well, that's not quite right. If you can find her, she'll bring you a drink, but she maintains a pretty low profile, says she doesn't like to bother people.

Now as we talk, I find I can't stop myself from staring. She's the most beautiful thing I've seen since I've come to California. Sure beats the hell out of watching some dripping redwood trees. Like a boob, I've travelled three thousand miles to move from one miserable climate to another. But Susan, now she's something I'd never see in Maine.

She'd look like she's on break from a Virginia Slims commercial, if you could ignore her tacky belly dancing outfit and that sword she's balancing in her left hand. Can't imagine a more unlikely exotic dancer. She's about as exotic as a stewed dumpling. Sue Ann's an advertiser's dream of the girl next door, all long legs and squeaky clean California looks.

Every afternoon I get a private performance and every afternoon I end up shaking my head. I am incapable of dealing with beautiful women. My heart stutters, aches, and falls silent. Only God can protect me from such women. My own defenses have never been sufficient.

"Do? Not too much, nothing very exciting. When I finish up my work I want to be alone. I don't want to see or talk to anyone. So I hang out at my cabin, read, maybe go down to the ocean to watch the sea lions. Dull, I lead a very dull, boring life. It fits my personality."

"Well gee, maybe you'd like to go to the ocean with me one day?"

"Huh?"

"I mean I just thought it might be nice."

"Sure, anytime at all."

"Are you certain?"

"Yeah really, anytime at all, I'd love to."

"Next Tuesday?"

"Tuesday?"

"It's a day of the week, Richard. There should be one coming up pretty soon."

"Yeah next week, next week's okay."

"Just stop by the house then."

Susan gives me a smile. I stand and look into that smile, hand still etching circles on the cracked plexi–glass with my rag. I may be in love. My face breaks slowly into a grin as I smile back at her. Who is it she reminds me of when she smiles like that? Never mind, it'll probably come to me in a minute.

Susan puts on her jacket and waves goodbye. I watch as she waddles out. She may be an exotic dancer but she walks like a pregnant duck. I don't care. She could bark like a dog or slide on her belly like a reptile. It wouldn't make her any less wonderful.

That lamentable bitch, fortune, has finally decided to wink in my direction. The golden girl of all my sweaty teenage dreams has just asked me out on a date. Who says it doesn't pay to wait? Well this time I'm positive that my luck has changed. Katherine's slimy curse won't be worth a glob of spit on a hot fire. Bleah, Katherine. What made me think of her? From now on I'm thinking only happy little thoughts. This time I'm positive that everything is about to click into place. I can feel it, honestly, I really can.

Relaxed for once, my mind races ahead, grinding out another episode in the surrogate life of Richard Davis. Scene One: Winter in New England –Sitting next to Susan by the fire, I look knowingly into her eyes and say …

"Been trying pretty damn hard to wax your old cucumber, huh Hoss? Must be if what I hear tell is true. They're saying our little belly dancer's been paying you some house–calls. Now that's what I call right neighborly of her."

Shit, it's Nick. Well that puts the old smash to any more of my daydreams. I don't know how I missed hearing him come in. Nick swaggers. He doesn't know how to just walk into a room. What he usually does is to announce his presence like an actor taking a bow on stage. Down in L.A. good breeding probably doesn't take you very far.

"Cram it, Nick."

"Whoa there boy, time to lighten up a notch. Everyone here knows you're sweet on Susan. No way you're gonna tell me otherwise. So you just listen to me now. You can count yourself damn lucky that I happen to be your friend. Some bar managers I know might not take too kindly to one of the help mouthing off like that."

Can't push Nick too hard. All that will get me is fired. For the moment, I need the job. What choice do I have but to stare silently into a dusty fizz glass searching there for next Tuesday's reflection.

***

Peeking out the window I spot Susan as she waddles her way up the rise to my cabin. I rush to the bathroom for a final check, scanning myself in the mirror for any obvious flaws. Not too easy to tell, what with all that Andecker beer advertising covering most of it. I can only catch an occasional glimpse between the printing. Another example of gratuitous self denial, little niggardly bits of saving that end up costing me more in the long run, like the times when I try to fix my car and have to pay some mechanic to repair the additional damage. And these goddam miserable suspenders, the uplift always seems to keep some of the juice in after I pee. That's all it takes. As soon as I stuff everything back inside, those last few bonus drops come dribbling down my right leg. Just like a junkie, I usually leave a bathroom sporting a fresh set of tracks. All these small–time affectations, I always paying for them in the end.

Hurrying back into the front room,I casually arrange myself on the picnic bench and grab a book. Wouldn't do to appear too anxious, don't want to spring at her before she even reaches the door. I try to force myself into a cool, off–handed mood. Damn, my bowels aren't convinced. I let the excess gas escape before Susan knocks. Amy Vanderbilt strongly advises against serving up raspberries on a first date.

"Hi Richard, I hope I'm not too late or anything. I'm awful about being on time."

Susan gives me one of her high wattage smiles. I still can't figure out who she reminds me of. Damn, I must be blocking it out.

"Something wrong?"

"No, you just remind me of someone when you smile like that."

"Stan Laurel."

"What?"

"I remind you of Stan Laurel when I smile."

"Yeah that's it … No, I don't think I really want to say that."

"Sure you do, but I don't mind. He was sort of a cutie in his own little way,don't you think so, Richard?"

"Can't say I've given it much thought."

"Well anyway, I'm sorry if I kept you waiting."

"That's okay, I was just sitting here reading."

"Do you smell something Richard? I think maybe you forgot to turn off the gas."

"I doubt it Susan, but I'll go check."

And every time I see this woman she looks even more radiant, definitely a dangerous situation. In the distance I think I can hear that old love bus pulling up. If I'm not careful it's going to stop and I'll have to climb aboard. There's really no choice. When it happens you find that scenic cruiser by your side, door open, driver tapping impatiently on the steering wheel.

The last thing I need now is to fall in love. I'm no longer twenty years old. I know love can't provide any answers to my problems. At the very beginning of these affairs I already see the end, the parting and the sorrow. I'm not prepared emotionally or physically. I have too much to do as it is, dealing with all the Florentine intrigues down at the bar. God, let her be a hopelessly egocentric bimbo. Keep me from doing this.

"So I hear you're the new bar manager, Richard."

"Yeah, sorry I couldn't make it on Tuesday, but I've really been jammed."

"You don't sound all that excited about your promotion."

"I'm not. I've been working around bars too long to be happy about my prospects. All it means is long hours, lots of hard work and endless headaches."

"I know what you're saying. Rickey, he's my ex–boyfriend, was managing this resort up near Vail, you know, back in Colorado. He ended up working day and night for those people. They totally took advantage of him. I hardly ever got to see Rickey that year, and when I did it was a complete waste of time. He was always too tired to do anything. You know what I mean, he was hopeless."

"I'll take care of myself."

"Well, maybe you shouldn't take the job. I mean, why not go on being a happy little bartender? You could spend more time at the ocean."

"Because I can't. If I turned it down, I'd have to leave. They'd give the job to some complete derelict."

"Couldn't be any worse than Nick."

"I could deal with Nick. There are some people around here who I can't come to terms with. What about you sweetie, and everyone else who works down there? I can at least try to take care of you and all the rest of them."

"Is that me or you?"

"What are you talking about Susan?"

"Well, I just thought that smell might be me. I can't break the habit of eating raw onions."

"That's okay."

"Oh, you're just trying to be nice, Richard. There are days when I stink. Deep down I'm nothing but a dumb little Okie. But you know what? I've had some guys who've actually kissed me when I was reeking from onions. And that's nothing. There was this one sucker who wanted to kiss my feet."

"They are kind of prehistoric."

"Sure, what can you expect from dancing barefoot for over four years? Now Richard honestly, no one in his right mind would want to put his mouth to one of these beauties."

"Well, you know how it is with sex …"

"Yeah, I know about sex all right. Ever since I turned fifteen and my hormones started popping I've been thinking about nothing but sex. Maybe I shouldn't be talking to you like this."

"No, go right ahead. I don't mind."

"So I know there's a lot of peculiar stuff that goes on, but really, he wasn't even tripping or loaded."

"You're a very attractive woman, Susan. You must realize that."

"But my feet aren't for shit … Oh, do you really think so?"

"Hm?"

"What you said."

"Sure, but I don't have to tell you that."

"Go ahead anyway."

"Be glad to … You are an incredibly attractive woman, Susan. I feel honored to know you."

"Gee, that's nice Richard. You're really sweet, not like the rest of the creeps around here."

"Who do you mean?"

"Oh, like that sleazy Nick. He's not a close friend or anything? I keep doing that. I start ragging about someone and then it turns out the person I'm bitching to is a wife or something."

"Nope, it's okay. Nick is your basic bag of shit."

"He touched me once and I felt like going home and getting into the tub."

"I thought you liked him?"

"Me?"

"Yeah, that's why he hired you."

"What?"

"That's how Nick hired all the waitresses when he was running the bar."

"Not me, he didn't."

"Well, what was all that about insisting he come to the wedding? And why did you go out to lunch with him?"

"Who told you that stuff?"

"Nick, who else?"

"Oh, that asshole makes me so sick. It wasn't like that at all. I got into town a couple of weeks before Tod and Deanna's wedding. They didn't have a phone yet. So one day I was down here trying to call L.A., you know from that booth opposite the Grove. I saw this guy smiling at me and signaling like he wanted me to come on over. Well, I walked across the street and he started asking me all these questions –Who am I, where do I live, how long am I going to stick around –I can't remember them all. Then he offered me a job. Now Richard, you've got to understand that I didn't have a bean. So I thought, why not? I mean my job in Colorado does't start till fall. And when he insisted on lunch the next day I said okay. What harm could it do? Besides, I love eating in restaurants."

"What about the wedding?"

"I was being polite. I didn't make a big deal out of it … So you must've thought I was just another one of Nick's little bimbos?"

"The thought did cross my mind."

"Ooh, that makes me so mad. What a no good jerk! … Is that why you've been keeping your distance?"

"I don't know. I wouldn't hold it against you. Bad taste isn't exactly a crime."

"Well, why then?"

"Huh?"

"Why were you so distant?"

"I'm not too sure. Could be I was afraid. I'm basically a pretty shy person."

"Oh no, are you being serious?"

"It's true. That's the way I am."

"Well then I'm glad I decided to ask you first."

"And I'm glad you did too."

"Really?"

"Can't think of anything I've meant more."

"I've had enough wine, thanks … well okay, but we'll have to get going pretty soon if we want to make dinner."

"Don't worry, we've got plenty of time … So how are you making out with Tod and Deanna?"

"Okay."

"You're not getting in each other's way?"

"No, Tod is too zonked most of the time to be any problem."

"But I thought Deanna was this real close bosom buddy of yours."

"Is that what she told you? Well it's true, sort of. We knew each other back in Colorado. What happened was she stopped me on the street one night and asked me to give her dancing lessons."

"Right there?"

"No, not on the street Richard, at her home. I was really surprised. I mean strangers did say hello to me all the time. I was kind of a minor league celebrity around there. But Deanna just planted herself in front of me and demanded lessons. She has that sort of steam roller effect. I think she likes to be in charge."

"Is that why she married Tod?"

"He's actually a very nice guy. But she does dump on him all the time. Like last Halloween, oh Richard, you should see what happens in Vail on Halloween."

"Can't be any worse than around here."

"No, it's wonderful. Everyone dresses up and goes crazy. Vail's like the 'Land of the Lost Boys' before Wendy arrived."

"So what were you saying about Deanna?"

"Well, we were all sitting around this table in some bar. Deanna had rigged herself up like a gypsy, you know, in order to show off her big fat boobs. She kept leaning over to give all the guys there a good eyeful. And she spent the whole night practically throwing herself at one of Rickey's friends. I don't even know why. It wasn't like he was super attractive or anything. I guess she just felt like doing it. It was making everyone else pretty uncomfortable. I mean Tod was sitting right there. Didn't seem to bother Deanna a bit."

"Yeah, she's like that."

"Did she ever? … no, don't tell me. I'm not so sure she's such a great friend. I know that's what Deanna told you, and I am living with her, but I think she actually resents me. It really burnt her when I was making it as a dancer. She thinks it's unfair for other people to get what she wants."

"She doesn't make much of an effort toward doing anything."

"That's just it. I don't mind her sitting on her butt all day. It's having her complain about the results that gets me. She's caused me trouble before with her little routines. Like the time Rickey was managing in Vail. We had this big argument before I split."

"About what?"

"It's not important. Besides, we've busted up, we're through with each other now."

"Is that why you left Colorado?"

"Not exactly, but let me tell you about Deanna first. Rickey asked me as a favor to be a maid there for a few months. He needed someone he could trust. So Deanna finds out and decides that she also wants to play maid. Like suddenly it had become some sort of glamorous position or something.

"Rickey didn't want to do it. He knew how Deanna operated. But she kept pushing me and finally I got Rickey to agree. So we're up there cleaning rooms and she doesn't want to do a thing. Mostly she just sits on one of the beds and tells me about her sex life. Meanwhile I'm stuck with cleaning the rooms by myself. I did start getting pretty darn angry but then somehow Rickey found out. It was a mess. He really let her have it. Called her a 'lazy pig' and 'totally worthless'. Deanna started bawling right there in the middle of the lobby. I guess I totally lost it because I hit poor Rickey over the head with my mop."

"You know she's asked me for a job."

"That's another thing. Deanna's really angry about that. I mean how you're teaching me to bartend. All I hear are cracks about how if she was willing to spend two hours in front of a mirror she could get a job too."

"The mirror would break long before the two hours were up."

"Now be nice Richard. Though you know, it's really true. She does have those pair of piggy little eyes and she's built like a college linebacker. But that doesn't matter. She'd always have some excuse. She'll never admit that the reason she doesn't get a job is because she isn't willing to work. It was the same with her dance lessons. Most of the time all she wanted to do was to sit and gossip … Besides, I do not spend two hours making myself up."

"Don't bother listening to her. Look, there's no way I would've hired Deanna."

"Well, I thought …"

"Susan, I don't hire people on those terms. I'm not like Nick."

"I know that, Richard. You're a real nice guy."

"Are you sure you wouldn't like another glass of wine?"

"Well, we should be going soon, but maybe just one more … Thanks, how did you know rose was my favorite?"

"I didn't. One of the reps gave me a bottle to try out. I'm usually not too crazy about rose."

"No?"

"Mostly it's for people who don't know what they like, you know, a typical mediocre compromise."

"Thanks."

"Gee, I'm really sorry Susan. I always do that. I insult people without realizing it. I didn't mean to say you had no taste."

"Oh, but it's true. I know it. I like all those cheesy wines you're supposed to make faces at."

"Are you sure you're not upset?"

"That's really sweet of you, but I'm okay. I was only trying to give you a hard time … Listen, you're lucky. When we go out you can always order off the bottom of the wine list."

"Does that mean you're thinking of going out with me again?"

"As long as you keep your mouth shut when you chew. I told you, I'm always ready for a free meal."

"That's not …"

"Now, I've done it, haven't I? That's not the reason I want to see you. You're not to think that at all."

"Then maybe …"

"Richard, I don't want us getting too cozy before we even have dinner."

"Okay. So tell me more. Who've you been seeing? What's your life like?"

"Mostly just hanging out with Deanna. She doesn't seem to like me to be too independent. It's the same with all her friends. Have you noticed?"

"What's that?"

"There's something wrong with all of them. Like Luba next door. I mean she's a very sweet person but she is a little strange. She thinks she's Princess Luba from the star system Zarsky."

"Look, I know she has this thing about Star Wars ..."

"It's more than that Richard. She really believes it. I've heard her describe how she goes jumping into hyperspace. You can't tell me that isn't a bit strange?"

"Maybe that's why her eyes are so offset, she must have tried one jump too many. But Luba seems to manage pretty well."

"She's on S.S.I. You can't expect someone like that to actually hold down a job."

"No, it's probably a challenge for her just to make it to the store and back."

"Well Deanna thrives on people like that. They're easy to dominate."

"And you don't mind?"

"Sometimes I do. I don't want to be part of her little group. Luba and a few of the others are okay ..."

"But the rest?"

"Well, there was this dumb kid there last night with her baby. Everyone was smoking dope and this little rug rat was crawling around on the floor. He kept getting closer to a big wax candle in the corner. So I said, 'Watch out, Josh is going to burn himself.' Do you know what this woman told me? I mean she couldn't have been more than eighteen herself, but that's no excuse. She said, 'I want my baby to experience pain. It'll expand his consciousness.'"

"You're kidding?"

"Of course, she got upset when the kid started wailing, but I just couldn't handle it. How dumb can you possibly be?"

"Stop spending so much time there."

"You're right, Richard. There's no reason to be friends with a bunch of derelicts and baby burners."

"Well, it's not quite that bad."

"Yes, it is. I'm not even randomly maternal, but I still can't stand seeing that sort of stuff."

"You're not going to let go of that are you?"

"No I'm not. I'd like to smack her."

"It's just as much her old man's fault."

"She's by herself. Her old man split before the baby was born."

"So what else is new?"

"Richard?"

"Yuh?"

"Did you ever think of getting married?"

"Sure, I've thought about it. I almost did once."

"What happened?"

"I was lucky. It didn't come off. So how about you?"

"Well, I do get this urge every so often to have a baby. But the last time I had an abortion the doctor said she didn't ever want to see my face again."

"What does she expect you to do, use a coat–hanger?"

"You don't understand, Richard. It was totally my fault. She's a really super lady. But after three abortions your insides start getting screwed up."

"Three?"

"I told you, I get this urge and then I just somehow forget about those little pills."

"So then it's whoops?"

"But it never worked. Rickey wasn't about to settle down and become a father. He's always been too much of a party boy. Still, I keep worrying about getting too old. You must have heard about the risk of having your first kid when you're already past it."

"Susan, you've gotta be kidding. You're still just a baby yourself."

"How old do you think I am?"

"Well you must be at least twenty–one. You couldn't be working in a bar in California if you weren't."

"I said I've had three abortions. Do you think I make it an annual event?"

"I guess I wasn't thinking. But you look so sweet and innocent, like you just graduated from a Catholic high school last month. You still look like you're afraid some nun's about to rap you on your knuckles."

"I'm twenty–seven, Richard."

"Holy shit, you're as old as I am."

"Anyway, I am closing in on thirty, so now you understand."

"I can't imagine you pregnant."

"There'd just be more of me, that's all."

"Pregnant women give me the willies."

"Well, you'd be a real comfort to some woman."

"I know, I'd be terrible. It'd be rough to try to pretend. But it wouldn't work to tell your wife that she looked like a repulsive blob."

"Is that what you think I'd be?"

"I can't help it, Susan. It makes me feel all queasy, like seeing a cripple or a hunchback."

"I don't think we should talk about this."

"I'm not too crazy about babies either. Little wrinkled lumps of flesh always smelling like poop or strained carrots ..."

"Richard!"

"I know, I should learn when to shut up."

"Well, it's hardly what a woman wants to hear."

"Susan, I promise I'll be good. You probably already regret being here with me."

"That's not true, Richard. After all, I was the one who asked you. And besides, I think this is just as nice as going to the beach, a lot more cozy too."

"Okay, so how about telling me why you started dancing."

"Oh that's a long story."

"We have time."

"Well you have to promise not to laugh."

"I promise."

"You see it was right after Rickey left me for the first time. I was a wreck. I didn't know what to do. We'd been together since high school. About all I did for two months was to sit in this dingy little apartment in Modesto and cry. But finally I realized that I'd have to go find a job. I mean there was rent to be paid and all that other stuff. So I went to an employment agency but all they could find was this job at a factory. There wasn't much to it, mostly typing up the orders as they came in. The owner was kinda peculiar though. He wanted to hire someone real plain looking. You see, he was some sort of religious nut. His name was something like Mumsley, or maybe it was Malmsey. I can't exactly remember what he believed in. But, when I went for an interview, the first thing he said was that women were the source of all lust and fornication on earth. An attractive woman would only fan the fires of Satan in the misbegotten souls of his salesmen. I'm not kidding Richard, he really talked liked that … You know come to think of it, the whole thing makes a lot of sense."

"Are you serious?"

"I don't mean all that stuff about the fires of hell, but the other thing, the part about ugly women. He just wanted his employees to keep their minds on their work instead of looking up some secretary's skirt … Anyway, I got the job."

"What?"

"I was a total mess, I really was. My eyes were all red and puffy from crying, my hair was stringy looking and I was getting the tiniest bit pudgy around the hips. That's where I always put it on. So the guy hired me. Sure enough, I end up getting into this terrible relationship with one of his sons. Both of them were working there. I think we basically despised each other but held on out of sheer perversity. I mean it wasn't even fun screwing around with him. So I just got more depressed and put on even more weight. I was becoming a blob, you know the typical little secretary having an affair with her boss, gaining weight and doing mindless work all day. I started feeling dead. I was only twenty–two but I felt like I was slowly dying. Do you know what I mean, Richard?"

"A–hah."

"Well then it happened. I was at this laundromat one day when I noticed a small card stuck up on the bulletin board. Some lady wanted to teach belly dancing. I felt sorta silly but I went anyway. Richard, it was terrific! I really fell in love with that lady. I don't mean she was a great dancer or anything like that. She must've been at least fifty. I know you won't believe this Richard, but even at that age she still had this sexy little walk that totally knocked me out.

"So I decided that for once in my life I wouldn't hold back. I would put all my energy into dancing. What else did I have to do? And I found out that I could really let myself go when I danced, like I became another person. I didn't have to be shy or afraid of what I was doing. It's a lot like being able to fly. ... Does that sound weird?"

"Not really."

"Anyway, after a few months this woman suggested I continue dancing with some hotshot she knew in San Francisco. I guess I must've been getting pretty good by then. So I did it. I drove down from Modesto every Tuesday and Thursday night. Yeah I know, belly dancing in Modesto does sound pretty hilarious. Well, there I was dancing my heart out when Rickey calls. He was living outside of Vail and wanted us to get back together. I guess that's what I was praying for all along because I just packed my things and left. I quit my job and told the guy I was living with to shove it. And can you believe it, that little stinker actually threatened to kill me?"

"So, what did you do?"

"I took a plane out to Denver."

"No, I mean about that guy."

"I didn't have to do anything. I knew the gun wasn't loaded."

"Oh."

"Well, when I got out to Vail I found this restaurant that was pretending to be Middle Eastern, you know, the sort of place with lots of squishy pillows and too many slimy waiters serving plates of greasy lamb. But they had live entertainment. And that meant they might be looking for a belly dancer, like me."

"I can't imagine the competition out there would be too stiff."

"You're right. Most of the girls who auditioned were pretty tubby and didn't know how to dance. They thought all you had to do was go out on stage and shake it up a little bit."

"You mean that isn't the whole show?"

"No, it isn't. I know everybody thinks it's sleazy and real simple to do, like those flaky women, Rose and Coralee who dance around here. They don't know what they're doing. They just roll their hips and grunt."

"So what happened?"

"I was hired along with this other girl, a dark little Jewish princess. She couldn't really dance so she just subbed for me on my night off. Well, she tried to make my life miserable, spreading rumors and scheming to get me canned. Nothing worked, not even seducing the owner. But Richard, I am such a dummy. I knew what she was doing and I still felt sorry for her, I mean she was so screwed up I couldn't help myself. She ended up disappearing with my grandmother's necklace and about a hundred dollars in cash."

"How long were you there?"

"More than three years. Oh Richard, I know you're going to think I'm horrible but I really loved it. The place got to be popular and it would be packed every night. I would dance and the whole restaurant would go crazy. These Texans would be stuffing twenty dollar bills in my belt and everybody would be standing up and stomping on the floor. You see I was like this little celebrity. People would wave to me on the street or stop to look. It was just wonderful."

"Susan?"

"Yes, Richard."

"You know that tape you play?"

"Huh?"

"The one you practice to."

"What about it?"

"Is the first song supposed to sound like "Whistle While You Work"?"

"What?"

"You know, 'Snow White and Her Seven Little Dwarfs?'"

"Are you making fun of my dancing?"

"I guess you never thought of it quite that way."

"I told you Richard, I don't like being made fun of."

"Susan, you don't have to be like that. You've got nothing to be defensive about."

"I just hate it when people snicker. I know what I do is sorta tacky but it is dancing. I work real hard at it. But people go right ahead making their nasty little jokes and thinking all you have to do is to go out there and shake your unit in front of a bunch of horny guys. Even Florinda told me she's going to start belly dancing. She must think that stuff she does at the Grove amountss to the same thing."

"Florinda does most of her thinking with her unit."

"You don't think she's smart?"

"If she was any dumber she'd have to go out on a leash."

"Well, I don't know about that. All I do know is that Florinda's been all over me since I came to the Grove. She keeps telling me how terribly artistic and sophisticated she is. I didn't think she was too bright, but I can't be sure. I only had two years at the J.C. and I spent most of that time screwing around. I mean I know I'm uneducated and I guess I'm sorta slow, not dumb exactly, but not all too quick either."

"Don't say that."

"Why?"

"Look Susan, you're not just some dumb blond. You should push that thought right out of your head."

"But it's true."

"Do you think I'm stupid?"

"No, you're one of the smartest people I've ever met."

"Okay, then why would I want to waste my time with a dummy?"

"To get inside my underwear, I mean if I wore any."

"Yeah, I know that."

"Have you been peeking?"

"No, but next time try to watch yourself when you walk downstairs to Nick's."

"Ooh that sleazy bag of grease!"

"It'd be hard not to look."

"Yeah, I guess so."

"Well, you're certainly not modest."

"I'm not going to pretend I'm not attractive."

"Sweetie, you're beautiful."

"Do you think so?"

"I told you that before."

"Well, it never hurts to hear it again."

"Look, I want you to stop saying you're dumb … okay?"

"Not dumb just …"

"Susan, it's not so. I wouldn't be here with you if I didn't think you were bright."

"So you don't want to get inside my pants?"

"That's beside the point. I enjoy talking to you."

"Well, I like it too. But you don't have to say so."

"It's the truth."

"Well, why don't you come over and sit next to me?"

She's in the only chair I have, this redwood picnic bench I found outside my cabin. It's a tight squeeze even for the two of us.

"Richard, what are you doing?"

"Oh, is that your leg?"

"You're kinda sweet."

Control, I think if I try to kiss her right now my eyes might fall out. Good thing I'm wearing these extra sturdy pair of Wranglers.

"We better leave if we're going to make dinner."

"Am I making you nervous, Richard?"

"Susan, either we go to dinner right this minute or I'm going to rip off all your clothes."

"Is that an offer? … I'm only kidding sweetie. You're right, we better get going and listen, no more wine. One more glass and I might start ripping your clothes off."

"Hey!"

"Whatsa matter Richard, never been pinched before?"

"You are one wild woman Susan Madison."

"Is that good?"

"It's wonderful, and I think you're terrific."

"You forgot beautiful and talented."

"That too."

"Okay, I'm ready to eat now."

"I thought we'd go down to the Country Arbour."

"Is it any good?"

"No, but it's close and it's cheap."

"Oh, this must be their community night. I've never been to one of those before."

"Good, you'll get the chance to see all the local hippie elite."

I take Susan's hand and we walk down to the restaurant bumping gently against each other's body. I don't understand how she always manages to smell so good. Doesn't she ever sweat or have to take a crap? God, but I'd like to take a bite right out of her ass.

We thread our way through the dining room between partially cleared tables. At least there won't be the usual wait with all the other bargain basement gourmets. I look at one of the tablecloths, lasagna tonight.

"Two specials, Richard?"

"Sure Gillis, and bring us two glasses of rose."

"No Richard, no more wine."

"It's okay Gillis, bring the wine."

"I'm starving Richard, I'm hungry enough to start chewing on this tablecloth."

"Judging by its appearance you could."

"Oh Richard, I just love to eat. It's almost my most favorite thing to do. When I wake up in the morning, the first question I ask myself is, 'I wonder what I'll have for dinner?' No kidding, if I didn't watch it and keep up with my dancing, I'd be a little tub like my mom. She's still sort of cute, but she's let herself go."

"Where she live?"

"Over in the Valley with her little German derelict."

"Not with your dad?"

"No, she ran off with a cowboy when I was ten. This is number three."

"What about your dad?"

"Oh, he remarried too. None of the Madisons like sleeping alone."

"I'll remember that."

"Richard, keep your mind on your dinner and stop trying to shift gears with my knee."

"Do you mind?"

"That's none of your business. Besides, you have to get to work in another twenty minutes."

"Well ..."

"Richard, stop that. I like you, but we can't start pawing each other the first time we have dinner together."

"Why not?"

"Because you're sloshing tomato sauce all over the front of my blouse."

"Here, let me wipe that off for you."

"Richard you clown, what do you think you're doing? I can tell the difference between wiping and squeezing. How about if we just eat and talk ... This isn't bad for two bucks."

"I still wish Danny would stop using 10/40 on the salads."

"Is that true about Lila and him?"

"They started screwing around last week."

"How do you know?"

"Lila told me."

"Do all the waitresses at the Grove fill you in on their sex lives?"

"Actually they do."

"Doesn't that make you feel weird?'

"I don't mind."

"But, I mean, what if you were interested in one of them?"

"Well, I was sorta thinking about Lila?"

"Are you serious?"

"Don't forget, my options weren't so attractive before."

"Now you stop that ... Well I still can't imagine what Danny sees in her."

"She's okay if you like cheerleaders."

"Have you ..."

"Not really, just fooled around once."

"I wonder if she dyes her hair that color."

"No, it's natural."

"How do you know?"

"You're not the only one who doesn't use underwear."

"Do you guys just hang around with Nick, craning your eyes up?"

"Only some of the time."

"But I thought Danny was married?"

"His wife doesn't mind."

"That can't be true."

"She's a lesbian. In fact, I thought that was the reason her sister came to stay at the Arbour."

"Why would she want to fool around with her sister?"

"No, for Danny, to keep him occupied and stop him from stepping outside the family. But I guess he wanted Lila instead. I can't understand it. That sister is really good looking."

"Maybe she's a lesbian too."

"Could be. She's standing over there, why don't you ask her?"

"She is really cute."

"Maybe she'd go out with you."

"Stop that, Richard. I can't help it if I like the way women look. I mean, I do like guys' bodies too, but I get so darn confused. Do you think there's something wrong with me?"

"I like women's bodies myself."

"I'm not saying I've ever done anything like that, but I've thought about it."

"Nothing wrong with being bisexual."

"Do you mean ..."

"No Susan, not me. I've had friends, known other women who were."

"And it didn't make you feel creepy?"

"No, why should it?"

"I'll have to think about that."

"Why don't we think about going pretty soon. It looks like they want to clean up."

I wish I knew where this was going to lead. Probably nowhere at all. Best not to get my hopes up. One day they're falling all over you, the next day it's as if you don't even exist. I can't understand these women. If they think I'm so fucking wonderful and nice why do they keep holding themselves back? In fact, most of them seem to find exercising restraint pretty damn easy.

"What's that lump you got there?"

"It's my wallet, Susan."

"Is that so?"

"Don't go poking at it."

"Funny sorta wallet you got there."

"Didn't your mother ever teach you not to grab?"

"Why, doesn't that make you feel good?"

"Look, either reach in and shake hands with Gidney or just lay off."

"Sorry Richard, couldn't resist trying to give you a hard time."

"Next time, see if you can try a bit harder. Now c'mon, I'll walk you back."

"You don't have to do that."

"I'm not trying to run an escort service. I'd enjoy doing it."

"Well, I don't want to make you late."

"I think Johnny can handle the Tuesday night crush for an extra fifteen minutes."

"Did I tell you that Rickey was coming for a visit this week?"

"I thought that was all over."

"Oh that part is, but it doesn't mean I don't want to see him. We're always going to mean a lot to each other."

"Will you be able to cover your schedule?"

"Sure, I'll bring him over to meet you."

"Good, I'd like that."

Actually I'd like to see him swallowed up by a crack in the earth, but it doesn't pay to go berserk. I can wait till he leaves. I'm good at waiting.

"Well, thanks for the meal, I had a really super time."

She gives me a surprisingly soft kiss then disappears inside Tod and Deanna's cabin. I'm definitely not ready to bartend.

What am I going to do? I think I may be in love with Susan, but I don't want to be in love. I don't like being in love. I'm no good at it. It will be a guaranteed disaster if I decide to go for it. I should just sit on my heart till the damn thing cools off. Besides, she's splitting in a few months. ... But she is wonderful, no question about that. I really have to do something. Susan is going to think I'm nuts if I tell her I love her after one cheap dinner. But it's enough for me. I know I'm right. You can always tell about these things, I swear you can. Well, maybe she won't think I'm weird. I mean, it is possible. I've heard about it happening. Not to me of course, but there's always a first time ... God do I sound sappy. But look, if I don't do anything, it's for sure nothing will happen. I really can't just let her slip by without making some sort of effort. I'll wait until her old boyfriend leaves then I'll see how things look. I mean, what do I have to lose, right? But I sure am tired of feeling like a complete jerk. Okay, I'll do it, but not over the phone, that never works. I've had so many people say no to me over the phone that sometimes I feel like an encyclopedia salesman.

"Sorry I'm late, Johnny."

"Nothing doing yet anyway. How was dinner?"

"Wonderful."

"Are you okay buddy? Dinner down the street was wonderful?"

"No, it's Susan who's wonderful."

"Oh Christ, I thought you were finished with all that romantic crap. Remember, I've seen how it all turns out."

"This is different. I've never met anyone like her."

"Be serious Richard, sure she's pretty, but there are always pretty women hanging around bars."

"She's not like the rest of the women around here. That's what I noticed right off. I think it's the contrast I like."

"I know what you mean, but what can you expect from a place where Halloween is more important than Christmas."

"Yeah, remember last year?"

"We opened the doors and a guy walked in dressed as a used tampon, pulled up a seat at the bar, and ordered a Michelob."

"And then things got worse."

"I still remember you emptying a salt shaker over Lennie's head. What the fuck did you think you were doing?"

"It was either that or remove his vocal cords."

"You know you're a real lunatic, Richard."

"At least I didn't try to pull a biker head first over the bar."

"I should've never let Jeannie work that night."

"Is it true she locked herself into the hall bathroom for two hours?"

"She couldn't take it. It was a snake pit out there on that dance floor. When that goober bit her on the ankle she completely freaked out."

"Well she's not used to it."

"And I don't ever want to see her getting used to it."

"You're lucky Johnny. I should've latched on to a nice Maine girl like Jeannie."

"C'mon Richard. You remember what happened when you thought you had. Just watch yourself with this Susan person. Try to go slow."

"I won't say a word till next week."

"Then what?"

"I'll ask her to marry me."

"Buddy, I'm going to wrap you in a wet blanket if you don't calm down. You can't keep pulling stuff like that."

"Why not?"

"Because it never works you madman."

"But it might this time. The odds have to be in my favor."

"Richard."

"Yeah?"

"Sit down over there and let me make you a strong drink."

"Do you think I should ask her before or after her shift?"

"I give up buddy. Go ahead and bash your head against the wall. Just try not to do yourself in."

"Don't worry Johnny. I've got everything under control this time. I can take care of myself."

"Sure you can Richard."

"You'll see. This time's gonna be different. You just remember what I'm telling you."

"I'll remember, but that's gonna be the least of your problems."

"Are you guys paid to serve drinks or are you here to discuss your love lives?"

"I'll take care of it, Johnny … Okay Mac, sorry to keep you waiting. Now what can I do you for?"

"Do you know I've been here for ten minutes."

"I said I was sorry. Now do you want to order or are you gonna just stand there badmouthing?'

"I don't know what's wrong with this place. Every time I come in here I get the same old song and dance. Can't get any service. Drinks never taste right. When are you people going to get your act together?"

"Yeah, well why don't you take yours down the street?"

"You trying to tell me something?"

"Look pal, the door's right behind you. Use it."

"You can't talk to me like that."

"Why not, it's real easy."

"Listen you asshole, I'm gonna speak to the manager about this."

"Okay by me Fido, go ahead and speak, I'm listening."

"No wonder this place sucks so badly."

"You should know. You must spend half your life here."

"Wait until I tell the owner what jerks he has working for him."

"Well, when he gets back into town, I'll set up an appointment. Now move your ass out of here."

"This won't stop here, you fuckhead. I've got friends you know."

"Well excuse me while I wet my pants. Now hit the hardtop and hit it hard."

One day, these stupid gorillas will stop backing down. It'll be a case of reconstructive surgery without the anesthesia ... I wonder how long it takes to get used to a set of dentures.

"That wasn't necessary, Richard."

"No, but I enjoyed it."

"Bad sign buddy."

"I know, I know, I should get out of this business. Okay, as soon as I marry Susan I'll try to lead a normal life."

"Sure buddy."

"And you shut your goddan trap Nick! I don't want to hear a word out of you." "What the fuck you talking about? I just walked in."

"Well watch yourself or you can just walk right back out."

"Is it true what I hear Richard? Have you been keeping a watch on that new neighbor of yours? You know, the one with the long blond hair and the pretty little ..."

"I'm warning you Nick ..."

"What's eating him Johnny? What she do at that dinner tonight, bite his dick?"

"I think you'd better leave him alone, Nick."

"Who me? I wouldn't do anything to old Richard here. I'm his friend."

Sure, some goddam friend. I'd be better off keeping company with a rabid dog … And how does he already know about that dinner? Is there anyone in town left who doesn't?

"I don't want to hear another word about Susan coming out of your filthy mouth."

"Don't worry, Richard. You can't expect to have her slice your sausage the first time out. She'll come around."

"Nick, if you're planning to hang on to your own sausage, what you're gonna do, and do it right quick, is to shut up."

"Okay Hoss, no need to get all upset."

"I'll be back in half an hour Johnny. Give my 'friend' Nick there a drink if he can behave himself."

I'll do it next week. I won't give it a thought till then. I've got to try to let my mind go blank. Otherwise I'll start pre–planning the whole scene. That's bound to be a loser. The point is to live through an experience, not to memorize lines.

***

"C'mon Richard, we both want to see you with your clothes off."

"Wait up Susan, I've got something to tell you … No, you go ahead Lila, we'll catch up with you in a minute."

Christ, I thought that drummer would never leave; sucking up to Susan, asking her when she got off. Good thing Lila didn't open her big mouth and invite him to go hot tubbing as well.

"So what uh, I've been trying to say is uh, Susan you see uh, ever since last Tuesday, well it's just that I um …"

"Yes?"

"I ah … I love you Susan."

"You mean you're not going to fire me?"

"Listen, Susan, this is serious. It isn't easy for me. Don't go making it any harder."

"But you don't even know me, Richard."

"I know you well enough to realize you're the most wonderful woman I've run across in years. I can't risk losing you. Listen to me Susan, this is important; I mean for you, too."

"No, you listen Richard, this is crazy. I like you, I really do. You're a nice guy. I'm sure we can be friends, but this other stuff, you can't go around telling people you love them after knowing them for only a week."

"Why not?"

"Well, you just can't, that's all there is to it."

If Susan doesn't stop this soon, I'm going to end up hitting her over the head with a bottle of scotch. What a complete bummer reality can be.

"Think about it. You can at least give it some thought."

"But Richard, it won't work. It's totally impossible."

"What if I send you a self addressed stamped envelope? Could I become your lover then? Will you at least put me on a waiting list? You could notify me in case of some last minute cancellation."

"You see, even you know it's nuts."

"Oh c'mon Susan, it won't kill you to consider it. You're making me feel like a complete dork."

"Okay, but listen, don't you go getting your hopes up."

"Yoo hoo, Richard! Water's all nice and comfy."

"Keep your muff on Lila, we'll be there in a minute ... coming Sue Ann?"

"Sure sweetie, I'm dying to see you show off your cute little buns."

Great, I'm opening up my heart and she's completely zonked out of her mind. It's a wonder she managed to hold onto her tray tonight.

I let her go on ahead, watching as she works her hips across the road. The hot tub is in a small grotto next to the swimming pool. I can hear Lila splashing around, her dress neatly folded on the grass. Then for a moment I'm looking at Susan's smooth white body before she disappears into the water.

There are times when I wish I could remember more of my classical education, like those lines in Homer about Thetis of the shining breasts and the other descriptions, the ones that featured a whole caseload of nymphs and neriads. That's what the moment calls for. Though I'm damn glad I'm not some blind poet right now.

"Don't be shy, Richard. Show us what you've got."

"That's right sweetie. Lila and I are laying bets."

I guess I'll have to forego the epic dithyrambs. Unfortunately, I'm still not Californian enough to do without underpants. It's those brown stains I worry about. The trouble is I haven't bought a new pair in five years and what I've got on is all pretty much torn and baggy.

"Catch a load of those shorts."

"Ooh, very chic."

"How about keeping it down ladies?"

"You first, Richard."

"Yeah sweetie, doesn't look like it's about to come down any time soon."

I hop into the tub amidst shrieks and jeers. Opens up a whole new possible career for me.

"This is really nice, Lila. Sometimes you can actually come up with a pretty decent idea."

"Haven't you been in before, Richard?"

"Nope, never got around to it. You should've dragged me here months ago."

I make my way over to Susan so that we're just barely touching. She turns toward me and smiles.

"Did you say something, Lila?"

"You understand about love, don't you Richard?"

I nod politely but turn my attention to Susan and the intricate delicacies of her body. Where does Lila find her dialogue? Well, maybe for once she'll be quiet. She doesn't seem embarrassed watching the two of us. That's okay with me, just as long as she keeps her trap shut. I'm not shy about performing. Only Sue Ann seems among the undecided in our little hot tub drama. She hasn't said a word. I wonder what's going on beneath that shiny exterior. Better make it my business to find out. Uh oh, Lila is gearing up for one of her monologues. I glance over. Naked, she's the image of the Poppin Fresh Doughboy. I wonder if she'd giggle if I poked her in the belly?

"Oh Richard, have I told you how much in love with Danny I am? I mean really and truly in love. And this time I'm certain … No need to say anything. I can see it in your eyes. You understand me, don't you Richard? You understand what being in love is all about. No one else but you, because you've been so special to me since I came up here. You've been like a brother to me, haven't you Richard? I know how much you've tried to look after me. No, don't shake your head, don't try to deny it. I'm grateful Richard. I want you to know exactly how much I appreciate all you've done for me."

I give her ass a small squeeze hoping that will slow her down. A wrong move.

"That's right Richard, tonight I want to show how much I love you … and Danny. Because now that I'm in love I know how happy that must make you feel. It's the two of us Richard. Only the two of us know what love is all about."

I'm nodding my head, keeping time like some dislocated metronome. If she doesn't shut up soon there's liable to be a third hot tub fatality in California this month. Meanwhile my tongue is lazily exploring the inside of Susan's upper lip. But Lila isn't concerned. Her hand closes slowly over my genitals as she launches into another monologue.

"Oh Richard, I'm so happy for you too. Because it's only your happiness that can make mine complete. You know you mean so much to me Richard, you do know that don't you? And do you know what I really want? The one thing that can make me truly happy?"

Yeah, but I can't figure out how I can service both you and Susan at the same time.

"I want you to be as sweetly in love with your Susan as I am with my Danny. And I am Richard. This time I really am. I am so totally and completely in love. I've never felt this way before Richard. I know I can tell you about it because you understand how I feel, you've always known, haven't you Richard? You're the only one that does understand. You really understand what love is all about, don't you Richard?"

If she keeps pulling like that, understand will be about all I'm capable of doing in the future. I give her a hard pinch hoping to loosen that death grip of hers.

"Oh Richard!"

"Uh Lila?"

"Richard, you do know what love is all about."

I glance at Susan. It's time for me to make a move. Why bother with cheese whiz when there's brie for the taking?

"Lila, isn't Danny waiting for you?"

"What?"

"Danny, the man you love, the only one you'll ever love."

"Who?"

"Danny. You're supposed to meet him tonight, remember? When his wife goes to bed you two meet down by the boat dock."

"Hold still Richard."

If Lila was as quick with a cocktail tray the bar would double its take. Finished, Lila pulls herself out, sending ripples echoing off the sides of the tub. She's still flapping her jaw, but I'm not capable of listening. I feel like I did when I was a boy and the Mets were scheduled to play a twilight doubleheader. I hear Lila whisper goodbye in my ear but my mind's already on the batting line–up for the second game.

Alone now with the enigmatic Susan Ann Madison I find myself glancing upward, checking the skies for any stray lightning bolts. Something drastic has to happen. Though, actually I'm more afraid that I'll start shaking. I do that whenever I think something wonderful is about to happen. I don't think I'm constructed to absorb too much pleasure. Sometimes in the middle of humping a girl, my right leg will start quivering so badly that I have to completely give it over.

Susan seems finally ready to stir herself. She's whispering something in my ear. Sounds like the ground rules for tonight's main event. I hope she keeps them simple. I have a hard time remembering too many.

"Richard, I can't do this."

"Sure you can, Susan. It's like falling off a bicycle. Once you learn you never forget."

"That's not what I mean."

"If it's about Lila ..."

"No, Richard, that doesn't matter. You just don't understand. I promised myself that I wouldn't get involved like this again. I can't explain now, so you'll have to try and trust me. I've been so good this last month, just like a little nun. But it's so hard sometimes, Richard. I get crazy and I can't stand it. I feel like going out and attacking someone. There must be something seriously wrong with me. I can't stop thinking about sex.

"And then there's that other thing I told you about. I've always really liked the way women look, you know the way they're put together. You must think I'm sick. I know what you said in the restaurant, but tell me the truth, do you think I'm some kind of closet lesbian? I bet you don't even want to touch me now."

"Susan, none of that matters."

And that is the truth. Women's bodies are pretty damn exciting. Why shouldn't they realize that themselves? Probably a lot of them do but they're all too well trained to mention it.

Besides, right now I would accept anything Susan says or does. If she confessed to being sexually aroused by Fig Newtons I would be equally as supportive and understanding. I am absolutely and totally in love with this woman.

"Well, maybe it'll be all right as long as you promise me there'll be no sex."

"Don't worry."

Anything she wants. I was satisfied just being in the same tub. But now given the chance, I can't seem to touch her in enough places at once. I keep pressing against Susan but never get as close as I need to. Her skin, her smell is what I want to taste Our kisses linger, tongues pulsing with our hearts ... The hot tub shuts off. I reach over and push the button, requesting another ride on this erotic merry–go–round.

"Richard?"

"Hush Susan."

"I've got to go."

"Soon, we'll leave real soon."

I start rubbing my hand lightly across her bottom. Our mouths grope for their familiar positions. Too much happiness, something is bound to go wrong, something sure as hell is getting set to pounce and pounce hard. But right now, if my toes could smile, they'd be laughing out loud ... I wonder how long we've been in. Must be more than an hour or we wouldn't be so wrinkled. Well Susan is certainly the prettiest prune in California ...

"That was really wonderful."

"Yes."

"I meant it, Susan. I do love you."

"Don't say that Richard. You don't even know me.."

"I know that you're wonderful and I know that I'm glad you moved here."

"No more. It's late. We can talk about this tomorrow."

"And Sunday at brunch?"

"Maybe all of next week too. There's no hurry."

I hold on for one more luxurious kiss with Susan's body smelling fresh, her skin moist. My hands rub up and down her ass like a conscientious housewife polishing the family silver. Our tongues are glued together as I start to press harder, then harder still. I don't want to stop. I want this to continue and not to end. I'm definitely in danger of becoming a pleasure junky.

Like a gear clicking into place some hidden reserve activates and Susan pushes me gently away. I ease back, trying to get my stubborn glands to toe the line. Shit, maybe I should just go for broke and jump her.

"Good night Richard, thanks for everything."

"Sure."

"I've really got to go."

"Okay."

"Richard, leave go of my hand."

"Sorry Susan, I didn't notice."

"Now say goodnight Richard and go home."

"Goodnight."

"Please Richard, don't be difficult. Look, I do like you but I want to get some sleep. You have to go home."

I turn and drift off in a romantic fog. I'm halfway to town before I realize I'm headed in the wrong direction. Once in Italy, walking the empty streets of Rome at four a.m., I felt like this. If I knew how, I would've tap danced on the cobblestones. Nothing really ever came of that but a few letters and a collection of Swedish postage stamps. Damn, I'm in love with the most wonderful woman I've ever met. And it looks like maybe, just maybe, this time love won't be a one–way street. So please God, no tricks this time. I can't take having things fall apart again. Please oh please, please, please let them go right ... Now just stop that. You know that never works. If you want something that badly, it's bound to come up a loser. Relax and stop trying to force the play. You'll find out tomorrow.

***

"Hi sweetie."

Susan goes steaming right on by, totally ignoring my existence. Some son of a bitch has switched scenarios on me again. This isn't what I had scheduled for tonight. I casually follow her to the waitress station. She's standing there, back set against me, making elaborate preparations with her drink tray. I look at her and feel a warm softness threatening my sanity.

"Susan, what's wrong?"

"Oh Richard, how could you?"

"What ..."

"All that groping and attacking. What did you think you were doing?"

"Well ..."

"I kept telling you not to, that I didn't want that."

Our reels have gotten totally jumbled. Not only is tonight's feature unscheduled, but last night we were watching completely different films.

"Look Susan, I just thought ..."

"Well you were wrong, Richard. I'm not like that and I especially don't appreciate some guy pawing me all over."

I look past her and see another boat load of my romantic dreams listing badly on the horizon. Now, just wait a minute, wait one goddam minute. This wasn't meant to happen. Someone must have gone and switched those reels. I have it right down here in black and white—8:00 p.m. – *The Magic Theater of Richard Davis*: Beautiful Susan Madison falls madly in love with dashing young Richard

Davis.

So whose idea was it to pre–empt that lovely romance with a remake of *The Bride of Frankenstein*? I have no desire at all to imitate Boris Karloff coming for his newly created beloved. But Sue Ann here sure seems willing to rev up for some serious Elsa Lanchester type shrieking. Who the hell put a hair up her ass? In one day she goes from playing Miranda to being an avenging fury. Who's she planning on dressing up as tomorrow?

I don't need any of this. No way I'm gonna be able to deal with these daily psycho–dramas. I'm too smart for this sort of crap. I've served my time on the frontlines. I don't need to check into the heartbreak hotel for a refresher course. So okay, Richard old buddy, there's really no problem, right? Just forget about her. Go back to screwing Dusty or some other River bimbo and get on with what you were doing.

What a dope. I should have known this would happen. Christ, I must be cursed. All I asked is for one break and the skies rain turds on me instead. Well, there's nothing I can do. There's certainly no way I could get away with murdering the silly little twat.

"I really like you Richard. I think you're a nice guy and I do want to be your friend. I've told you that before, but not if you're going to behave like you did last night."

Maybe if I lifted up her skirt I'd be able to break through some of the rubbish she's been feeding herself. At least she'd have to stop handing me that nice guy routine. I've had it with that number.

"Look Richard, it's not like I'm only thinking of myself or something. I'm saying this for your own good."

Sure you are, sweetie. Every time some woman starts looking after my well being I wait for that two by four to come crashing down on my skull.

"I suppose that means you don't want to go out to brunch tomorrow?"

"Whatever gave you that idea? I've never turned down a free meal in my life."

Swell, now I'm reduced to being a free dining ticket. "Nnm," I grumble.

"Oh Richard, don't be so serious. You know I'm just giving you a hard time."

"Ha, ha, ha."

"Now come on, Richard. I'm sorry, really, I wouldn't ever try to hurt you. You know that."

She doesn't have to try. She's been absolutely dead on without giving it a thought.

"Don't act that way, Richard. I really do like you."

Sue Ann gives my hand a little squeeze and smiles. That's supposed to make it all better. Maybe it does for her, now that she's arranged things to her own personal satisfaction it's easy to be generous.

"Run along and manage the bar, Richard. We can talk about this later."

I can't believe this. It's happening again. I'm going to be locked into another disastrous relationship and I'm not even going to get the girl in the final frame. I don't understand. I've been patient all these years. This time I did everything right. Susan's definitely the girl I've been waiting for, but she's refusing to walk off into the sunset with me. Maybe I should go back. Maybe if I cried or groveled at her feet she'd change her mind. No, Sue Ann might be the type to enjoy that. I should've learned years ago. Happy endings are for other people. If I can't understand that by now then I deserve all of the ridiculous pain that I feel.

"Wait up there Hoss, aren't you going to say hello to your old buddy?"

Nick, just who I need to see right now. I can't possibly deserve the life I'm living. There must be a mix–up somewhere.

"I'm busy Nick."

"Seem to have time enough to talk with your little honey in there."

"I said I was busy."

"C'mon Richard, tell me how it was."

Nick gives me that furry laugh of his. Always reminds me of bugs being squashed.

"I don't know what the hell you're talking about."

"Don't be so closemouthed, Richard. You trying to tell me you haven't found your way into Susan yet, you mangy old dog you?'

"Nick, come on over here for a second."

"What's up?"

"I have something important to tell you."

I draw up close to his right ear as if to whisper. Instead I let loose at full volume.

"Go fuck yourself with a window pole you slimy old bag of piss."

Turning around, I jam my boot heel down onto his toes and go stomping out the front door.

My friends and my parents always ask me what I'm going to do with my life. It's not that they really want to push or pressure me. It's just that we're all hooked on happy endings. That's all they want from me. Maybe that's all I want too.

9

JAM TOMORROW

... and when Rabbit said, "Honey or condensed milk with your bread?"
Pooh was so excited that he said, "Both," and then, so as not to seem greedy, he
added, "But don't bother about the bread, please." – A.A. Milne

In the dream, death and destruction rain down from above. Sirens
and alarm bells scream in an unending monotone of doom. Will they
never stop? Is there no place left to hide?

"Shit."

My hand slaps wildly on the floorboards. Where is that clock? No
avail, my hand keeps coming up empty, fingers wriggling in mock
disbelief as the alarm continues to clatter. Like a small persistent
child, the noise keeps tugging me awake.

No way out. I'll have to turn on the light. I yank the cord and a
murky light spreads through the loft. I stare at a cobweb overhead.
Spiders, how come I never see the spiders, only their webs? Damn,
the clock must be on the other side of the loft. That's right, I put it
there so I'd have to get out of bed. I was going to leave it downstairs
but I thought I might break my fool neck skidding down the ladder.

I'll have to get up. Okay; one, two, three – I slither out of my
sleeping bag, stumble over to the clock and kick it onto the floor
below. Silence. Diving back into the sleeping bag I lay on my back,
eyes blinking, mind completely blank.

Damp, it's goddam May and it's still damp and cold up here. My
fingers are throbbing from last night's bar shift. In the light they look
red and bloated like bundles of cheap blood sausages. A faint whiff
of decay clings to my cuticles. I squeeze my left forefinger and a
stream of pus shoots off toward the far corner of the loft. I think I'm
going to be sick.

I wonder what time it is. Maybe I set the alarm wrong, maybe it's still early and I can catch a few more hours of sleep. Christ knows I didn't get in till after four. I'd go back to sleep if I didn't have to pee. But, I can feel that water sloshing in my bladder whenever I turn. I can't ignore it. Maybe for once I'll just let go. Nah, not in my sleeping bag. It'd get all cold and sticky and then I'd have to throw the damn thing out.

Wonder why I moved that clock. Oh damn, damn and damn again, Stanford. I have that appointment down at Stanford today. I'll be absolutely frigging late unless I can get my little body moving.

Damn, damn, damn, what a way to start off the morning. I swear I'm falling apart. I can't even take a simple piss anymore without screwing it up. My penis shoots off at an unexpected angle and I end up watering my feet, or the floor, or even zipping some into the shower. Most of my shorts have yellow stains on them by now. I keep forgetting to shake out those last few drops. This must be what it's like when senility sets in. All these little housekeeping chores become paramount. Bodily functions turn tyrannical when you can no longer perform. I wonder if saints ever have these problems. Never seemed to figure much in those devotional tracts Sister Theresa had me read.

Okay, a shower should warm me up. What's that there? Better not be a herpes blister. I thought those little hickeys were gone for good. And the goddam shower still doesn't drain. After five minutes the water's slopping all over the floor. I've plunged the crap out of the thing, poured gallon after gallon of Liquid Plumber and still nothing. It's a constant battle to get any water past that drain. The pipe needs to be replaced. Fat chance of that happening. If I'm fool enough to live in a cabin with a view through to the ground, I'm obviously not the choosy type. The cheap lawyer who owns this dump has me pegged. He wouldn't replace the wood stove until it collapsed and nearly burned down the place.

My one overriding desire when I dream of being rich, my one fantasy is to live in a house where toilets flush, sinks drain, taps shut off. Not very romantic, but I've spent five years of my life nursing sick johns back into operational health. If only I could flush without running back to jiggle the handle or plunging my hand into the cold slimy tank to adjust the float. You'd think I'd learn. Inevitably the top of the tank is covered with an assortment of toiletries and other junk. Instead of removing them, I always try to balance everything when I lift off the cover. A hairbrush usually plops into the open bowl. Sometimes I think I'm spending my life blindly bashing off of one wall, then straight back into another like a giant slug gone berserk.

Stanford. I know this is going to be a total waste of time. Well, I guess I should make some effort for my parents. It's the least I can do for them in their declining years. Declining years? Yeah, they'd really love hearing me talk that way.

God knows I do little enough for them. Well I tried. It wasn't my fault Harvard Business School dumped me. Okay, so I did screw up the application. It was still mostly their own tight–assed attitude that did it. My parents were outraged; not at me but at Harvard. They wanted to sue, reverse discrimination, or some such crap. That didn't sound right. I'm not in any majority I know of. How many other loonies like me do I see let loose on the streets? Still, they've gone to a lot of trouble to set this up. I owe them.

It hasn't been easy for the poor dears, what with me being a compulsive underachiever. There's all that worrying they've put in over the years, like when they thought I was becoming a dope fiend.

It was in the air in those days, all the CBS specials and magazine articles. Of course they had no real way of telling if I was looped or not. All they had was Ann Lander's advice. And I was a hard one to pin down, being mostly out to lunch whether drugged or undrugged. There were all those freaky affectations I had back then. I spent one year wearing sunglasses night and day, indoors and out. Considering that I couldn't see under the best of conditions, I'd say suspicions were justified. Naturally they thought I was trying to hide my drug dilated pupils. Or was it constricted? Who can remember now? They actually asked me if I was experimenting with drugs. What a choice expression. It made me feel like a Robert Louis Stevenson creation, you know, like I was about to sprout fangs and shred the draperies.

So what should I wear? My usual patched jeans and bright red suspenders? Nope, I promised to play it straight. Where's that suit? Good, there's hardly any mold worth mentioning on it. Usually my style of dress is what I would call shabby nondescript. It's just a ragbag of gifts plus some miscellaneous clothing I've scavenged from a handful of bars … And the boots, I'll wear my Frye boots. All they need is a bit of brushing. God, here I am preening like some empty–headed bird. A lot of good it'll do me.

Wouldn't you know it, I've spent half an hour getting all lah di dah'd up for this Stanford gig. I have my suit on, boots shined, hair somewhat brushed and then I end up taking a messy dump, the kind that sticks to those little hairs around your asshole. No matter how hard you wipe, it just seems to cling there. It's typical. First I can't manage to take a clean piss, now this. Too late to do anything about it. Wonder how many other foul assholes lurk beneath three–piece suits. Probably more than I'd want to think about.

I hope my parents appreciate this. Besides, they really don't get any grief from me these days. It's not like it was five years ago … back from Europe for my sister's wedding I was trying to readjust to being home by nibbling at a late morning breakfast. In those days, coffee was still a mainstay of my existence. I was going through the cream and sugar routine, swiveling slowly in my chair, bare back sticking against the Lucite. It's always so damn warm in that house I end up spending most of my time wearing only a raggedy pair of cut–off jeans. So there I was hunched over my coffee. On the wall in front of me, some schlock landscape my sister painted when she was fifteen.

"So how's Dorrie been holding up? Bet you thought neither one of us would ever get married, huh Mom?"

"Now look Richard, you've had a year to bum around. That's long enough."

"What?"

"I said I've had enough of this. You should be settling down."

"I heard you the first time, Mom. I understood you the first time. My hearing and intelligence are still functioning adequately thank you."

"Now, Richard …"

"I want you to tell me what you mean. Is this a threat? Are you going to refuse to put me up when I visit?"

"You know I love having you. I only wish you would stay longer."

"Okay, then what do you mean? Just how do you intend to put that threat into operation?"

"It wasn't a threat. I didn't mean it that way. I'm your mother, Richard, I would never threaten you."

"Then maybe you'd better decide what you did mean. And while you're at it, maybe you'll begin to realize that there's not a damn thing you can do about how or where I live."

Cruel, there was no need to be that cruel. No real excuse either ... Damn, the phone. I don't have time to talk. If I was smart I'd just shine it on and get going ... Fat chance, no way I can resist a ringing phone. It's my upbringing. I always think it's going to be something wonderful.

"Hello."

"Richard, it's me, Dorrie."

"What's up?"

"Nothing much, I just wanted to see how you're doing ... Well?"

My sister never calls without wanting something. But damn if she'll come right to the point. First we've got to work our way through a whole string of preliminaries, only then does it become possible to accidently stumble across the main event.

"Well, nothing Dorrie. I'm just working most of the time."

"Do you know many people there yet?"

Boy that question drives me crazy. And my sister always asks it. She still thinks life is centered around a high school conception of popularity, the Willy Loman litmus test.

"I haven't got that much time, Dorrie. Why don't you tell me what's wrong?"

"I told you, there's nothing the matter. I thought I'd give you a call. Can't I give my own brother a call without there being something wrong?"

"Dorrie, if all you want to do is chat, that's fine. I'll call you back as soon as I can. If it's something important, I'd rather talk to you now."

"It's nothing much. I just thought you'd like to know that I talked to Bruce yesterday."

"Bruce, you've got to be kidding. Bruce called you?"

"Not exactly, I called him."

"Why would you possibly want to do a thing like that?"

"Well, he's always been very nice to me."

"Look, the guy's an asshole. He was an asshole when I knew him five years ago and he's an asshole now."

"I don't think you're being fair."

"I don't care about being fair. I've told you before what I think of him. I've told you what he's done and how he treats people. But if you still want to fuck around with him, go right ahead, enjoy yourself."

"He's just a friend. It's not like I want to go to bed with him or anything. I think I can still do better than Bruce Adams for that. But listen Richard, don't you think you're being too hard on him? He had a really traumatic childhood you know."

"Yeah, so did William Bonny."

"Who?"

"Billy the Kid … Listen Dorrie, you're trying to tell me he has feelings. Okay, I know he has feelings, but all that makes him is an asshole with feelings. So his parents were divorced and he was forced to live a luxurious but unloved life. Well, too bad. I mean my heart bleeds for him. But that doesn't excuse the way he leads his life. You should've seen how he treated his girlfriends."

"What did he do?"

"I've told you."

"No, you didn't."

"He abused them. Treated them like shit. I don't want to talk about it."

"Well he was always a perfect gentleman with me. I don't know why. Maybe I remind him of his grandmother."

"The guy is a total asshole. I'm not saying this because I'm upset. That was all a long time ago. I just don't want to have anything to do with him now."

"He told me he still feels very close to you."

"Well that just makes my day. Listen, you better take care of Mickey. I can hear him screaming in the background."

"Don't worry about it. He's just trying to get my attention."

"Well, he's doing a damn good job of grabbing mine."

"Quiet Mickey, I'm talking. Hold on a minute Richard."

"Sure."

Imagine calling your kid Mickey because he was born on Mickey Mouse's fiftieth birthday ... So, I can stop this conversation easily enough. All I have to say is, 'Dorene, I know Bruce fucked you seven years ago in a Jersey motel. I know because he told me. He told me where and when and that you were a good fuck. You enjoyed it. I know you've been having problems with Bernie and you want some reassurance from another man. You want to be admired, to feel appreciated.' See, it's simple. That's all I'd have to say. Nah, I don't think so. It wouldn't be simple. I'd have to spend the rest of my life dodging my sister.

"Hello, are you still there?"

"I'm still here, Dorrie."

"So anyway, he's coming for a visit."

"To the apartment?"

"Where do you think?'

"Look, that's not very smart."

"Why, I don't see why I shouldn't see him?"

"That's not what I mean. What about Bernie?"

"Why should I care about him? I wouldn't take that creep back if he came crawling. Not that he would or anything but ..."

"You're still not paying attention. Didn't you tell me he was making noises about a custody fight over the kid?"

"So?"

"So dear, I don't think your helping your cause any by having old Brucie decorating your apartment."

"I know that. I'll tell people he's my cousin."

"It's not going to work. Things like that always come out."

"So what? I really don't care anymore."

"Trying to revert to your teenage days, is that it?"

"Looks that way."

"You're thirty–two Dorene."

"Shut up."

"What's the problem now?"

"I don't want to hear about my age."

"It's no big deal, so you're getting old."

"Just shut up and stop talking about my age."

"Okay, but you're still no teenager."

"I like the excitement."

"Sure you do, until you get burned."

"What's that supposed to mean?"

"I mean when the bill comes due on this little escapade, you're not going to be so eager to pay up."

"Maybe …"

"Yeah, well try to keep that in mind."

"I still don't think there's anything wrong with my seeing Bruce."

"Do what you want."

"Those other women must've deserved what they got. You wouldn't catch me putting up with any of Bruce Adams' crap."

"That's how relationships go, Dorene. One person abuses, the other's abused."

"I don't believe that. I don't believe that at all. Maybe that's your experience but it doesn't have to be like that. I don't like being abused. Oh, I know what you're thinking. You're thinking about Bernie and me. It's not true. I don't care what Mommy's been telling you. That woman's always had it in for me."

"She hasn't said a word."

"That's it. Go ahead and stick up for her. You've never taken my side."

"Listen Dorrie, please stop crying. Let's not go through this again."

"Right Richard, go ahead, be like that. You've always been afraid to give your opinion. I was the one who stood up to Mommy and Daddy. I had to stay and listen to them while you ran off. You don't know how it's been all these years. All you ever did was visit."

"You didn't have to stay there."

"That's easy for you to say."

"Yes, it is."

"I call up to talk to my only brother and all I get from him is a complete load of crap. You've always been mean like that. All you care about is yourself."

"Listen Dorrie, I really have to go. I have an appointment. I'm late."

"That's right, run away. Little Richard always runs away if there's a problem."

"Please sweetheart, don't cry. Listen to me … calm down willya? Listen, I'll call you tomorrow. I promise. I'm really sorry if I said anything to upset you."

"You know how sick I get when I'm upset. I can't help it if I'm emotional. That's just the way I am. I can't be all cold and controlled like you."

"I'm sorry. You're absolutely right. I don't give you enough support. How about if I call you tomorrow? I promise. If I can manage some time off maybe I'll fly in. Okay?"

"Well, I'll talk to you tomorrow then."

Fantastic, what an absolutely gorgeous way to start the morning. She's what, thirty–two, and still going at it with our parents. I don't know how Bernie put up with it. Jesus, as if it were my duty to close ranks with her in some Holy Crusade against Mom and Dad. She's right though, I did take off as soon as I could. Damn if I'll feel guilty about that. Staying at home wouldn't have done anyone a bit of good. I'd only be miserable today, just like Dorene is. Though I kind of doubt that I'd be as efficient as she is at spreading that misery around.

The phone rings once, twice. I stare hypnotised, as if by some venomous cobra. This isn't fair. Usually days go by in complete silence. What right does the outside world have to continually break into my life, especially now when I need to get going? If it's Dorrie again, I swear I'll scream. I pounce on the phone angrily.

"Yeah."

"Is Bonnie there?"

"I'm sorry, you must have the wrong number."

"Is this 843–3852?"

"That's right."

"Well she must be there. I'm her mother."

"Look lady, if she lived here, don't you think I'd notice?"

"Who am I speaking to?"

"Excuse me, you have the wrong number. There is no one here but me and I am not your daughter."

"Why won't you let me talk with Bonnie? What have you done with my daughter? Answer me young man. I said …"

I slam down the receiver. Careful buddy, it's far too early in the morning to start losing it. God, look at the time. I'm really late now. Dusty's waiting and there's no way I can avoid hitting rush hour traffic over the Golden Gate. Damn that Dorene!

***

I always get confused going up this hill. It's impossible not to get lost, short of leaving a trail of breadcrumbs. The road is nothing but one continuous switchback. Of course I'm the type of person who gets lost walking around the block, you know, the type who leaves a building and instantly heads in the wrong direction.

Wonder why Dusty lives up here? That's a dumb question. It's cheap. Well it should be considering she has no indoor plumbing to speak of. She's something, though. If you're planning on screwing old Dusty you'd better remember to pack a lunch. She's a woman who's serious about her sex. When she sucks on the old banana it's no piece of polite chit chat. More like being attacked by a vacuum cleaner.

Actually, sometimes I think the only other thing we have in common is *Cushingura*. We've both seen it three times. It was the warm–up for our first night together. There we sat, eyes glued to the screen, frantically rubbing each other's body. Understatement always appeals to me. I mean the film, you know, the way it imitates the sparse beauty of a Japanese watercolor. Christ knows what Dusty sees in it. No matter, it's still a point in her favor. But somehow a mutual interest in a four hour Japanese film doesn't seem enough to sustain a relationship. Sure there's a lot of oral sex, but even so, the time's bound to come when your mouth is free for conversation.

"I couldn't find a sitter for Andy. Is it okay if I bring him? Now don't look at me like that, Richard. I tried. I was going to leave him with Terry."

"Who's stopping you, Dusty?"

"I'm trying to tell you. Terry called me about an hour ago. She has to go into Santa Rosa. Her old man's been busted again."

"Drugs?"

"No, drunk and disorderly. He pissed on some deputy's front tire."

"Brilliant."

"I tried calling you. Your line's been busy all morning."

"I know. I got tied up with my sister."

"What sister?"

"I'll tell you about it later. We gotta get going. I'm late as is."

"You sure you don't mind? Andy really won't be any trouble. He promised."

"It's okay."

"You look nice. I mean it. I don't think I've seen you dressed up before."

"Thanks, you don't look so bad yourself. I didn't know you owned a dress."

"C'mon Andy, get in the back seat."

"There's no room back there, Mom."

"Sure there is. Just push that stuff over. That's okay Richard, isn't it?"

"Sure."

"Hi, Richard."

"Yeah, hi kid."

"Aren't you heading the wrong way, Richard?"

"No, I want to stop at the Post Office and check my mail first."

"I thought you were in such a big hurry."

"It'll only take a second."

The usual collection of dust greets me as I swing open the door to my P.O. Box. No marriage proposals, no sweepstake winners, no job offers. Michael Anthony, where are you when I need you?

Outside two small boys argue. The younger one is near tears. An elderly woman tries to help.

"Cram it up your ass, grandma."

Gorgeous. A goddam sterling generation we're raising out here. Makes you really proud to be part of this community, to be upholding our shared values and all the rest of that crap. Well, we had to end up somewhere. The sixties ran its course. Single mothers and broken marriages are all that's left of my generation.

"Here Dusty, take the map and play navigator."

"Okay, take your first right up ahead."

"Very funny, Miss Smart Mouth. I think I can find my way to Santa Rosa."

"Well, I was just trying to help."

"Look ace, why don't you cool it till we get down to San Francisco."

"Okay, but don't act so grumpy. You've been bitching ever since you got here ... Well, are you going to tell me about your sister? I didn't even know you had a sister. You never said a word about having a sister. Do you have any others, Richard?"

"She's enough."

"You don't like to talk much do you?"

"Nope."

"Why's that?"

"Maybe it's because when I was a kid I had this speech defect."

"What sort of speech defect?"

"I was all screwed up. I Elmer Fudded my r's, mixed up s's and h's, couldn't make an l. You name it and I would fuck it up. No one could understand what I was trying to say. Except my sister, for some reason she always knew. She translated, you know, like some sort of United Nations session."

"What was wrong?"

"My ears, it turned out they were chock full of wax. Guess I never heard right from the beginning. It must have been like trying to hear under water. Christ, there were globs of wax the size of peas when this doctor finally douched them out. On top of that it took about three years worth of speech therapy to repair the damage, you know, before I could speak some recognizable form of English."

"Okay, then what's the explanation?"

"I told you, it was all that goddam wax. I mean I wasn't feeble or anything."

"Richard, don't play dumb. Just try to answer my question. What does all that stuff have to do with you usually being so close mouthed?"

"Simple. You see people didn't understand what I was saying. They didn't wanna try. Some of those bozos even laughed. So then I started to get careful. I made sure about what I was going to say before I let it out. I became pretty damn sensitive about opening my mouth. Besides, I figured out that most people weren't all that interested in what I had to say. If I could avoid talking I did. I'd much rather listen. You learn a lot more. So maybe that's why you don't see me flapping my mouth as much as some people do."

"Are you referring to someone in particular?"

"Yeah sweetie, like your mind is on vacation but your mouth is doing overtime."

"What did you say?"

"Nothing, it's just an old blues song. Popped into my head ... Now Dusty, you're not working yourself up, are you?"

"Me, of course not. I'm just a dumb bint, I don't have any feelings."

"Christ Dusty. Look, I'm sorry, don't be so damn sensitive."

"Richard, you might not think I'm very bright but I know when I'm being put down."

"I said I'm sorry. I don't want to fight. Just forget about it, huh? Besides, it wasn't true."

"What wasn't?"

"That whole story about a speech defect. Never happened. I made it up."

"Why, why would you ..."

"Don't know. It was pretty spur of the moment."

"Richard, how many other? ..."

"What's the time, Dusty? Do you know what time ..."

"No you wait a minute, I want to know if ..."

"That was the only time, I swear. Everything else has been straight."

"Well, okay. So, is she older or younger?"

"Is who older or younger?"

"Your sister."

"Older."

"What's she like?"

"Nothing like me."

"What's that supposed to mean?"

"Mean? Look Dusty, how would you describe me?"

"Pretty mellow, mostly a nice guy. I don't think anything ever bothers you."

"Okay, my sister's the opposite."

"How's that?"

"Just what I said. For instance, she's not too keen on listening. She only hears you if you say something she agrees with. That's why I never really talk to her. Any conversation always verges on becoming an outright hassle."

"I still don't get it."

"She has no patience. It's hard to explain exactly. Okay, let's suppose you knew, I mean positively knew you were always right. Well, you just might get impatient having to listen to a bunch of ignorant bozos who kept disagreeing with you."

"C'mon Richard, she can't think she's always right."

"I'm not making this up. Here's an example. Remember the film Z?"

"Yeah."

"Well, I once told her that I thought it was nothing but a bunch of slick propaganda, that it wasn't a good movie. God knows what possessed me to say that. Anyway, she just wouldn't let go. She kept picking at me, demanding that I change my opinion."

"I liked it."

"That's not the point. I don't care if you liked it. You certainly wouldn't persecute me because I didn't."

"So what do you say to your sister?"

"I don't. I try to limit it to sending her a birthday gift. It's always an art book, one of those forty dollar coffee table deals marked down to ten. She must be getting sick of them by now. Lucky for me, she's too vain to admit that she isn't wildly mad about art."

"Why do you keep doing it?"

"I'm cheap."

"You don't believe that."

"Well I can tell you this sweetie, my sister would never shop for a bargain. Shopping's her religion. Being influenced by price would be a sacrilege, like Monet switching to sculpture because the price of clay dropped."

"Is she married?"

"Separated with a kid."

"What's her husband like?"

"Patient."

"So what's the problem?"

"He ran out of patience."

Damn, traffic's jammed and we're not even to San Raphael. Well, if I'm late I'm late. Not much I can do about it now.

"Dusty's not you're real name is it?"

"No."

"Well what is it?"

"Desdemona."

"Desdemona?"

"I know. You see my father was in this play in high school."

"I think I know the one."

"Anyway, you can't go through life expecting people to call you Desdemona."

"Why not?"

"You just can't. Are you trying to be difficult, Richard?"

"But where does Dusty come from?"

"I told you, my real name is Desdemona."

"I don't get it."

"Dusty is short for Desdemona."

"It is?"

"Yes, it is."

"I don't remember that being in the play."

"It isn't in the play. It just is. Listen, are you trying to make fun of me again?"

"Who me? Never, I would never do that."

"Well sometimes I'm not so sure. You're always nice to me, and I like being with you, but sometimes I have this sneaking suspicion that you think I'm really dumb."

"Don't worry about it."

"And what's that supposed to mean?"

"That you're imagining the whole thing."

"Are you being straight with me?"

"Why would I lie?"

"Well, I guess that's okay."

"So tell me more about your father."

"My father?"

"Yeah, tell me about yourself."

"I can remember my father taking me aside one day when I was seventeen, looking into my face, and saying, 'Daughter, I know that you're beautiful but I hear you've fallen into evil ways.'"

Beautiful? I wouldn't exactly say beautiful; a great fuck, yeah, but not really beautiful. Well, you can hardly expect some father to say, 'Daughter, I hear you've become a really great fuck.'

"Religious, huh Dusty?"

"Mormon, everyone's a Mormon in Salt Lake."

"I didn't know they were that strict. I thought they just made lots of money and spent their spare time singing hymns."

"Are you trying to make a joke?"

"No, I really don't know a thing about them."

"Well, we're not supposed to drink or smoke and it's the church that has all the money. My father never had a dime. But he sure was strict with me and my sisters. Wouldn't let us wear makeup or go on dates. We couldn't even have non–Mormon friends. Afraid we'd marry outside the Church."

"It really worked."

"Huh?"

"With you, you're some model Mormon."

"Yeah, well I had other interests."

"I just bet you did."

"Is that supposed to mean something?"

"Will you cool it, Dusty. You've been jumping on me all morning. Are you having your period again?"

"Look Richard, you've been making nasty cracks about me all morning. You think the only time I get upset is when I'm hormonal? Here, I'll prove it."

Dusty grabs my hand and tries to shove it up her dress.

"Christ, I'm trying to drive. You want to get us killed?"

"Distracted you, didn't I, Richard?"

"I can't drive with one hand."

"How about now?"

"No, go ahead, knock yourself out."

"Well, you could be a little more responsive."

"What would you like me to do, wiggle my ears?"

"I know some guys who would be a lot more appreciative."

"I'm sure you do."

"That's nasty Richard, you didn't have to say that."

"Will you be careful. They're not detachable you know … Okay, I'm sorry, I really am. I just couldn't resist."

"Then try harder."

"I will, I swear to God I will. I don't know what's gotten into me today."

"Well okay, but watch it from now on. I'm warning you."

"Andy still sacked out in back?"

"You don't like Andy, do you?"

"I wouldn't say that."

"You don't have to. I just get this feeling about it. A mother can always tell these things."

"Well, he's a little on the hyperactive side."

"He's not that bad you know. He's a pretty good kid compared to some others I could name."

"Yeah, I guess you're right."

"I am. And I think I'm a pretty good mother too."

"I'm sure you are."

"You know Richard, I don't let Andy smoke dope, not like some of the other mothers on the river."

"How old is Andy?"

"Four."

"Yeah, well maybe you'd better hold off for a while."

"I did give him a hit a few months ago but he didn't get high or anything."

"That's good."

"I know I didn't start smoking dope until I was about twelve or thirteen."

"Must have been the same year I got started."

"Oh yeah, how old were you?"

"Eighteen, I ran with a very slow crowd. But I thought you said you were a Mormon. I mean you said you lived in Salt Lake."

"So?"

"I just never imagined anything like that going on there. The city's so clean and bright. Somehow I expected people to spend their time sweeping the sidewalks in praise of the Lord."

"You can buy dope there."

"Yeah, I guess you can most anywhere."

"That's why I left."

"Because you couldn't buy good dope?"

"You're not listening. Because of my father. You know, his religion, the way he treated me."

"What about your mother?"

"She died when I was just a little kid. I don't even remember her. But the first chance I got I took off with Gary. That's my ex–old man, you know, Andy's father. He's down in L.A. now selling scuba equipment. Back then I was only a senior in high school. I thought he was real hot stuff. Boy was I ever wrong."

"How so?"

"Well after we got married he started slapping me around, you know, whenever he was pissed off or something."

"Is that why …"

"Don't be cruel Richard. That's how my nose looks. It's not broken."

"I wasn't going to …"

"Sure you weren't."

Now that I think of it, her nose does look like a bent letter opener.

"Yeah Richard, I know I'm not your type. I've got these big all American boobs and a real fat ass. Don't bother denying it."

"It's fine. You look just fine."

"No, come on. It's Susan you're hot for. When I pounce on you, you let me, but that's about all you do."

"Leave Susan out of it."

"Why, it's true isn't it? Everyone knows she's the only one you care about."

"Look Dusty, I'm glad you're here. I'm sorry if I've been nasty. It's been a bad morning for me but I am trying to keep it together. Do me a favor and don't mention Susan. I don't want to talk about her."

"Okay Richard ... But don't you miss living with someone? I mean you live all by yourself up in that cabin."

"Of course I miss living with someone. You think I'm not human or something?"

"What do you miss about it?"

"I'll tell you, Dusty. I've never admitted this to anyone else before, so I want you to promise me you won't repeat it."

"Sure."

"See, I've given this a whole lot of thought ... You know how it feels when you're stuck in some grubby laundromat waiting for your clothes to dry; and then you take them out and start folding them? Well after I finish folding all my clothes, I still have the sheets left. It's when I'm struggling to fold those damn sheets by myself that I think, 'Gee, it sure would be nice having someone here to help me out.'"

"Richard, you're hopeless."

"Yeah, I guess I am."

Of course she's right. It's Susan I want to be with. But here I am listening to Dusty chatter away. And it's not like we have anything to say to each other. Christ, it's not even purely physical. I don't mind bopping her once in a while but the whole thing seems sort of pointless. Uh oh, I've gotta watch myself. Pretty soon I'll start talking about deep meaningful relationships ... and what's the difference? She seems to like me okay. That's one thing about old Dusty, when she gets tired of the game she just picks up her jacks and goes off to the next court. Maybe I should try smoking some more dope.

"Okay Richard, follow that sign that says 101 through San Francisco. Well maybe not, maybe we should take this turn off here for Highway One. You see if we keep going until …"

"Dusty …"

"Huh?"

"We're taking 101."

"I thought you wanted me to navigate."

"You're doing an absolutely splendid job."

"I told you not to be sarcastic."

"What could possibly lead you to doubt my total sincerity?"

"Richard, stop needling me. I don't like it."

"Okay."

"Is that all?"

"I'm sorry I was sarcastic."

"That's better."

"You mean I don't have to write it on the board one hundred times?"

"I give up."

I wonder what she thinks she's doing down there with my wiener. She's misinformed. This is not supposed to be a taffy pull.

"Dusty, you know what the worst venereal disease is?"

"Huh?'

"Venereal disease. I know you've heard of venereal diseases."

"Herpes."

"Nope, not even close. It's scabies."

"Scabies?"

"Yeah, most people haven't heard of it. You see Dusty, there are all these little mites that like to work their way under your skin. And then they just screw around like crazy, laying their eggs as fast as they can. Next thing you know, there's a billion of these teeny buggers using your body as a cheap motel. The pisser is that they're only active at night. Just as you're about to knock off, all these oversexed parasites begin to hop around. So your skin positively burns just when you need to grab some sleep. It's unbelievable. And contagious, you can catch it by shaking hands … yuck, just thinking about it makes me shudder."

"You're telling me stories again, Richard."

"I wish to God I was. I had it back in Maine when I was working as a waiter."

"I thought you said it was contagious?"

"I needed the money."

"That's disgusting."

"I don't know if it is. People are freaky about things like that. I mean, it's not like I touched the customers or fondled their food."

"Still …"

"Let me tell you about the cure. The cure was a real beauty. You've got to continually wash all your clothes and sheets. And then you've got to rub this goop all over your body. But when they start dying off, it's even worse. Your bloodstream becomes clogged with all of these tiny little corpses. You get seriously feverish and every last one of your bones aches. It takes about a week to get all that crap out of your system. Makes you want to take up ping pong instead."

"It can't be any worse than crabs."

"Piece of cake."

"Well, I had gonorrhea once."

"Who hasn't? A couple shots of penicillin in the ass, you walk funny for an hour or two, then it's over."

"Are you sure you're not putting me on?"

"Listen Dusty, do me a favor, if you ever get it, let me know."

"Why?"

"Because I'm staying clear of you that's why."

"Thanks."

Andy's sure quiet back there. Well that's one piece of luck. Maybe he won't wake up till we hit Stanford. Let's see, I should have just about enough gas to get there.

"Richard?"

"Uh huh."

"What was the most embarrassing thing that ever happened to you?"

"What brought that on? We playing *Reader's Digest* or something?"

"Dunno. Maybe it's just that we've been together for two months and I still don't know a thing about you. I didn't even know you had a sister till today."

"I tell you whatever you ask."

"I'm asking now."

"Okay, Easter Sunday, 1976."

"Huh?"

"That's when it happened, in Boston. I was down in Boston. I had to take care of some business."

"What business?"

"Had to see someone."

"About what?"

"Look, it has nothing at all to do with the story."

"Then why won't you tell me?"

"I went to the Harvard School of Business. I went there to talk to one of their admissions people. Satisfied?"

"Like today."

"Yes, like today. They didn't like me much then, and Stanford doesn't care for me now."

"Why?"

"What is it with you? Do you want to hear this story or do you want to play twenty questions?"

"Richard, stop being so touchy. I was only being curious."

"Look, maybe they don't like me because I'm just not good enough or maybe I don't package myself right. Maybe they're assholes or maybe I am. If you're so damn interested you can sit there with me today and ask the dork why he rejected me."

"How do you know he's a dork?"

"If he wasn't a dork he wouldn't be director of admissions."

"No?"

"No. Only dorks are allowed to be directors of admissions. It's a federal regulation."

"But you told me you were once thinking of doing that for your old college."

"Who says I'm not a dork?"

"Are you upset?"

"No."

"Are you going to tell me the story?"

"What story?"

"You know, about Boston."

"Are you going to keep interrupting?"

"No."

"Like I said, I was planning on staying in Boston. So I called this girl I knew. She once told me to give her a call if I was ever going to be in town. So I did. I asked her if she'd put me up for the night. Can't say Denise sounded any too thrilled. She started into this hemming and hawing routine instead. Said she was living with a guy now and that while he was really large, the apartment was still really small. So I said a couch would do me just fine. Well, then she said there was a Great Dane sleeping on the couch. That was okay by me, I was willing to share. Finally she agreed."

"Do you still keep in touch?"

"With whom?"

"That girl."

"No, I haven't seen her in a couple of years."

"What happened?"

"How the hell do I know what happened to her? Maybe she eloped with the Great Dane. I thought you weren't going to interrupt."

"Sorry."

"So as I was saying, when I got there we went out for a few drinks. There we were just sitting, chatting in this bar, having a nice enough time. And then she says, 'I know what we can do. Let's make last call over at the Prudential.'"

"The what?"

"It's in the center of Boston, the Prudential Building. It has this bar on top. Very hokey, you know, dark bar, dramatic view of the city skyline. Could be worse, at least it doesn't revolve. Anyway, to reach it we had to cut across the Common. You don't know Boston do you?"

"Never been east of Salt Lake."

"It's very historical, one of those big time Revolutionary War totems. You know, Paul Revere once took a dump there and all that sort of crap. But I forgot to tell you. Before we left the bar, Denise goes off to take a quick whizz. While I'm waiting, I start to feel like maybe I should do the same, but then I think, if I do, I might not be out when she comes back. Well, by the time she's through, the clock's closing in on last call. It's only a short walk, so I decide I'll just hold off till we get there. I mean I'm a big boy and everything.

"But Denise decides to make a quick detour and pick up some toilet paper. By now the pressure's pretty intense, but no worse than it's been at other times in my life. So half way there my bladder cuts loose, you know, like the bottom of a paper sack giving way, just one big sudden whoosh. So it's bad enough that I've pissed my pants and don't even have a change of clothes with me, but, the urine decides not to go sprinkling all over the sacred soil of the Common. Oh no, all of it makes a circuit down my pant leg and flows neatly into my right boot."

"You're making this up."

"Dusty, I sincerely wish I were."

"So what did you do?"

"First, I did what I always do in a crisis. I closed my eyes and said, 'This can't really be happening.' Then I realized there was nothing I could do. I could hardly turn to Denise and tell her that I'd just peed in my pants."

"Why not?"

"Yeah, laugh all you want, but I can tell you, I was feeling none too gorgeous squishing my way through that park."

"Squishing?"

"Every other step, every time I came down on my right foot I made this soft, squishing sound, sort of like stepping on a dead slug."

"Ugh."

"Disgusting, but I had no other choice. Lucky for me the Prudential Bar was dark. I ducked into their washroom and tried to sponge off my jeans. I couldn't bring myself to take off that boot. Old Denise didn't seem to notice. I guess she was pretty well snockered by then. I mean we even managed a few kisses before I bunked in with the Great Dane for the night. He didn't seem to mind either."

"So that was it?"

"No, the worst part came next morning. Like I said, I didn't bring a change of clothes. So when morning came I had to pull on that urine soaked sock and those foul jeans before I went off to Harvard."

"Gross."

"Nothing else I could do."

"Are we almost there, Richard?"

"Stanford? Another fifteen minutes."

"Well, aren't you going to ask me?"

"About what?"

"My most embarrassing moment. Aren't you curious?"

"Nope."

"And why not?'

"I can't imagine you ever being embarrassed."

"And exactly what's that supposed to mean?"

"Oh, stop being so damn suspicious. It doesn't mean a thing."

"You're making another one of your nasty cracks, aren't you? I told you I didn't like that."

"Which way do I go, Dusty?"

"Oh gee, I'm not sure. Let me check, just wait a sec willya?"

"Don't think I can do that right now."

"Oh sure, I've got it, you should have made a left at that last light."

"Great."

"You're not mad are you, Richard?"

"Why, am I starting to foam at the mouth?"

"That's what I like about you. You're always so mellow."

Yeah, me and a piece of moldy cheese. Well at least she's stopped her bitching.

"Nothing to be upset about Dusty. I'm sorry if I was grumpy. It must have been that phone call this morning."

"That's okay, I understand, I really do."

"Do you have that campus map I gave you?"

"What map?"

"I didn't give you a map?"

"Uh uh."

"I must have left the damn thing back home."

"Mommy, where are we?"

"It must be somewhere around here … Dusty, you'll have to ask that guy over there where the Business School is."

"Why me?"

"My horn doesn't work."

"Mommy, I want to get out."

I slow down the car trying to ignore Andy's whining.

"Excuse me … uh, pardon me sir?"

"Talk louder Dusty. Pretend you're ordering a drink."

"Hey Buddy!"

"Way to go, Dusty."

"Are you talking to me Miss?"

Of course, a genuine dork. That's what I get for not checking my calendar. I forgot, today's National Dork Day.

"Yes, could you please tell me where the Business School is?"

"Who's that man you're talking to Mommy?"

"You mean you don't know Miss?"

Christ, does the dork think we're riding around campus taking a survey?

"No, I don't. I wonder if you could tell me?"

"Good, you're doing real good, Dusty."

"Certainly Miss, do you see that building over there?"

"No."

"That one, the large white one with the red tile roof?"

"Yeah."

"Well, the Business School's the third from the right."

"Gee, thanks a lot for the help."

"No trouble at all Miss; and, I hope you have a nice day."

"Yeah fellow, you too. … Dusty, any idea where we should head?"

"I think so. Let's park and start walking."

**

"Good afternoon Mr. Davis."

A dork, another dork. This is statistically impossible. This guy looks like he'd do up the top button on a Hawaiian shirt.

"Mr. Hutchins. This is Ms. Evans and her son Andy."

"A pleasure to meet you Miss Evans and you too young man. Planning on applying here when you grow up?"

Andy makes a few very satisfactory noises. Dusty excuses herself and hustles him out the door. Score one ice cream cone for the little rug rat. I wonder why the dork is staring at me. You'd think he'd never seen an unzipped fly before."

"Excuse me, I don't mean to stare, it's just that you remind me of someone I know."

I'm probably cursed with an archetypal sixties face. People always seem to greet me by saying, 'You know, you remind me of someone.' Actually it's probably their Aunt Matilda. Is this some sort of an advantage? I'm not sure if it means that I have a memorable or totally forgettable appearance. I'd better figure that one out before I turn to a life of crime.

"Sit down Mr. Davis. A bit warm for that three piece suit today. Why don't you take off your jacket and make yourself comfortable."

I give him a polite smile. Score one for the dork. I knew I should've worn my overalls and shit kicking boots. Always better to be rejected on your own grounds.

"... And as you can see, your academic record and G.M.A.T. scores put you right up there in the running. We definitely gave your application every consideration."

Another insincere smile. I'm starting to get bored; and hot. Not much of a view from up here, no air conditioning. The guy is a light weight. Mid–thirties, probably a grad who couldn't cut it. I bet he plays a decent game of racquetball though.

"... So you see we currently have twelve applications for every available position. Do the arithmetic yourself. There are bound to be qualified people, people like yourself, who we've been forced to turn away."

"I've heard you weren't satisfied with my work experience."

"Who told you that?"

"Let's just say I heard it."

"Of course that's one of the things we take into consideration. How an applicant has made use of his time since graduation gives us some indication of how he'll fare at Stanford."

"So then it's okay for a woman to waste her time?"

"Excuse me?"

"Nothing. So what it comes down to is that you think restaurant work is a waste of time."

"Now I didn't say that. I'm well aware that it can be quite difficult to find proper employment. I have friends who were forced to work as waiters for a time. I don't doubt that it's hard work."

You wouldn't know hard work buddy if you sat on it. 'Some of my best friends' – shit. Maybe I should just heave him out the window.

"Look Mr. Hutchins, let's say I spent the last five years working in a bank, perhaps as a loan officer."

"I'm sure you're well aware that we have no strict guidelines as to appropriate work experience. In fact we specifically try to get a diverse and well rounded student body."

"But still, my chances would have improved."

"Mr. Davis, I don't mind telling you it wasn't only your work experience that left something to be desired. Your letters of recommendation could have been far stronger. Only one came from a former professor. The others came from employers or friends."

"After more than six years it's not so easy to dig up academic recommendations. Besides, everyone knows they're basically meaningless."

He's reaching now. I must have him on the ropes. Letters of recommendation my ass. Of course I was lucky enough to scrounge up even one letter. I sure as hell cultivated enough enemies during that college stint. Those were definitely my bridge burning days. Uh oh, here it comes. I can tell by his smarmy little smile.

"No, you're wrong there. Everything is given equal and careful weight."

Okay, one last try …

"Look Mr. Hutchins, maybe this is a bit beside the point. Maybe I'm even out of line for saying it … You can go ahead and snub working in bars, but it gives you a better insight into people and how they operate than any of those pantywaist paper pushing jobs you approve of."

"I hardly think any of that is relevant Mr. Davis. It seems to me that next time you might be better advised not to put all your eggs in one basket. After all, we're not the only business school."

That tears it. Just what I needed, a touch of false humility. At least he didn't mention my career aims.

"And while we're on the subject; Stanford doesn't usually accept applicants who see our master's program as only a stepping stone to a further academic career."

That should teach me to be honest. "I fail to see how that makes me any less qualified."

We both know that business school ratings are based on job placements. I could wreck their salary profile.

"Richard, are you through yet? It's getting kinda late."

"Right you are, Miss Evans. Your little man must be quite famished by now. Well I won't keep you a moment longer. Mr. Davis, a pleasure meeting you, and by the way, I did like your story."

"You did, huh? Well an equal pleasure I'm sure in meeting you."

"Richard, what story is he talking about?"

"Wait till we're out of the building. Quiet Andy."

***

"Okay, what was that about?"

"I wrote this Winnie the Pooh story as part of my application."

"I didn't know you could write."

"I can't"

"But you said …"

"It doesn't matter what I said."

"I want to read it."

"Sure."

"Well he seemed nice enough."

"Who?"

"That guy."

"You mean Hutchins? He's a dork."

"I wish you'd stop saying that. What makes you so clever?"

"Of course he's a dork. He even has red hair."

"Does that make him a dork?"

"Damn right it does. I bet that jerk had his jockey shorts on backwards. Besides, why are you so keen on defending him? You like being patronized? Miss Evans my ass."

"Okay, I'll take your word for it. You're the one who talked to him ... Well, how did it go?"

"It didn't."

"Are you upset?"

"I'm sure not feeling any too gorgeous right now ... Thanks Dusty, that was really nice ... again ... now just do that one more time ... You know, you're okay sweetie."

"I know."

"So how about some lunch? We could stop off in Sausilito."

"Do you mean that?"

"Absolutely."

"Andy too?"

"Of course Andy, too. Did you think I was going to lock him up in the trunk?"

"Don't wanna go inna trunk Mommy. Don't let Richard put me inna trunk."

"Hush, no one's going to lock anyone up baby."

"Look kid I'll buy you an ice cream, okay?"

"No you won't."

"What's got into him?"

"Please honey, we're going to have lunch in a restaurant. If you're good you can have ice cream."

"And a Shirley Temple?"

"Yeah kid, and a Shirley Temple."

"Richard?"

"Yah?"

"Where are we gonna have lunch?"

"Anywhere you want."

"Some place on the bay."

"Sure."

"Richard?"

"Huh?"

"You're not still taking all that vitamin C are you?"

"Sure, why not?"

"It's not good for you."

"Can't be true. I haven't had a cold all year."

"Well maybe, but I've heard too much vitamin C makes you impotent."

"Get out of here."

"No really, it makes sense. I mean it's not anything Linus Pauling would notice. The lead's been out of his pencil for years."

"Well professor, we'll just have to test your hypothesis some time."

"You can always trust one of my diagnoses."

"Then I'll just leave the matter completely in your hands."

"Won't be the first time."

"How about over there?"

"Huh?"

"No, I mean lunch. That place looks okay?"

"I guess so."

"Good, there's a parking spot right over there. Why don't you clean the snot off of Andy's face and then we'll go in."

… If this restaurant isn't the complete California cliché; hanging plants, lots of light wood. At least we get a chance to sit out on the deck and dodge the sea gulls.

"All we have now is our light lunch menu, sir."

"That'll be fine."

What an easy mark I am. Being a waiter for years always gets in my way. I can't seem to enjoy myself in a restaurant. I'm too conscious of the behind the scenes stuff. It's impossible to completely tune it out. Well, at least I don't stack my plates anymore.

"And a spinach salad, but go light on the sprouts please."

"Anything else, sir?"

"No, I think that's it."

The waitress tucks the menus under her arm and ambles off to the kitchen. I watch her ass twitch as she goes.

"I thought you liked sprouts Richard."

"Yeah, but not so that I feel like I'm gnawing my way through a bird's nest."

"I'll be right back. Make sure Andy doesn't play around with his food when it comes."

Dusty lumps off to the bathroom … Here comes our order. Good thing they were quick off the mark with the food. Must be able to identify a hyperactive kid when they see one. So for a change Andy's preoccupied with slurping down his soup. I lean back and close my eyes, giving the bright California sun a chance to warm my face. I was right. Completely wasted my time today. Didn't realize how pissed off I'd become until I practically swallowed that first glass of wine. I open my eyes and stare across the Bay. The woman at the next table is also temporarily deserted. We smile at each other. Well, gotta do something to fill in the gap.

"You've got a nice looking son there."

"Thanks."

"He looks quite a bit like you."

"But he's not …"

"Eat your soup Andy … Well, thanks again. People often say that, but I think he takes more after his mother."

"Oh no, he definitely resembles you, especially around the eyes. He has such lovely eyes."

I flash one of my warm encouraging smiles to keep her going.

"Do you and your family live in the city?"

"No, up in Sonoma County, near the coast."

"Oh my, that must be beautiful."

"It is."

"I know, I go up there occasionally on weekends."

"Really? You should stop by if you're in the neighborhood. Here, take one of my cards."

Boy do I feel like a jerk doing this. Card my ass. She must think I'm some sort of rising young successful type, what with this silly three piece suit and my stack of business cards. Still …

"That would be very nice. Thank you uh, Mr. Davis. I think I just might."

"No problem. That's the bar I manage. Stop by sometime. I'll buy you a drink."

Footsteps. We turn around, preparing ourselves for imminent re–partnering. Hm, they're coming back sort of close together. Wonder if they were playing the same game. Probably not. If Dusty was interested, she'd just hump him in the men's room.

"Mom, that lady thought …"

"Have a roll kid."

"Didn't she bring your omelet yet, Richard?"

"Uh huh."

"Richard!"

"Yeah I know, I gulp my food. You don't have to tell me that. When I was growing up my father would stare at me while I ate. Then the old fart would scream right in my face, 'Chew your food goddamit!' Everyone was supposed to eat exactly like he did, the last of the methodical chewers. What a miserable old tyrant. He made mealtimes an absolute treat. You can imagine how I felt. I wanted to kill the bastard. I kept quiet though. I was too busy shoveling roast beef down my throat."

"Roast beef?"

"Sure, you think I was always an organic vegetarian type? My grandfather was a butcher. Sundays my mom would cook two chickens. One for me, the other for the rest of the family. I figure I've eaten my share of dead flesh."

"But you're so thin."

"Well I don't eat like that anymore. Christ, I used to be an Olympic eater. At college I could swallow a dozen hot dogs for lunch."

"How could you do that?"

"Metabolism, I shit a lot."

"Nice talk, Richard. Here, do you want a taste of this?"

"Sure."

"Good isn't it?"

"Hey you're right, that is good."

Dusty watches as I wolf down half her quiche. I wonder if those tiny specks are pieces of meat. Fuck it. A little bit won't make my pecker fall off.

"Richard you pig, get out of my lunch."

"Don't be so greedy Dusty, I just want a taste."

"Greedy, you've eaten half of it already."

"Try some of my salad."

"I don't want any salad. I want my quiche."

"You let my mom's food alone."

"Eat your soup, Andy. I've told you not to interrupt me when I'm talking to Richard."

"But Mom …"

"Didn't you promise me that you'd be good?"

"I don't like the soup."

"Well if you don't eat it, Richard will."

"No he won't. Don't give him my soup Mommy."

"Who says I want it kid."

"I don't have to listen to you Richard. You're not my father.'

"Look kid, do you see that bay."

"Yeah."

"Well how would you like to learn to fly over it?"

"You're silly Richard."

"No I mean it. Just like Superman. Here, I'll help you out. See, I pick you up like this and then I just swing you out …"

"Mommy!"

"Richard, what do you think you're doing? Put him down. It isn't funny."

"Funny, it isn't supposed to be funny. Andy isn't laughing, are you Andy?'

"No."

"And you're going to sit down now and eat your soup. Right, Andy?"

"You're despicable, Richard."

"I was just explaining the situation to your son. We understand each other now, don't we Andy?"

"Haveta go to the bathroom."

"Richard, take him to the bathroom."

"Wait a minute, how about you? He's your kid."

"Oh, you know very well why not. Don't be like that.'

"Sorry Dusty. C'mon kid, let's go."

"Don't want to."

"You heard your mother. You're a big boy now Andy. You just can't pee in your pants … I said, let's go."

"I'm scared."

"Are you satisfied now, Richard?"

"Okay. Look Andy, I promise I won't hurt you. I swear. When did I ever lie to you?"

"My ice cream."

"Huh?"

"Want my ice cream. You promised."

"When we get back. You can have it after you're done."

"And the Shirley Temple."

"Sure."

"With two cherries."

"Look kid, don't push it."

"Try to be nice, Richard."

"I am being nice, goddamit. Please Andy, just give me your hand."

We walk into the dark bar striding along easily. So this is what it's like being a father. Feels all right.

"Do you need any help?"

"I'm not a little kid."

"Don't be so touchy. I wasn't trying to insult you."

"I'm through, Richard."

"Are you sure?"

"Course I'm sure."

"I know, you're not a little kid."

Andy runs ahead to report on our outing.

"Did everything go okay, baby?"

"I pissed in the toilet Mommy and Richard watched."

Terrific, it makes me sound like some kind of a voyeur.

"Want my ice cream. You promised."

"Miss, excuse me?"

"Yes, anything else sir?"

"Yeah, do you have some ice cream for the kid here?"

"I'm sure I can find some."

"And a Shirley Temple too. You promised."

"What flavor would you like, young man?"

"Choclate, no vinilla, no I want choclate and stawberry ..."

"Wake me up if the kid ever decides."

"Baby, how about a nice plate of chocolate ice cream?"

"Okay Mommy."

"So we have one plate of chocolate ice cream. And what about you sir?"

"No thanks, I'm fine."

"Richard, can I have some dessert?"

"Jesus Dusty, of course you can have some dessert. You don't have to ask my permission. What are you, scared of me too?"

"Just trying to be polite."

I look out over the water as Dusty and Andy conscientiously spoon up their desserts. The place is empty. I'm trying to keep myself from getting edgy. I'm always aware of a waitress' eyes burning holes in the back of my neck, willing me to leave. At least that's what I always did when I was a waiter.

"That was real nice, Richard."

"Glad you liked it. Should I drop you off at your place?"

"Well I sorta thought we could leave Andy at Terry's and then go back to your cabin."

"What did you have in mind?"

"Oh, I thought I'd might jump on top of you."

"Sounds okay."

"Well don't get too excited or anything … Hey, not in front of Andy."

"You convinced?"

"Okay, just save it till later."

***

In all the sleazy detective novels I've read, at some point in the story, a parting will be followed by the line, "And I never saw her again." But life's not like that at all. I always see these women again. People I know, I see again. Farewells aren't edged with foreboding. Dusty isn't about to mysteriously disappear. No matter how much I might prefer the drama of such a solution, she'll be here tomorrow. She'll be here until she gets tired of me and leaves.

"Lucky Terry was there to help us out, Dusty."

"Yeah, she just got back from Santa Rosa. Too bad about her old man."

"The guy's a dork. She'd be better off without him."

"What is it with you today?"

"Just forget I said anything. C'mere."

"Richard, wait until we get inside."

"Anything you want, Dusty ... Push the door open, it's not locked."

"That's one nice thing about the river. You don't have to lock your door, or worry about break–ins, or ..."

"It's not trust, Dusty. I've got nothing worth stealing. The lock's broke and I've got nothing worth taking. You think somebody's gonna sneak in and rip off my copy of Hegel's *Lesser Logic*?"

"Your phone's ringing."

"I hear it."

"Well, aren't you going to answer it?"

"Nope."

"No?"

"That's right."

"What's going on? Why won't you pick up your phone?"

"Because it'll either be someone I don't want to talk to or some very bizarre wrong number."

"I don't get it. How can you know that?"

"I just know."

"Well, I think that's totally screwy."

"So you don't believe me?"

"No."

"Okay, don't believe me. I'll prove it to you ... Hello?"

"Hello, it's me."

"Oh, hi."

"How are you?"

"Fine."

"Did you like your card?"

"Sure."

"Wait a minute, you're not my Timmy."

"That's right."

"Gee, do I have the wrong number?"

"Seems like it."

"What number did I call?"

"What number did you want?"

"843–3852."

"That's my number."

"But you're not Timmy."

"No, I'm not Timmy."

"Then where's my Timmy?"

"I don't know lady, I'm sorry."

"So this must be a wrong number."

"It must be."

"Did I disturb you?"

"Oh no, not at all."

"It's been very nice talking to you, young man."

"And you too."

"Well bye bye then."

Christ, I should never get involved with telephones. They've given me nothing but grief. Either I stare at a phone that refuses to ring or some girlfriend spends half an hour telling me what a complete dork I am.

"Who was it?"

"Wrong number."

"Wrong number?"

"Look Dusty, it's not worth trying to explain. Everyone gets wrong numbers but not the kind I get."

"That's okay, don't tell me. Be like that."

"Wait a minute there sweetheart. I don't have to listen to this. It's not what I came back for."

"Oh you drive me crazy, Richard. What do you want?"

"Here, I'll show you."

"Mmmm … That feels good."

"It's supposed to … And now Miss Evans."

"Yes, Mr. Davis."

"Have I ever shown you my loft before?"

"I believe I've had all the finer points demonstrated."

"Don't be so sure. I think we might've missed a few tricks the last time through."

***

Dear Dad,
The enclosed bill should be self explanatory.

Thanks a bunch,

                                        Richard

Gas	$18.25
Oil	.85
Tolls	1.25
Lunch	19.65
Tip	5.00
Total	$45.00

10

IN PURSUIT OF VIRTUE

Can you tell me Socrates – is virtue something that can be taught? Or does it come by practice? Or is it neither teaching nor practice that gives it to a man but natural aptitude or some other way? –Plato

"You know Richard, I just don't understand these people."

Johnny and I are sitting on the steps outside the Grove. Almost time to get ready for tonight's performance. It's still light out and I can see Jesse shuffling across the road. I nod hello. Nine o'clock in the morning I see him heading toward town, paper sack beer tilted to his cracked lips. He puts in a full ten hours hanging out in front of the Coop with the other local heroes. They all look like badly maintained replicas of the sixties' culture. Summer, his face is red and blistered, almost barbecued by the sun. I doubt that Jesse notices.

"All these people out here, the only thing they want to do is to hassle you. It doesn't make sense. People are supposed to come to a bar to enjoy themselves."

"Well Johnny, maybe that's what they enjoy."

"And it's not that I like to complain, Richard but …"

I give Johnny one long hard glare.

"Okay, so I do enjoy bitching. Everyone in the bar business does. It's one of the few fringe benefits. Still, you know what I mean. No way was it this bad back in Maine, not even close. Sure a lot of those fishermen were assholes. Yeah, you're right, there was Butch bringing in that dead bear and Mad Dog riding in on his motorcycle but …"

"Aren't you forgetting the time they reduced Greta to tears by shouting, 'Fuck, fuck, piss, piss; oh what a relief it is,' for the first hour of her shift?"

"Sure, but it wasn't personal, Richard. That's the point. They weren't out to get you. That's just the way they behaved. They didn't know any better. Once the locals got used to you, they were pretty straight. New faces tended to upset them, like rearranging the furniture or something.

"Here, they're strictly after your blood. Worse, you have to listen to their crap about brotherhood and sisterhood; you know, that whole love, peace and share routine. 'Hey bro, buy me a drink. I'd help you out if I could.' I'm getting tired of it, Richard. Anytime one of those derelicts calls me bro I hold onto my wallet."

"Burnt out hippie trash."

"I was talking to Jeannie the other night about it. You know it should be sort of sad, all these sixties' casualties on either crazy disability or A.F.D.C. It might be interesting if you were writing some damn novel, but I have to deal with them buddy, week in and week out. They're not fictional characters, they're my reality. It's getting to be too much. I can't stand their constant nickel and diming much longer."

"You can't desert me now, Johnny. You gonna leave me with the likes of Florinda and Chacko? A lot of help they are. If you go, who will I have?"

"There's Anita."

"Yeah, Anita's good but I can't figure out her angle. There's something on her mind."

"She's still your best waitress."

"My only one. Look, give it a few more months. Who else around here can I trust? I'll figure something out by then."

"We'll see, buddy. Right now, I just don't know."

"Time we both got into gear. Susan's probably getting anxious."

"Nice deal she has. Comes in late, leaves early."

"Mn."

"How's things going with you two?"

"Mmnn."

"I've gotta hand it to you, buddy. You sure know how to pick them."

"Death wish."

"Yeah, well like you said, I should relieve Susan."

Jaime is camped by the door, a monument to his own hugeness. He punched in about thirty minutes early again. I'll have to have a talk with that boy. But maybe I should wait till he stops fighting with his old lady. I hear she's buying him a bike for his birthday. That'll keep the dumb ape happy.

"What's up, Jaime?"

"Sheila wants to see you."

"What she want with me?"

"Must be looking for a job. I hear she gives really good interviews."

"Okay buddy, don't strain yourself trying not to smile. I'll be back and help you out with the door."

"Don't mind me, Richard. You just go right ahead and take your time. I don't like to see a man rush himself."

"Eat it, Jaime."

Sheila is rubbing her ass against the service door and sticking out those big tits of hers. All she needs is a sign around her neck reading, 'Fuck me', or maybe 'This space for rent'.

I can't be with her for more than five minutes without checking to see whether my zipper's closed. She might even be attractive if she wasn't such a sleazy airhead.

"What's up, Sheila?"

"I wanna job."

"Any job in particular?"

"I wanna be a cocktail waitress."

"Why?"

"What's the difference? I have plenty of experience."

"Yeah?"

"I worked down at the Cafe."

"Why'd you stop?"

"I quit. There's no money down there."

"Well the Grove isn't exactly the Cafe."

"Look Richard, I know the people around here, I'd bring in a lotta business."

Yeah, but for whom? I heard about the deals she was running at the Cafe. That's why Arte canned her.

"Okay, why don't you fill out this application and I'll let you know."

"I've already told you all you need to know."

"Then just put down your name and phone number."

"I don't have a phone."

"Well somewhere I can find you."

"You don't have to worry about that. I'm always available if you want me."

One more of those sultry looks and I'm smearing butter all over her face.

"Good Sheila, then write your name on the application and I'll let you know if anything turns up."

"Can we go in the back room for a minute?"

How the hell does she know about that?

"I don't see why?"

"I wanna tell you something, Richard."

"Go ahead."

"Not here."

"No need to be so shy. We're all friends at the Grove, just one big happy family."

Sheila hesitates, then reaches up and grabs my ear between her teeth.

"I give great head."

"Did you include that on your application?"

She pushes off a little and stares. Sheila can't understand what's happening. It's not the way her world works. Her hand drops down to my crotch. Reassured she smiles. Old Wilbur down there will jump at anything. Unfortunately he doesn't do the hiring.

"I'll be back to check in a few days. I hear you leave your afternoons free."

"Sure, thanks for stopping by."

She parts her mouth to give me a final penis swelling smile. I watch her wiggle her ass out of the bar then dump her application in the dustbin. Sheila is the very last person I'd hire, and for that matter I'd sooner fuck a corrugated douche bag. She's disgusting. Touching her would be like fondling a banana slug. I half expect to see a trail of slime glistening faintly behind her. It's not just her physical presence that's repulsive. It's that whole atmosphere of sleazy sex. Every time I see Sheila I get an urge to cram all her orifices shut with mayonnaise. Maybe I should hire her on those terms. Nah, she'd probably accept.

"Richard, it's Veray."

"Okay Jaime, what's her game today?"

"She won't pay the cover charge."

"Of course she won't."

"And she's taken the admission stamp."

"How did that happen?"

"We started arguing and she grabbed it."

"So what do you want me to do?"

"I need my stamp."

"Okay, I'll get your stamp for you. Just go back and stand by the door."

Jaime's manhood is being threatened again; probably some subsection violation of his biker's code. I'm being paid as a bar manager, but I end up spending most of my time doing psychological counseling.

"Hey, Veray."

"Hi Richard."

"You know why I'm here, Veray."

"Well, I'm not moving."

"It's nothing personal. Those are the rules. We're just trying to do our jobs."

"Richard, I've been to your cabin. I've seen the pictures on your walls. This isn't you. Why are you acting like this? What do you have against me?"

They all think they have some exclusive insight into my soul. I must make it too easy for them. I should stop letting these women create my personality; maybe I could try to be more forceful. Nah, why bother.

"Look Veray, Jaime is only trying to do his job. I won't let you hassle my employees. You should understand. You've worked in bars before. So why don't you be a good girl and give the stamp back. If you don't want to pay the cover that's fine, but you'll have to leave when you finish your drink."

"Richard, I know you're not like this. Why are you letting yourself be forced into this role?"

Probably because I've spent too much time dealing with assholes like you. Maybe if I talk real slow, the meaning of my words might seep into her acid soaked brain.

"I'm not trying to come down hard on you, Veray. It's nothing personal. But I've got responsibilities. The band has to be paid. Florinda, Johnny and everyone else would like to stay employed. I'm trying to keep the place going. Do you understand, Veray? It's not you."

"It's not right."

"Look, are you gonna give me that stamp?"

"Why are you doing this to me?"

"Okay, how's this? You give me the stamp and behave yourself and I'll buy you a drink."

"I wanna stay."

"You have to pay the cover. That's the band's money. I'm not going to rip them off."

"Can't employees invite a guest?"

"Once in a while."

"Well, I can be your friend."

"I have no friends."

"This place owes me, Richard. You owe me."

"Now wait a minute, Veray …"

"You took this job from me and you took my cabin. I was promised that place, Richard. I was about to move in. You were even there when the power went off at the laundromat while all my clothes were still in the washer."

"Why don't you quiet down, drink your drink, and give me the goddam stamp back."

"No! You pay me what you owe me."

"Okay, do what you want. Stay where you are or roll around on the ground. You can bark like a goddam seal for all I care. Just don't ever say another word to me again, understand?"

"I don't understand, Richard. You used to be such a nice guy. You're working too hard. Loosen up, it's really not worth it."

You can't expect to have a rational convseration with the brain damaged. With any luck she'll o.d. in the bathroom tonight.

"I got it, Johnny."

I jump on the phone, any excuse to get away from Veray — What was that business about her laundry? — Otherwise, I'd be the last person in this place to pick up a phone. No wonder so many places use recorded messages. Drives you crazy answering the same questions over and over again; who's playing, what's the cover, how do you get there from Santa Rosa?

"River Grove, largest dance floor in Sonoma County."

"Who's playing tonight?"

"Harlowe."

"Who?"

"Har–lowe."

"Hullo, whattya mean hullo?"

"It's the name of the band." What does this jackass think it is — the Soviet women's wrestling team?

"Yeah, I know that man, but I'm asking what they do."

"They play instruments and sing."

"Don't try handing me any of that shit, Jack. Just tell me what kinda music they play."

"Uh sorta progressive reggae with a kinda laid back, country–rock beat."

"Oh, you mean like, fusion."

"Sure, fusion."

"Any good?"

"Listen bro, they are just about as hot as a band can get."

"You giving me straight shit or what?"

"Sure it's straight. Wait till you see the bass player. She is one powerful little tootsie."

"Tasty stuff, huh?"

"If you want, I can arrange for her to sit on your face while she's playing."

"Stop shitting me, Jack."

"Don't believe me. It's your loss not mine."

"You expecting a good crowd?"

"I'm expecting nothing. They're already here. The place is almost packed right now."

"Any women?"

"Crawling with them."

"So what's the damage there, bro?"

"Two dollar cover."

"Two bucks for the Grove on a Wednesday night!"

"It's a bargain sport. You'd pay twice as much anywhere else."

"Okay smartass, name one other place."

"The Blue Lizard Lounge, Sioux City, Iowa." Huh, the little bastard hung up. Maybe he thinks I've insulted him. Well, I can live with that.

"Richard, mind if I catch a quick smoke before the band starts?"

"Might as well Johnny, nobody's here yet."

The guys at the end of the bar are signaling. I open two Buds and amble slowly in their direction.

"Hey man, don't fuck with any of that shit."

"Heavy."

"It's a total downer man. You snort some of that crystal, next morning you wake up dead."

"Really heavy man."

"It's a dollar seventy for the beers."

"I'm giving you nothing but the straight shit man."

"A dollar seventy please."

"I heard you man. You'll get your fuckin money."

He reaches down into the recesses of his jeans and comes up with two dirt caked dollar bills. He tosses them on the bar and they go skimming across a small puddle of beer ...

"Don't forget the change, huh bro?"

"Wouldn't dream of it, bro."

I ring up the sale, shove the bills into the register and walk slowly back with the change. Carefully I place one quarter and one nickel in the puddle of beer by his elbow.

"Thank you, my brother."

In the bar business it's essential to establish a proper rapport with your clientele. A good bartender understands his customers. He senses subtle shades of mood and adjusts accordingly. And what I can clearly intuit is the self evident fact that I'm dealing with a bunch of jerks.

To these people, bartenders are no more than mobile furniture. They shove money at you and you pour them drinks. Speak to them out of that role and you might as well be a talking sectional sofa. Do they really think we're all devoid of any human sensibility? Machine can be insulted with impunity because machines don't fight back. But once they reduce us to mere servo–matics, there's no further need for restraint. What's worse, customers feel no sense of shame. It's the bartender who's always forced to bear witness. Night after night you overhear a continual stream of depressing conversations. Other people's ragged, shabby dreams pour over you; sad horny guys or frightened single mothers trying to pick each other up. And it's too much to take on, all that unending pain. No wonder I treat them as units to be serviced. Fuck the tips, just pay up and get lost.

"Thanks for the break buddy, I can handle things if you want to take off."

"In a minute … hey, what the hell's this, Johnny?"

"You got a problem, Richard?'

"No, I don't have a problem, this fizz glass does. Not only is it filthy but there's a big lipstick smudge around the rim. Looks like it's been kissed by a Ubangi."

"Lip gloss."

"What?"

"Lip gloss. These little bimbos around here don't wear lipstick. Maybe it was someone up from Mill Valley."

"I don't give a damn whose lips they were. Look, don't you start giving me a hard time as well. You're supposed to be the only one left I can count on."

"Okay buddy, calm down. Do you want me to wash it for you?"

"No, I do not want you to wash it for me. I just want to know who was working this afternoon. There's precious little to do but prep the bar. Instead the glasses are caked with crud, I have two trays of moldy lemons …"

"Susan."

"Susan?'

"You got it buddy."

"Yeah, how could I forget? She left maybe an hour ago. Well, I'll just have to talk to her."

"Uh huh."

"I will. I'll take care of it."

"Sure."

"You don't believe me? You think I won't do it?"

"Richard, you are incapable of saying one harsh word to her."

"I just don't like to see her get upset, that's all. You know how sensitive she is … and there's nothing wrong with that. I mean it's not like she doesn't try. So she must've had a good reason … She really does try you know."

"So what's gonna be the story?"

"The glasses'll be clean from now on."

"You're not thinking of doing them yourself?"

"I've got time after work."

"At three a.m.?"

"It doesn't take all that long."

"But your fingers will be a complete mess."

"I'll wear gloves and use the dishwasher in the kitchen."

"You're already stocking the beer coolers for her in the morning.'

"I'm here early anyway."

"You're a sap Richard, d'you know that?"

"Yeah, I do … Well at least she smells good."

"You should know."

"Yeah, I should … You tell me Johnny, why do these River women wear that patchouli oil?'

"What?"

"Haven't you noticed it?"

"You mean that's intentional?"

"Yeah, I know, you thought they just weren't into washing."

"No one would want to smell that way."

"You're wrong. These women actually want to smell like a

thousand dead cigarette butts."

"Why?"

"Christ knows. Maybe they think it's earthy and natural. So's a pile of warm shit. You'd think they'd realize it makes a guy nauseous."

"Maybe they don't care."

"No, it's not just the lesbians. Probably they don't realize how they smell. Who'd tell them? Can you imagine going over to Florinda there and telling her that she smells like a freshly manured field?"

"Yeah, I see what you mean."

"Speaking of Florinda, where'd she come up with that outfit? Looks like she swiped that number right out of the Coop freebox."

"It's her artistic temperament … Look Richard, I've been meaning to ask you. How come you always work with Anita while I have to deal with the two bimbos?"

"I did my time before you got here. Besides, I should get something other than grief out of being the manager of this dump."

"Florinda is a bitch to work with. One of these days I'm gonna lose it. Even Chacko can't deal with her."

"They deserve each other."

"Like Florinda and Frank."

"Yeah, good thing they found each other. That way only two people end up being miserable instead of four."

"I like that."

"Yeah, so do I. It's not my line. Someone said it about an obnoxious poet and his wife. Fuck, who was it, you know, the one with the bird?"

"I don't know any of that stuff buddy."

"Wait a minute, the Ancient Mariner. That's it, *The Rime of the Ancient Mariner*. Coleridge and whoever the hell he was married to, Mrs. Coleridge no doubt."

"Right."

"What d'ya mean 'right'?"

"I remember the poem, that's all. We had to learn it in school."

"Doesn't matter. I think it was actually Butler referring to Carlyle. Can't seem to get anything straight anymore."

"I know what you mean."

"Hey, did you ever see Florinda's mother?"

"You mean that sleazy old bag she had with her last month?"

"Yeah, the painted whore of Guatemala."

"That's the way Florinda's headed for sure."

"Almost makes me feel sorry for Frank."

"That asshole?"

"I said almost. You know I used to think that fuzzhead knew something, that he was holding back on me. He has that way of staring deep into your eyes like he's finally figured you out. But then I realized it was only brain damage."

"I don't believe a word he says."

"You mean about playing with the Cubs or jamming in New Jersey with Jimi Hendrix? No, who would believe that? He's a pathological liar but he does tell a good story. You know, he hired me. I had to keep after him but he was the boy who brought me here."

"I thought Nick was managing."

"Nick was between Frank and me."

"Why would anyone want to hire Frank?"

"Supposedly Lydia had the hots for him."

"No?"

"Yeah, I think it's true. You should have been here when he came down with the flu. Lydia did everything but tuck him in."

"But isn't Mike …"

"He doesn't give a damn about Lydia. He just wants to be left alone to fool around with his secretary."

"Doesn't he own the place?"

"Along with Lydia."

"But it keeps losing money."

"It's a tax shelter, Johnny. He's raking in the old dough and he uses it for tax purposes. Besides, it keeps Lydia busy."

"So why not be a pal and work with Florinda tonight?"

"I deal with her enough as is. You know that slut went whining to Mike last month, complaining about the scheduling."

"You mean about Thursdays?"

"Both Susan and Florinda are totally worthless as waitresses."

"So it might as well go to Susan."

"Damn right. She tried to tell me she was head cocktail waitress."

"What?"

"Yeah, I fixed her. I made Susan a bartender and hired Anita to take over her schedule, Thursdays included."

"At least Anita knows what she's doing."

"Sure, but it's the way Florinda patronizes Susan that I don't like. I don't want anyone treating her like some kind of dumb cunt."

"I know what you mean."

"You're talking about Jeannie. Not quite the same thing buddy. She snubs Jeannie, but she does the same thing to Anita and Lila. I'd actually feel better if she just ignored Susan. It's her goddam attempt to be nice that's infuriating."

"Maybe, but I'd still like to slam my fist between her legs when I see her acting that way to Jeannie."

"Be my guest. But listen, that reminds me, did I tell you about her sponge?"

"What're you talking about?"

"Susan runs into Florinda in the bathroom and she asks her for a tampon. So Ms. Natural says, 'Don't use those, use one of these sponges.'"

"C'mon Richard, whatya mean a sponge?"

"You know, one of them little animals … or is it a plant? Damn, I really can't remember anything anymore."

"Are you telling me she uses a sea sponge with sand and bits of crap sticking to it?"

"Get out of here. They must sterilize the damn things first. She doesn't just pick them straight up off the beach. Anyway, Susan told me the thing kept popping out no matter what she tried to do with it."

"Wonder how Florinda keeps it in?"

"She probably has one of her harpy friends ram it up there with a poker."

"Ugh."

"I bet she doesn't even bother to take it out to let Frank fuck her. It must stay up there sodden with blood all month, period or no period. If you listen hard enough you can probably hear her squish as she walks."

"Buddy ..."

"Next time she asks me for a damp towel I'll say, 'Florinda, why don't you just reach up into your cunt and pull out your sponge'?"

"Enough."

"Yeah, I do get carried away."

"You gotta watch that stuff buddy. It's not healthy."

"I'm okay, Johnny, it's just that Florinda's such a sneaky little slut. Though I have to admit it, she does have a real nice ass."

"Well, why don't you go up to her and bite it if you're feeling so hot and bothered?"

"Look who's talking now. On second thought, maybe I will. Hey Florinda!"

"Don't do it buddy."

"Did you call me, Richard?"

"Yeah sweetheart, could you do me a favor and turn around."

"What for?"

"Just do it will you?"

"Listen to me, buddy ..."

"What's going on here?"

"Please Florinda, trust me. Just turn around. I'm asking for a very simple favor. I'd really appreciate it if you would."

"Well okay. How's this?"

"There, didn't I tell you, Johnny?"

"I still don't understand. What's wrong with Johnny?"

"Nothing, I was just telling him how nice you looked and I wanted him to see for himself."

"Oh, well thanks, Richard. That's really nice, I guess. I've got to get back to my tables now."

"Richard, you shithead."

"Had you going, didn't I? By the way, notice that little trail of blood that seeped down her left leg as she turned?"

Johnny nails me with a bar rag and goes over to wait on another drunk. I wonder if I'm getting out of control. Nah, didn't fold in New York, I won't fold here.

"How are you my brother?"

Trouble, I can smell trouble and it smells exactly like Ray.

"Can't complain, Ray."

"I must speak with my brother about business. This deal you are saying we have, it is not to my liking."

Imagine booking a band like Harlowe? Lydia must be mixing her valiums with Elavil again. Either that or a head cold is blocking her hearing. Ray plays the guitar like a mongoose attacking a python, but he's not the real problem. It's those women. They all look like extras from a Petticoat Junction revival. About as much chance of one of those little juicy fruits being a musician as of me playing a Chopin etude on the nose flute. You can tell that they're really serious musicians by the way they push their crotches out on the downbeat and try to get maximum bounce from their boobs. I can't figure the keyboard player though. He doesn't seem to fit. Looks like a hitch–hiker they picked up on their way down.

"Same deal that I always give. You get eighty percent of the door, half price on drinks, free coffee and soda. I expect you to play four fifty minute sets unless you're told otherwise."

"You listen up right, my man. We trucked all the way down from Mendocino to play a Wednesday night. This deal you tell me is for shit. When we play up north the clubs cut us a few rounds. Some do much more than that, my brother."

"No."

"What are you saying, my brother?"

"No, as in So–No–Ma county, which is where you are, my brother."

"You should not try to do me, my brother. The Grove does not work that way. It is Lydia who will be hearing from me."

"It works the way I say it works … my brother."

Quelle drama. Maybe I should curl my lip and speak out of the side of my mouth. Or, I could crack a bottle of Bud over the bar and threaten to cut him up a bit. Better make that Michelob, the Buds are deposits. Chiselers, this place must have an absolute fascination for them. Ripping off the Grove has become the local pastime. Just one day, that's all I ask, just one day off from weasel patrol, from watching these leeches trying to do me to death for a dime.

"Lighten up my …"

"It's nine–thirty Ray. Contract says you've got a set to play. We'll talk about it later."

Getting a band to start on time is like trying to coax a pregnant woman onto roller skates. Mostly it's a matter of persistence. No sense of time at all, but basically musicians just have no sense. Some of them are okay people. The majority though, the majority are either on some sort of star trip or fucked–up or both. Must be all them drugs they take, as my mother would say.

Well, at least they look good, sort of a road show version of Beauty and the Beast. Christ, the shorts on that blonde are unbelievable. Probably comes close to orgasm just zipping them up. 'Okay Jerome, you can climb back down into your boxer shorts and relax.'

I'm really surprised. They're even worse than I imagined. Mostly it's nothing but feedback from Ray's guitar. Those girls should replace him with a donkey. At least that way the customers would get to see what they want without having their hearing ground down by a lot of emery board music. Might as well tune out for the night and play bartender instead.

"Hey, hey you, you bartender!"

I get through with the whiskey soda and point at the loud little peckerhead. I should change my name to Haywood Yew. Seems to be what my clients think it is. Well, who am I to argue?

"Listen bartender, know how to make a good separator?"

I stare down at him.

"I'll take one of those and a Bud, but listen, make it a good one, understand?"

Wonder what's biting that guy besides being five–four? ... Okay, glass, ice, brandy, Kahlua, cream: fish a Bud out of the bin behind me. If nothing else, I'm still a good bartender, or at least a good mechanic. It's the talking I hate. I just can't stand talking to any of these fuckheads.

"Two seventy–five."

I watch as he counts out his nickels and dimes. Could've broken into his piggy bank while I was making the drinks. Sports, this bar is lousy with them.

"Richard, I'm gonna take a quick break."

"Sure Johnny, no problem."

"Two white bulls, vodka collins, pitcher, two Buds."

Set up the glasses, ice, both hands moving, open the tap, shake the collins.

"Nine ninety–five, Richard."

"Got it, Anita. Let's see, three seventy–five and two and nine ninety–five it is."

Anita's usually on top of her addition, but I've got to check. Some of the other bimbos either can't add or they try to do a little business on their own account.

"White wine, Lydia?"

Good old Lydia Miller, part–time owner, full–time victim. Too bad I wasn't here three years ago when she had her breakdown. Must've been a trip seeing her roll around naked in that gold tub upstairs. I don't really believe the rest of the things Frank told me. Not even a crazed Lydia would do that. But who knows what she's into? Hm, that's two weeks in a row she's worn that studded denim jacket. Makes her look like a dangerous broom handle.

"God Richard, they're awful."

"Yeah, aren't they? Don't bother booking them back unless they add the donkey."

"Huh?"

"Forget it."

It might give Lydia ideas. Six glasses of wine a night and two olives. Helluva diet. She actually thinks her old man will notice if she starves herself to death. Good thing Lydia never hankered after me. Puts me in a very select group. Christ, it'd be like poking a goddam skeleton. Now her daughter's a completely different matter, maybe I'll screw her daughter, the little slut.

"Next month's calendar ready yet, Lydia?"

"I want to talk to you about that first."

"Tomorrow, stop by tomorrow afternoon."

With any luck she'll be reasonably coherent. More important, she seldom plays 'daddy's little girl' until it gets dark. Old habits can keep people reaching for the same tarnished brass ring year after year. She must have been hot shit in fifty–six when she was the queen of upstate New York. Damn, here I am laughing at a perfectly nice woman whose husband is shitting all over her. She just isn't made for this California open marriage crap. She was brought up to give dinner parties for her husband's colleagues. Instead she ends up boozing and going home with the local talent while her husband sticks it to his empty headed floozy of a secretary. Yeah, that's why I laugh, there's nothing I can do for her.

"Richard."

"Can I get you something Mouse? Tanqueray and grape?"

"Yeah, but listen Richard, I've been hearing things about you?"

"Like what?"

She leans well over the bar, parking her equipment on top, and gives me a loose attempt at a coy look.

"I heard you were pretty good."

Christ, what should I do now; paw the ground, show my teeth, whinny? Or I could just slap my dick on the bar ... Hm, I wonder if she really doesn't bother to take her boots off?

"Who's been telling you things like that?"

"It gets around."

And now that sure shot on the River ratings, the old geater with a heater himself, fulfilling every single mother's desires, back from a whirlwind tour of many dark bedrooms ... I wonder who's been giving me the good marks? Women must be able to sense when you're fucking around. They come sniffing like a dog to a hydrant.

"The Grove's closed Monday night, Mouse."

Poor Richard Davis, the little boy who couldn't say no.

"I'll be over about six."

"Just climb the hill till you hit a redwood cabin on the right, cabin number eight."

"Well, I'll be ready for you, lover."

She winks heavily then slowly runs her tongue over her lower lip. Subtlety has never quite caught on around here.

"By the way Mouse."

"Yeah, Richard?"

"That's a buck–fifty for the drink."

Band's on break. I can relax now. Everyone else is rushing

out to toke up for the next set. They'd be better off stuffing those joints in their ears. Wonder where Jeff is? Nearly ten–thirty and still no swamper. The dirty glasses are starting to pile up. Can't expect Johnny to do my share. Damn, my fingers are going to be little oozing puffballs tomorrow. I'll be lucky if I'm able to put my hands in my pockets.

"Richard, you got these drinks screwed around. The bourbon's on the rocks, the scotch is up."

"No problem, Anita."

"What do you think you're doing?"

"Switching the ice."

"Gross."

"So don't watch."

"Listen Richard, Jesse won't leave me alone. He keeps rubbing against me every time I go by."

"Tell Jaime."

"He said to tell you."

"Great, I'll be there in a minute."

I signal to Johnny.

"What's up?"

"Jesse's doing his routine with Anita."

"Anita?"

"Yeah, he's not the discriminating type."

"I thought that was Jaime's responsibility?"

"Rubbing against Anita?"

"Don't be a sap."

"He's bucking his responsibility like everyone else in this joint. What do you expect for four bucks an hour? Hey Johnny, have you noticed anything peculiar about Anita?"

"What's to notice about Anita?"

"Is it my imagination, or is she wearing black pajamas?"

"Yeah, you're right, they do look like that."

"Maybe it's Ho Chi Minh's birthday or something."

"Dunno."

"Also, she's not packing any underwear."

"Wait a minute, I thought you said you've been swamped all night?"

"I'm never that swamped. I've seen Anita wear the same outfit just about every night for two months. And, she always wears a bra like any well behaved little Catholic girl from Biddleford, Maine."

"But how do you know about ..."

"Watch when she bends over."

"Okay, so tonight she lets loose."

"Yeah, and the question old buddy is why? She's not displaying her charms for Jesse's sake. Well, what the fuck, maybe it's a full moon, maybe the grunion are running. Doesn't matter, she can wear whatever the hell she wants as long as she gets the drinks out."

"How're your fingers holding up buddy?"

"So–so. If Jeff doesn't get his ass here soon I'll be hurting."

"Let me know, I'll try to help out."

"Thanks, I think it'll be okay. I can't see them throbbing yet. Look, I'll try to be back soon."

"No problem."

Jesse is leaning against the sound booth. I give Jaime a sign to stay alert. Anita picks her way through the crowd, tray held aloft like a sloop dancing over a heavy sea.

"Hey Jesse, how about trying to keep your hands to yourself?"

"Hold on a minute there man. You can take those heavy vibes and go sit on them. What makes you think you can lay your head–trips on me?"

"Pay attention fuzzhead. I'll say this real slow so you'll have a shot at understanding. The waitresses are here to serve drinks, not to assist in your personal physical therapy program."

"You trying to tell me that I've been molesting somebody, man?"

"I'm not trying shit, buster. I'm telling you. What's more you're going to apologize."

"For what? I haven't done a thing. I'm not apologizing for nothing. I don't care what that little ..."

"Shut up, Jesse. I'm not giving you a choice. I've got a customer and three waitresses who saw you. Now either mellow out or get out."

Jaime strolls up behind me during our exchange. Jesse eyes him.

"Look honey, I didn't mean anything by it. I was just playing around. You know I don't mean no harm."

"You satisfied, Anita?"

"Sure, about the best you can expect from him."

"Well then, terrific." I shake my head and turn back toward the bar. At least that big lump Jaime finally earned his pay.

"Richard! … Richard! … C'mere for a minute. I want you to meet someone."

I whirl around trying to track down the voice. I've got no sense of direction at all.

"Oh, it's you Evening Sky, what's up?"

"I want you to meet a real close friend of mine down from Humboldt County. Richard, this here is Rainbow Cloud. I've been telling her what a nice guy you are, even if you do manage a bar."

I'm supposed to be an educated person. I've even read some Heidegger. How can I possibly stand here, straight faced when I'm introduced to a woman with an ersatz Indian name like Rainbow Cloud? And, what's even more bizarre, I'm being introduced to young Rainbow Cloud by my good friend Evening Sky. She's making a special point of doing this. It's her way of showing she likes me, that my karma is correct. I'm twenty–seven years old and I'm playing Indians with two women who are probably named Jill Smith and Amy Tannenbaum. The point is I don't find anything peculiar about it, except perhaps for the way old Laughing Waters smells. I could say, 'Grow up kids', but why bother? Women up here pierce their noses and smell like manure. If they want to change their names, stop shaving their legs and wear plates in their lips, that's okay by me. I think it's meaningless and mostly a turnoff, but why the hell not? What harm does it do?

"I know how guilty you must feel selling this stuff, Richard."

"It's a job."

"You can't fool me. I know you feel it inside. You don't like being a poisoner. It's a shame the way this country forces someone like you to do this kind of thing."

"Yeah, a real shame … Look I'm sorry but I've really got to run. Uh, nice meeting you sweetheart, maybe I'll see you around later on."

I will not feel guilty. I will not feel guilty. Why am I always besieged by surrogate mothers? So people get drunk and puke, or maybe drive off the road. That's the way it goes. I'll take whatever responsibility's involved but I won't pretend to feel evil. Maybe I just don't care. I'm not even sure anymore. Who knows what the answers are? But I wish these women would join the local chapter of Mother's Anonymous and leave me alone.

A swarm of drunks are gesturing wildly at the bar.

"Sorry to take so long, buddy," I shout amidst orders for separators and tequila sunrises.

"No problem."

I can depend on Johnny not to give me any grief. That little twerp Chacko would have had at least two shit fits by now.

"Yeah yeah, I hear you, just wait one damn minute." I lean over and scoop up the phone.

"River Grove."

"Richard, Richard Davis."

"Speaking."

"This is George, how's the old sausage?"

"Georgie, good to hear you buddy. How're things back in Maine?"

"I said Richard, oh Richard, how's your sausage Richard?"

Uh oh, George is wasted again.

"Have you seen Megan? Is she still ..."

"Richard, put your sausage on the phone. I wanna talk to your sausage."

"George, why don't you hang up and go to bed."

"Listen Richard, it's important."

"What is George?"

"What I have to say to your sausage."

"George, I'm hanging up now. I have to go."

"No, no, no ..."

I hang up. He won't remember. Might as well save him some money.

"Guess who that was Johnny."

"Ethel Merman."

"Close, it was George."

"What's happening with him?"

"He was shit–faced."

"What was he mumbling about this time?"

"Nothing."

"C'mon buddy."

"He wanted to talk to my sausage."

"Oh yeah, did you let him?"

"My sausage was not receiving calls."

"George is gonna kill himself."

"Wonder if he's still working at my old job?"

"Sure, as long as he can keep his hands from shaking."

"Damn, the band's coming back."

"You gotta do something about them, Richard. Talk to Lydia."

"Yeah, I know, they really eat it, more like something you'd expect at a high school prom."

"High school prom nothing. Listen to that drummer. She can't even keep a beat."

"Well …"

"She's paid to do better than fifty percent of the time. I thought they only had bands as bad as this back in Maine."

"Yeah, okay Johnny, but what's the difference? You don't like any of the bands that play here."

"I liked that band last month, you know the one with the black woman."

"Who?"

"That little black woman with the accordion."

"Oh, the zydeco band from Oregon."

"Huh?"

"Zydeco, you know, polka rock."

"Yeah, that's the one. You should book them back."

"What do you care? You wear those earplugs most of the time."

"You think I want to end up like you?"

"What?"

"I said, 'Do you think I want to end up deaf like you?'"

"What did you say?"

"I said … screw this routine. Go take care of the consumers."

"Can I help you, sir?" A tourist for sure, probably up from the city.

"Have any cognac?"

"Martell, Couvoisier, Remy Martin."

"I'll have some of the Remy. What goes good with that besides coke?"

"Beats me."

"Well, better make it a Remy and coke then."

"Hey Johnny!"

"Yo."

"Can you set me up a Remy Martin and coke."

"Sure, right after I finish making this Chivas Regal and cream soda."

Hm, poor guy seems to have split. Maybe I should hold off on that drink ... Damn, the phone again. I scrooch down beneath the bar, put a finger in one ear and shove the receiver against the other.

"River Grove."

"Hello?"

"River Grove."

"What? I can't hear you. Is this the River Grove?"

"You'll have to speak louder."

"Who's playing out there tonight?"

"Look, I still can't hear you, the music's too loud."

"All I want to know is the name of the band."

"Two dollars cover."

"No, the band, the name of the band."

I hang up. My ear is throbbing. A thing like that could go on all night. I unplug the phone. Fuck the information service.

"Hey, Richard!"

"I'm busy, Jesse."

"You know what, man?"

"I said I was busy."

"I've fucked your girlfriend, man."

"Sure."

"You ask Dusty, man, go ahead, see what she says."

Dusty. I thought for a minute he was talking about Susan. He probably has fucked Dusty. There's not too many people on the river who haven't.

"You have my blessings."

"Huh?"

"I said, 'Good for you,' now scram."

"You don't understand man. I said, 'I fucked your girlfriend.'"

"Listen Jesse, get out of my sight."

"Hey man, does it bother you, man? Don't you like having me screw her, man?"

"I don't mind, Jesse, but if I catch you humping my dog again I'll bash your face in."

"What are you talking about man, you don't have no dog."

"That's the only reason you didn't hump her. Now get the fuck out of my face."

"Okay man, I hear you. No reason to get so heavy, I mean it's only some dumb cunt."

Maybe he'll cut his lip on a beer can and develop lockjaw. Maybe I could pay his brother to run his motorcycle over him. It'd be consistent with that Dennis Hopper image of his. Susan's right, dealing with these derelicts is no way to live.

"Johnny, I'll be back in a little. I have to talk to Polly."

Couldn't have lasted another five minutes in there. I've got to find some other way to make money. I carry a rocks glass of Southern Comfort across the small hotel lobby and knock on the office door. Time to build alliances. Polly screams to come in. She's on the phone. I wait in the kitchen idly scanning the walls. One wall is covered with a collage–like display of woman's movement material. Polly is very concerned about being her own woman. She even wears Wonder Woman t–shirts while cleaning the hotel rooms. She's divorced and undergoing a permanent identity crisis. Meanwhile her twelve year old son is going down the tubes. Arnold hangs out at the Coop, chain smokes cigarettes, drinks, does dope, but he's only a kid. Polly's decided to disown him. Refuses to give him any more time or attention. She says she has to start thinking of herself, her own needs. I don't say anything. I like Polly. She's a really nice lady, but what the hell is she talking about? Sometimes I think she's waiting for a shower of romantic love to descend on her as gently as a soft spring rain. What a complete waste. I wish she'd forget about her crises and get on with her life.

"Sorry to keep you waiting, Richard. Some woman called up about the suite and I had to go on and on about it."

"You rent it?"

"Don't know, she's supposed to call back. Doesn't matter, I can always rent the suite."

"Where do people come up with all that dough?"

"Haven't the slightest. For all I know they're pimps and dope dealers. Is that for me?"

"Yeah, a bit of petty largesse."

"Is this on Mike and Lydia?"

"No, it's on my own hook."

"You shouldn't bother. Look at the way they're squeezing me."

"How's the lease coming?"

"It's not. Mike's trying to ease me out."

"How come?"

"Now that I've built up the hotel he wants to cash in on it."

"What, with Lydia managing it?"

"So what do you want, Richard?"

"Who me?"

"Look I don't mind, but you're not the visiting type."

"Okay, it's Nick."

"What's he up to now?"

"He still has his keys doesn't he?"

"Uh huh."

"He's pushing it too far, Polly. It's not the liquor so much as the glassware. He's ripping off cases."

"That shithead. He's supposed to be your friend."

"Yeah, well there was this tacit understanding and he's broken it."

"I'll talk to him."

"Thanks, Pol."

"Are you okay, Richard? You look sorta beat."

"Fine."

"It's Susan isn't it? When she leaving?"

"A month."

"Aren't you going to do anything about it?"

"Nope."

"Don't be such a fool, Richard."

"There's nothing to do. I'm just going to have to deal with it."

"You act like it doesn't matter."

"Let me tell you a story, Polly. When I was about twenty I fell completely in love with a wonderful girl. Things were up and down for a couple of years. Then I was living in Europe, writing to her, and she writes asking me to come back, saying that we can meet at my sister's wedding and talk things over. So I flew in from London. Everyone thought I was being such a good brother but I knew I was coming in to see her, the wedding was just an excuse. There I was on that plane and I knew she was going to leave me hanging. And sure enough she did, she didn't show. So I call her up and we talk and we talk. Finally I say, 'Okay Lisa, the next move's yours. You want to see me again, you'll have to do the dialing.'"

"What happened?"

"I never heard from her again."

"But, Richard ..."

"Sure I wanted to call her, but I got over it. After three years I hardly thought of her."

"I couldn't do that."

"Yeah ... So what's happening with you? I haven't seen Tim around recently."

"That's finished. I've got a real gentleman looking after me now."

"Anyone I know?"

"Promise not to say anything?"

"Sure."

"It's the Sergeant."

"But he's ..."

"I know, married and Catholic, but very sweet. He brings me flowers and reads me poetry."

"You're kidding."

"What's wrong with that?"

"Nothing, Polly, I'm just surprised. He doesn't seem the type. Look, don't let yourself get hurt again."

"I can take care of myself."

"Well, come and see me if there's a problem."

"Thanks, Richard."

I give Polly a quick hug and leave. The lobby looks awfully inviting; dark, big comfortable chairs, even a fire. The evenings are always chilly here, summer or no summer. Nope, gotta be an adult. Besides I can't just desert Johnny.

"Well hello Jeff, so nice of you to drop by. Did you just get here? I certainly hope it wasn't too inconvenient for you."

"Hey man, I'm really sorry I'm late. I was at this wicked party up in the hills. But listen man, even though I was dancing with this really foxy little lady and smoking a dube, I was still thinking, 'Hey, I've gotta go, gotta get to work.' It's not like I was trying to shine you on or anything. Believe me man, I was thinking of you, but see this Nancy girl, she kept wanting me to dance some more and I thought, 'Hell, why not smoke one more number before I go?' That's the truth man. The time just sorta got away. But I didn't want you getting all uptight about it. I mean, I'm your friend, man."

"Me, upset? Why would I possibly be upset? What's a couple of hours between buddies. I mean you're my friend, man. It's not even last call yet."

"That's really beautiful, Richard. Here I thought you'd be bummed out or something. But you're being totally mellow about the whole thing. That's nice man, I can really dig where you're coming from."

"Thanks Jeff. Now do you think you could maybe get behind the bar and wash a few glasses?"

"Sure man, don't worry. I've got it covered."

So much for the power of sarcasm. I'd better save that for the East Coast where people aren't dead from the neck up. Uh oh, Johnny looks like he's ready to stuff Florinda's cocktail tray down her throat.

"Take a break Johnny, I'll handle things for a while."

He walks off discussing the merits of euthanasia in a low muttering tone. Florinda reappears. I give her my warmest, most sincere smile.

"Oh hi Richard, where's Johnny?"

"On break."

She puts her tray on the bar then leans forward to make herself heard over the music.

"One scotch and soda, two ..."

"Hold it Florinda, can't you see there's a couple of people in front of you?"

I mix five drinks.

"I want one ..."

"In a minute Florinda."

I deliver the drinks, ring up the money, return the change. I wipe my hands on a bar towel and look up at Florinda. She's mumbling the drinks to herself, writing them down, trying to remember who ordered what. I wait for her concentration to peak.

"Okay Florinda, I'm waiting. I don't have all day ya know."

Hatred pours out of her eyes. I respond with my most congenial smile.

"One scotch and soda, two bourbon rocks, gin and tonic, Tanqueray and tonic, two shots of gold, two separators, one pina colada, two Heine lights, one dark, two Buds and a draft."

I put a draft in front of her. "Okay Florinda I got the draft. What else was there? ... Oh gee Florinda, you have a really interesting little vein right in the middle of your forehead. Don't think I ever noticed it before. Look at the way it's throbbing to the beat of the music. That's really neat Florinda, what else can you make it do?"

She slams down her drink order and goes off to sulk in the lobby bathroom. Johnny's caught the tail end of the performance.

"What's the matter with her, Richard?"

"She's got a turd in her pocket."

"Warren Beatty?"

"McCabe and Mrs. Miller."

"Thanks for the help, buddy."

"You know Johnny, she didn't use to be this bad."

"Uh huh."

"Look you gotta admit she has a pretty nice ass."

"It's not her ass I have to deal with."

"Okay, I know I should fire her and Chacko, even that worthless Jaime at the door. I should fire Lydia too, but she owns the goddam place. I hate firing people, even the jerk–offs who deserve it. It's just not in me."

"Look Richard, they don't give a fuck about you."

"Yeah, I know that … Maybe they'll quit."

"Fat chance."

"Well maybe Florinda'll sprain her mouth at one of those women's rituals she goes on."

"Say what?"

"Didn't she ever tell you? Remember last Friday when Susan worked for her? Well, she was off conducting a ritual, some sort of mystic, earth mothering, touching souls with your sister experience. That little harpy, Victoria Windsong, runs them."

"Who?"

"Florinda's mentor?"

"Mentor?"

"That's the word Florinda uses. I'm giving you an exact quote."

"I still don't know who you're talking about."

"I know you've seen her around. About the same size as Florinda only wider, dark hair, long nose; looks like a witch. You know, the one with the herb shop who always seems to be conducting workshops at fifty bucks a whack. She must be raking in the old moola with that holistic song and dance of hers. I don't trust that douche bag at all. I bet she really leads a double life. Probably rents an apartment in East Oakland so she can eat fluffernutter sandwiches and watch General Hospital."

"Well, what are these things, these whatchamacallits?"

"Listen Johnny, I really don't pay much attention when Florinda opens her mouth. I just smile and think about ramming a pole up her ass … Okay, they probably roast ox pizzles and then roll around on the ground. It helps open up their bodies to the mother goddess."

Hm, I wonder what screwing old Florinda would be like. Probably hokey as hell. I bet she'd expect you to talk. Christ, I hate people who babble in bed. If you're enjoying it, you shouldn't want to do anymore than grunt. If you're not enjoying it you should just get up and leave. Well it might not be so bad if she'd agree to be gagged. Yeah, she might actually be into that.

"Hey pal, would you mind barfing outside and not in our trash can?"

Fucking 'A' surreal. What a way to earn a buck. Thank God there's only an hour and a half left.

"Richard?"

"Hey Wren, what can I get you?"

"No Richard, c'mere. I've got to tell you something. It's private."

"What's up?"

She leans close to me.

"I've just been in the ladies room."

"Oh, good for you."

"No you don't understand. Someone's taken a big crap in there."

"Those things happen."

"But it's on the toilet seat, right on top of the cover."

I stare.

"I thought you'd want to know. I mean you'll want to do something about it. You will won't you? That's your job, isn't it?"

I nod my head. Do, sure I'll do something. I'll stand here and pretend that I don't understand a word she's said. It's Gary's turn to clean the bathrooms tomorrow. It'll keep till then ... Uh oh, Lydia's steaming up to the bar. I wonder who told her about the turd?

"Richard ..."

"Yo Lydia, here you go, a glass of white wine."

"Thanks, but it's Jesse."

"No, it couldn't have been."

"Well I think you should do something about him. He's been standing in front of that bass player."

"Has he opened ..."

"He still has his pants on, but I think you'd better hurry."

I leave Lydia standing by the bar, waving her hands, and motion to Jaime. Jesse is standing about a foot away from the bass player staring straight at her crotch.

"I'm gonna bite right through that denim. I'm gonna teach you all you need to know about rhythm, you fat little slut."

She looks nervous. Can't blame her. Jesse doesn't just mouth off. I hook one arm, Jaime takes the other. We lift, walk across the dance floor and deposit him outside, very hard.

"Say goodnight Jesse or we arrange a nice chat with the deputies."

"Lighten up man, I wasn't doing anything."

"Tomorrow, Jesse."

I watch him hobble off. I should just ban his ass from the Grove. We go through this routine maybe twice a week. Makes you want to believe in euthanasia.

***

"Nice job, Richard."

"Yeah Johnny, like putting out the garbage."

"Oh, the guy down at the end of the bar was asking after you."

"Who's he supposed to be?"

"Dunno, claims he knows you."

"I'd better go down and see what his problem is."

"Hey there Richard, how ya doin' old boy?"

"Fine, what's new?"

He holds out his hand. I'm supposed to remember who this gopher is? What sort of memory does he think I have; random access, 18Kb C.P.U. with optional floppy disc?

Here comes the tricky part. What sort of handshake is he expecting; the standard firm pump, a brotherhood grasp, or a funky official N.B.A. slap? You guess wrong, you end up flailing about like a wrestler looking for a hold.

"It's Grant, Nick's friend. I could see you were having problems remembering."

"Sure, I heard you quit down at the Inn. You still bartending?"

"No, real estate, I'm selling real estate. Just a minute and I'll give you my card."

Christ, does everyone in California become a certified agent at birth? Who can they possibly be peddling the stuff to, each other?

"Still drinking Heineken?"

"There's a bartender for you, can't remember my name, only what I drink."

"Have one on me … How's it feel getting out of the bar business?"

"I don't miss it. Last week I worked at the Inn I took five stitches."

"Difference of opinion?"

"Yeah, some joker didn't think it should be last call."

"I'll tell Nick you stopped by."

"Where is that slimy bastard? I thought I could take him in a quick game of liar's dice."

"Last time I thought I could do that I lost fifty bucks. Nick's been gone a couple of days."

"He still going with the same honey?"

"You mean Linda? Nah, she dumped him."

"She didn't look that smart."

"They surprise you some time."

"So, she go off with another guy?"

"Nah, left for L.A. with another woman."

"You're shittin' me."

"I know, hit old Nickie where he lives."

"His balls must have shrunk an inch."

"Yeah, and most people think brass can't shrivel. Look, I'll catch you later."

It's close. I get through this set, holler last call, count the receipts and breeze home by two–thirty. All I want to do is get some heavy duty sleep and try to forget about Susan. I don't think I'm gonna take her leaving real well. My goddam insides feel like they're being pushed through a cheese shredder.

"Almost over Johnny. How have you been getting along with Florinda? Ask her out on a date yet?"

"You know Richard, when I heard that Frank and her were getting it on I couldn't believe it. She'd been bad mouthing him for months."

"Way before you came."

"Can't last. Florinda makes damn sure you know how artistic and talented she is. What can she see in a dumb fuck like Frank?"

"An orgasm. Besides, she's not so goddam bright herself."

"What do you mean?"

"Well don't tell anyone, I mean besides Jeannie. This is supposed to be confidential and all that crap, but it's too good not to repeat."

"So what's the dirt, buddy?"

"Remember when Florinda was out a couple of months ago?"

"Uh huh."

"She had an uterine infection."

"So?"

"So it was caused by her I.U.D."

"I don't follow."

"She kept the damn thing in for ten years and it dissolved on her."

"Hee, hee, hee."

"There's more, Johnny. Remember that article in Mother Jones about the Dalkon Shield? Well, that's what it was. Florinda kept one stuck up her wazoo until it finally disintegrated."

"What a bimbo. Wait until Jeannie hears about this."

"And you know that line she hands out about being a great poet with a deep sensitive soul?"

"How could I avoid hearing it?"

"Did you ever read one of her poems?"

"Uh uh."

"Hold on. I've got a copy here somewhere."

"Where'd it come from?"

"From Florinda, she gave it to me."

"Why'd she want to do that?"

"We used to be on pretty good terms, all buddy–buddy when I first started working here. Well one night after work we were sitting, talking in front of the lobby fireplace. Had quite a nice blaze going that night."

"You weren't uh …"

"Fucking around? Nah, not really. She was living with what's his name? You know, that guy with the bandanna; the one who always tangos to rock music in his bare feet."

"Temple?"

"Yeah, Temple, another supposedly great artistic soul. Anyway, she wasn't so obnoxious back then, not out of control like she is now. I thought she was kind of attractive."

"Florinda?"

"My taste tends to get quirky sometimes. So we were just mostly talking and she asked me if I'd like to have one of her poems. What else could I say?"

"How was it?"

"Here, make up your own mind."

Staring into the depths of my vacuous soul
I see the outline of my lover
gleaming blood red in the silence of a dusky nightfall.
Spinning, as water turns, bouncing obliquely
off impediments in its progress,
I unfold my wings only to hear the filaments
creak in protest at unwatched rapture.
In such a sea dark night
no caresses by my lover's side
fills the longing which drops ever
yearning at the trembling precipice of my
sleek black, tormented, desire engendering
loins.

"Phew, that's awful buddy."

"No, not just awful."

"A no talent epic."

"Try listening, straight–faced, to Florinda recite it at three in the morning."

"Pretty brutal. I was always suspicious of Florinda's artsy fartsy talk."

"She has all the sensitivity of a Portuguese panderer."

"Portuguese?"

"Yeah, but she does have a nice ass, Johnny."

"Has to be her only redeeming feature."

"Don't know that it rightly redeems her."

"Isn't that Sheila's old man down there trying to get your attention?"

"You gotta be shittin' me. Barry, goddam Bicycle Barry is Sheila's old man?"

"Where'd he get that name?"

"Something to do with his sexual preferences. I'd better go down and see what he's after. Has to be some angle."

If he thinks he's going to pressure me into hiring his slut of a girlfriend ...

"You the manager here, right?"

"That's what I'm told."

"Listen man, are you or aren't you?"

"Okay, I'm the manager."

"And you know who I am?"

"I've heard."

"Did you hear I got some pretty heavy connections."

"So?"

"So you do me a favor, I do you one. You follow?"

"I'm keeping up with you so far."

"You pour a Tanqueray and tonic and I give you a buck. I got some nice sensei coming in next week."

"It'll run you one–fifty."

"Hey man, I said a buck. C'mon, you like a little smoke. It'll make your old lady happy."

"One–fifty."

"Look, I've seen you eyeing my old lady before. Well, Sheila gives really great ..."

"One–fifty."

"What the fuck's the matter with you? Can't you hear? I said a buck. Your record broken? Can't you say anything but one–fifty?"

"Yeah, get the hell out of my sight."

"Big mouth son of a bitch, aren't you? Well, you can't talk that way to me, man."

"It's easy, Jack. Now either move yourself out of here or get moved."

"Who's gonna do that for you, man?"

"Why those two nice deputies behind you."

"Barry causing you any trouble, Richard?"

"Who me? No man, I was just leaving. I'm not causing any hassles. I don't go looking for no trouble."

"Okay with you, Richard?"

"Just as long as he leaves, Sergeant."

We watch Bruce head for the door.

"You want to make sure he doesn't hurt himself, Bob."

The other deputy trails after Bruce.

"Coffee Sergeant?"

"Cream and sugar."

"Anything happening out there?"

"Some trouble down at the Pink."

"Anyone I know?"

"Jesse bit some biker on the nose."

"Nice to hear he's keeping busy. Much of him left?"

"We moved in pretty quick. He'll be walking by the end of the week. Heard he was causing a ruckus in here."

"Yeah, we tossed him out. Started pulling down his pants again."

"Bad for business."

"Ask anyone on the River. It's a complete turn–off."

"Is it true …"

"About the ribbon? Nah, he stopped wearing that."

"Gift wrapping didn't make it, either?"

"Doesn't look that way."

I wonder if he knows Polly once screwed around with Jesse. Maybe the sergeant wouldn't be quite so keen to follow down that path. Polly's a damn fool, he'll never leave his wife.

"Thanks for the coffee."

"Anytime, appreciate the help."

"It's my job."

"By the way, Sergeant."

"Yeah?"

"Polly's a good woman."

"I know that."

"Well, take care."

First time I think I've ever seen that guy blush. Maybe he does read poetry.

I glance over at the clock and give Johnny the high sign as the band grinds up their last number.

"Hokay boys and girls it's last call. Buy it now or pack it in."

"Rock and roll, rock and roll!"

A band this bad and some drunk is yelling for more. Being fucked– up can't make them sound any better. This must be what's meant by mental torture. Well, I'm about ready to lose it. I guess I'll have to give up being a practicing stoic. Christ, you'd think the vocal cords on that bozo would snap like two overstretched rubber bands. No such luck. Just two more minutes and then I'm going to find out how much this professional dork likes having a bottle of Jim Beam shoved down his throat, blunt end first.

"Look Mac, the music's over. Why don't you hit the road?"

"You talking to me, man?"

"Is there someone else sitting there?"

"I'm just having a good time, man."

"That's nice. Now it's time to go home. If you can't find it, Jaime there will give you a hand."

"That's all right, man. I can handle it alone."

"Hey, Jeff."

"You ready to roll man."

"Listen, I don't want you giving the band drinks while I'm out back."

"Even the chicks, man?"

"If I catch you, you'll be out on your ass but quick. Got it?"

"Don't sweat it, man. No one gets drinks."

"Buddy, I'm cashed out."

"Okay, I'll be back there in a minute, Johnny."

I give Jaime a nod.

"Time to rap it up everyone, closing time … hotel–motel time, my friends. You don't have to go home but you can't stay here."

Drinks are slowly finished, glasses picked up, people herded out the doors leaving a backwash of debris.

"Can I have a damp rag?"

"Sure Anita, catch. Let me have your bank when you're ready."

Damn, some woman's pestering Jeff at the bar.

"Is there a problem here, Jeff?"

"There sure in hell is. Your bartender won't give me a drink."

"I'm sorry but last call's been given."

"Well there's no tequila in this margarita."

I love it when some drunk calls me a crook. All she has to be is a little bit nice and say the drink doesn't taste quite right. Instead she starts screaming like I've just tried to pick her pocket.

"Did it take you half a drink before you noticed?"

"You don't have to be so snotty. All I want is a decent drink."

"That's what you got right there in your grubby little paw."

"I want to talk to the manager ... And I want to talk to him right now."

"Okay sweetheart, talk."

"Listen smart mouth, you can't treat me like this. I'll have your job."

"Believe me lady, you wouldn't like it. The hours are terrible ... Here, you want some more, I'll give you some more."

I upend a bottle of tequila; fill her glass, then watch as it runs over and onto the bar."

"Satisfied yet, lady?"

"Well you are the rudest ..."

"Why don't you just crank it up your wazoo lady?"

I've gotta get some time off soon, maybe starting now. Two months ago I wouldn't have done that. But back then I wasn't muttering to myself at the end of the night. Good thing that bitch didn't have some gorilla trailing after her. One day my face is going to be permanently rearranged, free of charge.

"So this guy comes in here wanting nothing more than to get himself laid. He pays two bucks at the door. After buying at least ten drinks for as many different women and chugging six Buds himself he has nothing else to look forward to the next morning but a hangover and thirty fewer bucks. So here it is two o'clock, people straggling or being shoved out the door. This poor jerk is standing there faced with certain failure when a thought somehow creeps into his little beer sodden brain."

"There's always the cocktail waitress."

"You got it, Anita. If worse comes to worse, there's always the cocktail waitress, those lumpen proletariat of the sexual reserve army."

"Hey Lila, can I have your bank?"

"I haven't counted it out Richard. I'll give it to you in ten minutes."

"No problem sweetheart. I'll be in the back room."

"Anyway there I am after elbowing my way through this crowd

for five hours, hair plastered to my forehead and smelling like a cheap brewery. While I'm scrubbing down these sticky tabletops and picking crap off the floor, this yo–yo comes up, fixes me with a drunken romantic stare and says ..."

"You know, you remind me exactly of my mother."

"You too, huh?"

"Tried it on me last week."

"Unbelievable."

I automatically give the service door a shove with my foot. Nothing. The door doesn't budge. Some gopher has got his back shoved up against it. That hitch–hiking keyboard player is talking to someone in there.

"No sheet, so y'all come from Louisiana too?"

"Sho do."

"Learned to play down there in the clubs."

"Well, I sho do admire the way you play."

"Yah do?"

I don't need this. They're taking far too long to reach a predictable conclusion. No one guaranteed that he'd be able to sweet talk some little bimbo in private. Let him check the contract. If anyone's going to hump back there it's going to be me. But right now business comes first. I rap hard on the door. No response. I try again. He has no intention of breaking his concentration. Should try taking his music half as seriously. Okay, so much for the warning shots. I give the door a vicious shove. The knob grinds into his right kidney. I think that caught his attention. He shuffles aside and I push through. The girl stares at me bewildered. She wasn't expecting a commercial break to enter into her true life romance.

"Band needs you to pack up. Tell Ray I'll have your money in about half an hour."

The keyboard player meets my smile with narrowed eyes. He takes one step forward but then remembers about the cash. Greed outweighs other considerations. Instead, he settles for aiming cancerous psychic vibrations at my balls. I'm not about to lose any sleep over that. Too many other problems are already waiting patiently in line by my bedside.

"Old busy fingers and his southern belle still romancing out there."

"I suggested that they relocate down to the levee."

"You is one hard man, Richard."

"Sure Johnny, a real son of a bitch. Here, I brought you a beer."

"Thanks buddy. I'm all done. Bank checks out. I did four and a quarter."

"Here, count out the tips and I'll whip through my register."

"What's this, the March of Dimes?"

"We'll be lucky to clear four bucks a piece. Just give me a few minutes to count this out ... Yah, who is it?"

"Richard, it's me Florinda?"

I get up to open the door and send rows of quarters flying.

"You have your bank Florinda?"

"Richard, you know I have a bad back."

"Huh?"

"I can't lift those heavy upholstered chairs."

"Get Jaime to help you."

"Jaime won't do it, claims it's not his job."

"What's wrong with your back?"

"I've got a weak disc. You know that, Richard."

"Yeah, so what happened, did you hurt it dancing out there tonight? Maybe you should give it a rest."

"It's not dancing that's the problem. I just can't lift heavy objects."

"Florinda, if you can spend half the night squirming on the dance floor, then you're sure as hell gonna spend the remainder trying to do your job. Now get back out there and clean up your station."

"I do my job, Richard. But I'm not going to deliberately sprain my back. Not for you and not for this place."

"Listen sweetheart, there's four of you out there. Do you think maybe if you, Anita, Lila, and Jaime each grab a leg and heave at the same time you could get the goddam chairs up on the goddam tables?"

"Well, you don't have to be so mean about it."

The door slams. Johnny looks over.

"Hold on, Richard. Come on buddy, uncross those eyes. It's not important. Don't let it get to you like that."

"First I'm going to tie her down. Then ..."

"That's Jeff shouting for you, buddy. Go on, see what he wants."

This time I plow into a pile of dollar bills as I open the door.

"Richard, pick up the phone. Young lady wants to talk to you."

"Hokay, I got it."

I hear the clunk of a receiver being cradled roughly in place. I wonder who plugged in the bar phone? I wonder why the phone didn't ring out here.

"Hi Richard."

"Shelly, how ya doin' sweetie?"

"Look Richard, uh, would you like to come over?"

"Okay."

"Are you sure, you're not too tired or anything?"

"No, everything's fine."

"Well, when can you get here?"

"Let me see; finish balancing the registers, security check, drive over. Um, it's after two now, say three or maybe quarter after."

Christ, I sound like a dentist making an appointment with a patient.

"Good."

"See you then Shelly."

"Oh Richard?"

"Uh huh."

"Do you think, well, would it be alright, if you, uh, brought over some wine. It wouldn't be too much trouble or anything?"

Shelly always regresses into a teensy little girl's voice to ask favors. It's not winsome or appealing. It's pathetic. Wonder if she realizes it?

"Sure sweetie."

"Thanks, Richard."

An auto mechanic, more like an auto mechanic. Adjust the carburetor, change the points, lube and oil. Terrific, I'm starting to think of myself as an all night service station. Well I may be alienated, but at least I still own the means of production.

Good thing Shelly only expects me to hump her. I'm too bushed to talk and hump at the same time. Katherine, now Katherine wanted me to say things like, 'I love it when you suck my cock.' Tacky, molto tacky. Sounds like dialogue from a cheap smoker. That girl was so verbal, she dribbled. Nm, nm, nm. She just couldn't stop flapping that mouth of hers. When I fuck I fuck, when I talk I talk. There's no need to keep up a running commentary like some fifth rate Howard Cosell. A few grunts or an occasional moan but not, 'Do you like it when I shove my finger up your ass?'

"You're gonna wear yourself out that way, buddy."

"I'm doing okay."

"Give up the twenty–four hour service and get married."

"Yeah, I could ask Susan again and be rejected."

"It doesn't have to be Susan."

"What if I told you it didn't have to be Jeannie?"

A key turns in the lock. The door flies open sending me sprawling into the small change.

"Richard, how'd we do tonight?"

Like a microphone ready to record, Lydia wobbles in and parks her groin about half an inch away from my face. I think she's starting to wear out that tape.

"Just shy of a thousand."

"That's good isn't it, for a Wednesday night?"

"Yeah Lydia, that's good."

"Mike'll be pleased."

"I imagine so."

She sways unsteadily, scattering money like a four year old run amok in a monopoly set. Good thing I'm not her type. Otherwise she'd try to do more than just sit on my face standing up.

"I'll see you tomorrow," I say walking her to the door. I pat her on the shoulder and she smiles back, eager to please. At forty, she's still playing daddy's precious darling to each and every available male.

"Richard, Mike and I really appreciate the job you're doing here." She gives me a demure peck on the cheek and slowly makes her way out of the bar.

They should be satisfied. How often can you find a sap willing to work eighty hours a week for two bills. Especially someone who isn't intent on fleecing two professional victims like Mike and Lydia.

"Oh Lydia, dear Lydia, Lydia the tattooed lady."

"What's that you're mumbling, Richard?"

"Just an old song, Johnny. I remember seeing Groucho Marx skipping around a stage singing it."

"They're showing reruns of his show."

"You mean the one with the duck?"

"Yeah, Jeannie and I watch it when I get home."

"I remember watching the originals when I was a kid."

"You can't be that old."

"Johnny, I'm so old that the songs I danced to as a teenager are now being played on elevators … That wasn't a knock was it?"

"Sounds like."

"This can't be happening. There's no one out there left to knock."

"Keep quiet, maybe they'll go away."

"Hey bossman, open up."

It's that slimy toad Chacko. What damp hole did he crawl out of?

"Save it for the morning, Chacko."

"It only take a minute, mon. You all the time shining me on."

"I'm not trying to blow you off. I just don't want to be here all night."

"It's important mon, swear to God."

I deliberately kick the piles of quarters aside and open up. '

"Hey boss, when you gonna get us some raises? We can't keep working for these pigeon shit wages forever, mon. You gonna look after us or what?"

Maybe I should just pick him up and heave. Johnny sits stoically looking down at his beer. Chacko knows I hate being called Boss. He always makes sure I can hear the sneer in his voice when he says it. I'd sooner give Florinda a raise. The guy does fuck all. He should be thankful I don't can him altogether. Who else would hire such a classic California crybaby? The little rodent thinks the world exists to serve his ends. That's why he's whining now. Things aren't going exactly his way.

I reach down, select a stock expression, and plaster it on my face. "Well, Chacko old sport, I was talking about that to Mike and he said no raises. The place is barely making it as is."

"Don't give me that crap, mon. You should be fighting for us."

"Look, if you want to talk to Mike or the book–keeper go ahead. It's their signatures on your check."

That should shut down the little bugger. Mike's never around. Gary will automatically say no. Ebeneezer Scrooge seems to be his role model. Johnny hasn't said a word. Why should he? I got him a raise two weeks ago.

"I'm trying to be upfront with you mon, but you're just shitting on me. I've been working here twice as long as Johnny and he gets all the good nights."

"Well Chacko old pal, I know Johnny won't fuck me over. I don't see how I can say the same about you."

"Listen mon, I understand you wanting to help your friend, but you're not playing fair. Now you think you can insult me."

"All I'm saying is that I don't trust you, old buddy."

"What do you expect if you don't give me no trust? Like to like that's how it goes, mon."

"Nope, I can't see my way to letting you screw me over just to prove a point."

"Is that your last word, mon? Don't think I be afraid to talk to Mike."

"Just this, I've composed a little light verse in your honor Chacko old sport. I thought maybe you'd like to hear it."

"Sure boss."

"   'Oh do not say you're sorry
Or tell me tales of woe
You've never done a goddam thing
And your status will always be quo'
I think it has a nice lilt to it."

"So you're not going to get off your ass at all. You just be interested in trying to put me down."

"No Chacko, I'm not trying, I am putting you down. Now see if you can put yourself out of here."

"You talk real brave, mon. Well it not be like that for long. You see."

"What am I speaking, a foreign language? I said, 'Get the fuck outta here!'"

"I think you'd better go Chacko, it's been a rough night."

"Okay Johnny, I go but it not be ending here."

Chacko slams the door shut. As if I needed an additional excuse to call him an asshole.

"Nasty little asshole."

"Can him, Richard."

"Yeah, yeah … Do me a favor Johnny. See that everything's okay out by the bar. I don't want anyone copping a free drink, especially Chacko. I won't be much longer."

"Sure buddy."

Naturally as Johnny leaves, Anita slides past him. Has she been lurking outside the door or what?

"Are you busy, Richard?"

"Almost through. Why don't you grab a seat on that case while I finish counting."

"You count out the register on the floor?"

"No place else to do it."

"They could at least give you a desk."

"Okay, now what's the problem? I told Florinda to help with the chairs. She giving you any problems?"

"No, everything's done. C'mere a minute."

"Huh?"

"I've got something I wanna tell you. It's personal."

How could I be so dumb? That's the reason for the black pajamas. Well I'll have to duck. I don't want to hurt her feelings and she is my only decent waitress, but I've got Susan to worry about and Shelly's still waiting up for me. My life's complicated enough. And what about her old man? I've got nothing against him.

"Oh, did I tell you about your raise?"

"No, listen Richard, this is important. I want to give you something."

"Okay, what is it?"

Anita takes my left hand and tugs me toward her. Somehow I avoid all the rows of quarters. Well, here's the place to demonstrate a little of that famous self control. It's finally time for my moral rectitude to start shining through. Shouldn't be hard, I'm not even attracted to her. She's just a skinny little girl with crooked teeth. I've got enough problems as is. How do I expect to get some sleep if I carry on like this?

Anita puts her arms around my neck. So now's the time to duck, right? *Nah*, I say to myself squeezing her ass, *why bother*. My tongue pushes into her open mouth like a rotor rooter man faced with a balky drain.

"You make this gift all by yourself," I say coming up for air.

"Richard, you big dope, I've wanted you since that first day when I applied for a job."

"But Anita, I'm in love with Susan. I can't ..."

"Oh shut up and kiss me."

Funny how I always thought Anita was sort of scrawny. Seems to be enough here to keep me occupied. Christ, is Anita trying to crawl down my throat? If she keeps this up I'm gonna come in my pants. I move her onto the floor for greater comfort.

"No Richard, not here on the floor. That's not the way I want it."

"Sorry, I just got carried away." Once I start gunning the old engine I have all the inhibitions of a dog on Main Street.

"No I want to, but later. I'll figure something out."

"Wait a minute, Dennis, what about ..."

"I can take care of Dennis. Stop worrying."

"No, I can't do this. You don't understand. I love Susan. This just isn't right."

"I don't care."

Richard Davis you are one weak person ... Oh Jesus Christ she better stop rubbing against me like that ... I tense up, but it's no use.

"Are you okay, Richard? What happened?"

"I'm fine."

"No tell me."

"Hey Buddy I'm taking off."

"Hold on a minute Johnny, I'll be right out ... Look Anita we've got to be careful. Just hang on and I'll figure something out."

"I told you not to worry about Dennis, I can take care of him."

"You've got a really nice ass, do you know that?"

"About time you noticed ... Gotta run. Here, I brought you a joint, Colombian. I'll catch you later ... Oh hi Johnny, Richard says he'll be right out."

"Be seeing you Anita … Okay buddy, the coast's clear."

"Thanks Johnny. You better be getting home. Jeannie's probably waiting up."

He eyes my pants.

"Don't do it, Richard."

"Yeah you're right but …"

"Remember what happened in Maine."

"Plus ça change."

"Huh?"

"French for, what the fuck's the difference?"

"Just think about it some more."

"Yeah, I'll try. Say hello to Jeannie for me."

More delays. I can't go see Shelly looking like this. I'll have to stop by my cabin, change my jeans, clean up some.

"Been having fun, my brother?"

What the fuck are Ray and the bimbos still doing here? Damn, I forgot to pay them. Meanwhile they're all eyeing the damp patch around my zipper.

"Here's your two bills Ray. Why don't you give Lydia a ring about another gig?"

"What about those drinks before we go?"

"I've got to get up early. No drinks, it's time to go home."

"Not so fast, my brother. Where are those drinks you promised?"

"What promise? You've got more than you deserve. Now clear out."

"Just some beers for the road, my brother."

"Can't do it. It's against the law."

"I'm not liking all this heavy shit, my brother."

"I'm not asking you to like it, Ray."

Nose to nose with Ray again. I'd be willing to give the sucker a beer if he promised to stop eating onions. Now it looks like the bass player is going to make her pitch. She shoves Ray aside and stands in front of me her tits barely grazing my chest, a definite improvement in smell.

"There's no need for you two to go snarling at each other. We're not trying to pressure you. We're just asking for a favor. It's such a long drive back to Mendocino. You'll do it for me, won't you cutie?"

Shameless. She really thinks a little sexual titillation and a big smile is going to change my mind. She thinks that just because I can feel her nipples stiffening it's going to make a difference.

"One quick round, but you've got to drink it here and it's gotta be quick. I have to be back at nine."

"All right Richard, there's my man."

Not hard winning Ray's everlasting friendship. The blond gives me another squeeze and winks. Forget about her. I'm already overbooked and late. I pour them some beers and wait, my finger drumming on the bar.

"Aren't you having anything?"

"No, I'm serious. I have to be here in the morning."

Let me see. I can still get over to Shelly's before four if I skip the shower and settle for a quick wipe. Can I wrap it up by four–thirty? Nah, no way I can make a decent showing in half an hour. Besides it takes her a good ten minutes to put in her diaphragm. You'd think she'd have it ready. It's not as if she doesn't know why I'm coming over. Still, I bet it won't be in. Okay say five, that means I set the alarm for eight–thirty and I can just make it. Three and a half lousy hours. I'm going to feel like a fucked–out piece of cheese tomorrow. Better let Shelly handle most of the wine drinking.

"Richard."

"What's up, Polly?"

"I think some people are in the hot tub again."

"I thought you bought a new lock for the gate."

"That doesn't stop them."

"Local?"

"Hard to tell in the dark."

"Okay, I'll take care of it."

"Thanks Richard, I knew I could count on you."

That's a little extra that no one ever mentioned when I agreed to this job. Well I can't expect Polly to do it and she is a friend.

"All right, you'll have to come out. Look, I know you're in there. This isn't a public bath tub. Either clear out or the cops can help you make up your mind."

I can barely see them getting out of the tub. Damn if I'll open the gate. Let them leave the same way they snuck in. Don't recognize any of them, must not be locals. Imported scum, as if we didn't have enough of our own. Actually one of the women does have a pretty nice ass.

"Richard?"

"Yo Polly."

"Is it okay?"

"Yeah, they're leaving."

"Come in and have a drink."

"Thanks Pol, but I have to scoot. I'll talk to you tomorrow."

***

I never can understand how I manage to drive from one place to the next. Rationally I know it's impossible. I should be dead. Like a bumble bee, I shouldn't be able to fly. I'm not only talking about driving drunk or stoned ... Damn, right by the turn off to Shelly's ... Couldn't even find a clean pair of pants. Maybe I should pay someone to do my laundry ... Maybe I should find the money to do that first.

I especially hate driving stoned. Should've waited to smoke Anita's present. Needed something, though, to calm down, too much adrenalin flowing. So here I am, going about five miles an hour, the front tires feeling like they're coming off, and the steering wheel starting to collapse. At least I'm not outright hallucinating. Haven't swerved to avoid hitting any imaginary hitchhikers, yet. Well, I'm not an ace under the best of conditions. I can never seem to concentrate. But somehow my foot still taps the brake, I continue to steer and check the rear view mirror. It's as if my hands were doing my thinking for me. Without good reflexes I'd be a dead issue.

Sometimes I wish I were back in Maine. Right now though, my only wish is that Shelly lived a lot closer to the Grove. Maybe I'll try speeding up to fifteen ... I don't know, this whole California routine of sincerity and niceness is starting to wear on my nerves. It's superficial, like something sprayed–on from an aerosol can. I'm tired of everyone being so insufferably hip. All I hear are people flapping their gums about getting in touch with their real selves. Who do they think's been signing their checks all these years? These beanheads are so concerned with being upfront and communicating their innermost feelings that they have no time to listen to anyone else. You know, I'm starting to get a real hankering for a little polite hypocrisy, even a touch of puritan repression would do; anything but a stream of self–conscious jabber about becoming centered. If only I could get elected governor, I would force every last far–out, new age person in this state to read the complete works of Jane Austen. Not too bad, five miles in twenty–five minutes. Wonder if Shelly's asleep? I can see lights. She must be waiting. Neighbors look like they're having guests, there's all these cars around.

"Come in."

What's with the chorus? This is supposed to be a solo gig. Damn, there's half a dozen people scattered in front of the fireplace. Who arranged for a reception committee? Don't people know enough to be in bed by four? They look like Shelly's painting group. And, everybody seems to be in a jolly old mood. Oh yucko!

"Richard, this is Bob, Carole, Alice, Lizard, Ted, and Charley."

Lizard? I must be hallucinating, she couldn't have said Lizard.

"Richard manages the Grove."

Here it comes, the usual standard putdowns—'Oh I never go to the Grove. It's too: 1) expensive 2) rowdy 3) tacky. All the bands are much too: 1) loud 2) top forty 3) funky.'

"So you manage the Grove."

"Uh huh."

"Do you enjoy doing that?"

"Nope."

"Then why are you doing it?"

"I get to work long hours."

"You like that?"

"Yeah, I'm masochistic."

I don't think I'm making a big hit with Shelly's friends. Well I don't give a good goddam. I'm not being paid to be glib with these people. If they don't like it, let them eat me. All I want is for them to clear out so I can fuck Shelly and grab a few hours sleep. I don't need to be admired by the local River artistes. If only I'm repulsive enough maybe Shelly'll catch the hint or they will or both. No problem acting repulsive, it's a natural talent.

"I haven't been to the Grove in years."

"Yeah?"

"They just won't book decent music anymore."

"A hah."

"You agree?"

"We book whatever people want. I have no personal preference."

"Isn't that blatantly commercial."

"That's right."

"And you can get behind that?"

"I'm running a business."

"You're also dealing with music."

"As part of a business."

"Doesn't that bother you?"

"What do you do?"

"I paint."

"And that keeps you in potatoes?"

"Well hardly, I have a private income."

"Stocks and bonds?"

"A mutual fund."

"What's in your portfolio?"

"I don't follow."

"Do they invest in stocks like Dow Chemical or maybe General Motors?"

"So?"

"Does it bother you that your income depends on military spending or investment in South Africa?"

"You don't have to be so deliberately snotty."

"No, I don't have to be."

"Well, I don't have to listen to this."

"That's right, you can leave."

"I most certainly will. Are you ready Alice? ... Shelly my dear, thank you. We will see you again when you're not so unfortunately occupied."

Everyone freezes as they make their exit. Bob's managed a dramatic little departure. The others stir, make their good–byes, and leave more quietly. A problem of critical mass; move one you move them all.

"You're impossible, Richard."

"I didn't see you trying to step in."

"Well, it doesn't matter. I wasn't expecting them. They just popped in."

"This late?"

"They're like me, they stay up all night."

"I didn't think I'd be able to roust them so easily."

"It's their artistic temperament."

"Artistic my ass."

"No, you're wrong, Richard. They do spend too much time pumping up their own egos, but they all have talent."

"Would you say that if they weren't paying you for lessons?"

"You know better than that, Richard."

"I'm sorry. I had a rough night."

"I thought you weren't coming."

"The band held me up."

"How were they?"

"Thirsty."

"No, how did they sound?"

"Terrible."

"That bad?"

"Yeah, that bad. They played something that sounded like chainsaw rock. You remember Ray, he's their lead singer. No, that's right, he was before your time; one of the local heroes who hung out at the Coop. I didn't recognize him without his brown bag beer. Looked like he even washed his tee shirt for the occasion."

"I thought you might've been distracted."

"You mean a little bit of the old in and out with some local floozie?"

Now where did that come from? Right, *A Clockwork Orange.* Fuck, can't even write my own dialogue anymore.

"It's possible, Richard."

"I don't operate that way."

"Well, you do have your little affairs."

"Maybe, but no one gets ditched and certainly not you."

"Sorry, I know that ... Can I get you a drink or maybe some dope?"

"Oh, I almost forgot, here's the wine you asked for."

Shelly takes it to the kitchen, yanks off the cork, pours one glass, starts to pour another.

"None for me, thanks."

"Mm, good wine."

"It's that White Zinfandel you like."

"Yummy, you sure you don't want some?"

"No, I've got to be up early. If it's all the same to you, I'll just have some of that dope you offered."

Warmth, I crave warmth. Living under those redwoods is affecting my internal thermostat. Given a chance, I'd toast myself unmercifully. I cram Shelly's fireplace full of wood, using up almost all her kindling. Soon the fire's crackling.

We both sit staring into the fire, Shelly sipping her wine, me puffing on a joint. How often do you really make contact with another person? I don't mean talking at them, processing them, or falling into some familiar routine. I'm thinking of those rare moments when you feel somehow connected. It's no different with sex, mostly it's just mutual masturbation.

"I'm sorry about your friends. I just wasn't feeling social."

"Do you ever?"

"Usually I'm not so rude, or at least not so obvious about being rude."

"It doesn't matter about tonight. But you worry me Richard, you're becoming more detached as you grow older."

"Maybe I'm slowly disintegrating. About the only advantage I've gained from growing old is paying less for car insurance."

"You're certainly in a cheerful mood tonight, aren't you sweetie?"

"I'm being realistic. Sometimes I think the only rational response to life is despair and that's hardly a brilliant outlook, is it? Shelly, I wish my life was like one of those magic slates I had as a child. I would just lift the plastic flap and send all my unpleasant memories into the ozone forever. I could start all over."

"Sweetie, you would just fuck it up again."

"Yeah but it would take some time. I'm tired of carting around all these meaningless memories. You know how much time I spend trying to make some sense out of them? What would I miss? It's not like I've ever learned a goddam thing from them. I am such a dope."

"Ooh, you poor baby."

"That just proves it. Now I'm getting melodramatic."

"You sure are sweetie, not to mention all those nifty little existential epigrams you keep rolling out."

"Yeah, existential; Molly's parting words to me."

"Who?"

"Oh, some little bimbo I knew. It was maybe the third of four breakups conducted over the phone like all the rest. You know, I really have a score to settle with that wimp, Alexander Graham Bell. It's so much easier to blow off a disembodied voice than to confront someone face to face. You don't even have to pretend you're interested in the scene you're creating … Anyway, she said she could no longer tolerate my insufferable existential nausea – And some people have the nerve to say education's a good thing – I'd just turned twenty–one at the time. I was stunned. I thought, 'How can I possibly defend myself?' I certainly couldn't claim to be a logical positivist. I went upstairs and looked in the mirror. Nope, nothing new from that quarter, at least nothing I could notice. Same sleepy eyes and expressionless face starring back at me. Perhaps I was missing something. People were probably whispering behind my back, 'Richard Davis wears his angst on his sleeve.' I went downstairs and told Sam – You remember Sam; thin, glasses, drank too much – He laughed and threw me a beer. I sat down on the floor and thought about it. This was an improvement over the last time she dropped me. Then she cut the call short by claiming she had to go take a dump. No, I guess the difference was mostly aesthetic."

"So what happened?"

"Oh, you mean with Molly? I saw her again about a year later."

"Richard, the trouble with you is that you only want what you can't have. Did you ever fall in love with someone who wanted to be with you?"

"It's not so simple. I mean how can you tell when it first happens? Things usually start off great. There's no way I could've just looked at Molly and foretold the future."

"But you don't let go."

"Well, sometimes I think things are going to improve. I have these strong memories of those first few days and they take awhile to fade. But that's not so important. I just get a feel for a situation. Like that thing with Molly. I can't explain it but somehow I knew it wasn't over even when she practically pissed on me. The last time was different. There was nothing left to say. Whatever fascination or hold she had over me was gone. I stopped feeling anything either good or bad. I was bored."

"So is that the future for you and Susan?"

"Probably. You know she's going back to Colorado next month."

"And that'll be the end of it?"

"No, I've told you. I have a feel for these affairs. It hasn't run its course yet. But it's a funny thing, all these women that I've been so passionate about, I think I start resenting them."

"You said you just got bored."

"Yeah, I guess I haven't thought this through. I think in a way you can feel nothing but still resent someone."

"That doesn't make much sense."

"Yes it does. It's not them so much as the time I wasted with them. Or maybe even if I want to wish them well, I'm still pleased if they're snubbed or hurt by someone else."

"Of course."

"I know it's nothing remarkable but let me give you an example. Molly; I first met her in high school. She was a cheerleader. Can you imagine me with an ex–cheerleader?"

"An ex–cheerleader?"

"Sure, none of this happened while we were in high school. I was not a high school type person. She was one of those teenage golden girls; right clothes, right looks, right friends. I was definitely on the outside and too shy to say anything to her."

"You?"

"Yeah me. Aren't I allowed to be shy? You didn't have a lock on adolescent agony."

"Never thought I did."

"At least you were a girl."

"That was the rumor."

"I mean maybe you had the humiliation of not being asked, but you didn't have to deal with outright rejection … No, it probably was no treat either way."

"I don't think so."

"Christ, the hours I've wasted thinking about sex. I still remember when it first hit me. I was in seventh grade science class. Two seats down Barbara Grether was sitting hunched over her desk. I could see the bra strap underneath her yellow blouse. If I concentrate a second I'll be there; sitting very quietly, not listening to what Mr. Ziegelbaum is saying, seeing only that yellow blouse with the Peter Pan collar and Barbara's boobs surrounded by a cheap white bra. There's a couple of hairs sticking to the blouse from her short kinky hair. I wanted to rip that blouse off. Suddenly that seemed much more important than the larvae stage of the Monarch butterfly. What I expected to do afterwards, I don't know. I just had this overwhelming desire to strip little Barbara Grether.

"Since then I can't look at a woman without thinking about sex; old women, young girls, it doesn't matter. It's as if the world changed for me after that. I fall asleep dreaming about ramming it into one girl or another. There has to be a better way to spend my time. I mean I even think about it when I'm fucking. Can't keep my mind on anything."

"Richard!"

"Oh stop being so touchy, Shelly. You're not supposed to take this personally. We're just talking as friends."

"We are?"

"Yes we are … Okay, tell me about growing up, about all your conquests."

"That's easy. I was a total gawk, tall and skinny. No one would look at me, especially all the boys who were shorter. Finally I thought everything was changing. I started seeing this older guy. I was sixteen. He was almost twice my age, and a painter."

"Aren't they all?"

"No, he actually had sold some of his canvases, even got reviewed in the Times. He worked and lived out of a van, back when very few people were doing that. One day we drove and drove till we found a deserted beach. It was one of those few perfect days in L.A.; not too hot, sky miraculously clear. So we took off our clothes and went racing across the beach, splashing into the ocean until we found a sheltered cove. We started making love."

"Sounds like a million erotic movies."

"Except for the punch line. As soon as our bodies met I started screaming. My skin was flaming red. He lugged me back to the van but I was a total mess. I couldn't keep my teeth from chattering. And when he tried to cover me the pain became unbearable. The poor guy ended up rushing me to L.A. County Hospital. One of the worst cases of sun poisoning they'd ever seen."

"Certainly one of the most complete."

"You, my friend, have no monopoly on fiascos. But you were trying to explain something."

"Huh?"

"You know, about the woman who dropped you."

"Oh yeah, right, about resentment. I was talking about Molly."

"The cheerleader?"

"Yeah, the ex–cheerleader. The point I was going to make is that she'd been exceptionally pretty. Well I hadn't seen her for a few years, not since the last time she told me to take a walk. So I drive out to see her and she's gained all this weight; like there's at least twice as much of her. You should've seen the buns on this girl."

"But that didn't matter."

"No, whatever I wanted from her wasn't affected. I even felt melancholy; the whole snows of yesteryear routine. But deep down I was pleased. It was retribution for her being such a cunt. I can't remember ever being so delighted, except when someone told me that another girl who dumped me wore falsies. I kept imagining unhooking her bra and giggling at her itsy bitsy tits; maybe pinching them and going, 'Squeak, squeak.' I guess that makes me less than wonderful."

"I think it makes you human, Richard. I know you hate to admit it, but there it is. That's how people are. When Pete's latest girlfriend called me up to cry on my shoulder I tried to be sympathetic but I didn't feel it. She deserves to be buried in a ton of shit. Can you imagine the dumb gall that makes her come weeping to me?"

"It's your image, Shelly. If I ever wanted a shoulder to cry on, you'd be my candidate."

"That's different, Richard. I'd expect you to come."

"I know, but other people feel the same way."

"That's too much of a burden. They're not the only ones with feelings. Why should I have to mash down mine so that they can express theirs?"

"You don't have to."

"I can't break out of that role. I've been doing it all my life, comes from being the oldest in the family."

"If you say so."

"That's right, you wouldn't know. All you've got is that sister of yours."

"That's what I have."

"How's she doing?"

"Same as always."

"That bad?"

"Oh, did I tell you she had a kid a while back? I'm an uncle now."

"Your sister?"

"Sure, lots of people have them. Besides, if the kid's tough enough, he won't go down the tubes."

"What about you, Richard?"

"No, I don't plan on going down the tubes, at least not for the moment."

"Children, you wise–ass, how do you feel about children?"

"I don't give them much thought. Most of them aren't all that interesting, especially the infants, they're just little lumps of flesh."

"Some uncle you'll make."

"I'm sure the kid is being so buried with attention that mine would only be redundant. You wouldn't happen to have another joint around?"

Shelly gets up and I cram more wood into the fireplace. Well, why not? I give it to Shelly. No reason I shouldn't grab some of the advantage. Besides, this house is in direct competition with my cabin as the dampest hole on the River.

"You know what, Shelly?"

"What's that?"

"My life really deserves the rubber chicken award. If I thought about it from a certain perspective, it might even seem tragic. Actually it's been nothing but slightly absurd, especially if I set it against yours. Now yours has been a complete mess. I feel lucky compared to you … That didn't come out quite right, did it Shelly?"

"It doesn't matter."

"Yes, it does. It sounds like I'm sniping at you."

"You're just worn out."

"I know that, but I shouldn't be giving you any grief, not even unintentionally."

"I said it's okay."

"Look, I know it sounds like I've been whining …"

"That's right."

"Shelly, I'm just depressed with where my life's going. There's been no real development, only a string of disparate themes tried out and then discarded. I'm starting to worry that I no longer care. If I let myself get too goddam detached I'll probably end up incapable of feeling anything at all."

"You're scared Richard. You're just afraid of being hurt."

"Scared, no I'm not scared. Getting hurt can't frighten me. When you're alone in a cold Maine bedroom at three a.m. wondering where your girlfriend is, that's being afraid. There's a point when you can't seem to catch your breath, panic I guess. It's the fear of losing love that causes that panic. I don't think I'm able to feel that deeply anymore. You get numb instead. You start thinking of yourself in the third person."

"Don't fool yourself."

"I try not to."

"You know you wrote me a letter five years ago that said just about the same thing."

"Okay, I didn't want to fall in love with Susan, but when that bus pulls up and you've bought a ticket you've got to get on. And I did, Shelly. You can tell me that I should've known better, that I should've stayed away from bus stations, but it's too late for that now.

"The whole affair's brought me nothing but pain and hopelessness. Still that doesn't change what I said. My little heart may be broken, but nothing like it was five years ago. And next time, if there is a next time, it'll be even more superficial."

"So what's the solution? Are you going to lay off sex?"

"Why would I possibly do that? It was love I was talking about, not sex. I don't care that much either way about sex. Any woman who wants me can have me."

"Thanks for the flattery."

"Come off it, Shelly. We've known each other for over ten years. It's not the same."

"Why, do you do it differently with your other women, maybe swing from the chandeliers?"

"You know what I mean. We were both curious after all those years. We've got a friendship not a cri de coeur. Don't fish for compliments."

"Okay, then why let it happen? You know it can't work. Nothing good has ever come out of situations like that."

"Because they want it."

"So who elected you to be the local tooth fairy? It's not only you who gets hurt."

"Mostly it is."

"Aren't you being the slightest bit egotistical?"

"No, most of the time I let them drop me. I keep up a pretense of interest till they do."

"So they feel guilty instead."

"Nah ah. I reassure them. Look Shelly, I give them what they need for a little while. I can take whatever disappointment's involved."

"That's fucked, Richard."

"It isn't very romantic but it usually makes them feel good. What's wrong with that?"

"But what about you?"

"Doesn't matter."

"You're being impossible. It's just too damn cold blooded and calculated."

"Well, it beats hell out of being in love. Try asking Susan. I really love her and I've even tried to be restrained but I'm driving the poor girl nuts. I'm much more fun to be with when I'm mildly bored ... Don't look at me like that. I don't mean you. I count on being open with you. I like being your lover but not if I have to start watching everything I say. I won't pay that price."

"Oh, stop being so mature and come to bed."

Bed nothing, right here's good enough for this boy. I pull Shelly toward me. Our bodies slowly twist then pick up momentum. I'm straining against Shelly, trying to break down the barriers between us including her goddam underwear. With a roar I am pushing, defeating time, making my way into her panties when Shelly who has been going with me starts shoving me away.

"My diaphragm, Richard."

Damn Shelly and her goddam diaphragm. I knew she'd pull this. It's not like I dropped by unexpectedly for tea. I don't need this. It's like having an inconvenient timeout inserted during a touchdown drive. While she trips off to locate the necessary preparations, I'm left to hobble to her bedroom without the benefit of a halftime show. Not the same thing at all as downshifting.

I spoke too soon. I'm being treated to an entr'acte of watching her stick the damn thing in. Yeah, right in front of me to show how cool and West Coast sophisticated she is about her body and sex and probably all life in general. What does she think I'm doing in the meanwhile, drooling with anticipation? I'm just trying to stay awake. She pads over and stops a moment before me.

"You're really beautiful, Shelly."

Now what the hell am I telling her that for? Sure I like her, but I'm not passionately in love with Shelly, I've known her too many years. Besides, she is starting to get a bit dumpy. But, she was waiting for me to say it. What else was she posing there for? I'd feel mean not saying something.

So here I am pumping away, groin thudding irregularly against groin, our bodies sticking together. I alternate, increasing my speed then slowing down, almost stopping. Her vagina seems to be reaching out to pull me in like a small firm hand clamping down on my penis. It feels like two rows of hard even teeth are methodically shredding the poor thing to pieces ... I definitely have to lay off smoking dope.

I am just starting to spasm when Shelly shoves me off, rolls over, sets her alarm and goes to sleep. Well, she's honest if nothing else. I almost yell out, "Wait a minute, I'm not done yet."

This can't be right. It's incredibly morally corrupt. I mean I'm not emotionally crushed or anything but I am stunned at such hard–edged selfishness. What happened to the supposedly warm, giving woman I know?

I guess it serves me right for always bitching about how hokey women are in bed, all that desire for post coital romance. Cuddling is what Katherine always called it. I may have thought it was a bit sappy but still I did it. But here's Shelly who has her orgasm first and then immediately wants her sleep. There's a businesslike efficiency about it all that's upsetting. I suppose I'm sappy enough to expect some pretense of affection or even some communication, not this completely self-centered crap. This makes me feel like I'm being rented by the hour. I don't need all this fucking control. I'd be better off buying a stuffed animal. At least it wouldn't sweat or yank at the sheets.

No wonder women are furious. This must be how most men act. Well, it leaves me feeling like a used condom. You just have to make some effort. It doesn't matter what you feel like doing. A few more minutes of sleep aren't all that important ... Christ, I think Jane Austen is becoming my patron saint.

It's not really Shelly's fault, though. I think she's afraid of letting go. Considering her past record, she'd see no percentage in becoming vulnerable. Well, I should keep my mouth shut. She's my friend. If it makes her happy I can manage to lose some extra sleep. Anyway, she'll probably get tired of me after a while. They all do.

And that's not really the problem. For the last five years I've been running some kind of service for the women I know. I'm not so sure I entirely like it ... 'And there's always good old Richard. If I'm down or my old man's been giving me a hard time, I can always give Richard a call. He still loves me. He realizes what a wonderful person I am. He'll flirt with me, lend me money, or tell me I'm beautiful. There's always Richard to see me through. And when I'm feeling better, Richard will smile and tell me it was no trouble at all.'

Well, I've got some news for all you ladies. No more dial a lover. Old Richard has feelings too, just like a real person. I've had it. No more being squeezed dry and then tossed away like an old dish rag. From now on people who want an emotional commitment from me will have to pay in advance. Damn, I just flip flop back and forth. I feel like I should help out Shelly and all the others but I still resent being used. Then again, maybe none of it does really matter.

It's strange, I could never figure out why women didn't trust me. Susan for instance, I always feel her holding back, afraid that I'll hurt her. And I've wanted so much to find someone who was willing to be open. If she wanted to ditch me later on, at least she would come right out with it instead of avoiding me or trying to keep her options open. But now I think it mostly makes sense, this lack of trust. Usually I'm too polite to tell the truth. And I can't guarantee how I'll react to a rejection. I'm too damn erratic. Maybe it is better to let relationships die of neglect. No, I don't know that it's better. Sometimes it happens to work. The hell of the matter is there's no good way to tell how to play these things. You can't really measure someone's emotional needs in advance.

So here I am, six in the morning, a month away from my twenty– eighth birthday, listening to some woman snore damply beside me. I work over eighty hours a week and the only positive result I see is a bunch of A.F.D.C. mothers getting drunk off their collective asses. My fingers are rotting away, so is my sense of humor. I haven't read anything but murder mysteries in over a year. Even screwing is becoming a monotonous chore.

So is this what it's all about? I mean is this what life has to offer? Yeah, I guess it is.

11

A REWARD FOR WAITING

Whoever forgives and forgets throws away dearly bought experience.
–Schopenhauer

"That reminds me of visiting my friend Laurie back in Maine. I was there in the early spring. You know how those places are up country; one room, a loft, no running water. Well, we're sitting there talking around the kitchen table and I ask her how things have been going. She tells me that the two of them, her and her old man, didn't say a word to each other all through the last half of the winter."

"You're kidding."

"Not only that, but she was deathly sick most of February; and they both still wouldn't budge."

"Why didn't they split up?"

"Split up, when they had such a solid relationship going?"

"So that's how it is with you and Susan?"

"Could be that was the point of telling you the story, Johnny."

"I think the point of your story is walking up the road to see you. Isn't it about time for her to take off?"

"Tomorrow."

"Well, there must be something I have to do inside … Uh, if you need to talk later, I'll be around."

"Thanks, buddy."

So Susan has some conscience left after all. Thought she might be planning to split without bothering to stop by. I've spent the last two days trying to track her down. Not so easily done. Tod wasn't holding anything back, but that wasn't the story with Deanna. She had a smirk on her face like she knew I was being fucked over.

265

"Haven't you been getting any sleep, Susan?"

"What kind of a hello is that supposed to be?"

"You just look beat. Your eyes are all puffed out."

"Sometimes you don't look so hot yourself."

"More often than not, sweetheart."

That's what I call first striking, deflecting an attack by wallowing in the charge, sort of a sophisticated Uriah Heep approach to personal relations.

"Well, I'm sorry I don't meet your standards today. I thought I was always supposed to be so beautiful."

"It's your hair, what have you done to your hair?"

"My hair, what do you mean?"

"It feels funny."

"Maybe it's the new shampoo I'm using."

"Shampoo, what difference could that make?"

"Well you see I ran into Victoria last week and ..."

"What's that slut been telling you?"

"C'mon Richard. Stop being so darn negative. You know how much I hate that. What's wrong with Victoria?"

"Besides being a fraud, nothing at all. She's out there cashing in on her organic, earth mother image for all it's worth. Maybe I should respect that. It's the goddamed American way of life isn't it?"

"I don't see what's so wrong with that?"

"What, with being a fraud? You mean with passing herself off as Ms. Public Service while doing fuck all for the community?"

"You just can't be fair to anyone you don't like, can you Richard?"

"I've told you before Susan, I don't give a damn about being fair. People around here like Victoria make me sick. She's a fake, can't you see that? All of her herbal cures don't mean piss to her. I just bet she rents an apartment in East Oakland so she can shoot smack and gorge herself on hostess twinkies wrapped in Spam."

"That's not even funny."

"Besides, she's good buddies with Florinda. That should be enough to condemn anyone. I bet she talked you into paying ten bucks for a tiny bottle of some herbal gloop."

"It was only $8.95. But listen Richard, she said this was something brand new. It has placenta in it."

"What?"

"Placenta."

"Human placenta?"

"Uh huh."

"That's not very funny."

"No, I'm serious, it says so on the bottle."

"That's disgusting."

"Why is it disgusting?"

"I don't know why. I don't have to know why. It just reeks. That's all there is to it."

"Well I don't see anything wrong with it. Victoria says it's good for the scalp."

"Sure, if it's gentle enough for a baby it's gentle enough for your hair."

"You're being difficult, Richard."

"It's okay by me. Go ahead, run around smelling like a delivery room."

"Cut it out. I'm warning you."

"Throw the crap away, Susan."

"I certainly won't do anything on your say so. What right do you think you have? I can do whatever I like."

"Susan, you don't understand."

"Yes I do."

"Damn it! Give me a chance to finish. I don't want to see you becoming like one of these River women. You're too special. The first thing I noticed about you was that difference. You weren't like all the other scuzzy women around here. You always had this terrific fresh look about you. Now you're putting afterbirth on your head, wearing those ugly little braids and dousing yourself with patchouli oil."

"I am not."

"It's only a matter of time."

"I'm not dumb you know. I can think for myself."

"Who the hell says you can't?"

"Well you're always trying to tell me what to do. Maybe I'm not real smart but that doesn't mean I'm stupid. It just takes me a little bit longer that's all. I'm like my father. We both get there, but maybe a tad slower than most other people."

"For the last time Susan, I don't want to hear you saying those things. Look, am I some kind of dummy?"

"You know you aren't, Richard."

"Well, I don't hang out with airheads no matter how pretty they are. I know all your life people have cast you into this blond bimbo role. Listen Susan, stop believing that crap. You're a bright, intelligent woman. Your biggest problem comes from buying the garbage other people tell you."

"You're just saying that so you can try and get all cozy with me. That's all you ever want to do."

"Come off it, Susan. You're leaving tomorrow. What good would it do me?"

"I'm sorry Richard, I didn't mean to snap … Oh, the roses were real pretty. You didn't have to do that."

"So Deanna actually gave them to you."

"She wouldn't try something like that. It'd be too easy to check up on her. Anyway, she claims they won't open."

"I stopped by to see you."

"I know, Deanna told me."

"You weren't there."

"I know."

"So when are you leaving?"

"Tomorrow morning."

"Are you sure?"

"For the last time Richard, I won't marry you. Can't you get that through your head?"

"What are you talking about?"

"I couldn't possibly marry someone who doesn't believe in God."

"What?"

"You don't believe in Him. Don't try to deny it."

"Who me? I didn't even know God was a He."

"Oh you know what I mean, Richard. Don't try to be so cute. There's no way I'm going to have children with a man who doesn't believe in God."

"Children?"

"Yes. I want to have children, lots of them. I know you think that's hokey. Well it's what I want and I don't care what you have to say about it."

Definitely surreal, conversations with Susan are like that. I'll be doing just fine when suddenly a trap door opens and I'm in some uncharted realm of her subconscious. Right now I don't have the foggiest idea who she's having this conversation with. I know I'm standing in front of her, but that's only coincidental. Somehow, this has all turned into a very minor play by Ionesco.

"Susan, I didn't say one word about marriage."

"I know what you were thinking."

"No, you don't. Can't you just wait a minute; can't you wait until I actually tell you what I am thinking? You make up your mind beforehand and then dump on me for saying something I never said. I don't even get a chance to participate."

"I don't want to argue."

"Okay, so where were you the last few days?"

"Did I tell you my friend Mindy was in San Francisco last week? We had dinner."

"Where'd you go?"

"I can't remember. It was some sort of a seafood restaurant. I had abalone."

"That's nice."

"And we both had wine, a white wine. It was good even if it wasn't rose."

"What was it?"

"I don't remember."

"Dry?"

"No, it had a nice taste."

"Brown bottle?"

"I think so."

"Probably a Moselle, German."

"How do you know?"

"I'm supposed to."

"Is that a good wine?"

"It doesn't matter."

"But I want to know these things. I always feel like such a dope when I'm in a restaurant."

"Did you like it?"

"Yeah."

"Then it was a good wine."

"Well anyway, I thought I'd stop off and say good–bye."

"What time are you leaving?"

"Early tomorrow morning."

"Like I said, I came by a few times yesterday, but Deanna said she didn't know where you'd got to."

"Yeah, I know."

"Obviously you know."

"Look don't get nasty. There's no reason for me to tell you everywhere I go."

"I just wanted to spend some time with you. I've been upset about your leaving."

"That's too bad. It doesn't give you any right to try to monopolize my time. I've told you that. You've been a good friend but enough's enough."

"So where were you?"

"I said I don't have to tell you."

"What difference could it possibly make?"

"None."

"Then tell me."

"I don't see why I should."

"I want to know."

"Richard, I'm not responsible to you. If you don't stop, I'm leaving right this minute."

"Sue Ann, look at me. No I mean it, look at me. I've asked very little from you. All I want to know is where you were yesterday. It's all right. I'm not upset."

"Are you sure?"

"Trust me."

"Okay, I spent some time with Tim."

"Sunovabitch."

"Richard!"

"I'll kill him. I'll rip that sleazy motherfucker's head right off its hinges. I warned him not to do it. I warned that son of a bitch."

"Stop it, Richard!"

"Oh no, I had to be so damn sympathetic. 'Certainly Sue Ann, I understand. Of course Sue Ann, you're in love with some rock star in Colorado. I see, you don't want to get involved with anyone out here. Oh no, it's not you Richard, no I really like you but you do understand, don't you Richard? You're such a nice guy Richard, I know you'd never ...'"

"Shut up, shut up!"

"What a fool, what a goddam stupid fool I am. While I spend my time falling all over myself just hoping to make you happy, you're off humping my ex buddy Tim the first chance you get."

"It wasn't like that."

"No, of course not. I apologize. Now anything else you'd like to do before you go? How about pulling down your pants and taking a quick dump on my feet?"

"I don't have to take any of this crap."

"That's right sweetie, you don't. And guess what? I'm not putting up with any more of yours."

"Ooh I knew it. I just knew this would happen. I'm such a dummy. I knew I shouldn't have believed you. But I really liked you Richard, you were so nice. You kept telling me you understood. And I let myself believe it, like the dope that I am. Now look what's happened. I'll just never learn. I keep falling for the same old shit."

"That's right sweetie, abuse me for not rolling over. Maybe I should feel honored that you let me buy you a few dinners. A hot little bimbo like you always has other options than ..."

I see Susan's face, a tight mask set hard against mine. But it's only for a moment. She's gone before I can do any more damage.

"Son of a bitch! Son of a bitch!" My fist crashes repeatedly into the brown metal sheeting of the Grove. There's nothing else left to say.

***

"Hello."

"Tim, it's Richard."

"Hey Richie, what's up big fella? Long time no see."

"If I ever see you again I'm gonna break your no good, rotten neck!"

I can hardly get the words out. There's something hard stuck in my throat that won't let the words escape. My right hand slowly kneads the receiver while the other telegraphs into the wall board with short rhythmic snaps. I'm tripping dangerously around the borders of hysteria.

"So that's how it is"

"That's right."

"I guess we've got nothing to talk about in that case?"

"That's right."

"Well, I'll see you around."

"Not fucking likely."

I slam the receiver down into its cradle. It rebounds back. Dangling, the cord obeying some unknown law of physics, a metallic voice gurgles from the earpiece demanding that I hang up the phone.

"Eat it Pac Tel!" But like a well trained child I quietly replace the bright red receiver on its hook.

Some tough guy I am, practically blubbering while making my threats. Christ, how could she do this to me? She just doesn't give a fuck about anyone but herself. I try so hard and look what happens. All I wanted was to be able to love her. Is that such a goddamn crime? I should've known. No one wants what they can get too easily. And all my stupid, plodding sincerity must have been just one gigantic bore for her … Well fuck you Sue Ann … I'll just go over there, collect my books and leave. If she wants to give me her new address she can. I'm not going to be the one to bring that up. I'm through begging.

"Susan, can I come in?"

"What do you want, Richard?"

"I came for my Winnie the Pooh books. Remember, I lent them to you last month."

"Is that all?"

"I talked to Tim."

"You couldn't wait could you?"

"I guess not."

"What did you tell him?"

"That I'd break his neck if I ever saw him again."

"How can you be like that, Richard?"

"It's easy."

"And is that all you have to say for yourself?"

"Sue Ann, the trouble with our relationship is that not enough has been left unsaid."

"What's that supposed to mean?"

"Whenever I start trying to explain my feelings you just end up despising me."

"Don't be so melodramatic. I don't despise you, but you drive me crazy, Richard."

"I drive you crazy? What about me, Susan? Did you ever stop to think about how I feel? I admit it. Just one time I would like you to fuss over me. For once I would like you to make the first gesture. I'm tired of running after you Susan and being stepped on. I know I shouldn't care. I should just wistfully say, 'Oh no, Susan, no need to bother about little old me. Don't you worry. You just give me a call if you ever need help.' So I admit it. I'm not totally wonderful. Deep down there's some part of me that needs to know that you care. Look, you may not believe it but I do have feelings, just like real people do. Christ, why am I telling you this? You don't want to hear it. I really don't want to argue."

"Richard, you know that's all nonsense. I wasn't trying to hurt you. These things just happen. Like they say, 'All's fair in love and war.'"

"What?"

"You heard me."

"That's crap Sue Ann. Do you seriously think you can wreck someone's life, and then excuse yourself with some dumb cliché? It doesn't work that way. Whether you like it or not you're responsible. You've acted like a complete pig."

"I've told you Richard, I don't have to listen to that sort of talk.

How do you think I like being called a pig?"

"Jesus, Susan I'm sorry. I didn't mean it. I'm just upset. How could you and Tim do this to me?"

"It had nothing to do with you at all."

"Dammit Susan, I warned that sunovabitch."

"You warned him! What do you mean you warned him? You don't own me. I can do what I damn well please."

"You don't understand."

"All this time I thought you were such a nice guy …"

"Look goddamit, it's not the fact that you fucked him. I'm not upset with you."

"It wasn't his fault. He just happened to run out of gas."

"Sure."

"Well, he did. I'm not stupid. I can read a gas gauge. There was nothing else to do but to spend the night. We both tried really hard not to, but it was a pretty small bed."

"Listen to me Susan, that's not the point. Tim's supposed to be my friend."

"He likes you Richard, he told me."

"Yeah, I can tell that."

"Well, he does."

"Okay, just do me a favor and let me explain."

"I'm listening."

"Tim came to the bar a couple of weeks ago. Maybe the first time in a month I've seen him. So we're standing by the steps to the hotel lobby watching the band and talking. I guess I must've been feeling pretty down that night because I started to tell him how much I was going to miss you. Well he picked right up on the situation and decided to weasel his way in. There I am broken-hearted and he's smacking his lips like some vulture ready to pounce on a tasty piece of meat.

"Thanks a lot."

"Hold it, Susan. Can't you see what I'm saying? All he cared about was his chance to get a crack at you. I could see he didn't give a damn about me. So I even spelled it out for him. He knew I'd be totally pissed if he tried anything, A lot of difference that made."

"You had no right."

"Susan, I know you don't owe me anything but still …"

"He wasn't the first one you know."

"What are you saying?."

"Other guys around here were afraid to even come near me."

"I never said a word to anyone else."

"You didn't have to."

"Well, what about Rickey?"

"What about him?"

"He came to visit."

"And?"

"And nothing. I didn't say a word to him. Don't you understand, it's not you or what you did, it's that louse Tim. He did everything but smear my face in it."

"I don't believe that."

"You think I'm lying?"

"I'm not naive. You think I owed it to you, that if anyone around here fucked me you should be first in line. Well you can't buy me off Richard, not with dinner, plants, or any of the rest of the crap you tried to use."

"You won't let go of that will you, Susan? All I wanted was to be able to express my love. I didn't expect any response. When did you ever do anything but push me away? But you didn't have to kick me in the head. Christ Susan, all you had to do was take the damn plant and say thank you."

"You were trying to trap me."

"That's right, with a stupid plant."

"What did you want me to do? Carry it back to Colorado? Maybe remember you when I watered it?"

"I didn't give a fuck what you did with it. You could've flushed it down the toilet if that made you happy. I wasn't looking for anything in return. It was just my way of saying that I love you. Think a minute. Suppose someone did that to you."

"I don't force myself on people."

"Don't be so snotty. I hardly forced myself on you."

"What are you talking about? You were always hanging around

trying to get close to me. It got so I could hardly breathe."

"Stop trying to make me feel guilty."

"I can't make you feel anything, Richard. You're too concerned with your own damn sensitivities."

"Susan, you don't have the right to piss on me just because I was in love with you. You took every single decent and generous impulse I had and twisted it around. Don't you understand? I just wanted to do something for you, something to make you happy. You know, sometimes I'd be watching you down at the Grove and you were so damn lovely that I wanted to cry. I never schemed. I really didn't expect to get anything in return. Buying things for you was just a spontaneous response. Can you understand that? I was pleased that I could still feel that way about someone. So what do you do? You shit all over me for bringing you one lousy plant."

"What do you mean, 'was in love'?"

"I don't know what I mean. I'm confused. What do you care?"

"It matters."

"Don't tell me you're afraid your grip on me might loosen. I thought that's what you wanted?"

"I told you not to be so melodramatic, Richard. You know I care."

"Sure."

"Well I do."

"That's a great consolation to me."

"You're just not going to stop, are you?"

"Am I making it difficult for you? Well good. You're surprised aren't you? You can't believe I'm not rolling over and playing dead. I bet you think I should be grateful for the abuse. Well, fuck you Sue Ann and the car that brought you."

"Get out!"

"As soon as you give me my Winnie the Pooh books."

"Oh Richard, you're impossible."

"I know it."

"You know it? So stop, why beat on me?"

"Because I'm hurt and angry with myself. Because, I haven't been good enough for you."

"Don't, Richard. It just couldn't be helped."

"Answer your phone."

"Hello … yes … a hah … well I couldn't help it … No, I'm sure he won't."

"That's Tim, isn't it? C'mon Susan, I know it's him. You can tell Timmy I won't break his rotten neck. See you around Susan."

At this point in the story there should be a long tracking shot of me walking dejectedly along a deserted beach. Maybe the wind could be tousling my hair while my eyes expressed the anguish of a tormented soul. But somehow when women break my heart, I can't seem to find the time to wallow in my own self pity. Instead, I'm forced into the low comedy of mixing drinks and arguing with assholes. And I swear I meet more of them in one night than most toilet seats see in a week.

"Buddy, are you okay?"

"Fine Johnny, sorry I'm late."

"There's nothing doing around here. You sure you don't want to go home or something? I can handle things."

"I said I was okay. The band show up yet?"

"Richard, I saw you talking to Susan this afternoon."

"She's leaving tomorrow. We had a few things to say."

"Listen Buddy, how about coming around later on. I was talking to Jeannie and she said we never seem to get to spend much time together."

"Thanks Johnny. Don't think I don't appreciate it. But no need to worry, I'll pull through."

"I know you will. You're a real survivor, Richard."

"I'm afraid so buddy, I'm afraid so."

***

Dear Susan,

I did try. I just couldn't manage to pull it off. Sorry for walking out like that but I didn't want to start crying or make an even bigger fool of myself. So I'm leaving this note on your windshield instead. You may not believe me but I'm glad you came here and I had the chance to get to know you. If you ever need a friend, I'll be there to help. I love you very much,
  Richard

There's a small sunny spot by the steps as you walk into the Grove. I'm there at nine, trying to bake yesterday out of my mind. Wonder what she'll think of that note? I didn't know what else to do.

"Haven't seen you and Susan together recently."

"Mm."

"Hear she's heading back to Boulder."

"Huh."

"Don't feel much like talking, do you Slick?"

"You're real quick today aren't you, Nick? Sharp as a goddam tack, that's what you are."

"Lighten up there killer, won't do no good to go hitting on me. You remember when Linda flew back to L.A. last month. I felt like busting someone's face. There's nothing you can do about it. Sometimes the dice just roll that way. Look, maybe we're both better off. Okay, don't believe me … I tell you what … I go and buy you some drinks down to the bar tonight. Then maybe I describe for you the time my fourth wife pour hot water all over my spud. One beeg red tamale, you see what I mean?"

Damn it, I wish Nick would vanish. I suppose I should be grateful, but why do I always end up with people like him for buddies?

Nick lets loose with one of his nasty Mexican bandit laughs, like some small furry animal shitting down a drain pipe. Sue Ann pulls up in her sunburst V.W. complete with wooden bumpers and Colorado plates.

"Well, ain't that nice. Looks like your little honey's come to say good–bye."

"Nick?"

"Yeah, Bub?"

"Get out of here."

"Now no call to carry on like that, Richard. What about those drinks?"

"I don't want company."

"Okay, suit yourself."

"Hi, Richard."

"Well maybe you two sweethearts would rather I be off on my own business, isn't that so Pancho?"

"Don't hurt yourself laughing, Nick."

We both glare. Susan despises Nick. She claims she has to take a shower after just looking at him.

"I got the note you left on my car."

"Yeah, well, I'm really sorry about the whole thing."

"Weel ..."

"Susan, it's just that I tried so hard to get you to trust and believe in me. You don't realize. It tore me up all summer. I kept working at it, wanting to make it right. So then what do I go and do? I blow the whole damn thing in about five minutes. I know it'll never be the same. Everything I do from now on will never quite cut it. And it's all my fault."

"Look Richard, we'll just have to see. Okay?"

"I'd appreciate it if you would drop me a line sometime. And uh, you can keep the Winnie the Pooh books.

"Thanks, I'll try, really I will."

"Susan?"

"What is it, Richard?"

"I love you Susan."

"Take care of yourself sweetie. Find someone else, you hear me? There are other women out there."

Susan's car bumps and grinds its way out of town. So goddam fragile, my life is coming apart and there's nothing I can do to stop it. It's all very simple though. A woman fucks me over and I can't stop apologizing. The fact that I upset her bubble headed little life means more to me than my own emotional collapse.

I don't even know why I bother. Either I waste my time hanging out with some woman who totally bores me or I get cut to pieces by someone I really care about. It must just be a bad habit. I'd probably be better off raising nasturtiums. At least they don't have bad teeth or cold feet.

I've watched so many women I love walk away. This time I thought it would be different. This time I thought I would pull it off. And I almost acted like a decent human being. Susan will never trust me again. It doesn't matter what she says. You can't undo the pain you inflict on others. She won't forget. She thinks I'm a jerk ... and she's right.

12

REVEALED PREFERENCES

If all the girls at Vassar were laid end to end – I wouldn't be at all surprised
–Dorothy Parker

"So Carey, what's the news?"

"The usual, Jemina's been acting up again."

"How old's she getting to be?"

"Four last month."

"Four huh? Jason was hell on wheels at that age. He was either up and speeding in high gear or asleep; nothing in between. Wore me right out. But at least you've got Morley there helping you."

"How many of those separators are you good for Julie? Morley comes home at six, grabs a beer and waits for dinner to appear. If it's late, he's as cranky as Jemina when I won't let her cram her face full of Mars bars."

"You don't let her eat that crap?"

"I don't want her to but it's really hard. Morley doesn't care; he eats them all the time. I've given up on what he pokes down his throat. But Jemina wants to eat what Daddy eats. Great role model he is."

"So you've just mostly been hanging out at home with your kid?"

"Sometimes I get a call to substitute down at the school."

"Oh yeah, I forgot about your teaching trip."

"Did it for three years in the city before Morley talked me into coming up here."

"You two together down there?"

"Not really. We met at a Dead concert. Morley had these big plans. He wanted to cut loose and move out to the country. All he needed was to find the right woman. You should've heard him. He had that whole rap down; putting in a garden, raising a family, getting our heads together. Like a dope I believed him. He never explained that I'd take care of the first two items while he worked at getting his head together."

"Morley still working down at the Garage?"

"That's another thing. The guy has a degree in civil engineering from Berkeley and he spends his days up to his elbows in patched together V.W.'s. I swear he never gets that stuff off. I've got grease spots in some of the weirdest places."

"What do you do with Jemina when you're at work?"

"I day–care her with Angie."

"I wouldn't leave a mad dog with her."

"I've got no choice. I can't just tie Jemina to a tree and take off."

"Lucky you've only got the one kid to look after."

"Well two, counting Morley … What are you laughing at Richard? You've been eavesdropping, haven't you?"

"What Carey?"

"Were you laughing at me?"

"Who me? I was just standing here polishing a few fizz glasses, didn't hear a word you were saying … Uh, get you another one of those screwdrivers?"

"A little less ice this time."

Uncoded that means she wants me to go heavy on the vodka. Sure, why not. Carey's okay and I know she's tight up for cash. First time I've seen her around in months. Wonder how she talked Morley into looking after Jemina. He's usually here about now, downing Heinekens and letting his eyes rove.

"Buck twenty–five."

"Thanks Richard, you make a decent drink. Ever hear anything about the Grove?"

"Mike's turning it into some kind of private clinic."

"So no chance it'll reopen."

"Well, you're sitting at part of the old bar."

"Are you kidding?"

"Nope, sold everything off including the liquor license."

"Too bad, I used to love that place."

"That's what they all tell me."

"How come they closed? Whenever I went there the place was packed."

"People weren't spending any bucks. You don't get rich pouring glasses of water."

"Well, I don't get it. I know I always left there light by at least a ten spot."

"Carey, if all my customers were as nice as you, the Grove wouldn't be shut and my life behind the bar there wouldn't have been such a hassle."

"I never knew people gave you a hard time. Why would they want to do that? I mean, you were always so mellow back there. Julie, did you know anything about this?"

"Yeah, I heard about it occasionally. You know how some of the locals are."

"Well, I thought you did a good job."

"Thanks, Carey."

As I said, I like Carey. Julie, I could manage without. Anytime she runs across a line of coke she becomes a complete disaster, like the time she did that headstand on the bar. It's true what they say about River women. They don't shave their legs and they don't use underwear.

Well, thank God it's almost last call. Shouldn't take too long to clear the place out. Good thing the band played a short set. Harry must be getting soft in the head letting Mina talk him into booking her brother. That's what happens when Maggie takes a few weeks off; her ex–old man goes out of control. Frank may call himself the manager but he's too much of a wimp to say 'no'. It's bad enough working with Mina twice a week. I shouldn't be forced to listen to her brother trying to hit a right note.

"Hey there, white boy. We want some service down to this end of the bar."

Oh, I forgot to mention Mina's wonderful sense of humor.

"You trying to ignore a poor black woman? Ain't I good enough for you to talk to honey?"

"They teach you that at Bryn Mawr, Mina?"

"Hush up, white boy. I can handle the comedy my ownself. Now you just keep your mind on business and hustle me up another shot of Cuervo Gold."

"What about you Samantha, another keoki?"

"No thanks Richard, I'm fine."

Her good looking friend, Samantha, is another matter. She showed up about a week ago. Reminds me of the blonde, that actress, the one in that Woody Allen movie. Damn, can't remember her name. Anyway, there's something definitely provoking about her, though I'm not sure whether I want to fall passionately in love or just slap her across the face … Wonder why she bothers hanging out with a douche–bag like Mina?

Maybe I can get that woman canned. She's totally worthless as a bartender. Harry might do it if Maggie gave him a nudge. That's the reason Frank could never get his girlfriend on the payroll. Once Maggie makes up her mind there's no budging her. But it's always tricky pushing Maggie in the right direction. Even more so since she started falling into her tough dyke routine. First thing I should do is line up another woman for the job. Then I can let Maggie find out about the cash that's been slipping into Mina's pocket. It might work.

"Put those drinks on my tab."

"Sure Mina." What do I care? It's Maggie's problem not mine.

"So when are you and me gonna go stepping out, Richard?"

"Mina, you don't want to go out dancing with me."

"Sure I do."

"But everyone knows us po' white boys got no nat'ral sense of rhythm."

"You been saving that one up for me?"

"Wouldn't think of saving it for anyone else but you honeychile"

"Well don't you worry your head about that. Mina'll teach you all the right moves real quick like."

"Samantha, don't forget your package. It's in the fridge round back."

"Help yourself if you want. There's some havarti cheese inside."

"Thanks, maybe I will."

I'm leaning against the back bar, right in front of the register. Samantha's eyeing me. real steady like. She doesn't bother looking away. I give her a nervous smile. Maybe I should try hitting the 'no sale' button. She swings around on her chair, nudges Mina and they drift off toward the stage. Mina's brother Len lets a low chuckle slide across his brandy.

"They talking on you, boy."

Sure enough, Samantha and Mina are huddled in the corner whispering. I feel like a bull at a county fair. I wonder if I should stamp my foot and snort. Or my teeth, maybe they'd like to check out my teeth.

"Okay Len, what's that supposed to mean?"

"Now don't go playing dumb. You be up for grabs tonight boy and they deciding who be holding the short straw."

"Richard?"

"It's last call Samantha."

"No, I want to ask you for a favor."

"What's that?"

"Mina has to drive Len down to the city."

"She's too loaded to be driving."

"It's okay, Len'll drive."

"He's no better off."

"Look, forget about them. What I wanted to know um, I was wondering if you'd give me a lift. It's not too far from … Hey, what's Len laughing about?"

"Beats me … Look, that's no problem but you'll have to wait while I finish up."

"I'm in no great rush."

***

Damn, I don't want to be doing this anymore. Not just the bartending, I mean this whole boring routine. Maybe one day, if I grow up, I'll get past the urge of needing a response from every pretty woman I run across. I should stop getting involved. What does it matter if I hump this girl or not. I'll still be the same person, mixing the same drinks, and saying the same things to the people in this bar. I fell into this sort of life without thinking. Now I don't know how to get out. No, it's worse than that; I wouldn't know what to do or where to go if I did get out. Do I become an account executive, a computer programmer? What kind of a solution is that? I would just be drifting from one rut to the next. So why bother changing? If I could only think of something worthwhile to do with my time when I'm not working, that should be enough. Maybe I could learn French and read Proust in the original. Who am I kidding? I'll always be looking for a miracle to rescue me. But that solution is not about to come waltzing through the door. I know all that. But it doesn't change a thing. On the day of my death I'll still be sitting here waiting for my life to begin.

I think I've always been waiting for some sort of direction. When I was twenty I thought Lisa would be it. Having the right woman there to squeeze my hand would clear up all those other problems. Who knows, maybe it would. But what I really wanted was someone to make my decisions for me or at least to force me to make my own.

"You want a drink or something before we take off?"

"No, I'm fine ... Richard?"

"Yah."

"How long have you been working behind bars?"

"You make it sound like some sort of life sentence."

"Is it?"

"You know, sometimes I wonder if it is."

"If you don't like it, leave."

"Nope, it's not that easy. I've quit enough times, but then I need some quick cash or I've just moved into an area and, damn, you can always score a job as a bartender."

"That's a trap not a job, Richard."

"Comes to the same thing. I suppose I don't really expect much from a job except for a paycheck. To me it's time someone else holds hostage. But there are worse things than pouring drinks. I once had this girlfriend who worked at a Hickory Farms. Do they have them out here?"

"You mean that cheese place?"

"Yeah, I think I saw one at the mall in Santa Rosa. Anyway, she had to be to work by seven–thirty each morning to prep the store. The reason it took so long is that she had to scrub down all the cheeses with white vinegar first. It got rid of any of those green fuzzies that made a home there overnight. Put me right off that stuff for a while."

"Did that really happen?"

"Maybe she lied. Wouldn't have been the first time. Besides, people only remember what they want to remember."

"What about you?"

"Sure, me too. I'm no different. That's how I operate. My memory's as selective as the next, maybe more."

"I'm not following you."

"Most people have this thing about accuracy. They want to be able to verify their recollections. I don't care. I enjoy my memories as they come. I don't ask them to produce their pedigrees."

"You don't take anything or anyone seriously, do you Richard?"

"Sammi, I don't take myself seriously, I merely extend the courtesy ... You don't mind me calling you Sammi?"

"Nope, not particularly ... About ready to go?"

"Sure, here's your package. My car's the only one still out there."

"It's pretty beat isn't it?"

"We've both seen some hard times."

"Look Richard, there are rust holes big enough to put a baby through."

"Sweetheart, don't kick my car. It's light enough metal as is."

"I couldn't do it any harm."

"Humor me."

"Why are you coming around the passenger side, Richard?"

"It's the only door that works."

"Are you gonna hop over that hand brake?"

"No Samantha, I'm not into self castration. I'll lower it first."

"Now why are you turning the rearview mirror toward me?"

"I can't stand headlights glaring into my eyes."

"Then how do you see what's behind you?"

"See? I can't see a damn thing at night."

"You're joking."

"Samantha, just ease up on all the questions and I'll get you home. I'll pretend I can see. Works almost as well."

I have a distinct feeling I'm not impressing her. So what? One River woman more or less doesn't matter.

"Are you sure you're gonna be able to make it? I could drive."

"I said I can do it. Now where do you live?"

"Past the Lodge, you know at the flashing lights."

"You mean down among the troglodytes."

"What?"

"With the mushrooms and other fungus growth. Where the sun never shines."

"It's all those redwood trees."

"I know."

"What the hell is that?"

"Something the matter?"

"It's coming from your car, Richard."

"Don't worry."

"Look, are you sure it's safe? Sounds like you're grinding up a cat in there."

"Fan belt."

"That's supposed to make me feel better?"

"I need to tighten it, Sammi. It squeals on cold nights."

"It's summer."

"It doesn't have to be all that cold."

"Well what makes you think it won't fall off altogether?"

"If it did, the alternator light would go on."

"And you'd be left with a dead battery in the morning."

"So now you're an auto mechanic?"

"My brother knows about cars."

"Then get him to tighten it if you're so damn upset. There, it stopped."

"Aren't you going to open the hood?"

"Be sensible. If there's something wrong I'm not fixing it now. We've got no other way to get you home. Emily here won't let me down."

"Emily?"

"Okay, so you think it's stupid giving my car a name. Well I'm attached to it. Listen, if you'd rather hitch, go ahead. You won't hurt my feelings."

"It's three a.m."

"Be nice and peaceful hitching. You could meditate or something."

"You pissed off about your car?"

"Samantha, I will gladly take you home. I'd probably do it for anyone, but for you especially."

"Uh huh."

"Don't do it. Think what you want but don't hassle me. You're a nice woman. I like you. So why don't you ease up a bit?"

As I shift into drive I feel Samantha's lips on my cheek. That's a really sweet thing to do … Damn, here I go getting hooked up with another loony.

"You know Sammi, it's finally happened. I really can't see. I can barely make out the road. Fuck, my eyes are gone."

"The lights."

"What?"

"Try turning on your headlights."

"Hey, that's much better. Thanks a lot Sammi."

"Are you for real?"

"I'm sorta absent-minded."

"More than that."

"Okay, I'm a moron. Will that do?"

"No need to get all huffy."

"Forget it … What were you doing hanging out at the bar?"

"Any objection?"

"No, glad you did. I'm just curious."

"I thought I might run into Maggie."

"She split for a couple of weeks."

"I know, I'll catch her when she gets back."

"A friend of yours?"

"Well, do you know Nellie Weiss?"

"I thought we were talking about Maggie?"

"We are."

"Okay, I'm not sure that I know a Nellie Weiss. Is that the name she uses?"

"Of course it is."

"Sounded too ordinary for around here."

"I spent a year in therapy with her."

"Down in Santa Rosa?"

"No, she was up in Sebastapol then, handling family practice."

"What family were you practicing with?"

"My husband."

"You married?"

"Not now, he ended up with Nellie."

"Was that all part of the service?"

"Well, it did help."

"And is that the connection with Maggie?"

"Yeah, her ex and mine were friends. Before Maggie and Harry split, they went for counseling."

"To Nellie?"

"What's wrong with that?"

"Well, she doesn't sound like she's too good at saving marriages."

"You're missing the point. They wanted help, just like Eddie and me."

"Who?"

"My ex."

"Nellie's old man."

"That's right."

"So she convinced Maggie and Harry to split."

"You're still not getting it, Richard. The aim of the program is to let yourself go with your innermost feelings."

"And she did that for you?"

"Sure."

"So what did that involve?"

"Socking her on the jaw when she told me the two of them were humping during his morning session."

"And she did the same for Maggie?"

"No, it was in the afternoon."

"What are you talking about?"

"Nellie helped her realize her lesbian tendencies."

"In the afternoon?"

"She had group session in the morning."

"What about Eddie?"

"He and Harry played tennis in the afternoons."

"So everything worked out."

"Not quite."

"I thought you were telling me how absolutely wonderful Nellie is?"

"It's hardly her fault that Harry has a weak backhand."

"What about you?"

"Mostly it's my serve."

"Cut it out. I mean the therapy; did you keep it up?"

"I moved out to visit my brother. There's no need for therapy in Kansas. It's hard enough just staying awake around there."

"Are you goofing on me again?"

"Maybe."

"Be serious, I want to know what happened."

"With what?"

"Your old man, what's his name, Eddie."

"I outgrew him."

"Hold it, Samantha. People aren't pairs of socks. Don't you realize how insufferable that sounds?"

"It's what happened."

"I know, you made rapid strides toward a new found maturity while he remained where he was. So, like a snake shuffling off a useless old skin, you left him behind."

"Well, minus the hokey metaphor, you more or less got it."

"But that's completely bogus, Samantha. The guy's not some leftover youthful adventure. He's a real person, with his own feelings and thoughts; do you understand what I'm saying? What if someone talked about you like that?"

"Wouldn't happen."

"Why, are you so goddamn wonderful?"

"That's right."

"Are you trying to piss me off Sammi?"

"I'm succeeding aren't I?"

"Okay, a truce, just don't use those bogus expressions around me. Save them for someone else."

"There's nothing bogus about me."

"Sammi, it's a cruel uncaring thing to say. If you think people are no different than a pair of old socks you end up treating them the same way."

"Don't worry, Richard, I haven't outgrown you yet."

"You win Samantha."

"I do?"

"That's right. You've come out on top."

"Good, that's where I like to be."

I wonder if old Miss Stoneface over there would enjoy some physical abuse.

She's certainly trying to push me right over the edge. And I'm starting to think that I might enjoy cutting loose on her.

"Okay, I admit it. You are one tough broad. Is that what you want to hear? Excuse me, one tough woman."

"That's better."

"Should I ask to feel your muscles?"

"We'll discuss that later."

"Yeah, maybe we just might do that."

I can feel Samantha staring at me but I keep my eyes fixed forward as if I can actually see the road. I'm starting to get pretty tired of her.

"Are you pissed off, Richard?"

"What makes you ask?"

"Well, if you tighten your grip on that wheel any more it'll probably snap."

"I'm fine."

"Go ahead, admit it. Don't play Gary Cooper with me."

"I'd hardly mistake you for June Allyson."

"I'd hardly want to be mistaken for her."

"You've been listening to yourself. Answer your own damn question."

"Okay sweetie."

"What's this sweetie business?"

"I shouldn't be pushing you, Richard. It's a bad habit I've picked up ... Hey watch it. You're driving down the middle of the road."

"Am I? Thanks for telling me. I have a bad habit of doing that."

"Are you trying to scare me or are you being straight?"

"I told you, I can't see at night. That's how it is."

"You can't be serious?"

"Look, it's no game. I'll tell you one more time. What I try to do is to relax and pretend to see. Most times it works. Besides, I have good reflexes."

"Thanks for telling me."

"Listen Sammi, it's no use getting all lathered up about it. I said I'll get you there and I will. I've been driving this way for years."

"Well it sounds like a totally dumb stunt to me."

If she keeps this up, we may start spitting in each other's face in another five minutes.

"Tell me about your brother, the one in Kansas?"

"Are you trying to change the subject?"

"Either we do or one of us is going to get out of the car and walk."

"Don't threaten me, Richard."

"Please Samantha, just tell me about your brother."

"You don't really want to hear about him."

"Okay, I don't want to hear about your brother but tell me anyway. It has to be better than tuning in some easy listening music from Santa Rosa."

"He isn't in Kansas anymore."

"Why's that?"

"He's a captain in the Marines. He gets transferred around a lot."

"Now you're the one who's shitting me. I'm supposed to believe that your brother's a marine?"

"What are you, anti–military?"

"That's not the point. The reason I said ..."

"Don't dodge my questions, Richard."

"Okay, I'll play it your way. No, I am not particularly anti–military. I mean I don't get bent out of shape if I see someone in a uniform. I've known some people who go bananas if they see a marine, or a cop, maybe even a bus driver. That sort of stuff is pretty stupid. I never could understand the point of treating people like objects. That's not what confrontation is about. That's only self indulgence. But try telling them that."

"Do you?"

"Very seldom. With some people it's a waste of time talking to them. And it doesn't matter what their line of chatter is or if they're wearing brass buttons or dungarees. That type of person just doesn't want to hear. You know how it is … But the military itself, I mean apart from the question of individuals; I gotta admit, I'm not too crazy about the military."

"You were never in?"

"I sure in hell didn't enlist. You think I wanted to get blown up in some damn rice patty?"

"You were scared?"

"Damn right I was scared. Do I look congenitally stupid?"

"Like the people who did fight?"

"You think they weren't scared?"

"They didn't sneak out of going."

"I didn't say I avoided it. I just didn't have to go. I was lucky."

"A rich kid deferment?"

"Unfortunately sweetheart, I am not a rich kid. Nope, it was pure dumb luck. I was in that first lottery and pulled a high number … Christ Sammi, I still remember that insane night; everyone sitting by a radio, waiting for those numbers to be read out, waiting to face his destiny …"

"Don't go all dramatic about it, Richard. I'm not about to feel tingles up my spine."

"Look, it was important. How many times is your future decided for you in such an obvious way? You know, I didn't even want to be around anyone. I was way too tense. I snuck off to my dorm room alone and listened late into the night."

"And if you hadn't lucked out?"

"I don't know."

"You mean you didn't give it any thought?"

"Don't be absurd, Sammi. You were alive back then. What eighteen year old kid didn't think about Vietnam? It would be like forgetting about your left testicle. That was part of my life; or do you think I was always terminally out to lunch? I'm trying to say that I wasn't sure how I would react, I mean if I had to make that decision. I was way too unpredictable. I might have ended up in Leavenworth or firing tracer bullets on the D.M.Z. You know Sammi, that was what actually did it."

"Huh?"

"I was thinking about the anti–war movement. Nixon broke the back of that movement with the volunteer army. Once they stopped drafting college kids most of the steam went out of the protests."

"You're not being very fair."

"I don't care about being fair. I'm just telling you what I saw. Once they no longer had to worry about being shot up, a good chunk of them trotted off to become account executives."

"Except you."

"Do I look like I own a briefcase?"

"Is that my cue to applaud?"

"I'll let you know when it is."

"Quick Richard, take a left here. What's the matter with you, Richard? You went right by it!"

"I can't turn going fifty miles an hour. You should've given me some warning."

"I told you, right after the flashing lights."

"They weren't flashing."

"That's hardly my fault."

"Okay, where do I go now?"

"Take a right here."

"You gonna be able to direct me out of this maze?"

"Do you care?"

"Not really."

"So who do you hang out with now?"

"Besides you?"

"Don't take that for granted, sport."

What a drag. Not only is she obnoxious but she's also a snoop.

I should tell her to mind her own damn business, but what's the difference. Why bother being secretive? So who should I tell her about? I wonder if Sarah counts? Nah, that's only once a week and I could do without her altogether.

"I was seeing someone for a while but she left, went back to Colorado."

"Ditched you, huh?"

"Well she said it was because of a job offer but, you're right, I was dumped."

"What'd she do?"

"You mean work? She's a dancer. She dances up there."

"Ballet?"

"No, belly."

"Are you shittin' me?"

"Look, don't start knocking it. Dancing is dancing and she's damn good at it."

"You haven't shaken her yet, have you?"

"That's right. So just don't bring it up."

"I think that's sweet of you."

"I don't need to be patronized."

"You really must have been in love."

"What's so strange about that?"

"Nothing, Richard. Look, I'm sorry about hitting on you."

"That's okay, Samantha."

"When we get to my place, how about coming in for some wine?"

"I'd like that."

"Good, then it's settled."

"It is?"

"Hold on there Junior, not so fast. We'll see what happens."

"I can wait."

"Good, you'll have to … slow down and make another right, now a left at that cabin; not into the house Richard, onto the road there."

"Road?"

"I'm convinced, you are blind."

"That's what I've been telling you."

"It's the third house on the left in back of that plum tree."

"I can't tell one tree from another."

"Richard, pull over, park, and get your ass out of this car."

"You living here alone?"

"Sort of."

"What does that mean?"

"The place belongs to this friend of mine, or at least to her dad. She asked me to stay with her."

"So where is she?"

"She took off."

"Visiting someone?"

"Nope, I mean she disappeared."

"You mean like poof?"

"Don't be a jerk, Richard. No one knows where she is. It's happened before."

"So you're staying on?"

"It's okay with her dad. He wants someone to look after the place. When real estate agents come around he likes to have someone here."

"So that's what all those little white cards are from."

"Yeah, it's a multiple listing. Whenever I come back there's always at least one business card waiting for me."

"You don't mind?"

"I don't pay any rent."

"What happens when he sells the place?"

"Obviously I'll have to move. It's not like I come with the joint."

"Where will you go?"

"Somewhere else. I don't bother worrying. I can always manage."

"Pretty confident aren't you?"

"It doesn't take all that many smarts to find a place to stay."

"Sometimes it can be a hassle."

"Only if you let it, Richard. Look, how about some wine? It's a Moselle. Do you know what that is?"

"Yes, Samantha, I know what a Moselle is."

"Well, would you rather have something else?"

"Like what?"

"Juice, tea, coffee?"

"What kind of tea?"

"Chamomile, maybe some English Breakfast. I could look."

"No jasmine?"

"Yuck!"

"There something wrong with jasmine?"

"It's okay if you like drinking perfume."

"I'll have some wine."

"What was the survey for?"

"Just curious."

"You weren't maybe thinking ahead to breakfast tomorrow morning?"

"Nope."

"Well, don't start counting on it, sonny."

"I wouldn't think of it."

"No need to be so definite, Richard. You never know what may …"

"Like me to open that wine?"

"You trying to change the subject?"

"That's right. Now, how about handing over that wine?"

"You certainly don't bother to dodge around."

"Sweetie, I know when I'm outmatched."

"Smart."

"I give it a try now and then."

"I hope so for your sake. I get tired of most things real quick."

"How's that?"

"Nothing seems to last. Sure, I get excited at the beginning but then everything just starts to deteriorate. Once I figure something out, once I know what makes the damn thing tick, it becomes a bore. There are no more surprises left. When that happens, it's time to shine the whole thing on. That's the way it is with people. They become boring and predictable. So, I take off."

"Too bad."

"You think so?"

"Maybe not. If you wanta know the truth, it probably depends on how you look at it."

"That doesn't mean a damn thing."

"You've got it."

"What?"

"That's the point, Sammi. It doesn't matter that you're bored with people."

"I'm not bored by people."

"You said you were bored with people."

"Richard, if you're not going to pay attention I won't waste any more of my energy on this."

"Sounds like an exit line."

"I live here."

"Me, I'm the one that should be going."

"What makes you think you have to go?"

"You, sweetie. It sounds like you're throwing me out."

"Look buster, if I wanted you to go you'd know it. I don't fuck around."

"Why can't you just come out and ask me to stay?"

"It means that much to you, Richard?"

"I'm tired. Not only am I tired but I'm totally fed up with trying to be cool and hip. It's not worth my time learning the rules and the right moves. Bad enough some of that stuff rubs off anyway. So let's just use simple words so that even I can understand. Open your mouth and say, 'I would like you to stay.' See how easy it is to show a little concern."

"Why bother?"

"If you're having trouble grasping the concept, try thinking of it as a favor. Or, tell me to pack it in. It's all the same to me—there, you've got me doing it."

"You know, you're being extremely difficult over nothing at all. Okay, if it'll make you feel better, I want you to stay."

"See, I told you it was easy to be gracious. Next I'll teach you how to say please and thank you."

"Do you always have to be such a smart ass? It's starting to get on my nerves."

"You know, that's the cause of the world–wide population explosion."

"What, you being a smart ass?"

"No, you're supposed to say, 'What's that?'"

"Then what do you say?"

"Too many fucking people."

"You seriously expect me to feed you straight lines for bum jokes like that?"

"I thought you might."

"Try again."

"Okay, I was a failed abortion."

"I don't want to hear any more of your jokes."

"No joke. I was scheduled to be an abortion."

"Well no one's perfect, Richard."

"Don't be such a snot."

"Okay, you want to tell me about it, go ahead."

"Well since you're so enthusiastic …"

"Your mother didn't want a kid but she had you anyway, what else?"

"My folks had been through the wringer with my sister. They didn't need any more grief. So when she found out she was pregnant, my mother opted for an abortion."

"Not so easily done."

"Not back in 1951. I guess she had some bad connections. All she came up with was an old lady in the slummy part of town who gave her a bottle of pills."

"What did they do?"

"Made her shit green for about a week."

"Not quite the same as an abortion."

"No, not even very close."

"And was everything else standard for a little boy growing up in …"

"Ohio. I'm not sure. I get confused about childhood and adolescence. I keep thinking that it should be something like the stuff you see on TV."

"Don't be a maroon."

"Yeah I know, but it's hard to shake. I kept expecting my dad to be another Ward Cleaver."

"Who?"

"*Leave It To Beaver.*"

"Oh yeah, that show with Eddie Haskell."

" 'Good morning Mrs. Cleaver. My but you certainly look attractive today.' 'Why thank you Eddie.' 'I was wondering if Wallace and young Theodore might be up in their room.' Those two were always up in their room. Probably the only time they were allowed downstairs was for dinner. And good old Ward Cleaver hanging out in his den, we didn't even have a den."

"No one lives like that. How many mothers wear high heels and makeup to cook lunch."

"But you see what I mean. I kept wondering why I wasn't having good times down at the malt shop with the rest of the guys. People who claim they had wonderful childhoods are not to be trusted. I think they've just got short memories."

"Yours couldn't have been that bad."

"Difficult, not bad. I mean I know my parents cared about me. There's no denying that. But sometimes obsessive concern can become pretty damn claustrophobic. There were days when I wouldn't have minded a little benign neglect."

"It's worse the other way. Ends up making you feel all cold inside."

"I know. It doesn't even have to be intentional. Friend of mine was deserted in a department store when he was four. His father forgot he had him along. Drove home without giving it a thought. Good thing his mom wasn't totally out to lunch."

"Is that true?"

"Yeah, it was one of those family stories that everyone laughs about. In fact I think I heard it from his mother. I thought it was pretty funny."

"What about your friend?"

"He never mentioned it. Somehow I don't think he found it quite so hilarious."

"So which way is worse?"

"You got me there, Samantha. My parents were impossible in their own way. I once pissed off my father and he refused to talk to me for a week."

"That, I don't believe."

"No, it's too goofy not to be true. It took a formal apology conveyed through my Mom to break the ice."

"At least you didn't have inspection after reveille."

"Where?"

"Military for morning wake–up. Everything at my house was synchronized; alarm clocks, bathroom use, breakfast. If we were late for a meal we went without."

"That explains your brother."

"How's that?"

"Entered the family business, joined the Marines."

"It's not quite that simple, but it's true Dad was in the Army. Spent thirty years in, never made it past major."

"Did you like being an army brat?"

"What kind of question is that? Did you like being a boy? I didn't get to try out other alternatives."

"I mean, did you envy the kids who lived in one place? Were you an unhappy child?"

"It was mostly my father. He was impossible. The moving around was no big deal. I'm pretty adaptable."

"Even as a child?"

"Yeah, no different. Maybe I was odd but I never felt insecure. I made friends easy enough."

"So what was the problem with your father?"

"You can pin it down with a single letter. The bastard was a miser as well as a hard core martinet. You know what that means?"

"I have an unusually large vocabulary considering my socio-economic class."

Samantha flashes me one of her, 'Don't fuck with me Charley' looks.

"We had to stand at attention around the breakfast table till the little dictator strode in."

"Did you salute?"

"You know, I used to wonder whether he inspected Mom before they screwed. Probably conducted her through her paces by the numbers."

"Sounds pretty dismal."

"I could almost forgive him all that military crap. I doubt that he could help it. The army trained him to think like a metronome. It probably became the only way he knew to relate to other people. But the army wasn't to blame for his obsessive stinginess. Do you know he put my mother on a budget?"

"That doesn't sound too extreme."

"How many housewives do you know that have to master double entry bookkeeping in order to buy groceries? Dad would audit her accounts every Saturday night."

"Right before they humped by numbers?"

"Shut up Richard, it's not funny. My Mom would sit at the kitchen table with tears streaming down her face trying to balance her budget."

"What if she didn't?"

"She'd have to make it up out of next week's allowance. At some point Mom started fudging the figures. I can remember helping her when I got older."

"So you resent your dad because he mistreated your mother."

"Nope, that asshole was totally impartial. Sure I resented what he did to Mom, but I hate him because of the way he humiliated me. You know he used to dole out a small allowance to me and my brother and never let loose of one dime more. I can't ever remember getting an extra treat or a little surprise."

"It could've been worse."

"Okay, you want details? What about the time we were living in Italy? Dad was some sort of military attaché with the Embassy in Rome. Did you ever see that film, *The Bicycle Thief*?"

"Sure, De Sica."

"Good. Remember the scene shot at a flea market when they were searching for that crazy bike?"

"I think so."

"The camera pans over boxes and boxes of bicycle parts; horns, wheels, seats, every goddamned thing you could think of … Well, that's how I got my first and only bike."

"Huh?"

"Good old Dad haggled over each and every part, threw the

whole mess in the back of his car, and spent the next week piecing it together. Sure it sounds pretty funny but try to imagine a ten year old kid rolling along on a Salvador Dali bike. I would've cried but it took all my concentration to keep that abortion going. The front wheel wobbled something fierce."

"Anything else?"

"Richard, I could sit here all night without running out of stories. I'll give you one more example from the same year. We were living in this villa outside of Rome ..."

"Wait a minute, I thought you said he was such a cheap bastard?"

"He rented it from a West Point buddy at half the going rate."

"Sorry."

"Well Dad decides we need some chickens for the back yard. Figured on selling the eggs and picking up some extra lire."

"You're kidding."

"It was no joke. We had ten chickens clucking away behind the house."

"What about the neighbors?"

"He intimidated them. He had a flair for doing that. But the real point of the story is distribution."

"You mean of the eggs."

"Every Saturday morning my brother and I were handed a wicker basket filled with eggs. We were told to go from door to door until all the eggs were gone. Dad made it clear that he didn't expect to see a single egg returned."

"You're making this one up, Sammi."

"I don't need to make these things up. I can remember every last detail. My mother shaking me awake at seven o'clock, scrubbing my face and helping me put on a clean dress. I had a pair of those Buster Brown saddle shoes which I always wore with white cotton ankle socks. Before I left I had to sign a receipt for the eggs I took."

"Didn't your mom try to stop it?"

"What could she do? The poor woman was terrified. If she tried slipping me some money she'd have to juggle her accounts even more. And Dad would notice if we started having eggs too often."

"You must have looked sweet going door to door with your little basket."

"Sit on it, Richard. My brother did the Fuller Brush routine, not me. I would wait by the curb for an hour then toss those damn eggs down the sewer."

"I don't understand."

"I used my allowance to pay for the eggs. You think I was going to humiliate myself? I had maybe ten lire to spare."

"What's that worth?"

"I think at the time it came to about one cent U.S. I don't know what it'd be now."

"Not a whole bunch."

"That's right, sweetie. If I saved up for a month I could buy a small square of chocolate. Usually I never dared. I was always afraid Dad would raise the price of eggs."

"Balance of payments deficit."

"What's that?"

"Nothing, I was just thinking about international trade."

"Don't say it unless you want to explain it, Junior."

"It was nothing important."

"Then don't let it dribble out."

"Should I salute now?"

"That's not funny, Richard."

"Well what about your brother?"

"What about him?"

"Was he traumatized too?"

"Who knows? It's something we don't talk about. Look, enough of this childhood crap. Why don't you tell me more about your love life."

"What love life? All my former girlfriends are married and/or mothers. I think that's the first time I've ever thought and/or said that out loud. Makes me sound like some sort of a textbook talking. Anyway, it makes me feel old. Some days I feel about one hundred and five years old. Not very exciting, is it?"

"That's okay Richard, if you want to keep your little secrets, go right ahead."

"It's not a matter of secrets. There's just not much to tell. My love affairs are mostly a series of departures. If you wanted to shoot the film version, all the major scenes would take place in airports, train stations or bus depots. One minute I'm starting a relationship, the next I'm waving good–bye. I'm always biting on the promise of an affair, never chewing on the reality."

"Obviously that's what you want."

"Nothing's that obvious, Samantha. I don't really know what I want. When I was twenty I was a total romantic. I actually believed all that stuff you see in the movies, I mean my little heart yearned for romance. Some day, I thought I would meet the one woman who could truly love me. And then, all my problems would vanish."

"It doesn't work that way."

"I know that. It's not a solution. But that's not the point. At twenty, I believed that the reason I was unhappy was because I couldn't find the right girl. So I proceeded to make myself even more miserable."

"What's the point then?"

"That's exactly it. There was no point, none at all. Took me a good five years to figure that out."

"And so?"

"Nothing. It doesn't make you feel better but what does besides strong drugs?"

"Sex."

"Only sometimes. But coming face to face with emptiness certainly doesn't. What I mean to say is that I cured myself of romanticism but I can't say I gained anything in particular."

"No?"

"Uh uh. I don't spend my time yearning after every woman I see but so what? There's nothing wrong with yearning."

"It's pathetic."

"True, but it's probably more entertaining than self awareness."

"So you've given up on relationships?"

"Oh no, I'm still as big a sucker for a beautiful woman like you as I ever was. I just don't expect anything from it."

"Is that supposed to be a compliment?"

"You mean about you being beautiful? Hm, it might be. No, wait a second, maybe not. You're an attractive woman but I thought that was obvious."

"Well thanks. You know you can just come right out with it. I don't mind."

"No, I'm getting this all gummed up. It wasn't really a compliment because that wasn't my intention. Now, if I said, 'You have a smashingly beautiful face,' that would be a compliment."

"You think so?"

"Sounds like a compliment to me."

"No you idiot, about my face."

"Sure, but you must know that. Beautiful women usually do."

"Sometimes, but it never hurts to be reminded."

"Okay, but we're getting off the track. I was trying to explain how I feel."

"Why?"

"I don't know why. For some reason I thought you asked. Maybe it's just that we've still got half a bottle of wine to kill and I thought I'd fill in the time by talking. I'll shut up if you want."

"No, go ahead. I don't mind."

"Thanks a bunch … All I was saying is that I wasn't trying to compliment you. I was just telling you how I feel about relationships. I don't expect anything from them. Come to think of it I'm usually not disappointed."

"You probably set yourself up for what you get."

"Possibly, but I can't make myself believe in personal magic anymore. Relationships are futile."

"God, you're depressing."

"Yeah, well let's talk about something else then. Why don't you tell me about your name?"

"Samantha? You want to know why my name's Samantha? You're not exactly being original."

"You've got your choice, sweetheart. I've got two basic modes; depressing or boring."

"Are you trying to be cute?"

"Not particularly. Look, humor me. I know you've been through it umpteen times before, but it won't kill you."

"Okay, what do you want to know?"

"Well Samantha's such an unusual name."

"I like it."

"I didn't say I don't like it, but it feels unreal. People in storybooks have names like that. Witches in fairy tales are called Samantha."

"Are you saying I'm a witch?"

"No, I've just never known a Samantha before."

"Actually it's my middle name."

"Oh yeah?"

"Aren't you going to ask me what my first name is?"

"I'm afraid you'll tell me."

"Don't be an ass."

"Okay, what is it?"

"Sydney."

"Sydney?"

"I told you, my father was an army officer."

"So?"

"He was stationed in Australia when I was born."

"Wait a minute, there's no U.S. base in Australia."

"Are you sure?"

"Well no, I'm not positive but …"

"There you go."

"Then why don't you use it?"

"Are you kidding?"

"You end up being called Sammi, anyway."

"It's not the same thing."

"I don't see any difference."

"Look, how would you like me to start calling you Daphne?"

"I don't think I'd be too crazy about it."

"See."

"What? I don't understand."

"Obviously the question's settled."

"But why would you want to call me Daphne?"

"You can't let go of anything, can you Daphne?"

"I'm not getting very far am I?"

"Losing ground all the time."

"Okay Samantha, no more questions."

"That's up to you, it's your life."

"Thank you."

"No problem at all."

"Well the wine's about finished."

"Is that some kind of hint? Do you expect to fuck me now?"

"I'd like to."

"That's not what I asked."

"I try not to anticipate."

"Afraid of being shot down?"

"Not entirely. I'd just feel like a smug bastard expecting it to happen."

"But the thought did cross your mind?"

"C'mon Samantha. A nearly beautiful woman asks me to drive her home and I ..."

"Nearly beautiful?"

"You're an extremely attractive woman. I like how you look. Let's not quibble about aesthetics."

"And?"

"So of course I thought about it. What do you think I am, a human turnip?"

"Okay, go ahead."

"What?"

"Do it."

"Don't be so goddam condescending."

"Look you cretin, you're right. That's why I asked you in. So shut up and get started."

"Here, on the kitchen table?"

"Oh Richard, have I hurt your feelings again?"

"No, I'm just reeling from your overpowering charm."

"Come here ... Now take my hands and listen. It's okay, you're only reacting to me. I've been pushing you too hard. I know. I do that sometimes. Let's go to bed now and be nice to each other instead ... Hey you oaf, what do you think you're doing?"

Samantha isn't constructed for convenient carrying, too many long dangling limbs. Still, I manage to stagger toward her bedroom. "Mph," I grunt romantically. Samantha is squirming and making life generally difficult. We knock over one minor lamp but not before I find the right door.

"Richard don't …"

Well, why not go for a splashy finish? I hurl myself, Samantha included, onto her mattress. But, there's no reassuring oomph to break our descent. Instead, I'm victimized by Newtonian physics. Whomp, and the mattress is transformed into a nasty piece of plywood.

"Samantha?"

"Huh?"

"Were you about to warn me that your bed was a bit on the firm side?"

"I have a bad back."

"You're not the only one now."

"We've got to get up anyway to take off our clothes."

"Don't worry about that, just relax."

"But I don't even know your last name."

"Davis; pleased to meet you."

***

Well that really sucked. Here I am wanting to impress this bimbo and I totally blow it. Maybe I've forgotten some of the right moves. I'll have to go out and buy one of those inflatable love dolls to practice on, or I could always learn to yodel instead. Damn, I know I shouldn't feel inadequate but I'm sure Samantha's ready to pounce. I wouldn't be surprised if she held up a point total.

"What do you think you're doing, Samantha?"

"It's obvious isn't it?"

"Don't waste your time."

"Meaning?"

"Jesus Christ himself couldn't resurrect old Akbar down there."

"So that's it. huh?"

"Yep, show's over."

"Less than spectacular wasn't it, Richard?"

"Look toots, what would you like me to do, fist fuck you?"

"Don't be gross."

"Sammi, you're beautiful but I'm just too wasted."

"You're planning on dropping off to dreamland now, aren't you? Maybe you'd like me to hold your poor little head?"

She's hunched over me, tits swaying back and forth like salamis in a delicatessen window. This woman is becoming a distinct problem.

"Leave up, lady. Are you getting a kick out of needling me?"

"Okay Richard, no need to be so sensitive."

"I'm not being sensitive. There's just no need to dump on me. What if I started complaining about the shape of your cunt? Be pretty stupid wouldn't it?"

"Not the same thing."

"I don't want to fight about this. You're too smart to see it as some sort of dopey contest. It's not that I don't want to make you feel good. Sometimes it just doesn't work out."

"I know that. I've got to check, though. Some men are just pigs. I'm not here to be pawed over."

I reach up bringing her face down near mine and kiss Samantha carefully on each eyelid.

"We'll try another time, Sammi. Don't be upset."

"I'll think about it."

I was right to begin with. She'd be more responsive to a few raps in the mouth. This trial by ordeal business is nothing but the total shits.

"Could you set your alarm for eight?"

"Don't worry Richard, I'll make sure to roust you out of bed."

***

I hear Samantha get up and stumble to the kitchen. The dry throat and pounding head of a suitably respectable hangover urge me to make one last grab for unconsciousness.

"Richard, are you awake?"

"Mph, scxrnt."

"Here, I made you some tea."

To be able to open my gummed up eyelids on a beautiful woman is both undeserved and unhoped for. To have that same woman make some gesture of concern is overwhelming. Kindness is always unexpected. It leaves me defenseless. I'm a sucker for a small thoughtful act. At this moment, if Samantha would only promise never to get dressed, my devotion would be complete.

"Thanks, that's really decent of you."

"No trouble. Look, I'm going to take a shower. I'll be out in fifteen minutes."

"No need to rush off."

"I'm feeling grungy. I need to wash."

"I think you look terrific."

"That's sweet, but the only thing that's going to make me feel better is some hot water."

"Well …"

"No, Richard, not now. Why don't you take a shower with me?"

"No, you go ahead."

Now that I've registered as unclean, as well as a bum fuck, I can't possibly sink much lower. Actually it's my hair I'm worried about. If I take a shower it'll be hours before it dries. Then bits of it'll go shooting off, following its own aims and directions, till it resembles a basic *Bride of Frankenstein* cut. I can wash when I get home. At least this way I won't have to worry about clogging her drain with my pubic hair … Well, maybe she was satisfied with last night. Nah, couldn't be. I can sense these things, especially when I'm told straight to my face. Christ, I wonder why I was so clumsy. I've been wasted before.

"Richard?"

"What's up?"

"Did you know I had a tampon in last night?"

Well aren't I the compleat nerd.

"Oh yeah?"

That's what I admire about myself, never at a lost for some witty repartee.

"I just said so, didn't I? Couldn't you tell or didn't you even give a damn?"

If she thinks I'm getting involved in this sort of discussion she's dopier than I am. You think she could have told me it was her period. At least that explains the sliding door effect to her vagina. I thought things were a bit cramped.

"I'm asking you a question, Richard. How could you not notice?"

"I knew something was peculiar but I wasn't in any shape to make sharp distinctions."

"Well, that's just stupid."

"Okay, I'm a dummy. But what about you? It's your tampon and your period. You can't just disassociate yourself from that?"

"The point is not whether I put a tampon in."

"You could have mentioned it last night."

"It wasn't my responsibility."

"Well, it didn't bother me. There was plenty of room in there for all concerned."

"That's only because of your midget hard–on, Richard."

"If you're not satisfied, shop somewhere else. I'm not into performing."

"That's obvious."

"So what am I supposed to do now?"

"Oh nothing, I just thought I'd mention it."

"Cute, very cute."

"I think so."

Either I'm going to fall madly in love with this woman or I'm going to hack her into little pieces and mail them off in a series of hatboxes. Right now I'm leaning heavily toward the sausage option. Okay, I'll give it one more try.

"How about breakfast when you're dry?"

"There's nothing to eat in the house."

"No, I meant how about going out for something."

"Where to?"

"The River Front. It's close by and I know one of the owners."

"How's the food?"

"Decent."

"I can't go. I'm broke."

"I meant it as an invitation, my treat."

"Are you trying to bribe me?"

"That's right, I'm feeding you so you'll keep me company for a few hours."

"You don't have to do that."

"I know I don't. I'd like to take you to breakfast. You're not obliged to come."

"Obviously … Well okay, I think I will. Yeah, thanks a lot."

I really do feel like throttling her. Samantha has the manners and the innate grace of a warthog. But then here she comes damp from her shower, looking so terrific that I don't care if she is congenitally rude or even if she thinks I'm impotent. All that wild blond hair and that tight slim body; damn, I wouldn't mind slamming my tampon in her right this moment.

"You look really great."

"Thanks."

"Who's that?"

"Where?"

"That picture on your dresser."

"Oh, that's my brother. I told you about him last night. He's in the Marines. What's the matter with your memory?"

"Yeah, I remember now. Well, you certainly don't look like any Marine I've ever seen."

"Want to feel my biceps?"

"So how come you're house–sitting this dark crummy cabin instead of married to some nice lieutenant in Kansas?"

"Because I don't want to be in Kansas right now. Maybe next month I will, but not now … I know, let me show you my butterfly collection. It's in this box."

"You mean you've got one of those nets and a …"

"No, I just find them already dead. I wouldn't want to kill one."

"I can't remember ever seeing a dead butterfly lying on the ground."

"That's because you don't look. Here, I found this one in Kansas."

"It's pretty."

"It's more than that, it's a miracle."

***

"Are you sure this place is any good?"

"Trust me Samantha. Claude's my neighbor. He'll cook us up

something decent."

"Well, I'll take your word for it."

"Thank you Samantha ... Claude, what's the story around here?"

"Hey hey, Richard. Haven't seen your ugly puss around here for a while."

"You know how it is working in restaurants."

"All too well guy."

"How's Debbi been? What's she doing with herself these days?"

"Debbi's been sick, hepatitis."

"How the hell ..."

"From our drinking water. You know what a tight bastard Spencer is."

"I'm still waiting for that insulation he promised."

"Yeah, well remember how our cesspool always overflowed after a heavy rain? It finally started leeching into the well water."

"That would do it."

"I'm gonna sue that bastard. Debbi lost nearly twenty pounds, and then her hair started falling out. At least he could pay for the wig."

"Listen, tell Debbi hello for me. I hope she's feeling better."

"Thanks, I will. Now what can I getcha?"

"Thought I'd take a chance on one of your breakfasts. Learn to make an omelet yet?"

"Your boyfriend's a real panic, isn't he?"

"Why don't you just answer his question, sport?"

"Is that true, Claude?"

"Now wait a minute, Richard ..."

"No, up there on your menu. You really serving burritos?"

"Oh that, sure, started last month. They're going over pretty well."

"Can you make 'em with avocado and a little salsa?"

"Don't see why not."

"I love burritos."

"I could put one together for you. Wouldn't be too much of a hassle."

"No kidding. That's decent of you."

"Richard, you can't have a burrito at ten o'clock in the morning."

"So what's the word Pancho? You want for me to feex the beeg burrito con salsa?"

"She says I can't have a burrito for breakfast."

"Well, if Miss Emily Post says no, then I guess it's gotta be no."

"The name's Samantha, Samantha Doran. Why don't you just try minding your eggs and waffles, Clyde? We can make up our own mind without you leaning on us."

"Now wait a minute honey ..."

"Gee I'm sorry, Claude, I thought you two knew each other."

"I don't want to rush you, Richard, but I've got other orders waiting."

"Yeah, who from Clyde? Did that potted palm in the corner ask for one of your burritos?"

"Look sweetheart, I don't have to ..."

"I'm not your sweetheart you big ..."

"Samantha, why don't we just order."

"Stop trying to be so damn nice, Richard. You don't have to ..."

"The mushroom omelet, Claude and some of your oatmeal toast."

"Sure, Richard ... Uhm, I think your girlfriend would like you to get off her foot."

"I'm sorry, Samantha. Are you okay?"

"Don't think I won't remember this, Richard. Order me a spinach and cheese omelet."

"Are you sure about the spinach?"

"Don't argue with me, Richard."

"You heard her Claude."

"Oh I sure did. Ms. Doran will get her spinach omelet. Don't you worry about that. One spinach and cheese omelet coming right up."

"Look, I said I was sorry, Samantha. Now maybe you'd rather order ..."

"I know what I want."

"Anything to drink for you and the princess?"

"How about splitting a strawberry smoothie?"

"Does he use fresh strawberries?"

I grab Samantha and hustle her off to a table on the sun porch. Claude's an okay guy but he's been having some hard luck. Rumor says his partner's trying to screw him. I doubt that he's up for a go

around with old Sammi, but who is? What the fuck's the matter
with her? You'd think she had it in for every guy she runs across...
But when I see that beautiful face, even her snotty attitude becomes
appealing. I wonder what it takes to acquire normal tastes?

"Don't ever do that again, Richard."

"I'm not about to spend my morning apologizing to you or
anyone else. I'm not into early morning confrontations. It was just
easier to avoid a stupid scene."

"Shape up, buster. You'll never go forward in life if you're always
back–pedaling."

"Hold it Samantha. I really am sorry about your foot. If it'd help
I'd kiss every last little tootsie to make them all better. But I saw
what happened. You were needling Claude. You wanted him to
blow."

"Who me?"

"Okay, it's very funny. Smile all you want but ... Samantha, do
you realize you just poured a glass of water down my boot?"

"I consider the issue closed."

"Sweetheart, do you remember when you were young being told
a dirty joke and not getting it?"

"Yeah, like maybe last week."

"The difference is when you're thirteen you feel like you have to
laugh."

"Peer pressure."

"Sure, who's gonna admit to not knowing about sex?"

"I can never remember any of those jokes."

"I'm not asking you to tell me one."

"They're not even particularly funny."

"The point is not dirty jokes ... You know, I've never made that
connection before. Sex is dirty. What a bizarre mindset. Sticky
maybe, but dirty? I mean not unless you decide to hump on a mud
flat or something."

"You were about to make another one of your points, Richard?"

"Yeah, the point is, I'm much older now."

"That's not much of a point."

"And, I no longer feel obliged to laugh. If I'm curious I'll even ask for an explanation."

"Good for you."

"So I'm asking you now Samantha; what do you have against me?"

"That's certainly an indirect approach you've got there."

"I like to take my time getting to where I'm going."

"I hope so."

"We both do. Now what's the scoop?"

"Vanilla, chocolate, strawberry."

"You're not about to answer, are you?"

"I like to take my time getting to where I'm going."

"In other words, when you're ready, you'll tell me."

"You're a potentially bright boy, Richard."

"Yeah, I'm even learning to read without moving my lips."

"So, are you going to pick up our omelets or what?"

"I'll be right back."

"Don't forget about the strawberry smoothie …"

"What do I owe you, Claude?"

"For you, five bucks."

"Are you sure?"

"There's one catch."

"I know, I won't bring Samantha back."

"It's nothing personal, Richard, I just don't like dealing with her."

"Sure Claude, I'll catch you around."

I suppose I should've taken a poke at him but he has a point. She is a pain in the butt.

"How's the omelet, Samantha?"

"Don't look so damn smug."

"I knew Claude wouldn't have the sense to rinse the spinach."

"He did it on purpose."

"You're giving him too much credit."

"You could've said something."

"I tried to but … Hey, what do you think you're doing?"

"Switching omelets."

"Am I supposed to like grit in my breakfast?"

"Try taking it to that laundromat around the corner."

"Yummy, maybe, you'd like me to iron the leaves after the spin cycle?"

"You think that'd work?"

"Depends whether or not you use the right starch. Otherwise you might scorch the little buggers."

"Look, do you mind about the eggs?"

"Nah, I'm just fucking around. Go ahead and enjoy yourself. What I eat for breakfast doesn't matter much."

"That's nice, but how do you expect to eat when your hands are in my lap?"

"You noticed that?"

"Yeah, you forget how damn sharp I am."

"I was momentarily stunned by your beauty."

"You are bizarre, aren't you Mr. Davis?"

"I try my best."

"Well eat your breakfast and we can discuss my lap later."

"Okay boss, just one thing more. If I say something you think is funny?"

"Yes?"

"It's not that I don't appreciate a good audience, but I wish you wouldn't blow egg on my face."

"Sorry, Richard. Here, let me wipe that off for you … Did you know you've got little bits of omelet in your hair. You look kind of cute."

"Maybe you'd like to try rubbing marmalade into my mustache?"

"Oh don't be so dignified. There, I think I've got the last piece."

"Samantha, how about swallowing between laughs. I feel like I'm undergoing some strange new facial treatment."

"I can't help it Richard, it's your face."

"I know it's my face, but it's your omelet."

"No, the expression on it. You've got one of those rubber faces that registers whatever you feel."

"Okay, I'll admit to being a clown if you'll snort into a napkin from now on … Is putting butter on my nose suppose to amuse me?"

"Eat your toast."

"You think you can get away with this don't you."

"I know I can sweetie."

"What makes you so sure?"

"One, you're a nice guy. Two, we both know I'm attractive."

"We both know that?"

"A hah."

"And that's all it takes?"

"You gonna argue?"

"No."

"Besides, I take good care of you, Richard. See, I always clean up after playing with your face."

"I'm impressed."

"You don't fool me kid, you're enjoying this."

"Sure."

"By the way, there's a dork approaching us from 0100."

"So how's my main man, Mr. Richie doing?"

"Hey Mick, how's it going? Oh you know Samantha, don't you?"

That was close. Almost did it again. I always forget to introduce people. Pisses them off something fierce. Maybe I should try rereading *Pride and Prejudice*.

"Sure, I've seen her around."

"Where?"

"Did you say something, baby?"

"Where have you seen me before?"

"You know, like in the local clubs when I'm playing with my band. I'm not gonna miss a good looking honey like you."

"I'm not your honey, Mac."

"No, the name's Mick … am I upsetting you baby?"

"Your band needs a new lead singer."

"She's some funny lady you've got there, Richard."

"You think I can't hear you buddy? I'm sitting right next to you, you big hairy …"

"Now Sammi, he doesn't understand that you're only fooling around."

"Butt out, Richard. You don't have to protect him."

"Why don't you have a seat, Mick. Samantha and I were just

talking about your band."

"Thanks man, nothing I'd like better, but I really gotta split. I left Annie waiting outside for me in the car."

"I thought she was in New York this week."

"Yeah, I guess you're right. Look, I'll see you tonight, okay man. I've got this ton of work that's gotta get done ... Hey Richie, do me a big favor. Put some of these flyers up around town. I can't do it all by myself ... Thanks man, I really appreciate it."

We both watch Mick scuttle off. Maybe I shouldn't have bothered with the introductions.

"That was pretty low about his voice."

"Oh, is he the lead singer?"

"You're a real killer, aren't you Samantha?"

"What about you calling him on Annie?"

"It's not the same thing. That just slipped out accidental like."

"So what's the story with that guy? Is he supposed to be some sort of friend of yours?"

"Who Mick? I'm not sure. I think it's one of those deals where we both pretend to be friends. Neither of us really gives a damn about the other."

"Why bother?"

"Mostly because it isn't a bother. Mick's pretty harmless. I mean it's not like we hang out together or I fuck his old lady. There's no reason we can't be on good terms."

"Do you want to?"

"Fuck his old lady? Nah, not really. She's too Marin County slick for me. Though I think I could if I wanted. She's been trolling the neighborhood recently."

"She's a sleazebag."

"You know her?"

"I've seen her around."

"That's not enough."

"She'd blow sailors for a dollar."

"And how much do you charge sweetie, five bucks? Ah Samantha, if I let you step on my face later on will you put down that plate now?"

"You were lucky this time."

"I'm sorry, it just came out. But you didn't have to rag on that poor woman. She's never done anything to you."

"She's a slut."

"That's no way to talk about someone. How would you feel if …"

"I don't want to hear about it, Richard."

"Look, I don't give a damn about Annie, Mick, or anybody else in his hokey band. But you don't see me going out of my way just to be nasty."

"The band's okay but he can't sing for shit."

"You know you're terrific Samantha. I'm not sure why, but you are terrific … Hey, what are you doing to those flyers? Stop drawing zits on Mick's face."

"It's an improvement."

"Can't you ever leave go of something?"

"I'm not leaving go of you, sonny."

"Is that a promise?"

Oh shit on me. I am definitely falling in love with this loony. That makes me one very dumb person.

"You're being serious, aren't you Richard?"

"I'm trying to be."

"I'll think about it. Here, lean over for a minute."

"… Jesus Samantha, how'd you do that?"

"Did you like it?"

"I don't think you should do that too often. Might short out my pacemaker."

"Stop being silly."

"C'mon, let's get going."

"What's the rush?"

"If we don't get moving I'm going to come right in my pants … Stop that Samantha."

"Okay sweetie, let me help you up."

***

The truth is I like being with a good looking woman. I like to feel that I'm being watched, that I'm basking in reflected glory. It's nothing but dumb vanity, but I love it. I know that I do. I can't cure it, can't begin to defend it. So why bother lying to myself? It's not my only motivation, but it's there goddammit, it's always there.

"Must be almost two years since I lived here, Richard."

"In Greenfield?"

"Yeah, I mean right here; across the street above that laundromat. I roomed with this woman who gave French lessons."

"In Greenfield?"

"Stop repeating yourself, Richard. You sound like some goddamn parrot."

"That must've been awful."

"No, not at all."

"But this is such a sleazy little redneck town, and living over an all night laundromat—are you trying to tell me that wasn't depressing?"

"You're wrong, Richard. And you're gonna keep being wrong as long as you refuse to open those big beautiful eyes of yours. Why are you so negative about everything? I could take you by the hand right now. Ten minutes from here are places so wonderful that even you'd be forced to notice. Take off those blinders Richard. You've become trapped by your own ..."

"Okay Samantha, you don't have to keep on ..."

"No you listen to me, Richard. Sometimes when I was living over that dumpy laundromat, I'd get up at dawn and just wander around. Those places I was telling you about, you can stay there for hours without seeing anyone. And the people around here aren't just ignorant greasebulbs. They're as real as you are and every bit as interesting. Maybe one day we'll go visiting. There's a woman who knew Ferringhetti in the fifties and an old man whose father bucked redwood logs back when it took two days to get from here to the mill. Another had an uncle who worked on the coastal train from San Francisco."

"You've made your point."

"Don't knock everything, Richard."

"You're right, it's a nasty habit."

"Well you should do something about it."

"I could keep you around to restrain me."

"Is that supposed to be funny?"

"No, actually it might be quite nice."

"I can't tell when to believe you, Richard. I hear you saying some really sweet things but I don't know if you mean any of them."

"There's nothing I can do about that."

"You mean you don't want to bother."

"Samantha, believe me, if I could think of something that would turn the trick I would. I'd wear my underwear backwards for a month if it would work. But I'm old enough to know that there's no magic formula. It's your decision."

"Then I'll have to put my mind to it."

"I'm in no hurry."

And that's true. It's sunny out. I'm holding hands with a good looking woman and I'm feeling content. Well except for a stunning hangover, severe lack of sleep and a desperate need to shave and shower.

"Do you remember the words to that song Richard?"

"Which one?"

"You know the one that goes, 'I get no kick from champagne'."

"Mere alcohol doesn't thrill me at all."

"But tell me, what can I do?"

"Cause, I get a kick out of you."

Step out of your romantic fog, buddy boy. You're hung–over at twelve noon in front of a seedy laundromat singing Cole Porter. Try to squeeze some significance out of that. Besides, we sound terrible. She's the only woman I've met whose soprano is a match for my tenor. It's true though, Samantha is elegant. I've never thought too much about bone structure but that's what she's got. Not that it stops her from being sleazy. I don't know about that combination, sleaze and elegance. Still, in the right light she reminds me of that Goya portrait. No, not any of those hokey ones, more like that portrait in the National Gallery. I used to stare at that damn thing instead of looking for a job as a government flunkey. I guess I'm just a push over for any good looking woman, even if she's only oil and canvas. The coloring's all wrong, but for some reason Samantha reminds me of that portrait. It must be the elegance.

"Eleanor Roosevelt's had me to tea."

"That's enough singing, Richard. Are you working again tonight?"

"Yep."

"Then we better get going. Do you remember how to get back?"

"Not exactly."

"Just follow my directions after the first left."

"Anything you say boss."

"How much longer you going to be working there?"

"I'm not too sure, I may be heading back to school."

"That's good. You shouldn't be bartending."

"Why not?"

"Because you hate doing it."

"I can't see myself liking any job."

"Some people enjoy their work."

"I know, I've always admired people who could do that."

"It's not easy to find a job you like."

"Not just that, I was thinking more of those people who manage to have definite aims and goals."

"There's nothing particularly wonderful about that."

"Maybe, but I still think they're pretty amazing. They've all got this incredible need to hang on to an illusion of control. I'm downright in awe of it."

"So what's stopping you?"

"Huh?"

"If you find it so irresistible, why don't you go out and scramble?"

"Nope, I said I admired them, I didn't say I wanted to be like them."

"Afraid to fail on your own hook?"

"That's the obvious answer. It may even be true. I probably don't want to know if I'm a failure by choice or necessity, but that's not what I'm talking about. I was just describing my reaction. I truly am stunned by the whole process."

"Millions of people act that way."

"I know that Samantha. It has nothing to do with being unique. The most commonplace actions can still be amazing. Look, these people have their lives charted out. They talk about when they'll get married and what job they'll hold for how long. They probably plan out their bowel movements a week in advance."

"But you're too aware to fall for that crap."

"Nope, that also isn't the point. I don't feel superior to them or envious. I don't want to marry their sisters or play tennis with them. I'm only saying that they're an alien race. I could never believe in that sort of thing. I had more of a feel for the hustlers in the South Bronx."

"Not so very different."

"I know, the whole control routine. But it is different. The blacks down there didn't necessarily buy into their own fantasies. The goobers I'm talking about do."

"Richard, I wasn't suggesting you join an ad agency; just get out of the bar

business. It's not for you."

"How can you tell?"

"You're too private a person for the job. Do something more relaxed, something where you'd have time to think."

"Like what?"

"I don't know what, but it must be out there."

"Do I make a right Sammi?"

"No, just tuck your car behind the Lodge. I'm gonna use their pool."

"I thought that was only for guests."

"It's only for guests and for me."

"I should've known by now."

"That's right sonny, it's about time you started catching on."

***

Samantha lies sprawled on a webbed lounge chair. Some of the straps are broken and scrape against the ground. The pool looks stunted, trapped in a pygmy Olympic mode. At the bottom is a tacky painting of a dragon … I thought the place was owned by Italians. This must be another metaphor I'm missing here. But what could possibly induce a bunch of Italians to use a red and green dragon for decoration?

Eyes hidden behind sunglasses, lips curled in a sulky smile, Samantha has a distinctly dusky look about her. I'm not sure what that means but somehow I know it's distinct. I keep getting this feeling of smoldering. Maybe it's her hair. It has that color leaves take on in mid-October. Not around here; nothing ever changes around here. I mean back in Maine.

"Don't you have to get to work, Richard?"

"Yeah."

"Then stop looking at me like I was the prize in your box of crackerjacks."

"Well ..."

I bend down to kiss her. She meets me and melds softly with my lips, not holding back but still very much her own woman. Nice.

"I'll stop by the bar tonight."

"Will you Samantha?"

"That's what I just said."

"I'd like that."

"So would I sweetie. Now get out of my face; go home, take a shower, go to work."

At the gate I turn back for one last look. Samantha pushes up her sunglasses and makes shooing motions with her hands.

So she'll either come by or she won't. I never can tell about these things. I wouldn't mind if she did. Then again if she doesn't, maybe I could manage to snag some extra sleep. Can't really say which way I'd rather have it. But if she doesn't drop by I won't be the one to make the effort. I know that. I just don't care enough anymore.

13

ROASTED TURKEYS – A ROMANCE

If turkeys flew through the air roasted and ready to eat, man would still be dissatisfied. –Schopenhauer

Scuttling down the ladder like a crab, my bare feet rubbing against the smoothness of the rungs, I lower myself past the missing bar and fall to the floor with a small thump.

It's pitch black. Cold assaults my body but fails to thwart my progress. I won't be deterred. My mission comes first. I must stop that ringing. My hand shoots out and returns holding a telephone receiver. Puzzled, I stare. Only then do some of the pieces of an intelligible universe start slowly clicking into place.

"Hello, Richard?"

"Mmph."

"It's Sarah."

"Oh, hi sweetheart, what's up?"

"I didn't wake you, did I?"

"No, of course not."

Compulsive politeness, that's what I suffer from. Maybe Sarah's right. Maybe I am too repressed. It is possible to be too damn accommodating. I'm never asleep, never inconvenienced, always at everyone's service. Why don't I just start telling people to go fuck themselves like my sister does? Hah, that's some ideal to aspire to. Nope, I'm stuck with this laid back, nice guy image. If I could only figure out whether it's due to caring too much or not at all. Sometimes I think I was born with a teflon heart; baked on emotion removed with one easy wipe.

It's four in the morning. I have to tend bar at noon. What the hell else would I be doing but sleeping?

"Well what took you so long to answer?"

"I was up in the loft."

"Doing what?"

"Sweeping."

"At four in the morning?"

"Yeah, well I couldn't sleep and I noticed all the dust on the floor."

I wish to hell she would get to the point. I'm standing here naked in my kitchen, a kitchen containing all the warmth of some long forgotten romance. Trying to tell my body to relax isn't a solution. Those old Maine tricks don't work anymore. I can hear my teeth chattering convulsively like a pair of castanets in Madrid.

"Richard, can I come over?"

"Uh, sure."

"You don't mind?"

"No, it'd be great."

"You sure?"

"I'm sure."

"You're not just saying that, are you Richard? You know I don't have to come over. Don't go doing me any favors."

"Listen, if it wasn't all right I'd tell you."

"No you wouldn't."

"Well, maybe not."

"So what's it going to be? Should I come over or not?"

"I swear to God Sarah, I want you to come over … Please Sarah, would you please come on over?"

Yeah, just wonderful. No rest for this kid tonight. What's worse, no crawling back into my comfy sleeping bag. Instead the old boy scout routine, rubbing our bodies together and hoping for a spark. Which reminds me, how's old Rex the Wonder Horse going to perform tonight unless I get busy and start puffing on some dope.

"Well I'll be over in about fifteen minutes."

"Bye–bye Sarah."

That's another habit I should can; those insipid bye–byes. You can over–do this Peter Pan bit. Not even one of the lost boys would be caught dead saying bye–bye over the phone … provided A.T.&T. still hooks up to cave number five in Never Never Land.

Fifteen minutes to get stoned. I wonder when dope stopped being a sexual enhancer and moved on to becoming a sexual necessity. I know with Sarah it's a necessity. No dope, no show; like giving a broken–down race horse a shot before post–time.

But before I do anything else, my first move is straight into the bathroom so I can check myself out in the mirror. Well actually it isn't a mirror. It's an advertisement for Andecker beer, complete with a crack down the middle. As a mirror, as even a feeble stab at decoration, it's pretty dismal. Mostly it's just another example of my senseless self deprivation. Thank God for safety razors. Otherwise I'd look like a cast member of the "Student Prince."

At least my hairline seems to be hanging on. Christ I'm getting toward that age and I am nervous … What a disgusting case of vanity. This whole song and dance isn't even for Sarah's benefit. For Sarah's benefit? Hell, it's nothing but my own poorly suppressed vanity. I find myself primping even when I'm alone. Getting ready for bed can take me half an hour or more. But maybe it's only a question of aesthetics.

Crap, why am I letting this lackluster affair with Sarah dribble on, spreading an already thin emotion over a longer and longer period of time? Still, if that little twerp dropped me I'd be pissed. Why can't I scourge myself of this infantile self–infatuation? But I guess there's no real reason to stop seeing her. Mostly it's a way of marking time. Indifference creates the possibility of nearly perfect substitutes; one activity becomes as good as the next. I've withdrawn so far, relegated my concerns to such a limited area that what I do for large stretches of time is irrelevant.

Sarah would be some pleased to know she was reduced to pure filler, on par with watching a banana slug slither across the floor. Somehow though, I end up with a vague affection for them all, the ones that bore me, the ones that grate on my nerves …

Right, I've got to get busy on that dope. I yank open the refrigerator door. Yogurt, tofu, Grapenuts; the dope's in the crispolator hidden among reduced for quick sale Spaceway produce. What a shopper.

Slimy brown vegetables, stale bread, dented repositories of botulism; I buy whatever's cheap that day. Sort of a perversion of eating whatever's in season. I'm willing to impair my health, curtail any possible enjoyment I might derive from eating, to save maybe fifty cents ... Buy my new best selling cookbook, *Inedible Meals from Disgusting Ingredients*, soon to be available at all major airport terminals.

I'm becoming some sort of environmental equivalent to the Easter Seal poster child. I used to think that any fool could make money in this country. Deliberately being poor was evidence of my innate intelligence. So instead of making money, I've dealt with rising prices by consuming less. Now as I sit on my wooden stool, wrapped in sweaters, trying to turn the pages of a book with gloved hands, I sometimes feel that it may be time to rethink that strategy.

Yeah, I best use some of the dope that weasel Chacko tried to bribe me with last month. Mm, one paper or two? Better play it safe and make it two. I stitch a couple of E–Z Widers together. Looks to be enough room there for a family of pygmies. I slowly shake out the stuff and align it on the paper. Picking it up with the officially sanctioned dope roller's motion, I proceed to roll an absolute travesty, never could get my fingers to move to the right places. I would come in last at a convention of epileptic joint rollers. Half the dope sprinkles onto the table as I twist the ends shut. I examine my effort – a camel hiding inside a snake.

No time for niceties, she'll be here any moment. I light up. The paper flares, scorching my nose hairs and thinning out my moustache. I ignore the smell of burnt hair and puff on. That pleasantly disassociated feeling finally arrives. I gaze longingly at a corner chair and rub against the kitchen table. I'm ready for Sarah.

I hope she doesn't expect me to talk. I'll nod and listen but I'm just too tired to pretend to be articulate. I seldom do talk. I admit to occasionally chatting with people but talk, never. Non–communication is much more comfortable and reassuring. Talking turns into such an arduous process. Deep down I rather doubt that I care enough about people to make the effort. It's easier to be pleasant and agreeable. No trouble at all yielding when matters don't concern me. A good part of my image as a nice guy probably hinges on that indifference.

Well there's always sex, but even that's become mostly humdrum. I've heard all about the drive for immortality; breaking down the walls separating us, transcending time, death and rebirth. But still, orgasms can become as mechanical as parking a car. It's getting so that I fake them in order to give some pleasure to Sarah, or whoever else I'm with. Maybe I'm just confused. I never claimed to understand all that much about sex.

I'm not even sure where I picked up what I do know. All I know is it took me a hell of a long time, mostly the result of on the job training. In high school I couldn't quite get a hold of the mechanics of masturbation. What was all that talk about "shooting your wad" or "having a boner"?

I was either sixteen or seventeen before I had my first wet dream. I can't remember what the dream was about. For all I know it involved feeling up my aunt. But surprised, I felt like an innocent young girl having her first period. I was jerked awake by a rapid crescendo of pressure and then an explosion. My penis throbbed and burned. The end tingled. I thought the damn thing was going to fall off. I was fully awake now, lying in a puddle of cold sticky sperm. I don't even think I knew quite what it was. All I knew was it couldn't be piss. Pissing was never that dramatic. I can remember feeling panicky. My mother would make my bed in the morning and discover everything. So I quietly got out of bed, not making a sound, not daring to switch on a light. I changed my pajamas, furtively shoving the soiled bottoms deep into the hamper. Then a damp wash cloth, a towel over the offending spot, and a prayer that it would dry by morning. Ten years later I don't even bother to roll over. If it wasn't for the concomitant stickiness, I might not even remember in the morning. So much for my flights of ecstasy.

That must be Sarah clumping up the path. Please God, don't let her smile when she gets here. It makes her look like Charlie Chaplin. I must have a thing about early screen comedians. Sue Ann looks exactly like Stan Laurel when she smiles. My next love will probably be the dead image of Buster Keaton. Well, at least she won't smile.

"Well hi, Richard."

Jesus Christ, she's smiling. I'm already depressed.

"Hi Sarah, what's up?"

"It's that fucking George. I'm so mad I just couldn't sleep. I swear I'll kill him."

"Well why do you keep seeing him?"

"I don't know. I thought the three of us could go out tonight, you know, like civilized people, and enjoy the fireworks.... Bobby just hated the fireworks, he cried straight through them.... But you know, I thought for once we could have a good time. Fat chance, fat fuckin' chance.

"He starts in on me. Tells me it's all my fault that he's so screwed up. Like hell it is. That boy had his gears stripped long before he latched onto me. Did I ever tell you about the time we were living in Occidental?"

"Yeah, I think you did."

"There I am shivering in this dark shit–hole of a house. Bobby a permanent pale shade of blue, no money, no firewood and George comes home with a goddamn salmon. He stands there expecting me to cream over the big provider taking care of his little woman. He not only expected me to clean the damn thing, he expected me to be grateful."

"So what did you do?"

"What do you think I did? I kicked him in the balls. He can take that macho garbage and just shove it. I swear to God I almost strangled him tonight when he tried to fix my car. I told him if he put his head under the hood I'd turn on the goddamn engine. And I would have too."

"C'mon Sarah, give the guy a break. He probably only wanted to help."

"Richard, you don't know George. Everything he touches turns to shit. It's not just a lack of mechanical aptitude. He's a genius of destruction. Did I ever tell you about our trip to Tacoma?"

"Yeah, I think you did."

"Well he assures me that the car will make it. It's a hundred dollar car but he swears that he's got it all fixed up. So we're approaching the Oregon border; George, Bobby and me, yeah and some hitchhiker we picked up near Point Arena, when the car stops dead. I mean nothing, completely belly up. And it's fuckin' pouring and the rain's leaking into the car. George is outside playing super mechanic, tinkering with the engine like he knows what he's doing. That madman doesn't even know how to fill up a gas tank. So I mean I just had enough. I took Bobby by the hand and started walking down the road with George shouting after me. I hitched a ride back down to the river. George didn't show up till a week later."

"What was his story?"

"Who remembers? He probably spent the week screwing that hitchhiker in the back seat of that crazy old car. Hey, it's freezing in here."

"Yeah, well the fire went out."

"I thought you were up."

"I was. I'm just saving on wood."

"Well, maybe we should go on up."

"Yeah, maybe we should."

Clambering on the ladder like a performing ape, I yank Sarah up after me, almost dislocating her arm. I shrug off my bathrobe and dive into bed trying to keep my teeth from chattering again. Maybe I should have started up the stove. Nah, I'll be warm before long.

Sarah waits indecisively by my mattress. She seems uncertain whether to test out the waters or not. We go through the same charade every time. In a minute Sarah will crawl into bed fully clothed and act as if she hadn't the foggiest notion about what was going to happen. And, she always climbs into bed without removing any of her clothes. I end up fumbling my way through miles of tattered underwear. I'm tempted to ask her about it but I'd only end up provoking an argument. If she enjoys doing it, who am I to arbitrate bedside fashion?"

"Richard, it's freezing up here. Why don't you buy some decent blankets? These are totally worthless."

"Well sweetheart, why don't you come on over here and we'll see what we can do about warming you up." Pretty hokey I know, but I never claimed to be a Noel Coward manqué.

I click off the light. Darkness helps. My hand finds the small of Sarah's back beneath a torn t–shirt and I bring her close to me. Okay, here it goes. If I can just relax, blank out my self–conscious mind and let my body go, maybe this time it won't be such a half assed performance. In any case I'll try to give her what pleasure I can. It's not going to be easy. I just can't manage to delude myself into a grand passion. My blood seems unable to rouse itself past the tepid stage.

"Uh Sarah, uh sweetheart."

"Mm?"

"Sarah, the gum, how about taking the gum out of your mouth?"

Haphazardly the gum makes its way from her mouth to the rafter above. Ugh. Sometimes this L.A. low–rider routine of hers gets to be a real pain in the ass.

Rubbing bodies together, kissing, I slowly tug off most of her clothes and begin snaking my way down her body, making appropriate stops as I go. Well here I am, head between her legs, my nose nonchalantly doing reconnaissance work like a bloodhound casting about for the right scent. My tongue hunts slowly for the proper spot, slithering its way through tufts of fur. Sarah starts moaning softly, her pelvis working up and down, demonstrating the articulation of her ball and socket joints. Damn, I'm suffocating. The blankets are wrapped too tightly around us. They're shutting off my air. I speed up, tongue moving into overdrive, as I frantically try to finish the job before all oxygen disappears. As she gives a final shudder I burst into the clear, lungs heaving, hair matted wildly on my forehead. Sarah giggles as I lie exhausted on the mattress, gulping air like some out of shape marathon runner. My heart slows gradually as I await the next scene. Two to one it's reciprocity time, the mandatory exchange of oral sex acts. There must be some unwritten but universally acknowledged etiquette about this. I know it's not in Emily Post. I looked; no entries under either sex, oral; fellatio; or cunnilingus. Most women don't appear to be all that enthused about this part of the performance. They just give a few perfunctory slurps like an obedient child tasting a suspicious looking dish.

Sure enough, there goes Sarah earnestly working her way down my body like some Boy Scout searching out a good deed.

"Christ Sarah, it's not a brussel sprout."

"Hah?"

I reach down, place my hands on her head and draw her up to me. Pressing tightly I work my way in.

"Did you come?"

Now how hokey can you get? I thought women only said that in bad novels.

"You heard me Richard, I said, 'Did you come?'"

Uh oh. Nothing lascivious in the tone of that question; there's not the slightest sprinkling of wanton passion softening its edges. Sarah's voice is shrill, insistent.

"I don't know."

Sarah tosses me off.

"What! How can you not know? Look at me, I'm all wet, you must have come. What's wrong with you? I told you not to come."

Oh Christ, what a sordid nasty scene. The thing is, I'm really not sure whether I did or not. If anything, it was more of a dribble. Maybe I need a washer replaced. I put my finger in the fluid and sniff trying to determine whose juices they are. Hard to say.

"There's too much of it there to be mine, Richard."

Why argue. I shrug my shoulders.

"Okay, I'm sorry."

"You're sorry? A whole lot of fuckin' good that does. You're sorry."

What does she expect me to do? Draw it all back in like a syringe?

"Why don't you try jumping up and down, Sarah?"

"Very funny. You think I want to be pregnant? You think I need another child? I'm thirty–five years old. I've got enough problems."

Does she really think I want to have a child, especially her child? What a bleak prospect that would be.

"Look, nothing will happen. It'll be okay."

"Why, are you sterile?"

"I just know it will be okay."

"Sure, I've heard that one before. Where do you think Bobby

came from?"

I say I'm sorry. Then I say it again. I confess my guilt. I abjectly beg forgiveness. Slowly Sarah calms down.

"Well, we'll have to see what happens."

"Sure sweetheart, everything will work out."

She turns and snuggles against me. Gradually we regain our rhythm. All is forgotten for the moment. What a hassle. Maybe I should take up stamp collecting instead.

"Richard."

"Mmph."

"Richard, wake up."

"Wuznament."

"Richard, get me a towel."

"Sdont smthner."

"Fuck you, Richard. Either get me a towel or you try sleeping in this swamp."

Sarah punctuates her demands by digging her elbow into my ribs. That elbow of hers must be made of corrugated steel.

This has got to be one of the oldest running battles in the history of sexual combat. And I think the tide is turning against our side. Where did those happy days go, when women demurely and sedately placed their bodies over the damp sticky mess, playing Raleigh to our masculine Queen Elizabeth? But no use bewailing the change. Gotta roll with the times.

I swap places. On my back, trying to ignore the cold clammy goop underneath, I find myself fantasizing. Here I am lying next to a woman, though it's true that at the moment she's a bit inert. The bed's still damp from our exertions. I'm in the process of falling asleep. Falling asleep I'm fantasizing about women. Not the one next to me. No reason to fantasize about her ... Talk about mental masturbation. Why do I even bother with the physical performance?

Uh oh. Not Katherine, the last person I want to think about is Katherine. When I mention her name I cross myself like a Celtic monk hearing of a Norse landing. Those were a prime two years of torture.

Lila, I'll think about torturing Lila. Lila's the type of woman I'd probably enjoy torturing. Forgive me Ti–Grace Atkinson but it's true. There are some women whose nipples I would gleefully pinch. Not because I dislike them, not because I'm frustrated by them or feel any animosity at all towards these women. It just seems to be the only appropriate response I could make. Maybe I'm incapable of attaching any sense of reality to their presence. Torturing them would be the moral equivalent of punching the Joe Palooka boxing dummy I had as a child. I'd expect them to just bob back up smiling, ready for still more. Oh my, yet another urge to shove back into its Freudian cage, along with an intermittent compulsion to pull my pants down in front of the Spaceway checkout counter … Now if I could just pry some of these blankets from Sarah's grasp …

Morning. Wonder what time it is? My fingers throb as they do every morning. If I get a chance I'll try to squeeze some of the puss out of the cuticles. That should bring down the swelling. Bartending is slowly rotting away my fingers. Five bucks an hour doesn't come close to covering the pain. Got to find something else to do.

Sarah is huddled in an unattractive, blanket covered lump by my side.

Christ is it cold! Sunny California my ass. I scramble down the ladder and head for the stove. My body doesn't feel right, the joints don't seem to fit. Trying to think is like trying to crank a car in sub zero weather. The strain is felt but nothing turns over.

I spread last nights' embers around and look suspiciously at the ash. More than likely to smother the fire before it gets going. Methodically the steps are performed, trying to keep my body relaxed, trying not to feel the cold. Newspaper, cardboard box, two logs; newspaper already smoldering, I shoot some charcoal starter in. Bad for the stove and dangerous; I've already lost the right half of my moustache and sections of my eyebrows. But it seems to be working this morning. I watch the fire through the open door, blowing and huffing, waiting to get warm, trying not to breathe in too much ash or smoke.

Sarah mutters something from above.

"I'm going to the store sweetheart. Be right back."

"Richard, put some water on."

"Yeah, I'm going to get you some coffee."

Ten o'clock, work at noon, better get moving. Wash later. Christ I feel funky. Check my pockets for keys and cash, head for the door and check again. A constant paranoia of locking myself out or of not having enough money to buy groceries haunts me. Okay, I'm all set. Open the door and … damn the phone. If it's a wrong number I'll scream. Wherever I go I attract wrong numbers. The first time I answer the ring of a newly installed phone it's inevitably a wrong number. There must be some sort of cosmic or metaphorical significance to all this but damn if I can figure out what it is. Something's malfunctioning. Maybe I have a polarized aura or an inverted bio–rhythm.

"Hello dear."

"Hi Mom, how are you feeling?"

"Well enough."

"What does that mean?"

"No really Richard, I'm fine."

"Dorrie said you weren't feeling too well."

"Don't worry, it'll pass."

"Sure Mom, and so will you one day. Look, have you seen someone about this?"

"What's a doctor going to tell me? What do they know?"

She's got me there. I wouldn't see a doctor unless I had my right arm tucked under my left. The only doctors I trust are the ones that admit to not knowing what they're doing. Of course I wouldn't go see them either. What do they know?

"How about your diet Mom? Are you eating right? Getting enough vitamins?"

"Well enough."

"Listen I'll send you some vitamins, okay?"

"You don't need to do that dear."

I've definitely been in California too long. I've become fixated on diet and nutrition. Next thing I know I'll be suggesting a hair analysis.

"Richard, I'm having a hair analysis done next week. Dorrie found someone she likes."

"How's Dorrie doing?"

"You know Dorrie. She's Dorrie."

What in the hell is that supposed to mean? They probably said the same thing about Lizzie Borden. Better let it pass. I'm not up for a rundown of my sister's marital difficulties and other weekly tantrums.

"And now enough about me. Tell me how my son is doing."

"Fine. He's doing okay."

"What have you been doing?"

"Nothing very interesting."

"But Richard, I want to hear."

"Listen Mom, I work seven days a week. Some days I work fourteen hours or more. There isn't much time left to do anything else."

"Oh Richard, why do you insist on making life so hard for yourself?"

"It's not particularly hard."

"But you could do so much more. You've got a good mind. Why do you insist on wasting it?"

"I'm not wasting anything Mother. I've got nothing to waste."

"You're always tearing yourself down. I don't understand you Richard. Why can't you confide in me more?… Well maybe one day you'll find yourself."

"What?"

"Maybe you'll stop looking for yourself and settle down one day."

"First of all, I'm not looking for myself. Second of all, the reason I'm not looking for myself is because I know exactly where I am. I'm standing here in my drafty cabin talking to you on the phone. Third, I thought *Time Magazine* stopped running articles like that. You must have picked up an old *Reader's Digest* at the dentist's."

"Richard, why don't you move? You know Dad and I would be more than glad to help you out."

"I like where I'm living."

"Oh Richard, you know how I worry about you. I don't see how you can live like you do."

"Me neither. And, it certainly isn't getting any easier. Don't worry Mom. Really, I'm okay."

"Well have you made any plans for next year?"

"Not yet."

Some chance. I've never made a plan in my life. You can hardly call my sporadic shots in the dark planning. At best I'm able to conduct short range tactical maneuvers. It's not that I intentionally avoid planning out my future. I'm just incapable of doing it. Not incapable of carrying out a plan but of concocting one.

"Okay Richard, you'll be sure to tell me if you need anything."

"Sure Mom."

"You won't, will you Richard?"

"Won't what?"

"Call. You won't call, will you?"

"No, I won't."

"Oh Richard."

"Now look Mom, I don't call anyone. I just don't like talking on the phone. Really, it's nothing personal … Look, I've gotta run. Say hello to everyone."

"I love you Richard. Stay well."

"You too Mom."

Maybe a gift, some flowers or something. I certainly do little enough … If I weren't so hardhearted I'd feel terribly guilty. Gotta get on the old stick though, Sarah will be up screaming for coffee any minute now.

Sunshine, I crave sunshine. Living beneath the redwoods sounds picturesque but it's about as poetic as living in a morgue. It must be at least twenty degrees warmer once you get out from under these trees.

My car's parked down by the road. It still has Maine plates, one looped crazily in a homemade sling from the front bumper. The plates only serve to emphasize the obvious. This car has led one hard life. Poor old Emily Vega, she's not the auto she used to be. There's just not as much of her left anymore. Mysterious and long forgotten trim no longer adorns her perimeter. Holes up to eight inches in diameter trick out her sides. Front disc brakes are only a memory.

I open the passenger door, sidle over the hand brake and under the steering wheel. The other door tends to fly open unless slammed shut from the outside. I pump the pedal a standard twenty–three times and turn the key. A brief flurry of excitement as the engine catches, pauses indecisively and dies.

"Come on baby, come on sweetheart, Richard will change your oil if you're a good little girl and start."

I pump the pedal another fifteen times and try again. Close, very close that time.

"Okay honey, and I'll add a quart of Mystery Motor Oil."

Christ knows what that glop does. I regard it more as a votive offering to a mechanical deity. Yep, that's what she wanted to hear. The engine roars into life spewing a requisite number of black particulates into the surrounding atmosphere.

Might as well stop at the post office and check my box. Getting my mail is the closest I come these days to a religious experience. I always approach it with trepidation bordering on awe. For years I've thought that somehow, someday, something wonderful would make its way through the U.S. mail solely in order to enlighten me, to finally awaken my soul to its spiritual possibilities. I would be touched by the hand of God, return reply requested. The trick was that the unfolding of this event, the moment when that state of blessedness would come raining down on me, could only occur if I was not expecting it. A conscious wish for such a letter would produce instead a thick wad of junk mail. Only by not desiring would I be found worthy. A bit of Karmic reasoning left over from the sixties but still, why spoil the possibility? I blank out my mind and insert my key.

Looks pretty packed. I yank out the contents, ripping the first few pages of this month's two week late folio from Pinko Pacifica Broadcasting. I flip through the letters; Friends of the Earth, A.C.L.U., New East African Fund, circulars announcing the opening of the New Age Transcendental Business School plus fifty percent off any purchase at Holistic Wallpapering Ltd. I must be on every left–liberal mailing list in the country. Damn, K.P.F.A. must be selling their subscriber's names again … University of California,

Berkeley, I wonder what that's about, too early for any decision. Better get a move on. I round the corner and go into Brixton's for coffee and muffins. Okay, what aisle is the coffee in? I wander up and down the aisles, ignoring the evil looks from the Iranians who own the place, finally spotting it between the candles and dry cereal. Good coffee, should be something drinkable but instant. Can't make real coffee, nothing to make it in. Can't remember what the good brands are, years since I've drunk coffee. Price, I'll use price to decide, buy something medium expensive. That can't be right. You don't get what you pay for. Never have, never will. Better watch it or I'll start babbling about rugged individualism and the free enterprise system. And muffins, I refuse to buy any more of those whole wheat honey bran ones. They taste like they were made with sand.

"Richard, long time."

"Hey Chacko, what's happening?" Now how can I get out of this conversation, damn me and my Jane Austen politeness.

"You know, same old same old. I ..."

"Great, good seeing you. I've uh ..."

"Heard you got a job over at Bogart's."

"Uh huh."

"Who else is bartending?"

Here it comes.

"Matt and Janie."

"Matt's a good man.

"I think so."

"You think they might need someone else?"

The little dork is going to try and weasel me out of my job. "Can't say."

"Frank still managing?"

"Last I heard."

"Maybe I should go over and have a talk with old Frank."

"Well maybe you should do just that."

"Well maybe you could mention it to him."

"Yeah well maybe I could."

Yeah and maybe I could twist your scrawny little neck you fucking sleazepot.

"Good seeing you Richard, old buddy. Stay in touch."

"Sure."

How's that for a complete bummer? This time if Chacko causes me the least bit of trouble I'll squash him like the little scaly bug he is.

Out of Brixton's, past the usual group of 'Heroes' in front of the Coop. A human junkyard, it's a frigging wrecking yard for defunct human beings. 'Yes son, over there's a `67 San Francisco hippie. Yep, that's it parked right next to the teeny bopper circa 1965. Nope, sure don't make `em like they useta.' I nod vaguely in the direction of glazed eyes and sun–burnt faces as I go by.

"Sarah, hey Sarah!" Sarah's still not up. "Hey Sarah, eggs for breakfast?"

"Mmph."

Let's see, still half a dozen eggs left over from the dozen I bought on sale last month. Maybe if I scrambled them with some of these 'reduced for quick sale' avocados. My eating habits, as always, are dictated by the vagaries of Spaceway's pricing policies.

Just cut some of this grey mung off. Get the water boiling. Toast muffins in my toast one side at a time toaster. Should I warm the plates? Nah, it's only for Sarah.

"Hey Sarah, get a move on before the eggs get cold." She fumbles down the ladder looking like people do first thing in the morning.

"This is really good Richard. How come you didn't make an omelet?"

"Can't make omelets."

"Well this is good. I mean it."

We sit side by side on my wooden picnic chair. Furniture has never been my strong point. Absent mindedly I start patting Sarah's leg. Mornings I've got nothing to say. But my fingers seem to be embarking on a project all their own. I glance at Sarah …

Now why did I do that? Tacky, very tacky. I seem to be bent on destroying my own romantic self image. Move, gotta get off the River. My mind seems to be filling up with green mold. And my moral character is going the same way as my manners. Those I buried years ago in the Maine woods.

"Sarah, I'm thinking of moving back to Maine."

"What brought that on, Richard?"

"Oh, I was just thinking about driving in Maine in the winter, you know, the snow and everything."

"Like when I taught skiing up at Larson."

"I didn't know that."

"Yeah, it was about eight years ago. I can't believe it was once important, I mean really important to me, to ski well. I was never terrific or anything but I was good enough to be an instructor, at least to instruct beginners. Anyway, I had to be up there at seven. I was living in a little cabin down in the valley and I would get up about five. It'd be freezing, the sky still dark above me, and I'd jump into this beat up old car I had. I'd drive up that scarred old mountain and it'd be silent, like the world was just being born. And everything would be covered with these great masses of snow.

"Then sometimes I'd be driving home late, past midnight, and I'd be creeping along. The snow would be falling like crazy and there'd be no one else on the road. I'd be all nervous about sliding off the road and getting myself stranded. Christ, you couldn't even tell where the road ended and the country began. But other times I'd just relax and the snow would be falling in thick soft heavy flakes, my car slowly making its way home. My headlights would pick out trees all covered with snow, and I felt as if I'd wandered into some fantastic sculpture garden. The trees looked like they were made of snow, and the smallest branches were just so much delicate filigree. I'd be riding along and feeling so happy, not caring when I got home or even maybe if I did."

Sometimes I think I sell Sarah short. It's really too bad I'm not physically attracted to her.

"Gotta get going, Richard."

At last, I barely have time for a quick nap before work. I'll just have to show up a little late.

"I'll walk you to your car."

Tromping on the redwood needles, I shift my gaze right and left. I'd rather not be seen with Sarah. What vanity. Silly really, everyone knows everything you do around here. Just as well to relax and not worry about it.

There's her grey battered V.W. squareback. I get ready for the obligatory kiss. I wonder what that letter from Berkeley is about.

"Bye sweetie, see you tonight."

"Okay, Sarah."

I flap my hand as her car putters off toward the Pacific. Good, that's out of the way, now for some sleep. All this screwing around is disrupting my sole remaining pleasure. It's impossible to grab a good night's sleep when someone else is bumping into you, snatching at the covers, generally keeping you on edge all night.

I wave to the various A.F.D.C. mothers and S.S.I. fathers who comprise my neighbors as I make my way back to my cabin. Picking the Berkeley letter off my spool table, I rip it open.

Dear Mr. Davis:

The School of Business Administration has accepted you into its Master's Degree program for the coming academic year. Official notification will be sent out within the coming month from the Director of Graduate Studies at which time we will apprise you of the status of your fellowship application ...

Hot shit. At last, my ticket out of oblivion and into the golden realm of the professional middle class. All those years of struggling against the mainstream, of trying to maintain my integrity. Am I going to forget about my ideals just for a pile of consumer crap? Am I going to surrender to the sordid greediness that plagues this country? After all these years am I finally going to sell out? Damn right I am.

EPILOGUE

Things are bad, and then they get worse. –Philip Freedman

"Huh?"

"I have a collect call from Susan. Will you accept the charges?"

"Wha?"

"Richard?"

"Please wait until your party accepts the charges. Will you accept the charges sir?"

"Susan?"

"Will you accept …"

"Yeah sure."

"Were you asleep Richard?"

"Susan, how can it be you?"

"I didn't mean to wake you Richard. It must be later where you are."

"It's been five years Susan. How did you know where to find me? Why did you call?"

"Shelly gave me the number."

"Well, how are you Susan?"

"I wanted to apologize to you Richard."

"What?"

"For being a jerk. You were so sweet to me and I just gave you a lot of crap."

"Nah, it's okay. That happened a long time ago."

"Are you seeing anyone now?"

"Ah … not really."

"You should."

"Yeah, well maybe."

"I don't know how many times I've wanted to call you these last five years."

"I don't understand."

"I really love you Richard."

"Who me?"

"I even thought … no, that's ridiculous."

"What?"

"No, I can't tell you."

"Susan, if you can wake me up at three in the morning, you can share your little secrets."

"Oh gee, 3 a.m. I didn't know it was that late. Maybe you should go on back to bed."

"Believe me, I'm up. Why don't you just say what's on your mind?"

"I heard you got a really good job."

"Susan!"

"Marry me Richard."

"Huh?"

"Don't you love me anymore? You said you could never stop loving me."

"Okay."

"Then you'll marry me?"

"Sure, why not."

"I just knew you would."

"Look Susan, there's no need to insult me. If you think after all these years I'm going to …"

"No Richard, you don't understand. I spent all yesterday praying. And then He said you would."

"He?"

"Oh Richard, don't you see, I've found Jesus!"

www.ingramcontent.com/pod-product-compliance
Lightning Source LLC
Chambersburg PA
CBHW060938030726
47503CB00003B/646